EZEKIEL'S SONG

YAHWEH'S LEGACY BOOK TWO

NAOMI CRAIG

ISBN: 978-1-951839-66-6

Celebrate Lit Publishing

304 S. Jones Blvd #754

Las Vegas, NV, 89107

http://www.celebratelitpublishing.com/

PRAISE FOR EZEKIEL'S SONG

"In Ezekiel's Song, Naomi Craig offers a key to unlocking confusing prophetic mysteries. Impeccable research and exciting fiction carry readers along the hostage trail from ancient Judea to Babylon, building to a crescendo in a cataclysmic vision. Ezekiel's passion for speaking the truth is only exceeded by his wife's passion for praising in song, and their burden for their people is second only to the Lord's."

~ Dana McNeely, Author of Rain

For Ella Mae and pastors' wives everywhere. You are seen and loved.
For Rob. I'm so thankful to serve alongside you.

CHARACTER LIST

Jerusalem

**Amram Chief Musician*
Baruch *The prophet Jeremiah's scribe*
**Chesed Shiri's cousin, Musician in the temple*
**Dvorah Shiri's ima*
Ezekiel *Levite, aide to the governor of the temple*
**Gilead Valiant warrior, Archer*
Hananiah *False prophet*
**Ibraham Shiri's abba, Former Chief Musician*
Jeremiah *Prophet, Priest*
**Keziah Shiri's childhood friend*
King Coniah (Jehoiachin)*King of Judah, Jehoiakim's son*
King Jehoiakim *King of Judah, vassal to Nebuchadnezzar*
Nebuchadnezzar *King of Babylon*
Pashur *Chief governor of temple*
**Rabgar-Nebo Chaldean captain*
**Samuel Water boy in the temple*
**Shiri (Shiriel) Musician in the temple, Ezekiel's wife*

Babylon

**Atta Shiri's friend*

Ahab *False prophet*

**Dumah Elder in the synagogue, Atta's new husband*

**Huz Musician in synagogue*

**Keli (Kelila) Ezekiel and Shiri's daughter*

**Perez Elder in the synagogue*

Seraiah *Quartermaster of Judah's army*

**Vakhtang Chaldean general, Gilead serves as personal body guard*

**Yassah Shiri's friend*

Zedekiah (Mattaniah)*Appointed by Nebuchadnezzar as King of Judah,*
Coniah's uncle

Bold *names are mentioned in the Bible and/or historical documents.*
**Denotes fictional character or description.*

The word of the Lord came to Jeremiah concerning all the people of Judah, in the fourth year of Jehoiakim the son of Josiah, king of Judah (which was the first year of Nebuchadnezzar king of Babylon…"I have spoken to you, rising early and speaking, but you have not listened. And the Lord has sent to you all His servants the prophets… but you have not listened or inclined your ear to hear. They said 'Repent now everyone of his evil way and his evil doings and dwell in the land that the Lord has given to you and your fathers forever and ever. Do not go after other gods to serve them and worship them, and do not provoke Me to anger with the works of your hands and I will not harm you. Yet you have not listened to Me,' says the Lord.

~Jeremiah 25:1,3b-7a

PROLOGUE

And Jehudi read [the scroll] in the hearing of the king...And it happened when Jehudi had read three or four columns, that the king cut it with the scribe's knife and cast it into the fire... until all the scroll was consumed... Yet they were not afraid, nor did they tear their garments.
—Jeremiah 36:21a,23-24a

Jerusalem, 604 BC

Ezekiel searched the faces of the people mingling before him.

None seemed put off by the king's soldiers patrolling the temple courtyard, their marching a tempo for the droning chants coming over the western walls from Jerusalem's Second Quarter—Baal's priests conducting their afternoon rites.

Even those he knew who only offered sacrifices to Yahweh did not seem fazed by the competing sounds of temple musicians and worshippers of Baal.

Oh, Yahweh! That You would open the eyes of those who are spiritually blind so they would see the error in their ways. Wake up Your people to their sin. Ezekiel rubbed at the ache in his chest and brought his attention back to Baruch, the prophet Jeremiah's scribe.

Baruch's expression mirrored Ezekiel's soul-deep pain as they climbed the semi-circular steps dividing the Court of the Women from the Court of the Priests. On the third step up, they turned and faced the courtyard filled with people blind to the folly of their ways.

Baruch's gaze darted to the soldiers—their intimidation tactics and disregard for the ways of the Lord casting a constant dark shadow over the temple grounds—setting all on edge. He scratched his neck.

Ezekiel clasped the scribe's shoulder. "Set aside your nervousness. Now is the time."

Moistening his lips, Baruch shifted from side to side. "Seventy years of bondage..." His voice squeaked out, barely reaching beyond the step where they stood, and he tucked an ink-stained hand inside his dark cloak.

Ezekiel angled his shoulder against the scribe's arm to infuse him with courage.

Baruch met Ezekiel's gaze, drew in a couple of breaths, and fixated on the portico leading to the outer courtyard as if he could see the choir and the musicians competing for the congregation's attention.

Opening the scroll, Ezekiel held it before Baruch. "You can do this, my friend. You must read the words."

The older man swallowed hard, and his gaze darted to the archer staring at them with narrowed eyes and crossed arms.

"Think of the people, Baruch. How can they turn from their wicked ways and follow Yahweh if they don't hear?"

A man and woman with a young boy wandered close to the steps where Baruch and Ezekiel stood.

"We already were at this place. Why are we here again?" the child whined, tugging at his *ima's* arm.

The mother glanced at Ezekiel's Levitical robes. "No, son, that was the temple of Baal. This one is for Yahweh."

How could they visit two temples and not be convicted of their sin? Ezekiel's chest ached. "Please, Baruch."

Baruch's expression grew grim. He pressed his lips together and took Jeremiah's scroll from Ezekiel. He cleared his throat. "From the thirteenth year of Josiah the son of Amon, king of Judah—"

Ezekiel nudged the scribe. "Louder."

"—even to this day, this is the twenty-third year in which the word of the Lord has come to me and I have spoken to you, rising early and speaking, but you have not listened." Baruch's voice lifted, becoming strong and sure. He attracted the attention of the boy's father and began imploring him directly. "Repent now, every one of his evil ways and his evil doings, and dwell in the land that the Lord has given to you and your fathers forever and ever."

The father paused, his eyes darting across the back of the scroll as if he could read through it.

"Hiram, what—" The woman's eyes widened as she turned back to see why her husband didn't follow. She tugged on the boy's arm, bringing him to an abrupt halt.

"Why are we stopping, *Ima*?"

"Hush. Your *abba* is listening."

Baruch bent slightly at the waist, emphasizing the words Jeremiah had dictated. "Do not go after other gods to serve them and worship them and do not provoke Me to anger with the works of your hands; and I will not harm you."

"Why is the scribe angry with me?" The boy's whisper disguised nothing.

At the woman's questioning glance, Ezekiel smiled and crouched low, softening his voice to not interrupt the reading. "Baruch is not angry."

"Then why—"

"He speaks of Yahweh, the one true God."

"There is also Baal. We worship Baal too." The boy tipped his chin in confidence.

"Hush, son. Let the priest explain." The boy's mother turned her questioning gaze to Ezekiel.

"Apprentice to the priests," Ezekiel corrected. Apprentice to the Levites, actually, but few cared to distinguish between them. Two more years, then he could officially be sworn into service in the temple. "Yahweh is the one true God. The God of our fathers. He created us to worship and serve Him alone. Remember the Shema?"

Ezekiel tapped his forehead. "Hear, O Israel, the Lord our God is One."

The boy formed the words as Ezekiel spoke them.

"Yahweh is angry because He loves us so much and we choose to not love Him. He has pleaded with our people again and again to repent. To return to worshipping Him so He can stop being angry."

The woman fiddled with her sleeve, eyes wide. "And if we don't?"

"—Nebuchadnezzar, King of Babylon, will utterly destroy this land and all its inhabitants." Baruch's timing was perfect. "He will make them an astonishment, a hissing, and perpetual desolation…"

"Not Jerusalem. Yahweh wouldn't allow it." The woman shook her head and placed her hand on the boy's shoulder, steering him away.

"Wait." Ezekiel rose, stopping himself from grasping her arm and shaking reason into her. "Please listen. Yahweh doesn't want to destroy Jerusalem—but if we don't turn from idolatry, what choice does He have? It goes against His character to allow us to desecrate ourselves with the works of our hands by worshipping gods we have made."

"So He will destroy us instead?" she scoffed. "That doesn't sound like a loving God."

"Wait. I want to listen." Hiram snagged her wrist, never looking away. "The scribe speaks truth. I can feel it."

Ezekiel's surprise mirrored the woman's. She turned her face toward Baruch, eyebrows raised.

"—Behold, I begin to bring calamity on this city which I have called by My name, and should you be utterly unpunished?" Baruch's voice softened. "Repent while there is still time. Humble yourself before Yahweh alone."

Hiram sank to his knees, tearing at the neck of his tunic, and groaned.

Heads turned and gazes shifted from Hiram to Baruch. Some stared openly—their faces lined with curiosity and hesitant understanding. Some hurried away in obvious discomfort, and others pretended not to notice while casting furtive glances over their shoulders.

Baruch's words faltered as the king's soldiers advanced toward the steps from all sides, most with imposing scowls and hands resting on sword hilts.

Ezekiel stepped close to the scribe and whispered, "Remember Yahweh's promise. Your life is your prize. You will not be killed for speaking this truth. Be faithful to the task."

Widening his stance, Baruch braced himself and lowered his gaze to the shaking scroll.

Ezekiel put his hands under Baruch's wrists. Just as Aaron and Hur supported Moses' arms in battle long ago, he would stand by Baruch and the truth.

"Behold, My judgment has already begun." Baruch stole a glance at the nearest soldier. "Did not Nebuchadnezzar take away ten thousand of our young men and princes? Even King Jehoiakim who had been returned to us."

Ezekiel winced. The faithful priests had all hoped King Jehoiakim would be deposed permanently, his wicked ways the cause of many Judahites straying from Yahweh. Though Prince Coniah—newly appointed as co-regent—had already displayed his *abba's* tendencies, he was a mere eleven years old. Still young enough to be influenced for good.

Nothing could delay Yahweh's judgment, though, and Jehoiakim had returned to Judah, flaunting his sins.

Scanning the uplifted faces, an urgency pressed on Ezekiel's spirit. The time to repent was short. If these people standing before him didn't turn their hearts back to Yahweh soon, their chance would slip away.

"Men and women of Judah," Baruch's eyebrows knit together, and he sounded close to tears. "We have arrived at this day of fasting to petition Yahweh to preserve our nation. Even now the Arameans and Moabites sit on our borders to destroy us."

The soldier with the bow slung across his back sank to his knees and braced his hands on the steps. "What can we do?"

Astonishment flashed across Baruch's face. "Turn from your evil ways. Present supplication to the Lord, not only for the nation but also for your sins. It may be Yahweh will yet relent and forgive us of our iniquities."

Hiram let out a wail, and the soldier began weeping. Hiram's wife held tight to the boy's hand and knelt, staring at the ground. The circle of those affected by the conviction of Yahweh's moving spread like the ripple of a stone tossed into a pond.

An incredulous smile tipped Baruch's mouth, and he nodded to Ezekiel.

Thank You, Yahweh. Ezekiel raised his arms and shouted with all his might to overcome the din of the musicians, the people mingling, and the clopping hooves of the livestock. "Let us pray. Have mercy upon me, O God, according to Your loving-kindness. According to the multitude of Your tender mercies!" His chest swelled at the sound of his people joining him in repentance. "Blot out my transgressions, wash me thoroughly from my iniquity, and cleanse me from my sin!"

Movement from behind Ezekiel drew his attention to a priest staring with eyebrows raised to his turban at the dozens kneeling—soldiers and commoners alike—confessing their sins to Yahweh.

A scribe in black robes wove with timid steps through the kneeling crowd. "What are you doing?"

Baruch extended his hand. "Gemariah. We are reading the words of Yahweh. His spirit is calling to the people. The time for revival is now."

Gemariah wrung his hands. "But the king's guards—"

"Behold." Ezekiel pointed to the archer kneeling with hands braced on the step before him.

Gemariah blinked twice.

The archer met Ezekiel's gaze. "How can we turn back the coming wrath?"

Ezekiel's throat closed. He swallowed. "Turn to Yahweh. Repent. Before it is too late. Great is the anger and the fury the Lord has pronounced against our land. He has sent prophets to warn us of the evil of our ways, and we have not inclined our ear."

Hiram moaned at Ezekiel's feet. "What should we do?"

"Tear down the Asherah poles and idols of Baal you have erected in the land and in your hearts."

Gemariah surveyed the crowd, tapping his finger on his lips. "Look at these people! Their repentance seems genuine. Imagine if they stood strong and we turned back Yahweh's wrath."

Baruch exchanged a glance with Ezekiel. "What are you thinking, Gemariah?"

"You have to spread the word farther. The more people who repent…we might convince King Jehoiakim." Another tap. "Come with me."

"Where are we going?" Baruch rolled up the scroll carefully.

"My chambers overlook the New Gate. With all the people arriving for the fast and the evening sacrifice…more will hear."

Only Yahweh could arrange this. Ezekiel paused. What of the people here? How could he leave at this time of uncertainty? *But what of the opportunity for more?*

He frowned, shifting his attention from the departing scribes to the afternoon sun.

Returning to the top step, he smiled at the upturned faces, desperate for truth. The laws of Moses flowed off his tongue with ease, his big, clear voice—a gift from Yahweh and always noticed—projecting to the corners of the courtyard. "Recall the words given to Moses! 'I am the Lord your God, who brought you out of the land of Egypt, out of the house of bondage. You shall have no other gods before Me.'"

The silver trumpets sounded, summoning the people to the evening sacrifice. Still, his little flock remained rooted to the spot, hunger in their eyes. Ezekiel declared the law of the Lord despite the curious glances of priests and Levites climbing past him, leading the lamb for slaughter. He shared with the rapt listeners the declarations of the Lord.

As the dusk deepened, Hiram's boy squirmed. "*Ima,* I'm hungry. Let's go."

Ezekiel couldn't dismiss these people for physical food when they were spiritually malnourished. Hiram hastened the decision by succumbing to the boy's demands. Others glanced toward the darkening sky and followed suit.

"Return tomorrow," Ezekiel called out, "I will continue to tell of Yahweh's instructions."

The people left the temple courtyard as swiftly as if they had been on the exodus from Egypt. He bit back his frustration. The archer was the last to leave and kept glancing over his shoulder.

Please, Yahweh, protect these people till they hear more. Revive our hearts and heal our land. His shoulders sagged as he wandered out of the Women's Court and turned toward the Levites' quarters.

"Ezekiel!" Sandals slapped the hewn rock.

He turned and blinked to see Baruch running, his arms flapping in an undignified way. "What is it? What's happened?"

Baruch bent over, hands on his knees. He caught his breath while scanning the empty courtyard. "The people… they heard. They responded. Such a repentance as of the days of King Josiah! Gemariah's son Micaiah told all the scribes in the king's house. All the princes were there."

Ezekiel gripped Baruch's shoulder. "Then what?"

"They summoned me, and I read Jeremiah's words. The whole scroll." Baruch's eyes danced. "All who heard were convicted!"

Ezekiel's breath hitched. He lifted his hands to the soft colors of evening sky. "Thank You, Yahweh."

"There's more." Baruch tugged on Ezekiel's arm. "Jehudi, the messenger, is being sent to declare the warning to the king."

Jeremiah's latest prophecy spoke against national security—warranting the king's attention.

"That is good news!" Ezekiel laughed. He could run with the speed of a gazelle fueled by that hope.

"Will you accompany Jehudi?" Baruch flushed. "They told me to go into hiding along with Jeremiah. Is that lack of faith, since Yahweh promised me my life?"

Ezekiel studied the scribe's downturned face. "I don't think so. Your assignment was to read the scroll here. I will go with Jehudi."

Baruch exhaled and smiled. "Jehudi leaves for the winter palace at first light."

Ezekiel embraced the older man. "I will bring you the report of Jehoiakim's change of heart."

"Revival, Ezekiel! Yahweh's people will turn back to Him!"

By mid-day, Jehudi's entourage arrived at Jehoiakim's winter palace in the arid region of Jericho. Ezekiel dismounted and surveyed the cedar-paneled doors painted red with vermillion. He shook his head in disgust.

When Pharoah Neco had appointed Jehoiakim to the throne four years prior, the king had imported cedars and expensive vermillion to update the palaces. Jehoiakim indulged in the opulence despite the nation's crumbling financial state. He had refused to pay the laborers their wages, claiming truthfully to have no funds in order to pay tribute to Neco.

Lord, Jehoiakim has mistreated Your people. Convict him of the error of his ways.

Where did the tribute funds come from now that Nebuchadnezzar of Babylon had overtaken Judah? Not from the barren treasuries, but likely from the backs of the people.

One of the scribes who met their party, Elishama, straightened his robes and rumpled them again as a servant escorted them through the echoing halls. "Perhaps I should store the scroll in my quarters. We'll feel out the king's reaction."

Jehudi relinquished the scroll, and Elishama broke off from the group and melted into the shadows as they approached the guard stationed outside the throne room.

"State your business."

"We come on matters of national security as told by the prophet Jeremiah." Jehudi's brow glistened with sweat.

The soldier's beady eyes traveled the length of their motley party. His lip curled and he crossed his arms.

Jehudi's shoulders angled forward and his arms stiffened. "As you know, all threats must be presented to the king in a timely manner."

After an annoyed huff, the soldier instructed the herald and flicked two fingers, allowing entrance to the throne room where the king and the young co-regent sat enthroned in splendor.

Ezekiel stared. More cedar-paneled walls. More extravagance at the cost of the people. The tapestries on the wall were garish and gaudy, matching the sultry music swirling around dancers clad in sheer linen.

"Oh King, live forever." The herald announced Jehudi and his assignment from Jeremiah.

Jehoiakim glared from his ebony throne. "I don't wish to hear what that bag of wind has to say." He waved his hand, and the musicians increased their volume.

Ezekiel averted his eyes from the dancers' seductive movements.

Please, Yahweh, change his heart.

Jehudi strode forward and tore a flute away from a musician mid-note. The music broke off in a clang of dissonance. Wide eyes darted to the king.

"I must insist, sire," Jehudi's voice rang boldly through the stunned silence. "It is regarding your alliance with Babylon."

King Jehoiakim gave an exaggerated sigh and waved his hand.

Jehudi bowed with more respect than Ezekiel would have been able to muster. "Thus says the Lord of Hosts, 'Because you have not heard My words, behold, I will deploy the armies of the north,' says the Lord, 'and Nebuchadnezzar the king of Babylon, My servant, and will bring them against this land, against all its inhabitants, and against these nations all around, and will utterly destroy them, and make them an astonishment, a hissing and perpetual desolations—'"

King Jehoiakim propped his elbow on the side of the throne with a bored expression. His gaze roved over the dancers, standing uncertain against the wall, and he summoned a young woman to his side.

Why did the young co-regent, Coniah, react with tilted shoulders and clenched fists as his father fondled her? Ezekiel studied the girl's face and his jaw dropped. He had seen that haughty beauty paraded through the streets of Jerusalem at Coniah's marriage feast. It was Coniah's bride. A stone of revulsion settled in Ezekiel's belly.

King Jehoiakim raised a hand, halting Jehudi's recitation. "This is from Jeremiah?" He retrieved the knife the scribe had left at his station beside the throne and fingered the handle. "This isn't his style. Where is his scroll written so there is no mis-com-mun-ica-tion?"

Jehudi shifted a glance toward their group and moistened his lips.

"Fetch it, dog!" King Jehoiakim hurled his knife with deadly accuracy, impaling Jehudi's foot.

A woman screamed and a collective gasp rose to the arched ceiling. Jehudi paled. Ezekiel and the group of scribes pressed close behind Jehudi, ready to catch him should he fall.

"Here it is." Elishama appeared from the side, holding up a scroll. He glanced apologetically at Jehudi.

"Read it again, dog."

"Yes, my king." Jehudi's breathing was shallow.

"But first, bring me the knife."

Jehudi blanched, bent, and began to topple.

Ezekiel caught his arm and hauled him upright.

A soldier strode forward and mercilessly yanked the blade from Jehudi's flesh. The scribe cried out, and blood spurted on Ezekiel's robe. Ezekiel drew in breaths through his nose to calm the riot in his body.

The king accepted the knife, and his mouth twisted in a sardonic smile. He regarded Jehudi and licked the blood from the knife. "Proceed."

Ezekiel's mouth soured with the threat of the contents of his stomach rising. He wiped his mouth but couldn't avert his eyes—Jehudi's blood one direction, women's indecent bodies another, and the king's vulgarity before him. *Oh, God of my fathers, help me be strong for Your name.*

Jehudi unrolled the scroll, and somehow his voice was still strong. "Take this wine cup of My wrath, declares the Lord, 'for behold I begin to bring calamity on this city that is called by My name. Should you be utterly unpunished for you have walked in the evil ways of your fathers?'"

King Jehoiakim threw back his head and roared with laughter. "My fathers, Manasseh and Amon, didn't begin to know how to make Yahweh most angry. But I say to you before this audience, the only thing Yahweh has given us is the light of the temple. A light we no longer need. This is all we need now." He lifted his golden goblet.

Jehudi ground out words with labored breath. "Nebuchadnezzar acts upon Yahweh's instruction. He *will* destroy Jerusalem. Your people will be *slaves* seventy years—"

A shadow passed across the king's face. Remorse? "Bring it here."

The scribe limped forward, grunting with each step. He handed over the scroll with a dip of his head.

"Do you have ink? No? No problem, this will suffice." King Jehoiakim dipped the tip of his knife into Jehudi's blood seeping onto the tiled floor. With a flourish, he scraped the dagger across the papyrus.

"No!" Jehudi grabbed for the scroll, and Ezekiel lunged forward, only to be restrained by a guard's fist to his eye.

King Jehoiakim spread the scroll wide. "Yahweh is of no use to us. I am lord of this land. This is what I think of Yahweh's empty threats." He stabbed the dagger through the scroll and yanked downward with a vicious expression. The sound of tearing cloth rose over the gasps of the crowd.

The king crumpled the section of Yahweh's words he had cut and tossed it into the gilded brazier at his side. The papyrus ignited with a crackle and belched forth smoke.

"Read." King Jehoiakim slapped the scroll against Jehudi's heaving chest.

Horror was tangible in the throne room as Jehudi read the next four columns, and the king destroyed it in the same manner, showing blatant disrespect for the words of Yahweh, burning every last bit. Blows from the guards silenced the scribes' protests.

Heat screamed through Ezekiel's limbs. He glanced through the slit of his swollen eye at the bruise forming on Elishama's face. What could he do?

"Is there anything else?" A sinister smile slid across the king's face. "If not, then I'd like to continue with my evening."

He clapped once and another contingent of guards materialized. "Escort these men out. And hunt down the prophet Jeremiah. He and the man who penned this drivel die tonight."

Concern for Jeremiah plagued Ezekiel as he followed the trail of Jehudi's blood out of the palace. Apprehension wrapped around him as snugly as the linen bandage they wound round Jehudi's foot.

The nation's blood would surely seep through her temporary bandage soon, refusing to be staunched any longer.

1

Thus you shall separate the Levites from among the children of Israel, and the Levites shall be Mine…So you shall cleanse them and offer them like a wave offering. For they are wholly given to Me from among the children of Israel.
—Numbers 8:14, 15b-16a

602 B.C.
Two years later.

"It is time."

The boy's voice broke through the stillness of Ezekiel's meditation.

After serving as an apprentice seven years from his thirteenth year and doing the menial work of the temple, Ezekiel would be ordained this day as a Levite in the house of Yahweh, Most High God.

He rose from the ground and smoothed his white linen tunic. The boy waiting outside his chamber tipped his chin and studied Ezekiel solemnly.

Anticipation made Ezekiel's pace swift. He briefly closed

his eyes and slowed his steps to keep behind the boy. Dignified. Respectful. He served in the house of Yahweh, not some play yard. The stately pillars lining the corridor imbued ever-present wonder as they stood sentinel in this hallowed place. They crossed the outer courtyard and turned into the Courtyard of Women. Ezekiel made the pilgrimage from east to west through the Court of the Women and the Court of the Israelites to the sound of the musicians tuning their instruments in the outer courtyard. Soon the gates would be opened for morning worship and offering.

Drawing in a deep breath, Ezekiel stepped onto the smoothed stone slabs of the Court of the Priests. A cool breath of air washed over him, even as he felt the heat emanating from the altar where a small group waited.

A servant held the leads of two bulls at the base of the altar, and another held a blue and scarlet sash. Jeremiah—wearing a matching sash—stood with the other priests, a smile warring against the weariness and sorrow etching lines to his face.

Thank You, Yahweh for Your continued protection on my friend. Ezekiel met his mentor's steady gaze.

One bull tossed its head and tried to back away. In the absence of his *abba*—may peace be upon him—who had purchased the bulls? In these uncertain times of raids and famine, the animals would have cost a steep price.

Jeremiah gave a slight nod. "I'm glad to do it. To have you serving before Yahweh with a pure heart is worth the cost of my life."

"Thank you, my friend," Ezekiel murmured as he bowed at the waist to the priests. Hopefully it wouldn't come to that. This calling—handed down by a long line of priests before him—pressed on his spirit from the first time he accompanied his *abba* in the week-long service.

The priest ushered Ezekiel to the bronze sea.

Ezekiel knelt.

"May you always distinguish between holy and unholy. Clean and unclean." The priest dipped water from the sea and poured it over Ezekiel's head.

The water dripped down Ezekiel's clean-shaven head and face. He closed his eyes and lifted his hand. "You alone are holy. I will wash Your people to present them before You, clean."

Holy purpose swelled Ezekiel's chest and the back of his eyes burned. He rose and climbed the stairs to the altar where Jeremiah waited.

The bulls' hooves clopped on the quarried stone behind him.

"You stand before the Lord today, and tomorrow you will stand before the people. Your duty is to serve the priests and love these people and shepherd them in the ways of truth as Yahweh has indeed called out to our people over the centuries." Jeremiah's face contorted with sorrow. "Regardless of the danger to your own life and their hard-hearted ways."

Ezekiel swallowed as the man departed from the rehearsed lines. "I will lead these people as Yahweh leads me."

"Lay your hands on the bull's head." Jeremiah held the animal's face still as Ezekiel placed his hands and forehead against the broad face. The priests pressed close and put heavy hands on Ezekiel's back.

Jeremiah's voice lowered, "Yahweh, as this man dedicates his life to serving You, guide his steps. Give him wisdom. May his soul yearn for Your truth. May Your people turn their hearts back to You under Ezekiel's leadership."

Accept this offering as atonement for my sins. Ezekiel's throat closed as the bull snorted.

Jeremiah slit the bull's throat, and the blood drained into the waiting bowl. The Levites cut and skinned the bull with trained efficiency. Jeremiah pressed the sacrificial knife into Ezekiel's hand as the second bull was led forth.

Ezekiel scrutinized the knife he held. Could he truly live

up to this holy office? The weight of the people's waywardness pressed heavy against him. What made him think he could convince them to return to Yahweh, well-knowing the approaching doom? *Only by Your leading.*

He curled his fingers around the handle and the bull's head. Jeremiah's rough hand encompassed his and together they sliced through hide and skin, piercing the vein. The bull's life ended and Ezekiel's began.

After he cleaned his hands, he lowered his head before Jeremiah.

"My son, you are now consecrated to serve in the temple according to the order of King David and the priests faithful to Yahweh." Jeremiah wrapped the sash around Ezekiel's waist twice, tying it and allowing the excess to trail behind him on the steps. "I publicly dedicate you to service of the Lord as your *abba* did at your birth."

Jeremiah placed a priest's turban on Ezekiel's head. "Ezekiel, son of Buzi, you will serve in this role until your thirtieth birthday. Then, according to the law of Moses, you will be ordained as a priest. Do you vow to hold this office dear, and conduct yourself as though you already have the title of priest?"

If only Abba were alive to see this day. Ezekiel smiled somberly. "I do so swear. As Yahweh sees fit."

The quartered meat on the altar smoked, and flames licked the dripping fat. A trumpet sounded in the outer courtyard, and the gates clattered open. Ezekiel glanced to the sky. Just in time to prepare the morning sacrifice.

They descended the altar steps as the morning rotation of priests and Levites waited with the lamb. Ezekiel held his head high.

Most shifted their eyes from the sky to their party and adjusted their positions with airs of impatience. Did no one care for the sacred job they had been appointed to? The last priest on the left lifted his head and smiled slightly.

"How do you feel?" The shift in Jeremiah's voice drew Ezekiel's attention. By the expression on the older man's face, Yahweh had spoken to him.

"What can I do?"

Jeremiah surveyed the courtyard—now bustling with people—shoulders heaving. "You will report now to Pashur, the chief governor of the temple."

Ezekiel blinked. Serving the priest who scheduled all the comings and goings of the different Levites and priests would keep him close to the workings of the temple. This would confirm his trajectory to become a priest.

A gong sounded outside the temple complex, and the abrasive chants of Baal's priests overshadowed Yahweh's musicians. Jeremiah covered a sob.

"What is it?" Ezekiel gripped his friend's shoulders.

"They don't care. They know and don't turn away."

Ezekiel scanned the faces in the crowd, unable to shake the dread that settled in his stomach.

Jeremiah turned back to the steps, giving the indication he was closer to collapsing than sharing the word of Yahweh. "Thus, says the Lord of hosts, the God of Israel." Jeremiah raised his voice and hands.

Ezekiel reached out to halt a man walking by. "Listen to the words of Yahweh."

The man turned his eyes to the prophet.

"Behold, I will bring on the city and on all her towns all the doom that I have pronounced against it, because you have stiffened your necks that you may not hear My words." Jeremiah swiped away streams of tears only to have them replaced.

The man shook off Ezekiel's hand and stalked away. "He declares doom and gloom. He is mad. None of these so-called prophecies have come to pass."

"Wait!" Ezekiel reached out again. "Can you not see?

Judah's borders are even now encroached by Moab and Amon."

The man didn't turn.

Frowning, Ezekiel situated himself by a cluster of chatting women. "Listen, the prophet speaks truth." He gestured toward Jeremiah.

The women gawked at Ezekiel as if he had an extra eyebrow on his face.

"'—Judah and Jerusalem will fall by the sword before their enemies. I will break this people and this city as one breaks a potter's vessel' says the Lord."

"Bah! Yahweh will not allow His holy city to fall." The woman to Ezekiel's right brushed off her hands.

"'—behold, I will bring such a catastrophe on this place that whoever hears of it his ears will tingle. Everyone who passes by Jerusalem will be astonished and hiss because of all the plagues upon it.'"

"What are you doing?" Pashur, the chief governor, strode toward the stairs, followed by two soldiers.

"'—Your corpses shall be meat for the birds and beasts, you shall eat the flesh of your sons and daughters, your friends—'"

"Enough!" Pashur struck Jeremiah across the face, and the prophet sprawled down the stairs.

A gasp rose from the crowd. The people pressed around, more concerned with the spectacle than the message.

Ezekiel lowered his shoulder and ducked around a portly, balding man and reached the steps as Jeremiah pushed himself to his knees.

"How dare you speak such heinous words! Jerusalem is under Yahweh's protection." Pashur kicked Jeremiah's side, sending him colliding into Ezekiel's legs.

"Would you deny the words of Yahweh?" Jeremiah accepted Ezekiel's offered hand and struggled to stand.

"Yahweh would never destroy his inheritance." Pashur

snapped his fingers at the archer flanking him. "Take this man to the stocks."

"No!" Ezekiel stepped between the men.

Jeremiah's hand rested on Ezekiel's shoulder. "Serve the people regardless of the danger to your own life and their hard-hearted ways."

Ezekiel frowned as his mentor extended his arms for shackles. How could he stand by and watch Jeremiah endanger his own life?

"Remember your task." Jeremiah allowed himself to be led toward the New Gate.

"Be at peace, my people." Pashur smiled benevolently over the agitated crowd. "The prophet will be punished for his blasphemy. Yahweh has promised He would never leave us or forsake us."

The knot in Ezekiel's gut tightened as the crowd dispersed with a chuckle. Heads shook and tongues wagged, Jeremiah's name as much a byword as he predicted Jerusalem to be.

"You, there."

Turning, Ezekiel lowered his head. *Yahweh, give me the respect to match this man's position.* He unclenched his hands under Pashur's perusal.

"Are you a supporter of Jeremiah's?"

"I have studied under him these two years."

"Ah. Ezekiel, right?" Pashur placed gentle hands on Ezekiel's shoulders. "You should know Yahweh's truths by now. He has established our nation, this city. He will not abandon us. It is against His nature."

Ezekiel's vows of moments before did not entail backing down from danger or truth. The word of the Lord was a light to his feet and a lamp to his path—meaning he'd walk amongst darkness. Perhaps he was appointed to this position to illuminate the path for Pashur. "Jeremiah's words come from Yahweh. Can't you see the terror encamped around us?"

Pashur smiled and raised his hand. "You shall not be afraid of the terror by night because Yahweh is our refuge."

"But—"

"We'll have no more of this talk." Pashur led Ezekiel toward the gate house. "I know it must be hard to see someone you care about imprisoned, but it is according to Yahweh's plan. We cannot allow people to stir up trouble in the courtyard. The utmost focus should be on worshiping Yahweh in peace."

Ezekiel glanced to the sky as Pashur's soothing voice determined the order of things. Since the reign of Joash, two kings prior to Jehoiakim, the people of Judah had turned a blind eye to the turmoil beyond Jerusalem's borders, caring only that they could worship in supposed tranquility.

The priest of Baal droned on beyond the wall, and Ezekiel's head pounded.

Give me wisdom, Yahweh. This position was supposed to ensure influence. How could he change the course of their hearts? He felt as haggard as Jeremiah appeared—walking out of the gate in chains—and his first day had just begun.

2

And it happened on the next day that Pashur brought Jeremiah out of the stocks. Then Jeremiah said to him, "The Lord has not called your name Pashur, but Magor-Missabib. For thus says the Lord: 'Behold I will make you a terror to yourself and to all your friends; and they shall fall by the sword of their enemies, and your eyes shall see it…"
—Jeremiah 20:3-4a

Gilead glanced over his shoulder at his prisoner as they left the temple complex.

The weeping prophet trailed behind, still spouting off to unheeding ears. "Repent! Surely Yahweh will not restrain His anger against Jerusalem for much longer."

A sun-burned shepherd leaned forward and spat. "Your prophecies of doom are mere rainless clouds. All thunder and no moisture for our land."

Gilead's eyes narrowed and he stepped toe to toe with the man, twanging the bowstring across his chest. "Out of my way. Move along." He clamped his free hand on Jeremiah's shoulder and veered toward the Gate of Benjamin, avoiding an approaching crowd.

The chains clanked together as Jeremiah wiped his eyes, muttering,

"Why have You enticed me, Yahweh? I am derided daily."

Jeremiah seemed to be intertwined in orders from a superior officer, yet still had the freedom to engage in conversation as he would a friend.

Gilead shifted and cleared his throat. "Why do you continue to say the words? The people will not change."

Jeremiah blinked woefully at him. "I cannot hold it back. Yahweh's word is a burning fire in my heart. Have you ever had a fire shut up in your bones?"

"Sounds painful." Gilead arched an eyebrow.

The prophet scowled and strode ahead.

Gilead swiped away his grin. If he didn't know better, he'd think Jeremiah *wanted* to be imprisoned. He followed his prisoner through the narrow streets of hewn stone. The incline pulled on the back of his legs as they turned onto the market street and into a gathering crowd.

Sandals slapped the roadway behind them, barreling close at a frantic pace.

Gilead shifted to the side and glared at the harried woman. "What's your hurry?"

"The barley seller has just restocked!" She rushed on, nearly plowing over an old woman.

Gilead and Jeremiah steadied the fragile woman with hollow cheeks. Shouts erupted, along with the sound of a fist hitting flesh, and Gilead broke into a jog. He yanked a man back and shoved into the inner circle. These vendors grew more physical with each passing day.

His eyes widened. Contrary to what he expected, the seller cowered behind the bins watching the melee. The woman who had nearly run them over—now sporting a red mark on her cheek—grabbed and tugged on a basket filled to the brim with barley.

The owner of the basket was a woman with a pronounced forehead and a scream like a jackal. Her leg jerked out in a kick that should have knocked loose her opponent, but the first woman clung to the basket with white-knuckled determination.

"What is going on?" Gilead's uniform garnered respect with all in the crowd except the clawing woman. He stepped close and rested his hand on his quiver of arrows. "Step back, woman."

Obeying, she burst into tears. If she had been a man, Gilead would have struck her with a closed fist, but tears? He wrinkled his forehead and wheeled to the woman with the basket. "What happened?"

"She is trying to steal my barley!" The woman jerked the basket out of reach, spilling some in the process. She shrieked and knelt to scoop every last grain.

The barley merchant stacked his empty baskets, making no attempt to moderate the riot.

Gilead faced the sobbing woman. "Stealing will be punished."

"But she—"

"I suggest you move along before I arrest you."

"Thank you." The woman with the broad forehead rose, hugged her basket to her side, and scurried down the street, casting furtive glances over her shoulder.

Gilead glared down at the woman still standing before him, her shoulders shaking with sobs. "Get out of here."

"She has enough stockpiled already to last until next barley harvest." The woman fisted her hands. "Every time the seller comes, she purchases even more. Then there isn't enough for the others."

Gilead followed her soggy nod to the elderly woman still

standing with Jeremiah. He glanced at the vendor. "Is this true?"

The merchant shrugged, clearly not caring who bought his grain. And why should he? The day stretched before him, yet he had sold all his wares.

Jeremiah's forehead furrowed, and he put shackled hands on the old woman's shoulders. "There has to be more up the way. Walk with us."

"I can't afford what they ask at Elias' stall." The elderly woman's voice wobbled like her legs.

"We are heading that way." Jeremiah guided the woman up the arched walkway.

Who was the guard and who the prisoner? Gilead shot a glare the prophet did not see. Fine. The woman did resemble the neighbor who had looked in on him as a child. When they arrived at Elias' stand in Jerusalem's elite market, he too stacked empty baskets.

"Thank you, anyway." The woman turned.

Jeremiah restrained her. "Please, my lord, this woman is in need of grain."

"Can't you see I am closing up?" Elias spread his hands.

"I happen to know you have a reserve of the finest grain. Is there a more noble client than this fair widow?"

Gilead crossed his arms. If this convinced the vendor, Jeremiah was a worker of miracles.

"Well…" Elias' expression softened. "The barley remaining is the first fruits of my crop."

"The first fruit I'm sure you intended to take to the temple as your prescribed offering." Jeremiah tipped his head.

Elias shifted his weight, stammering, "Of course."

Jeremiah leaned closer. "Yahweh would rather have you meeting the needs of the poor and the widows than giving sacrifices to the temple out of obligation."

"It will not be cheap." The merchant cleared his throat,

casting a glance between Jeremiah and Gilead. "That is, I have to make a living."

Gilead smirked as the man patted his already fat money pouch.

Jeremiah tipped his head. "What's the best you can do?"

The vendor haggled and perspired more profusely as Jeremiah scowled at each offer.

Unbelievable. Without a word, the prophet allowed the man to haggle himself to cheaper than the merchant charged down the hill.

The elderly woman wiped away a wayward tear. "Thank you." She dug into her satchel for her coins.

"I'm surprised you don't pay after all that talk of caring for widows." Gilead leaned close.

Jeremiah turned grieved eyes toward him and indicated his simple, priestly garments. "I don't carry coins when I'm serving in the temple."

Gilead glowered at the expectation in the priest's eyes and dug the amount from his money pouch. "Fine. I'll pay."

"Bless you." The woman pulled his face down and kissed the top of his head as his neighbor had done all those years ago. Catching the prophet's intense gaze, he scowled. "Move out."

Jeremiah turned without further prompting and they marched in silence.

"You could've escaped back there." Gilead slanted a glance at the prophet. "Why are you still here?"

"You could've ignored the scuffle. Why are you still here?"

Gilead clenched his fist to keep from striking the man. "Because I have a job to do."

Jeremiah tipped his head and raised the shackles.

"Do you mean to tell me Yahweh wants you put in the stocks?" Gilead squeezed Jeremiah's shoulder until the man grimaced.

"I am saying Yahweh expects me to be faithful in whatever

He sets before me. He told me the people would not hear or obey."

Gilead leaned close to hear.

"Being untouchable doesn't make it easy."

"You call being beat 'untouchable'?" Gilead shoved the man forward.

Jeremiah righted himself. "On good days, I remember serving Yahweh is a blessing. A joy. Who would've thought that a king's soldier would pay for a widow's grain in a panic-induced famine?"

Nodding to the gatekeeper at the Gate of Benjamin, Gilead yanked the chain for show.

Jeremiah sat before the stocks and extended his legs into the grooves for Gilead to clamp the beam down. He turned his upper body north and gazed over the land of Benjamin. "What do you believe about what I say?"

Gilead fastened the lock and returned the key to his belt. "About Jerusalem being overthrown? I've seen the armies on the outskirts. I see how we aren't in a desperate place with food like the merchants would have us believe. Is it likely our land will continue to be invaded and overthrown? Yes."

Jeremiah turned his marrow-piercing gaze to Gilead. "What holds you back from following Yahweh's path?"

A cluster of youths exited the city, shoving each other and laughing. "Oh, a prisoner. What did you do, old man?" One scooped up small rocks and hurled them at Jeremiah.

The prophet shielded his face with his arms, yelping as the rocks pinged off his skin.

"That's enough." Gilead stood in front of the stocks.

"Do you think you're the only one who can afflict him?"

Gilead launched forward, snatching the insolent boy's tunic and pulling him a handbreadth from his face. "I think you will find yourself afflicted if you don't relent."

Fear flitted in the boy's eyes, and Gilead swung his glare to the others. They retreated as one, eyes wide and hands up. He thrust the boy away from him. "Move on." The boys darted off like scared rabbits.

"Be careful. You just defended a weak one. You might be in compliance with Yahweh." Jeremiah's voice held the hint of a smile.

Gilead didn't turn. "He called you old. I figure you and I are about the same age, and I'm not old."

The prophet chuckled, and Gilead allowed himself a smile.

The next morning, Pashur strolled out the gate as it opened. Gilead nudged the priest with the toe of his sandal. Jeremiah opened his eyes and stretched his arms high, grunting as a man who had spent the night huddled on the ground trying to rest.

At Pashur's signal, Gilead slipped the key into the lock and twisted. The stock's creak foretold the sound Jeremiah's bones made when he pushed himself to his feet.

"You understand why I had to arrest you." Pashur clasped smooth, uncalloused hands. "As chief governor of the temple, I cannot allow you to upset the people by speaking scandalous words about Yahweh."

"I understand perfectly." Jeremiah bent and rubbed the raw marks on his ankles. "Your eyes are closed to the truth in front of you. Yahweh has called you Magor-Missabib because you have prophesied lies. You shall be made a terror to yourself and all those you've misled."

Pity overtook Pashur's expression. "You accuse *me* of false prophecy? Yahweh will not destroy this place. He has put His name upon it. He has promised."

"He has promised to preserve the city only as long as we seek him."

"And we have. Do you not remember King Josiah's reform?" Pashur brushed off his beige robe. "Even now, King Jehoiakim allows us to continue worshiping Yahweh."

The prophet's eyes flashed. He drew in a breath. "You

think Yahweh will be satisfied with 'allows us'? King Jehoiakim has set the course of our demise in strong motion."

Gilead searched the hilltop. Nobody stood nearby to hear Jeremiah's treasonous remarks.

Pashur shook his head with a smile. "Jehoiakim wouldn't shut the temple down. He can't. I wouldn't allow it."

Did the man see nothing of Judah's unscrupulous king or her crumbling borders?

"King Jehoiakim has no power in light of Yahweh's judgment!" Jeremiah shook his finger.

"Enough! I will not have you continue to blaspheme Yahweh and speak ill of the king." Pashur turned to Gilead. "Remind Jeremiah of the folly of false prophecy and spreading his doom and gloom to the people."

"Yahweh will give all of Judah and its wealth into the hand of the king of Babylon." Jeremiah spread his hands wide, encompassing the city and the overlook of the land.

"Gilead! You will stop this." Pashur jerked his head toward the prophet.

Hesitating, Gilead glanced apologetically at Jeremiah—he couldn't afford to disobey an order—and struck the prophet across the face.

The man staggered and shouted to Pashur's departing back, "Thus says the Lord, 'you and all your household shall go into captivity in Babylon! You shall die and be buried there.'"

"He's gone. Let it go, prophet." Gilead put his hand on Jeremiah's shoulder. "He doesn't realize the devastation he brings on himself and others."

"Why do you make excuses for him? People are being deceived." Jeremiah pressed the back of his hand to his cheekbone. "They will endure a great hardship and die because their leaders aren't honorable."

Gilead shifted his stance. Through all his training and the battles he'd experienced, he'd neglected to view the people around him as anything more than practice scenarios. Were they as misled as the prophet indicated? Wasn't all mankind accountable for their own actions? The elderly woman's lined face came to mind. He'd disregarded the needs of the people he was sworn to protect. Had he led anyone astray? Nobody turned to him for wisdom. How could they?

"You should come to the temple." Jeremiah twisted his back side to side. "There is a group of us who study and live the law."

Buried records of wrongs that littered Gilead's past threatened to surface. He swallowed and avoided Jeremiah's probing examination. "You don't want me. I've done too many bad things."

A long moment passed. Gilead glanced up. As he figured, the prophet's gaze convicted, but Gilead hadn't expected the grace.

He cleared his throat against the discomfort of self-awareness. "What's the point? If Yahweh is set against us, what good would it do?"

Jeremiah's shoulders straightened, and he exuded confidence. "It's not too late. Yahweh needs shepherds."

Gilead's lip curled involuntarily.

"Figuratively. Leaders. People to care for the remnant. Yahweh will restore Judah. Eventually."

Longing pressed inside Gilead's chest. Could Yahweh use him to impact others?

"Step out in faith. Set aside your doubts," Jeremiah prodded.

Gilead rubbed his thumb across his bow string. If Jeremiah—Yahweh, really—extended a fresh start, he simply had to reach out and take it.

He consented with a dip of his chin. Moisture sprung to his eyes as the prophet embraced him, laughing.

3

'Thus says the Lord God: "Woe to the women who sew magic charms on their sleeves and make veils for the heads of people of every height to hunt souls! Will you hunt the souls of My people, and keep yourselves alive? And will you profane Me among My people for handfuls of barley and for pieces of bread, killing people who should not die, and keeping alive who should not live, by your lying to My people who listen to lies?
—Ezekiel 13:18b-19

599 BC

Three years later.

Ezekiel strode with rising frustration toward the closed New Gate. Workers couldn't enter until they had a way. This marked the second day in a row Hadar hadn't arrived at his post on time. The man refused to take his position seriously. With a shake of his head, Ezekiel reached underneath his tunic and brought forth the spare key to unlock the gate. In the three years he had been serving as aide to the chief governor of the temple, no man had irked him as much as Hadar.

All gates were to be opened upon completion of the long-concluded morning sacrifice, to allow entrance to the temple courtyard. The bolt thudded back and Ezekiel leaned against the gate, pushing it open, revealing a line of frowning people and their vocal animals.

"*Shalom*, my apologies." Ezekiel folded his hands in an effort to present himself as unrattled and in control. Inside, his thoughts swept over the different Levites on duty. Which gate-keeper could he call on to step in for Hadar?

As the surge of people funneled through the gate, two women approached with shoulders held high, gazing boldly ahead. They clustered together and clutched their brightly colored head scarves tightly around themselves. Too tightly.

Ezekiel stepped in their path and crossed his arms.

The shorter woman gripped her companion's elbow and lowered her face. "Is there a problem, your grace?" A jangle accompanied her friend's halt.

Ezekiel leaned forward, using his broad shoulders to intimidate the women. "What brings you to the temple today?"

"We came to prophesy, priest." The first woman kept her chin lowered and lifted eyes that conveyed a message opposite her demure posture.

Ezekiel narrowed his eyes. He took another step forward.

The second woman shifted back, and the pouch she clutched under her covering fell to the ground, its contents clanking together. She gasped and lunged forward with a flurry of fabric, but Ezekiel was quicker.

He scooped up the pouch and yanked it open, revealing grotesque charms and amulets. "Aha. And what do the prophecies from your own hearts say?" He dumped the charms to the ground.

The shorter woman whipped the scarf from her head, revealing more charms sewn on her sleeves. "The Lord says there will be peace. Behold, our brothers have already begun to build a wall on the south to prevent more raids from the invaders."

"There is no peace. The Lord's judgment will not be delayed." Ezekiel spread his arms and advanced, pushing the women out of the temple. "You hunt the souls of the people with your lies. Will it extend your days?"

"I have seen a vision…"

"Because you and your kind have spoken nonsense and blinded those who would seek Yahweh, He is against you."

The second woman planted her fists on her hips. "It is you who speak falsely. The Lord wants to protect His city just as the southern wall will divert raiders."

Ezekiel scoffed. "I have seen your wall and your untempered mortar. It will fall with a strong wind. Get out. You shall not enter into Yahweh's temple to pervert His people."

The shorter woman scowled and flounced out with a huff, and the second woman crouched to retrieve the charms before following.

If Hadar had been at his post, he would likely not have caught the impostors—or cared.

Ezekiel rolled his shoulders. *Help me be vigilant. Give me the wisdom of Solomon and the discernment of Samuel. Guard this gate with me.*

The women planted themselves to the side of the road, a stone's throw away, calling out to the entering worshippers and the animal handlers bringing in the day's contribution for the offerings.

"Move on." Ezekiel brushed the air.

"We aren't on temple property. You have no authority here, priest." The shorter woman draped veils over her arms, displaying their bright colors. Such distain flowed from their hearts.

Ezekiel's chest clenched. How long would they deceive themselves? He searched the courtyard for someone to relieve him so he could shoo them away.

"Listen to the word of Yahweh." The second woman turned a defiant expression to Ezekiel. "This priest would want you to believe Yahweh doesn't love us any longer. He would say Yahweh doesn't care about Jerusalem."

The shorter woman lifted her arms, the vibrant fabrics flowing as colorful waterfalls. "We are here today with a message of peace. Serenity that will drape across you and soothe your soul as surely as these lovely veils will drape across your shoulders."

A man lingered before them.

"We even have something for your noble height." The shorter woman draped a veil with blue tassels over the man's shoulder.

A wink of silver on the underside of the fabric caught Ezekiel's eye. "Pardon, my lord, that isn't a prayer shawl."

But the man had turned aside to listen to the women's ear-pleasing message. The second woman smirked at Ezekiel as her companion successfully diverted the man's attention.

Ezekiel strode two paces, halting as the second woman stepped to the opposite side of the path, edging closer to the gate. He ground his teeth and backed into the gateway. He must maintain the post. *Yahweh, show this man the folly of his ways.*

"Are you good here, or…" Hadar's lazy drawl drove Ezekiel's agitation level to the heights of the temple walls.

He angled himself to see the guard's hair unkempt and his robes crumpled. Did he not respect himself enough to put on fresh clothing after rising? "Where have you been?"

Hadar shrugged. "My apologies."

Ezekiel struggled for control. "If this gate is not open on time, the people are affected."

A slender woman in the off-white robes of the Levites approached the charm-peddling serpents.

"It won't happen again." Hadar's attempt at a promise

hung as false as the pretense of worship from the men entering the gates.

"You are correct in saying that. Tomorrow you will wash the priests' feet as they minister to Yahweh." Perhaps the humble station would produce a proper attitude. It also demanded less attention to outside distractions.

Hadar shrugged and raised his eyebrows.

The Levitess pressed something into the shorter woman's hand, shifted a long, wrapped object in her own, and turned toward the gate again.

"Beware of those women, they have tried to enter to sell their charms."

Hadar wiped at his eyes and leaned his shoulder against the gate post.

Ezekiel's growl snapped him to reluctant attention.

He gave Hadar his most intimidating glare and swung it to the Levite woman as she stepped through the gate. His calm and decorum evaporated with the rising sun, and he grabbed her arm. "Why are you even here?"

Her mouth rounded, and she blinked as he dragged her out of the throughway. "Unhand me!" Her voice shook.

Good. Let the idolatrous woman fear him. He released her with a shove. "You dare to come into Yahweh's temple after purchasing those trinkets? Yahweh will not be mocked!"

"What?" The woman backed out of his reach, hiding her bundle behind her back.

"Why are you here?" Ezekiel ground out the words. His fingers wrapped around the contraband item, and with a swift yank, he dislodged it from her grasp.

"Give it back!"

"I will not ask again. Why did you come into Yahweh's house today?" He tore the linen wrapping off, revealing a reed flute. Turning it over he shook it. If charms were hidden inside, they had been secured well.

"I am a musician. I'm here to worship the Lord." She rubbed her arm.

Lies. She might be a musician, but not here. Women weren't temple musicians. His insides churned. Ezekiel raised the flute with both hands and spun toward the wall. He'd smash the instrument of idol worship over his knee if he couldn't find a surface to assist.

"Stop!" The woman lunged at him and latched onto the reed. Her grip was no match for Ezekiel's strength, and her heels slid over the smooth tiles.

Her shriek drew the attention of the passers-by, but they glanced away and hurried on. Hadar's stance indicated he had already passed into the stage of oblivion prior to dozing.

Someone attempted to violate the temple, and no one could be bothered.

Ezekiel wrenched to the left, jerking the woman as well. The purity of the temple was at stake, he would not relent.

"What is going on here?" Pashur strode toward them.

Finally, Ezekiel would get assistance. Pashur might be misguided, but he took impurities in the temple seriously. "This woman purchased charms and is trying to defile the temple."

The woman gasped, and Ezekiel used her surprise to leverage the flute from her hands.

Pashur's eyebrows shot up as he glanced between the woman and Ezekiel.

Ezekiel relinquished the instrument to the chief governor. He cast a triumphant glare at the woman.

Her chin quivered and tears streamed down her face. "I don't know anything about any charms." Her voice pitched high, and she wiped the moisture coming from her nose. "I am Shiriel, daughter of Ibraham. I am appointed to serve this week under the chief musician."

Pashur's eyes widened.

"Since when has the temple employed women to lead worship?" Ezekiel raised his eyebrows.

"Since she is the daughter of our former choirmaster." Pashur bent at the waist and extended the flute.

"But a woman?" Ezekiel palmed the back of his neck.

Shiriel cradled the flute to her chest and tipped her face up. "My *abba* has retired. It is our family's week to serve, and I have no brothers. Abba has already made arrangements with Amram, the choirmaster."

"Of course." Pashur shot Ezekiel a look of censor. "As I recall, your family has served in the temple for many generations and is descended from the noble musician Hemen."

Shiriel tossed a withering glare to Ezekiel. "That is correct, my lord. My family comes from the line of Hemen's *daughter* who sang in the temple in the days of Solomon."

Perhaps the musician part had been explained, but what of the charms? "I witnessed you giving something to that woman—"

"Shiri?" A man near Ezekiel's age dressed in Levitical garb approached, face lined with concern.

Tangible relief flashed across Shiriel's face. Her shoulders sagged. "Chesed."

"Is there a problem, your honors?" Chesed edged in front of Shiriel.

Ezekiel surveyed the drum head protruding from the intruder's bulky pack. "Can you vouch for this woman?"

"Shiri—Shiriel—is my cousin, my *dohd's* daughter. I am...we are…musicians, serving the week appointed to our families."

Pashur tented his hands. "There has been a misunderstanding. We were just apologizing to your cousin so she could meet up with Amram."

Release her? "But the trinkets—"

Pashur glared at Ezekiel. "Thank you for your service to Yahweh, Shiriel. May His name be glorified."

"Thank you, my lord." Shiriel bowed to Pashur. She and her cousin turned toward the musicians' risers on the north wall of the temple.

Ezekiel glared at her retreating form. "I saw her."

No answer.

Pashur had left, and Ezekiel spoke to himself. He growled, straightened his sash, and returned to his rounds. Though all others disregarded the sanctity of the office, he still had to ensure everything moved smoothly. With so many different factors needing strategic placement and timing, the day-to-day operations of the temple were an elaborate undertaking.

He marched across the compound, his head held high and his arms folded behind his rigid back, but his mind kept replaying the exchange between Shiriel and the merchant.

Yahweh, if she pollutes the minds of these people, I'll never forgive myself. His stomach turned. He strode toward the choir and planted his feet in front of the risers and surveyed the musicians and singers, making note of the numbers for the record.

Chesed sat on a stool in front of the choir, his drum's base tucked under his arm. He alternated between rolling his fingers one after the other over the taut surface and tapping all four at the same time.

Ezekiel shifted his attention across the harps and stringed instruments with slender necks and finally to the flutes—both transverse and vertical. Shiriel followed the choirmaster's nonverbal communication. She lifted the flute to her mouth and blew, moving her fingers in a pattern only a musician would understand. An expression of peace spread across her face as the smooth, hollow sound floated on the air.

How had he not noticed the music before? He had always been aware of the numbers and of course the reputation musicians lived up to. At the end of each day, they flounced to their quarters, not lifting a hand to help with temple upkeep—as if they had already made the most important contribution to the temple.

Had Ezekiel ever stood still before them and listened as the choir led worship? He closed his eyes and quieted his heart, permitting the chanting to wash over him. The final note from the harp twanged and the company stood silent.

So Shiriel was a musician, by every count, genuinely worshiping Yahweh. What of her idolatrous ways? She couldn't mix the two and remain undisciplined.

Ezekiel turned on his heel and strode to the New Gate, clapping the sleeping watchman on the shoulder as he passed. Hadar startled and shook himself awake. Did none have good work ethic these days?

The women who prophesied from their hearts still sold their wares and turned people aside. They glanced up as Ezekiel stormed close.

"That woman, what did you sell her?"

The shorter woman smirked. "The girl you accosted?"

So the incident did come across as horribly as he remembered. "Yes. I saw her pay you."

"Did the holy priest allow a heathen to slip past him?" the second woman mocked.

Ezekiel's fist closed. "Tell me."

"Nothing."

"Why do you keep lying? I saw her give you money." Red blurred Ezekiel's vision.

The shorter woman laughed and jerked her chin toward the road beside them. "You'd better investigate more thoroughly before you condemn your next victim. I wouldn't give her a thing for what she offered."

"Come along. There is no shade here." They turned toward the city, and the second woman shot a parting glare over her shoulder.

Good riddance. Ezekiel bent to retrieve the small scrap of parchment they had left on the ground. He crumpled it tight in his palm, considered his actions, then smoothed it out once more. The need to know what lies to protect the people from was stronger than the desire not to taint his own mind.

"Hear, O Israel: The Lord our God, the Lord is one! You shall love the Lord your God—" Ezekiel frowned and turned the parchment over. Nothing but the words of the Shema.

Shiriel had given words to encourage these women to soften their hearts to Yahweh.

Heat rushed up his neck. He had put his hands on this girl and accused her. Her *abba*—or husband—would have his head. She had said she was under her cousin's guardianship, so possibly no husband…only an irate *abba*. He groaned. His only salvation was she would be there for the whole week. He'd find a way to apologize, to explain.

4

You will show me the path of life; In Your presence is fullness of joy; At Your right hand are pleasures forevermore.
—Psalm 16:11

Shiri rose with the chipper blast of the morning trumpet and stretched her arms high. Excitement and continual revisiting of her encounter with the priest at the gate had been her restless companions during the still of night. The footsteps and low humming of the Levite doing night-checks and the unfamiliar noises of the temple stirred her from light dozing time and again.

She rubbed her face vigorously and dipped her hands in the water basin beside her sleeping mat. The cool water refreshed her blurry eyes and invigorated her. Rolling up the mat, Shiri propped it in the corner of the narrow room—one of the few unoccupied by the men serving in the temple that week.

Thank You, Yahweh, for allowing me to serve in Your magnificent temple. Was there anything better than serving with the gifts Yahweh had bestowed upon her?

Excitement fueled Shiri's strokes as she combed her hair and wound her head scarf into a knot at her shoulder.

With a quick glance around her small quarters, Shiri unwrapped her flute and blew into the reed, her fingers flying over the holes for quick scales.

Once finished with her practice, she ducked under the tapestry and glanced around. "Where to go to break the fast?" Beyond the stately pillars in Solomon's Portico a stream of Levites and priests headed to the south.

Amidst the slap of sandals against the stone slabs, faint conversations drifted through the air like the hum of instruments tuning.

Shiri drew back her shoulders and merged into the throngs of people.

The flutist who sat on the stool beside her yesterday nodded a greeting. "That is a fine flute you have there."

"Thank you."

He re-engaged in his previous conversation before Shiri could tell him how her *abba* had made it for her. Worry nagged at Shiri's peace. With her here at the temple, *Abba* would have to spend less time on his flutes and more time caring for *Ima.*

Shiri mentally shook herself. Twice a year *Abba* had served his time at the temple. Yes, it disrupted the rhythm of the household, but what glorious purpose it was to know *Abba* served in Yahweh's courts. Now it was Shiri's turn, and her parents had been glad for her to serve—practically pushed her out of the home. Yahweh would not abandon those who were called according to His purpose. He would provide.

Yahweh, fortify my ima today. May her health improve. Send patrons to buy Abba's flutes. She rubbed her thumb over the smooth reed.

Abba had spent countless hours on this flute, as he did with all his flutes. But, this one he had lovingly fashioned just for her. In her mind she could see him sanding it smooth, the aroma of sweet almond oil tangible.

This instrument was a treasure for sure, but replaceable.

Why had she acted so rashly when that hotheaded priest snatched it? If Chesed hadn't come along when he had…

Was she meant to allow the man to destroy her instrument? How would she fulfill her duties? *I don't go around destroying his…whatever he needs to perform his responsibilities.*

The bruise on her arm smarted, commiserating with the blow her feelings had taken. Shiri rolled her neck from shoulder to shoulder, trying to release the tension evoked from her thoughts. If she allowed that priest to affect her, her playing would suffer, and she needed to be at her best.

"Good morning."

Shiri lifted her gaze from the path before her feet. As if her thoughts had summoned him, the same priest materialized beside her.

Her feet slid to a halt, and she thrust the flute behind her. Angry tears stung the back of her eyes. Shiri clamped her mouth shut, warring with the emotions suffocating her, pressing on her chest. Fighting the urge to flee, she sidestepped.

"Watch out." The priest reached out.

Shiri ducked away from his vice-grip and smacked into another Levite.

"Mind where you're going." The man glared at her.

"Your pardon." This time, Shiri turned her head and merged into an opening in the line of priests and Levites. She lifted her chin and marched past the gatekeeper.

"I am sorry." He fell into step beside her at an appropriate distance.

Shiri swallowed her tears and shoved her emotions down

before they betrayed her. She held the flute on her far side, away from his reach. Not that it had stopped him before.

"I'd like to explain—though there is no excuse for my rudeness."

Why wouldn't he leave her alone? She rubbed at her throbbing arm.

The priest hung his head. "I saw you give something to the women peddling charms."

That was what this was about? The back of her neck prickled.

He held up his hand. "I know now you were behaving honorably. I admire that, but at that time I thought…"

Come out and say it. Shiri crossed her arms then uncrossed them to keep her flute far away.

"I thought you had purchased those tokens of idolatry."

Shiri's mouth dropped open. "What?"

"I'm sorry. I'm sorry about your flute. I'm sorry I accused you, and I'm sorry I…" he lowered his voice and glanced around "…grabbed your arm."

"You thought I…" Shiri pressed her hand to heated cheeks. What kind of person assumed idolatry as a first reaction? Now her near-the-surface emotions pulsed with injustice and betrayal. Tears blurred her view of the Levite in front of her as they entered the corner kitchen, and the fragrance of fresh bread embraced her.

"I am Ezekiel. I serve as a gatekeeper." The impudent man still walked behind her.

"Why do I care? I won't be seeing you again." Shiri closed her eyes. That response displayed her as a petulant child rather than the woman she hoped to present. "After this week, we'll probably end up on different rotations."

Ezekiel shifted and accepted a portion of bread. He glanced up apologetically. "I also schedule everyone's service."

The bread's aroma no longer tugged at her hunger. If Ezekiel thought she was idolatrous, he wouldn't schedule her for duty. Her service would end after one day. She swallowed and a tear spilled down her cheek.

"Don't cry." Ezekiel reached out, then withdrew his hand.

Who was he to tell her not to cry? Her grand hopes of bringing honor to her *abba's* name were gone with one misunderstanding.

"I only meant you'll see me again as I assign the shifts."

Shiri plowed to a stop and gaped at Ezekiel. The face that radiated scorn yesterday, seemed sincere. His eyes and the hair peeking from his wound turban were not yet marked by age, his beard still full and dark. Broad shoulders hunched forward as he clasped and unclasped his hands.

Heat rose to her face. Staring at a man didn't help solidify her case as a mature woman. She averted her eyes. "You will still schedule me?"

Ezekiel's shoulders rose and he smiled, revealing slightly crooked teeth. "Yes, of course. We need as many faithful followers as possible at this time."

At this time?

Ezekiel dipped his chin to her and then angled toward the courtyard. "I must go prepare for the morning sacrifice."

Shiri stared at his departing back. What had transpired between them? She glanced at the position of the sun and sped to the north side of the complex. Though women were forbidden to play till after morning sacrifice, she needed to prove to the chief musician she was a good addition of her own merit, not for her *abba's* name alone.

Sliding onto her three-legged stool, Shiri rested her flute on her lap and inhaled through her nose, trying to steady her breathing. A portion of the choir and musicians mingled casually, talking and eating.

"Blessed are You, Lord our God, Ruler of the universe, who brings forth bread from the earth." The prayer steadied her jittery nerves. She knew how to play and to follow, she would do well.

A gentle breeze caressed her face and imbued her with peace. She belonged here. As she nibbled on her round of bread, the choirmaster arrived and men filled the risers and stood at attention.

Amram spread his arms with a flourish as if to embrace the musicians. "Let us warm up." He lifted his hand as the kinnor player plucked a chord across the thin soundboard.

The choir performed a series of vocal scales. Amram peered through the gate to the inner court.

Movement along the wall caught Shiri's attention. She suppressed a smile to see Chesed—late as usual—approach with stealth. He met her gaze as he sat on his stool and set his drum down without a sound. He wrinkled his nose at her smirk.

As a Levite led a lamb from the chamber where livestock was kept, Amram raised his closed hand. The men to Shiri's left raised silver trumpets and puffed out their cheeks. The sound of gates swinging open projected out from the corridor simultaneously with Amram's hand opening in a flourish, and the clear blasts filled the crisp morning air. A breeze swept the courtyard and carried the trumpet summons beyond the walls.

Shiri craned her neck to see into the corridor, and through a mere sliver of the inner courtyard, it was enough to observe the flare of the flame welcoming the offering. The choir began their monotone chant as the smoke lifted above the walls in a straight plumbline to the heavens. Shiri closed her eyes as the low, haunting tune of the vertical flute flowed around the vocalization of the choir, expressing the harmony in her soul. Upon completion of the opening psalm, the trumpeters sent a final blast to invite the worshipers into Yahweh's presence. All gates opened simultaneously and clattered against the compound walls, and Amram lifted both hands to the musicians and orchestra.

Shiri raised her flute to her lips, matching the movement of the flutist beside her.

"Ready... And..." Amram opened his hand to Chesed.

The rhythm of the next song thumped from the drum. Harps and strings responded to the flutes' call, and the singers added to the rich layers. "*Better is one day in your courts than thousands elsewhere.*"

Shiri inhaled air and exhaled praise to the God above all gods. They continued lifting the prayers and offerings of the people to the heavens for a length of time she could not measure. The music ushered Shiri into the place in her soul where she played unfettered for Yahweh. *Hear our prayer. May it be a sweet-smelling aroma before You.*

"We shall rest now." Amram closed his hand on the last note of the song. He applauded the company. "Well done."

Shiri beamed. To serve under Amram's masterful leadership would be a joy. She stretched her neck and fingers.

"Would you like water?" A small boy offered her a clay cup.

"Thank you." Shiri drank deeply, the water quenching the dryness in her mouth. "I'm Shiri."

"My name is Samuel." The boy lifted his jar to offer her more.

Shiri shook her head and wiped her mouth. "I see you serve Yahweh, just like Samuel of old."

Samuel's eyes widened. "You know about him?"

"Of course. He was a great prophet of Yahweh, serving in the temple as a boy."

"Bring the water here," a singer called.

Shiri winked at Samuel as he moved past her.

Chesed caught her attention. He lifted his eyebrows and flicked the hand-held drum she always teased resembled a tambourine. The familiar humming as he moved his thumb in a circle produced a sound akin to bumblebees.

Shiri smiled, and a hum vibrated her lips as she counted the timing. "*The law of the Lord is perfect, converting the soul. The heavens declare the glory of God and the firmament shows His handiwork.*"

The kinnor player joined in, plucking out the tune. Chesed began to sing, holding the melody steady as Shiri vocalized, her voice embracing his. By the second chorus, the vertical flutist and other singers had joined in their impromptu worship. On the last measure, all instruments and voices silenced as if they had rehearsed together, and Shiri sang alone. The choir applauded quietly, and the hair on Shiri's arms stood on end.

"Very impressive."

Shiri started and turned to see Amram smiling at her.

"The honored Ibraham's daughter is as gifted as he is. Possibly more."

Shiri blushed under Amram's scrutiny. "Thank you, my lord."

Amram stroked his well-kept beard. "Do you know 'The King of all the Earth'?"

"One of my favorites." Shiri lifted her gaze to meet the choir master's. All air escaped her lungs at the interest displayed across his face.

Light sparked in Amram's eyes. "Chesed, if you please."

Chesed tipped his head with a mischievous smile Shiri's direction. He started up the rhythm—too fast as always—challenging her in a battle to keep up. The vertical flute joined, chirping at Chesed's fast pace.

Shiri pursed her lips and narrowed her eyes but matched his tempo with claps. "*Oh, clap your hands all you people*—"

Amram held up his hand. "Begin again. You will get more air to support that lovely voice, daughter of Ibraham, if you stand. Again."

The flutist beside her reached for her flute as Shiri stood and slightly bent her knees.

Chesed began again, faster even than before. Shiri's foot

began tapping and she sang. This time a surge of power supported her voice. "*For the Lord, Most High is awesome*—"

Praise for this glorious day trilled in Shiri's chest, endowing purpose and a peace. Serving the Lord in this way was right. It was what she was created to do.

5

Thus says the Lord: "Will they fall and not rise? Will one turn away and not return? Why has this people slidden back, Jerusalem, in perpetual backsliding? They hold fast to deceit; they refuse to return. I listened and heard, but they do not speak aright. No man has repented of his wickedness, saying 'What have I done?' Everyone turned to his own course."

—Jeremiah 8:4b-6a

The hollow call of the shofar pierced Ezekiel's soul. He snapped his head to the sky, dread stealing the words from the end of his sentence as he stood before the faithful followers.

Just after mid-day. Much too early to signal a sacrifice. Did disaster besiege them?

Ezekiel's heart pounded within his chest as he surveyed the disbelief and shock on the faces before him, all turned to him for answers. The pristine walls of the backside of the temple gave no hints.

A temple guard peeled off the left side of the congregation, pulling the short sword from his side in a fluid motion as he rounded the corner to the north to investigate.

"What is it?"

The question roused Ezekiel from his stupor, and he raised his hands to dismiss the people. "Remember, do not waver. Share with your neighbors while there is still time to change, before the Lord's judgment comes."

He wiped his sweaty palms on the clean cloth hidden in his sash and strode around the corner of the temple toward the musicians' risers, drawing strange comfort as his flock banded behind him. His gaze flicked to the open New Gate and around the edges of the courtyard. Every station was manned. Relief soothed his harried thoughts, and he felt the push of exhaled breath on his neck from the congregation behind him as he loosened his shoulders.

The only thing out of place was the large crowd gathered by the musicians. Amram stood beside the shofar player, eyes closed. Someone slowly picked at a stringed instrument.

How did the man add variety to the unique sound produced from the ram's horn? The one time Ezekiel had picked up a shofar, he could hardly produce any sound, let alone variation and tone.

The shofar player lowered his instrument and Amram began to sing, his ballad haunting and smooth. This is why he served as chief musician. Ezekiel surveyed the worshiping crowd— the man to his right lifted his hands, some swayed to the music. The attitude of reverence bolstered the atmosphere.

Ezekiel's shoulders relaxed and he turned on his heel. Now that he had disbanded the fellowship, it'd be pointless to reconvene. The water level in the basin near the altar would be getting low.

A female voice with pure tones joined the lilting melody, matching Amram with perfection. Ezekiel searched the crowd and the musicians for the woman bold enough to sing along.

He blinked.

The heavenly sound came from the former chief musician's daughter. Masterfully, her voice carried over the whole crowd, embracing each one with life. If the experience was so enthralling here, how would it be in the front row?

Shiriel's eyes closed and her hand lifted—an extension of her song and soul. Amram seemed to be following *her* lead. Ezekiel leaned forward, trying to discern between the blend of the two voices. Amram was excellent, but Shiriel was…exquisite.

Ezekiel averted his eyes, regretting intruding on her prayers to preserve Zion. Within seconds, his gaze returned to her upturned face. The pure offering of praise to Yahweh—mesmerizing. The dip in Shiriel's chin added to the beauty of the moment. The crowd leaned forward with baited breath.

When the song concluded, Shiriel opened her eyes and glanced shyly at Amram's proud smile. Ezekiel remained spellbound for three more songs, until his duties forced his reluctant retreat away.

"We have to schedule Shiri more. I'll need her more than just two times a year." Amram sat before Ezekiel without so much as a may-I-join-you. "Have you heard her sing? Words cannot describe her talent."

Ezekiel glanced across the dining hall to where Shiriel ate beside her cousin. She laughed at something he said, modestly hiding her mouth behind her hand.

"Do you know how challenging it is to have musicians revolve from week to week?" Amram waved his hands and spoke rapidly. "Think of the joy she brings to the worship. Imagine the people she will escort into a humble position before Yahweh."

Lifting a hand to halt Amram, Ezekiel finished chewing

and swallowed. Amram's recounting echoed the list Ezekiel had already created. "I understand your position. Shiriel has a wonderful gift."

"Wonderful? Wonderful is roasted lamb served three times a week. Shiriel's talent is sensational."

Ezekiel pressed his retort down, closing his eyes while he composed his words. "There are more things I have to consider apart from her exceptional gift."

Amram scowled and crossed his arms. "Like what?"

"Her cousin acts as her guardian, sponsors her for propriety. We cannot allow a young woman to be at the temple without a sponsor."

"So, we will ask Chesed to come more often. Two solid musicians." Amram brushed off his hands as if he had solved the problem.

"Chesed lives in Anthoth, with his wife and ailing mother."

Amram growled. "It's like you are trying to make my life difficult."

Ezekiel scooped remaining lentils into his mouth with the last bit of flatbread. He concentrated on chewing until his patience returned. "I am not against you, Amram. I see her value also, but you must consider my position as well. Her *abba's* permission will have to be obtained."

"Ibraham led worship for twenty years. He will know the benefit of consistency."

"We'd have to find her a sponsor. Do we even know if she wants to?"

Amram's disparaging expression made Ezekiel squirm internally. Apparently, he knew nothing about music or musicians.

"I will pursue it. Does that satisfy you?" Best to allow Amram to believe it was all his idea, and Ezekiel did everything to accommodate him.

Satisfaction lit up the choirmaster's face. "Thank you,

Ezekiel! We've got something special here, I can tell." He strode away, shuffling his feet to an unheard melody.

Ezekiel stood, collected his and Amram's dishes, and shook his head. Amram personified the ancient call that musicians were exempt from all other chores and duties in the temple. He deposited the dishes in the wash basin and stretched his arms high. Another smooth day at the House of the Lord.

His thoughts traveled past ensuring the gates were locked for the night, past the sleep mat beckoning him, and onto tomorrow's agenda.

The inspection of the yearling lambs refused to remain on his mental list when he caught sight of Shiriel going up and down the aisles of eating mats, collecting abandoned dishes. Her stack rose high, yet she pivoted with the grace of a dancer. She approached the basin, and her cheeks flushed when she noticed him watching.

"You don't have to clean up. That isn't your job."

Shiriel blinked twice and glanced over her shoulder at the dining hall. "I like to help."

"Musicians are exempt from other duties."

"Should I use that as an excuse to not be a decent person and clean up after myself?" She tipped her head to the side, revealing hair the color of shadowed sand tucked under her head covering.

"No, of course not." Ezekiel frowned. Did he intend to convince her *not* to help? Why did he continue to press the issue? "I wasn't sure if you were aware…"

Shiriel took a half step backward and shifted the stack of dishes.

"Here, allow me to help you."

She stepped around his outstretched hands and plunked the dishes into the basin. Never taking her wary gaze from him, she dried off her hands. "Was there something specific you needed, my lord?"

Why *wouldn't* she be skeptical? He had told her not to help others, to act selfishly, and had insulted her intelligence in the span of two minutes. Not to mention their meeting on her first day in the temple. He swallowed. "No. Nothing."

Shiriel turned and walked away without a backward glance.

"You are very talented." The words flew out of his mouth against his better judgment.

She turned back with a hint of challenge in the tip of her chin.

"I was quite surprised. I didn't know you could sing." Ezekiel rubbed the back of his neck where sweat prickled his skin.

Indignation flashed across Shiriel's eyes.

Ezekiel frowned. "That's not what I meant. I meant 'sing *so well.*' You are a wonderful addition to the temple service."

"Thank you, my lord. Is that all?"

Oh, he hoped so. What other awkward thing would fly out of his mouth in the name of righting this conversation? "You may leave." Ezekiel winced as she exited the dining hall.

What had happened to the concise words and directions he normally possessed? It must be because he was accustomed to speaking with men. Women—though he'd get himself in trouble for thinking it—were more sensitive. "If I knew that, why didn't I proceed with caution?" Ezekiel muttered while stalking out of the dining hall to his quarters.

The next morning Ezekiel strode with purpose to the musicians' riser at the time of the early sacrifice. To ensure everyone was in the right place, of course. Unsanctioned disappointment flooded through him to see Shiriel sitting on her stool, flute in her lap, and a serene expression on her face as she watched the choir sing the psalm.

He frowned at his foolishness. Of course, she wouldn't be singing now. Tradition held that women didn't perform at the morning and evening sacrifices. He pivoted and marched toward the New Gate.

"*Your mercy, oh Lord, will hold me up in the multitude of my anxieties within me. Your comforts delight my soul—*"

The chanted words of the song arrested his attention, and he sank to his knees, facing the corridor to the altar. This was the time to be still before the Lord.

Forgive me, Yahweh. My heart is anxious within me to the point of distraction from my duties. When did serving the Lord become a duty and not a privilege?

"*—Uphold me with Your mercy, restore Your comfort to my soul.*"

Yahweh, why is this so hard? Your calling is so clear, yet few turn back. Heaviness pressed against his soul. How could he lead others if he allowed the prayers and sacrifices to become commonplace? *Regardless of whether others choose Your way or not, You are my God.*

Ezekiel remained on his knees until the three blasts from the silver trumpet sounded. He continued his duties in humility the rest of the morning, yet still the burden weighed upon him as he sat with Pashur recounting the day's events.

"Why are you so downcast, Ezekiel? The offerings are up. People linger long after they have presented their sacrifice."

Ezekiel's ears pricked. "That is good news, indeed. To have more worship Yahweh by choice is preferable to being forced to acknowledge His power by their destruction."

Pashur's brow puckered as if he'd eaten something bitter. "You've been listening to the fool Jeremiah too much."

Ezekiel pressed his lips together and inhaled through his nose. The man continued choosing to see but not comprehend.

The chief governor patted Ezekiel's shoulder. "You worry too much. People are returning to Yahweh. His scorn will dissipate, as it always has."

"Yahweh's mercy has run out. Our time comes to an end. We will surely be punished for our unbelief—"

"Enough." Pashur held up his hand. "We will discuss instead *why* the offerings have increased. Please spend time at each location offerings are given. If we can find out why, we can pour our attention into that which is successful."

Ezekiel inhaled. *Yahweh, how can I be of service to You if none will listen? Give me one more soul who would choose You.* He rolled up the scroll before him and placed it into the large jar. "Yes, Pashur. I will report back."

Instinct told him which station brought in more revenue, and he followed the enchanting sound of Shiriel's voice to the risers. The choir's monotone—the only accompaniment—a platform for her song to soar. Ezekiel angled himself where he could see both Shiriel and the offering box. Indeed, the people stopped at the risers both before and after they participated in their sacrifice.

The clink of coin against coin drew his attention. No one had deposited anything in the receptacle. His gaze landed on a woman straightening from a smaller wooden box directly in front of the riser. Shiriel smiled encouragingly and extended her hand to the woman.

Heat surged up his body and he crossed his arms. While singing about giving unto Yahweh His due honor, she had the nerve to accept donations personally? Another coin clanked in the unofficial container. How did this account for the rise in the offerings if she scammed it from the people? As a face of the public worship of the temple, she *should* be a pious example.

Ezekiel squeezed his eyes shut. He had already learned what came of plunging to conclusions with Shiriel. There could be a logical explanation.

Planting his feet to fight the urge to rock back and forth, Ezekiel's insides twisted at his own inconsistency. Others who put on the show of worshiping saddened him. Why did Shiriel's front make him so angry? Why did her potential deception bother him so…personally?

6

For a day in Your courts is better than a thousand. I would rather be a doorkeeper in the house of my God than dwell in the tents of wickedness. For the LORD God is a sun and shield; The Lord will give grace and glory; No good thing will He withhold from those who walk uprightly.
—Psalm 84:10-11

Six months.

How could Shiri possibly endure living away from the presence of Yahweh for the next six months? She still had the rest of today and the first part of the Sabbath, yet the conclusion of her week lurked, threatening to steal the joy of now.

Mentally she shook herself and returned her focus to the music. There would be time to grieve when she returned home. Clearing her throat softly, she lifted her gaze to Amram as he directed the choir.

Such a gifted musician. He had an ear for the nuances and themes of the songs, and his animated face demonstrated the deep passion he had for the music. What would it be like to share life with someone who appreciated the way music completed her?

The man beside her raised his flute and Shiri followed suit. Heat rushed up her neck. She should be watching Amram for musical cues, not daydreaming about a life together.

Amram turned his head toward them and opened his hand on the swell of the sound. His smile breathed life into her chest, her music. He turned her direction. Did he hear her devotion from her *abba's* flute?

Behind her, a syncopated rhythm was plucked on the kinnor. She covered the holes of the flute and blew, her breath resonating through the reed like wind rattling through dry grasses. The song ended and a breeze brushed Shiri's neck as if responding to her flute's call.

The crowd gave a smattering of applause, and the man directly in front of Shiri cupped his hand around his mouth. "Sing."

Amram thanked the crowd with a slight bow and flashed a smile at Shiri. Her stomach fluttered as he extended a hand. She stood, placing the flute on the stool.

Waving her close, Amram announced the song and signaled the strings players with two fingers. The low vibrations filled the air.

"*A psalm to King David, he plays the strings*—" Dampness made Shiri's hands clammy at Amram's closeness. She kept her face forward while extolling David's eyes, ever aware of a pair of beautiful eyes on her. The bridge came and Chesed's fingers rolled and thumped on his under-arm drum. She clapped twice on the offbeat, then three times. A loud clap behind her threw off her count.

Amram tapped his hand on his leg in time, helping her back to her place. He nodded to the choir and they began to chant. "*Saul has slain his thousands, and David has slain his ten-thousands. The son of Jesse exists forever.*"

Shiri joined in lifting the melody higher and then dipping

lower. She scanned the tapping feet of the gathering crowd. They worshipped Yahweh, and she had a part in it.

She almost lost her place again when her gaze landed on Ezekiel's intimidating scowl, his arms crossed over his broad chest. Did he disapprove of her singing or the way her hips swayed to the lively beat? She did nothing to merit the accusation in his eyes—even King David danced and sang before the Lord. Shiri had no intention of dancing like *that*.

At the last drumbeat, the crowd wildly applauded.

"Beautiful," Amram's whisper brushed her ear.

Her heart pulsed like Chesed's drum. A new sound registered—coins clinking into the offering box Amram had placed before the risers. "Thank you for giving to Yahweh."

"You have a beautiful voice, dear." An elderly woman grabbed Shiri's hand after depositing a coin.

"Thank you." Shiri kissed the woman's fingers.

"Such a gift in this uncertain time." She headed toward the West Gate, her head lifted and her steps sure.

Shiri smiled, but once again her gaze met Ezekiel's displeasure. What now?

The man raised his eyebrows and directed his gaze to the offering box. Did he object to the people giving to Yahweh?

"Thank you." She bowed her head to another worshipper.

Samuel and the other water boys brought around their jars and ladles, and Amram began the next song.

Shiri sat, angling herself to block Ezekiel from her view. Though her eyes only saw Amram, she couldn't avoid the scorn pressing against her back. She squirmed as she played. Didn't he have schedules to make and people to harass at the gate?

The song ended and Amram bowed his thanks to the musicians. "We shall adjourn. Return before the sun passes the riser's corner."

Shiri rose and twisted her back from side to side. She'd sing straight through the day and night if she could.

Amram knelt before Shiri to heft the offering box. "Shiri, my song, you are exquisite." He bestowed her with an appraising glance and a satisfied nod. Humming the line about David's beautiful eyes in a field of lilies, he rose and swept into the court of the Israelites.

Where was Samuel with that water? Shiri pressed against her fluttering heart.

"The offering bin is a nice touch."

Ezekiel's sarcasm snapped her out of her trance but did nothing for her dry mouth. "Yes, Amram believes the people will give generously, as in the days of King Hezekiah, if they have but the opportunity."

"How convenient. Amram provided the opportunity, and you receive the benefit."

She blinked at the Levite. Why did he despise her? "The greatest benefit is to sing in the courts of Yahweh."

Ezekiel swung his head away with a scornful click of his tongue. "You should repent now so that the Lord will act with compassion on you when Nebuchadnezzar captures the city."

Anger surged in Shiri's chest. "What is it you think I need to repent from, oh holy and devout keeper of the gates?"

Ezekiel shifted forward, leaning into Shiri's space. "Serving Yahweh with a double tongue."

Shiri narrowed her eyes. "How can you say that? You, who accosted me in the gate and accused me of idolatry while claiming to speak on behalf of the temple?"

He clenched his fists. "You accept money from the people's offering."

Coldness spread through Shiri's middle. She stammered, "Am-Amram takes the offering to the treasury. Search my quarters if you wish."

Ezekiel tipped his head and narrowed his eyes as if contemplating taking her up on her offer.

"What do you mean Nebuchadnezzar will destroy the city? It is Jerusalem."

Something akin to sadness softened Ezekiel's expression. "How long will the Lord endure Judah's blatant disobedience? Nebuchadnezzar is Yahweh's servant."

"He believes in our God?"

Ezekiel chuckled. "Yahweh will *use* him to chastise Judah, just as He used the Assyrians to punish Israel."

Shiri covered her open mouth. The people of Israel had been led into captivity over one hundred years before.

"King Jehoiakim hasn't paid tribute to Nebuchadnezzar for three cycles. How long do you think this brutal tyrant will extend favor?"

But Yahweh wouldn't…Judah was different. This was the holy city. Shiri glanced over her shoulder into the Court of Priests, taking in the temple furnishings stripped of the legendary gold and silver of King Hezekiah's day. Three years late on tribute. How could that be?

Realization swirled around her with the afternoon breeze. If King Jehoiakim had *wanted* to pay Nebuchadnezzar, were there funds? The land she loved was stripped bare of resources and food. Would Yahweh's presence be taken away as Israel's dignity had been?

The pillar of smoke still reached to the heavens from the Most Holy Place. She furtively scanned Ezekiel's face as he tracked Amram's progress from around the east corner. Some men seemed bent on spreading pessimism and were never happy unless they could affect the atmosphere like soggy wool blankets—reeking and heavy.

Ezekiel caught her staring. He passed a hand over eyes sunken in circles of gray.

Averting her gaze, Shiri plucked at her sash.

"Is there a problem, priest?" Chesed advanced, eyes narrowed and hands fisted.

Shiri shook her head, but her cousin didn't seem to care. He created a wall in front of her.

"Yes." Ezekiel shifted and directed his gaze to Shiri. "We are running out of time."

"Pardon me?" Chesed searched Shiri's face.

"I am sorry." Ezekiel bowed his head. "I assumed…again. Your cousin is very talented. Thank you for taking such good care of her."

Ezekiel turned and walked into the Court of Israelites in the direction of the treasury.

"What was that about?" Chesed stared at Ezekiel's departing back.

"He just—" What indeed? Did he accuse her again, or had he been talking about Nebuchadnezzar the whole time?

The choirmaster drew near, saving Shiri from having to answer.

Ezekiel's mournful expression unsettled Shiri. Whatever conspiracy Ezekiel believed drove him with the certainty of matched steeds before a chariot. His zeal for the purity of the temple was admirable, and he had the strength of character to apologize when he was mistaken.

Shiri shook the thoughts from her head as Amram smiled in her direction. All Ezekiel's oddities were nothing compared to the promises she saw in Amram's eyes.

"Now, Shiri, my song, I will teach you to control that marvelous voice." He rolled his shoulders back and forth, gesturing for Shiri to follow. "Your voice is like your instrument. There are certain techniques that will produce more quality sound."

That made sense. *Abba* had specialized—and had only instructed her—in the flute.

Amram reached toward Shiri's middle, halting as Chesed crossed his arms and glowered. "How can I teach her if I cannot demonstrate?"

Chesed stepped forward. "You may demonstrate on me."

"I suppose that will have to do. You see, Shiri, your neck

muscles are smaller than your middle and legs." Amram tipped Chesed's head to demonstrate.

Shiri put her hand to her throat as Amram shifted closer. She stared straight ahead.

"Take a breath." Amram's words tickled her cheek. "There, see? Your shoulders lifted. That shows you are using the little muscles. Breathe from here." He framed her with one hand behind and one in front, a handbreadth away from touching her.

Chesed cleared his throat.

Amram growled, swung around, and patted Chesed's middle. "From here."

Shiri put her hand on her jittery stomach.

"Yes! That's the spot. Can you tell the difference?"

Oh, she could tell the difference, but it probably had more to do with Amram stepping away—now she could actually breathe.

"Try again. Breathe low. Push out your hand with your belly." Amram prodded Chesed's midsection.

Shiri closed her eyes and stilled her shoulders. Why was breathing such a difficult task? Concentrating, she pushed out her hand.

"You've got it!" Amram's voice was close again. "Now sing."

An airy giggle escaped Shiri's mouth. She tried not to think of how close Amram must be. "What should I sing?"

"Sing about King David's beautiful complexion."

Pushing out her hand with her breath again, she began to sing.

"There it is! Can you hear the difference?"

"—*David was a shepherd in the lilies*—" Rich sounds came from her throat and her eyes flew open.

"Breathe again." Amram stood a handbreadth away, inhaling deeply at the natural pause.

King David must have had brown eyes flecked with gold like Amram's. Would any other eyes be as beautiful?

A satisfied smile spread across Amram's face, and his eyes darted towards Shiri's mouth. "Lovely."

"I didn't know it was possible, but I heard an improvement." Her cousin squeezed her shoulder, guiding her to the stool.

Shiri sat and pressed a hand to warm cheeks.

A member of the choir drew Amram's attention to the edge of the riser.

"Thank you for bringing me this week. I shall cherish this time for all of my days." Her eyes burned. "How will I last six months before we come back?"

At that moment, Amram glanced over his shoulder towards them.

"Mm-hmm." Chesed smiled knowingly, missing nothing.

Shiri's cheeks heated. "To sing. To be in Yahweh's presence."

"I'm sure that's all," his tone teased.

Shiri blew a fast burst of air on the high note in Chesed's direction before her gaze drifted back to Amram. Would it be wrong to have a second reason to miss the temple?

7

From the least even to the greatest everyone is given to covetousness; from the prophet even to the priest everyone deals falsely. For they have healed the hurt of the daughter of My people slightly, saying 'Peace, peace!' when there is no peace.

—Jeremiah 8:10b-11

"We'd like to invite your daughter to serve at the temple on a more regular basis." Ezekiel waited while the former chief musician clamped a reed between his knees and sent the hot rod into the hollow end. The scent of burning wood filled the workshop.

Had Ibraham heard him? Ezekiel folded his hands in his lap as mature priests did.

Shiriel ducked into the workshop. "*Abba*, I've brought you water. You know *Ima* doesn't like you to work out here too long."

Eagerness—and a good portion of nerves—flopped in Ezekiel's belly.

Shiriel halted as her gaze landed on him and her eyes narrowed. "Forgive me. I didn't know you had company."

"Serve our guest first, daughter."

"Yes, *Abba*."

The set of her jaw didn't give Ezekiel comfort. "Thank you."

Shiriel dipped her chin and turned to her *abba*.

"Why should I entrust my greatest treasure, and risk her safety, for the benefit of the temple?" Ibraham's gravelly voice contrasted the smooth sounds his flute made in Shiriel's command.

Ezekiel swallowed and kept his gaze trained on the older man. "In truth, my lord, you shouldn't."

The reed gave a pop as the rod penetrated the next chamber. Ibraham dug the metal deep into the embers of the fire and uncurled hands spotted with marks of time. "Explain."

"I am the one who…doubted your daughter's devotion and integrity." Ezekiel clamped his hands on his knees to resist the urge to wring them. "What sort of environment would it be to serve in the temple if the workers accuse the faithful?"

Ibraham massaged his hand and winced.

Best to present the whole case so the man could make his decision and Ezekiel could resume his duties. "I come, instead, on behalf of Amram."

A sharp intake of breath came from Shiriel's direction.

"He appeals to you, chief musician to chief musician, and asked me to implore on behalf of consistency and quality."

Ibraham's shoulders shrugged side to side as if weighing the merits on a scale. He exhaled a slow breath. "My daughter is an unmarried woman. I cannot ask my nephew to abandon his family more than his established commitment. I am needed at home to care for my wife. So…"

All arguments Ezekiel had considered. He brought his hands together and bowed his head. Amram would have to live with the disappointment.

"Please, *Abba*." Shiriel knelt by Ibraham's knee. "I want to serve. I want to play and sing in the temple. Remember how wonderful it is to be in Yahweh's presence? There is nothing sweeter."

Ibraham considered Shiriel's upturned face, emotions warring across his own. He tapped his fingers on his knee. "A woman is unable to enter the temple courts when she is unclean. You would be prohibited from serving one week each month."

Shiriel's back stiffened and red stained her neck. "*Abba!*"

"You think the scheduler of the temple is ignorant to the impurities of life?" Ibraham patted Shiriel's cheek. "He must make it his concern to maintain holiness in the temple."

Certain his face matched Shiriel's in color, Ezekiel inwardly squirmed under Ibraham's scrutiny.

"I am willing to consider one week a month—"

"Thank you, *Abba*!" Shiriel flung her arms around his neck, planting kisses across both cheeks.

"—if Ezekiel agrees to sponsor you."

Ezekiel's eyes bulged. He coughed. "Me?"

Shiriel covered her gasp with her hands. She shot a glance of absolute horror at Ezekiel.

"You can't be serious." Ezekiel pushed off the ground and stepped back. "How can you consider this after my disrespect toward your daughter?"

Ibraham rose, holding Shiriel close, and stretched his other hand to Ezekiel's shoulder. "From what Shiri tells me, and from my own observations when I served in the temple, the zeal you have for Yahweh and His house is evident. Your commitment to purity in this uncertain day elicits my trust. I know you would take the responsibility seriously."

Ezekiel's mouth dropped open. He averted his eyes from Shiriel's glare. Surely Amram would make a better sponsor. "I don't think your daughter would approve of reporting to me."

"Then she can serve twice a year at our family's appointed time." Ibraham's expression left no room for debate.

Sweat poured from Ezekiel's armpits. Could he add one more responsibility to grant Amram's and Shiriel's wishes? If she agreed, *would* she submit to Ezekiel's direction and leadership? He shook tenseness from his hands.

As aide to the chief governor of the temple, surely he could find a way to competently oversee a woman at the temple.

An odd pang struck his thoughts at the possibility she might refuse the terms.

"I will arrange for Shiri's escort to the temple after she has been cleansed from her monthly impurities. You may remain seven days as our customary time and then I will escort you back home." Ibraham turned to Shiriel and tilted her face up. "What do you say?"

"*Abba*—" Shiriel's gaze darted Ezekiel's way.

"Do you wish to serve?"

"More than anything."

"Can you respect Ezekiel's desire to serve Yahweh, and understand it was this drive, rather than a personal attack against you, that prompted his earlier actions?"

Ezekiel swallowed and nodded as Ibraham confirmed his words with a glance. For reasons Ezekiel could not identify, it was imperative that Shiriel understand his motives.

Shiriel appraised Ezekiel with a guarded expression, the cleft in her chin giving her an air of dreams yet dreamed.

"The scheduler's dedication is admirable." She drew in a breath. "I can serve under his authority."

Ibraham beamed and laughed, as if he were the one returning to temple service. He swung Shiriel in a circle, and Ezekiel had an urge to join their celebration.

Instead, he studied the flute Ibraham had set aside. The beautiful melodies that would be played seemed so effortless compared to the many hours of work represented in this reed. A basket of tall stalks sat behind the fire.

Ezekiel drew one out, scraping it against the side of the basket and its companions filled the void with a clatter. The reed he held in no way resembled the flute he had taken from Shiriel.

Peering inside, he discovered a very short chamber. Ezekiel didn't know much about music, but he knew the inner walls would restrict the sound traveling down the stalk.

Shiriel ran from the workshop and her footsteps slapped across the courtyard. "*Ima*! You'll never guess—"

Ezekiel sensed Ibraham behind him. "I have to admit, I didn't pay attention to the intricacies of the music until…" Ezekiel stopped. Which would offend more? To say he had ignored Ibraham's music all those years he served, or to say Shiriel's singing had captured his interest? "Forgive me."

"There is nothing to forgive. Your position requires you to see the full picture. To assure that all the small details have come together just right." Ibraham placed a finished flute in Ezekiel's hand. "Transforming a reed into an instrument is much the same."

Shiriel's voice carried into the workshop like joyful birdsong.

Ezekiel moistened his lips and narrowed his eyes, focusing intently on Ibraham's demonstration of how he fashioned flutes.

"As you maintain purity in the temple, I seek a reed that stands straight and true. I see the potential it carries and know the need it is to fill." Ibraham retrieved the rod from the coals and closed one eye to peer into the chamber of the reed. He pushed the red-hot rod into the opening, twisting it back and forth as the wood sizzled. Thrusting further, Ibraham burned through all the ribs except the last one. "This will serve best as a transverse flute. This wall remains."

Ezekiel examined the offered reed. "Fascinating."

Ibraham moved swiftly and efficiently—his tools an extension of his stiff hands—measuring the distance between holes, marking and puncturing the reed's exterior, and sanding down rough edges inside the holes.

"Now, you will have an appreciation of how an element composes part of your full tapestry." Ibraham blew into the flute. His head cocked to the side. Frowning, he selected a small saw and rested the flute across his knees. He sawed back and forth at the next rib until the piece fell to the ground.

The master flute maker examined his creation and raised it to his mouth. This time, a higher sound emanated in the small space. A satisfied smile spread across Ibraham's face. "As you know, if everyone under you does their part well, your job becomes easier."

Ezekiel pondered the application. "How do I convince those who serve to desire to put forth excellent effort?"

Ibraham rubbed oil into the reed's surface.

Had he heard the question?

"I am an old man. The best way I found to inspire sincerity in worship is to be sincere myself." Ibraham lifted troubled eyes. "Despite your best effort, each person must decide on their own to follow Yahweh. He allows us the opportunity to affect others, but often they choose to serve only when it is comfortable. Even then, in our comfort we forget to rely on Him."

Ezekiel's shoulders sagged. "So there is no hope? King Solomon spoke truly when he said all is meaningless?"

Ibraham smiled. "There is always reward in serving Yahweh. There is always hope. It is the perfect law of Yahweh that converts the soul—not our efforts."

"His judgments are true," Ezekiel continued the psalm in a whisper as he took his leave.

"Master Ezekiel," Shiriel waited for him at the gate. "I am honored to be asked to serve in Yahweh's house more often."

Ezekiel smiled at the first conversation of friendship.

"Will you thank Amram for me?

Had *Amram* petitioned her *abba*? Did Amram agree to sponsor an unrelated woman?

Ezekiel pushed a smile at Shiriel's hopeful expression. "Of course. We look forward to your next visit to the temple with great anticipation."

She dipped her head and turned abruptly, hastening to the house.

Ezekiel contemplated Ibraham's words as he walked alongside barren fields. *Yahweh, there* is *great reward in keeping Your ways. Allow me to influence one more soul before judgment comes, that we can be a light unto those who blindly turn away from You.*

He entered the temple courtyard at the seventh hour, reluctance weighing his steps. Why did he hesitate to share the victory with the choirmaster? If not for Amram's insistence, Shiriel wouldn't be returning in a month's time.

Amram turned away from the risers, as if sensing Ezekiel's approach, and rushed over. "Well?"

Ezekiel nodded. "Shiriel will serve one week each month."

Amram's expression changed from hopeful to disbelief—his excitement escalating at the tempo of the drumbeat from the riser. He grabbed Ezekiel's shoulders and kissed both cheeks. "Now you will see the people return in droves, with Shiriel's voice rising above all else."

Ezekiel wiped his face and scrutinized Amram. "With Shiriel's voice directing the people to Yahweh."

Amram raised an eyebrow. "That's what I said."

Something beneath Amram's charming smile and the exuberant way he whirled towards his station gave Ezekiel pause. "Amram, if I may have a moment?"

The chief musician pivoted—conducting an unseen choir. "Yes, what is it?"

Ensuring no one around appeared to be listening, Ezekiel stepped closer. "Tell me about the second offering box."

"It's a good idea, isn't it!" Amram beamed. "The people's

hearts move them to give. The offerings at my station have never been higher."

Ezekiel found no signs of deceit in Amram's amiable face, yet something felt amiss. "Why not use the official box?"

"With the smaller one, we offer the convenience of a better location."

Hinting at the subject would not evoke a straight answer. Ezekiel stiffened his shoulders. "Are you taking a portion of the offering for yourself?"

Anger sparked in Amram's eyes, and he crossed his arms. "Are you accusing me of stealing?"

The man walking by turned his head at the sound of Amram's raised voice.

Ezekiel paused. Did he assume again? The donations had substantially increased—to the point where someone could dip a hand into the offering and none would be the wiser. Amram *had* opened the door to suspicion when he began to use the small offering box. But if Ezekiel's hunch was misplaced…

"The official offering box is the one that we will be using." Ezekiel raised his hand. "The people can walk the short distance back."

A pleasant smile masked something in Amram's eyes. "But of course, my lord. I was merely trying to make it easier on the patrons." He gave an exaggerated bow and strode back to the risers.

Amram had done nothing to assuage Ezekiel's doubts. If anything, his distrust had grown.

Yet, even with the trumpet-shaped funnel depositing the offering into the official treasury box, how could he monitor the amount coming in compared to what was deposited in the treasury? Amram still had authority to deliver the coins to the treasurer.

Would the offerings decline this week in Shiriel's absence?

When she was on site, he could watch the offering box.

Ezekiel kept his posture rigid, though everything inside him squirmed. That would probably come across that he either didn't trust her, or worse, he was infatuated with her.

Great responsibility pressed on his chest. What had he been thinking to agree to act as Shiriel's guardian? He'd have to ensure the young woman's protection like she was his own—he had difficulty classifying Shiriel as a sister or a cousin. He didn't admire his female relatives in this way that bordered on attraction. However, Shiriel's expression of disdain had been clear enough. He had no business regarding her with anything but courteous regard.

He stalked toward the gatehouse. Pashur would set his head straight with duties and tasks.

8

"But if you will not hear these words, I swear by Myself" says the Lord, "that this house shall become a desolation... And many nations will pass by this city, and everyone will say to his neighbor, 'Why has the Lord done so to this great city?' Then they will answer, 'Because they have forsaken the covenant of the Lord their God, and worshipped other gods and served them.'"

—Jeremiah 22:5,8-9

"Ezekiel." Gilead ran his fingers through still-wet hair and shook his head vigorously, sending water droplets sparkling in the mid-day sun—a temporary fix to keep tired eyes open.

A smile spread across Ezekiel's face as he strode out of the New Gate, arms wide open. "Gilead! Welcome back, my friend."

Gilead clasped arms with the younger man and patted his back. *This* was why he didn't go to his quarters directly after battle. Though Ezekiel was fifteen years his junior, the man was Gilead's spiritual father.

Ezekiel's thick brows knit as he scrutinized Gilead's countenance. "What news of the Moabites?"

"They've retreated, but I think they bide their time. They prey on the unfortunate cities and slowly encroach on Judah." Gilead glanced at the people milling into the temple, each one oblivious to the impending doom. "There's more. Rumor has it Nebuchadnezzar has begun his trek west."

A pained expression took up residence on Ezekiel's face and his shoulders sagged forward. "Time is running short."

Gilead ran his finger down the bow string across his chest. There were no words.

"We need to communicate the urgency to the faithful." Ezekiel placed an arm around Gilead's shoulders. "Come with me to the west side. The men and women will arrive at the fourth hour for the time of listening and learning God's words. They will need to hear."

Gilead fixed his gaze on feet that charged into battle and the broad hands that released many an arrow and took numerous lives. "I can't, my brother. I have blood on my hands."

The priest glanced to Gilead's hands and his wet hair. "You have washed. Did you spend time outside the city?"

"Of course." Since he had committed to following Yahweh wholeheartedly, Gilead managed to implement the time allotted to decompress after battle. "I...being away so long wears on me. I am not worthy to come before the followers." He wasn't worthy to set foot inside the temple.

Ezekiel's jaw twitched. Disapproval flashed across his eyes. "That's when you need to come the most. Purchase a lamb or kid. Present your sacrifice to Yahweh and accept His forgiveness."

How could it be that simple, when Gilead felt so stained with sin? He worked among archers who lived for their own pleasure—women, raids, crude behavior—all his prior sins paraded before him every day. Though his body had restrained from joining in, his thoughts hadn't been so strong this time.

Ezekiel stiffened, staring at an approaching man and woman.

Gilead narrowed his eyes to place the man's gait and frame. "Isn't that the choirmaster?"

"The former choirmaster and more specifically, his daughter." Ezekiel frowned.

"Why the reaction?"

"Shiriel is here to sing, or play her flute—or both." Ezekiel cleared his throat and glanced over his shoulder.

Ah. A doting *abba* who thought his daughter had talent. A nightmare for any scheduler. "Can't she sing at all?"

"She can sing quite well." Ezekiel's smile seemed forced as he raised his hand in greeting. "I am to be... she is to be my ward for the week."

Why did a young woman reporting for duty rattle the bold and straightforward scheduler? How many times had the man personally prohibited idolaters from entering the temple? Ezekiel was as stalwart as a soldier.

Gilead clasped his wrists behind him and kept his voice down. "Don't you like her? Is she conceited?"

"On the contrary. She is nothing like the other musicians." Ezekiel stepped forward as the choirmaster and his daughter approached. "*Shalom*, Master Ibraham."

The man eyed Gilead with distrust.

See? I don't belong here. Gilead slanted his gaze toward Ezekiel.

"This is Gilead." Ezekiel placed his hand on Gilead's arm. "He is my friend and a valiant warrior for Yahweh."

"Ah." Ibraham shifted the tall basket to his other arm. "Yahweh is also a valiant warrior. He fights His enemies with a swift and powerful sword."

Gilead blinked. Could Yahweh approve of his fighting then?

"According to the prophet Isaiah, Yahweh dons the helmet of salvation and the breast plate of righteousness. He wears the garments of vengeance and zeal as a cloak." Ibraham crossed his arms and appraised Gilead. "If you are for Yahweh and direct your zeal toward Him, He will not forsake you."

"Thank you, my lord."

Inside, the temple musicians could be heard tuning their instruments. Ezekiel glanced from the gate to the sun's position. "Can you join us, Master Ibraham?"

"I wish I could." Ibraham tugged on his beard. "I must return home to care for my wife. She did not sleep well last night."

Worry tempered the girl's expression. "Perhaps I should go with you."

Beside Gilead, Ezekiel clenched his jaw. Sure enough, he held his breath.

"No, my daughter." Ibraham framed Shiriel's face with his hands and kissed her forehead. "It is right that you serve in this way."

Ezekiel's shoulders sagged. "I need to attend to my duties." He stepped towards the gate.

"I will return for you in seven days' time."

"Thank you, *Abba*." Shiriel reached for her basket of belongings.

"Gilead can bring her things." Ezekiel turned abruptly and strode into the courtyard.

A low trick to get him inside. Still, Gilead couldn't leave the young woman to her own resources. He accepted the basket from Ibraham. "I'd be happy to serve you."

After one more embrace and a wistful glance inside, the man turned and lengthened his stride in the direction he had come.

Gilead gestured toward the courtyard. "After you, Shiriel."

"Please call me Shiri." She gave a shy smile and glided

into the courtyard with the innocence of youth. Her attention was riveted on the musicians.

As uncomfortable as Ezekiel was with her there, Shiri seemed completely at home.

"Do you recall which quarters you are meant to dwell in?" Why hadn't Ezekiel given instructions when he volunteered Gilead's services?

"The west." Shiri pointed and led the way in a gentle rhythm.

Gilead followed, every step taking monumental effort. He plodded behind Shiri, his spirit heavy and burdensome.

"Are you well?" She glanced back at him with compassion in her eyes. "Your countenance, it seems…discouraged."

Gilead blinked. "I… Uh…"

"I'm sorry. That was too forward." Shiri faced front.

"You are right. I am discouraged." Not that he'd share details. "To have someone notice…means a lot. I'll be alright."

Shiri tilted her head and studied him. "I will pray that you find peace today."

After depositing her belongings in an unoccupied room in the small women's quarters, Gilead took his leave and purchased a yearling lamb. He waited in line before the altar where five men stood before him. Within minutes, his lamb was skinned, quartered, and burning. Without so much as an encouraging word, Gilead was dismissed.

Stepping to the side, he regarded the blood dripping into the basin.

Always blood, but no reassurance. He made his way down the steps to the outer courtyard, more weighed down than before.

The sun stood at nearly the seventh hour position. Perhaps hearing the words of truth would pull him out of this pit. He trudged back to the western section behind the temple and positioned himself—back against the wall—at the edge of the growing crowd.

Ezekiel effortlessly cast his voice so all could hear, exhorting the faithful to convince their neighbors to return to truth before Yahweh darkened the land and removed His light. "The time is coming, and even now draws close. We must humble our hearts before our great God. Nebuchadnezzar is Yahweh's servant. Judah *will* be overthrown."

Gilead scanned the faces before him. Most had worry etched around their eyes but seemed resolute.

The hair on Gilead's arms rose with a shiver. Ezekiel's urgency and exhortation presented a rousing battle charge. A battle not with flesh and blood, but for righteous living. Would these untried civilians hold true with this same tenacity when trials came? Or would they conform under the strain of what was to come?

Ezekiel continued to build up the people, sharing from the law and weaving it together eloquently to charge the people to rise up and be strong in their faith. "—fear not! For the Lord is with you. Do not be dismayed. For the Lord our God will strengthen you, help you, and uphold you with His righteous right hand."

Individually, these men and women—he himself—might cave, but there was good return for a multitude banding together.

The ropes binding Gilead's spirit slightly eased yet did not lift the melancholy weight that made his feet shuffle and his body long for a soft bed.

Gilead stepped away as the people congratulated Ezekiel on a wonderful message. The man took on a glow when instructing others. Perhaps when things quieted down, he'd have time to talk with a lost archer.

Yahweh, I know You forgive those who humble themselves, but I feel so far away from You. When did the sin offering, the teaching—

both things beneficial for restoration—take effect rather than just being ritual?

Gilead exhaled and scuffed his sandal against a mud stain in the path from the New Gate. "I guess I can report early to the palace for duty."

The passing Levite glanced around and raised his eyebrows. "Are you speaking to me?"

"No, sorry." Gilead bit back a smile. The twanging of plucked lyre strings drew him to the musicians' risers.

Shiri stood by the current choirmaster, eyes closed and swaying to the music. She opened her mouth and joined the simple melody. "*To you, I will cry, oh Lord, my rock. Do not be silent toward me. I become like those who go down to the pit. Hear the voice of my supplications. When I cry to You, when I lift up my hands toward Your holy sanctuary*—"

The young woman, who couldn't possibly know what it was like to be wallowing in the midst of sin, sang as if her heart would be torn from her chest if Yahweh didn't rescue her.

Gilead sank to his knees, closing his eyes and raising his hand. Her song spoke the words his spirit could not articulate.

"—*the Lord is my strength and my shield. My heart trusts in Him and I am helped. Blessed are You, oh Lord, You have heard the voice of my supplications.*"

The music and the words washed over him, filling the gaps and cracks in his foundation. *Yahweh, why do You still restore me when I stray off course so often? Help me to stay in Your refuge, my God.* He whispered, "Help me be strong."

When his fortitude had been replenished and his knees had stiffened, Gilead pushed himself up and hobbled stiff legged to the palace.

Assigned to overwatch in the throne room, he navigated up the stairs and down the service corridor. In the shadows of the balcony overlooking the king's court, he whistled softly through his teeth. Coming upon an archer unannounced meant an arrow through the shoulder.

The archer on duty turned his head and relaxed.

Gilead took his place on the bench and plucked his bow string. *Twang!* Perfect tension. "Anything new?" He reached over his back, fingers re-counting each arrow in his quiver.

The archer stretched his arms over his head and twisted his back side to side. He sneered. "The old windbag prophet is spreading the same cheery message." With a two-finger salute, he slipped away, one with the shadows.

Gilead leaned over the marble railing.

Sure enough, Jeremiah, shoulders and legs rigid, stood before King Jehoiakim and his court "—yet your eyes and your heart are for nothing but your covetousness. For shedding innocent blood."

The position of the overwatch angled behind the king's shoulder, cloaking his expression but providing a clear line of sight to any threats. *Except the worst threat to your person is your own arrogance.*

The co-regent's face was visible and usually gave insight into King Jehoiakim's mood. Young king Coniah yawned and examined the back of his hand.

Jeremiah struck his hands together. "Thus, says the Lord, concerning Jehoiakim, son of Josiah, the king of Judah. 'They shall not lament for him. He shall be buried with the burial of a donkey, dragged and cast out beyond the gates of Jerusalem.'"

Gilead straightened. Oh, to play a part in that glorious day. He reached back out of habit for an arrow. He could fulfill that prophecy right now.

"Is that a threat, prophet?"

The guards stepped closer in unison.

Instead of answering, Jeremiah turned and shook his finger at the adolescent. "As for you, King Coniah, though you were a signet ring on the right hand of Yahweh, even still He will pluck you off and give you into the hand of those who seek your life. Those whose faces you fear. Nebuchadnezzar, king of Babylon!"

"Enough!" King Jehoiakim raised his hand.

"You are a despised, broken idol, Coniah!" Jeremiah's voice rose. "The Lord will write you down as childless."

"Shows how much you know." Coniah glanced at his father with a nasally chuckle.

King Jehoiakim turned slightly, giving Gilead a clear view of his scorn toward his son.

Coniah shifted and his countenance did too. He cleared his throat. "That is, I already have five sons. And another child arriving any day now."

"I have a prophecy for you, Jeremiah," a voice heckled.

Gilead craned his neck. Hananiah, the man paid to fill the kings' ears with pleasant words and outcomes.

"You will die." Hananiah chortled. "As soon as you were born, you began to decay."

Course laughter filled the throne room. A blur of color whizzed through the air, striking Jeremiah's chest. The pomegranate fell, splattering its burgundy juice on the marble floor.

Yahweh is the saving refuge of His anointed. Gilead clenched the shaft between his fingers, dislodging the arrow ready to fly to the prophet's aid. Yahweh was Jeremiah's protection, not him.

Jeremiah stood strong in the face of adversity. "You and all your household will be cast out into the land of Babylon. You will die there."

Coniah shook his head. "Our relationship with Babylon is on good terms. Nebuchadnezzar respects our partnership. He couldn't rule this land without us." Another glance at his *abba*.

"Everyone's ears will tingle as they hear how Yahweh has overturned all nations in this land." Jeremiah rubbed his chest where pomegranate juice stained his tunic like blood. "All nations will know and shake their heads as they pass by, because you have forsaken the covenant of the Lord your God!"

Hananiah cupped a hand around his mouth. "The only thing that will 'pass by' is your doom and gloom."

"You are through." King Jehoiakim waved his hand. "Get him out of here."

The musicians struck up a lively tune, and Jeremiah pivoted slowly and marched towards the door.

Don't turn your back! Gilead nocked his arrow and swept the point across the throne room. A soldier moved to escort the prophet, hand resting open-palmed on his sword.

Gilead sighted the soldier's back until Jeremiah had exited. Only when the soldier returned to the revelry did Gilead return the arrow to his quiver. He flexed his hand, unable to shake the dread from his shoulders.

9

Bind up the testimony, seal the law among my disciples. And I will wait on the Lord, who hides His face from the house of Jacob; and I will hope in Him.

—Isaiah 8:16-17

Serving those who served. Leading others into an attitude of worship before the sacred altar of Yahweh. Fellowship with other brothers and sisters of truth.

And Amram.

Shiri's heart swelled with the beautiful privilege of being in the house of the Lord. She drank in the sight of those gathered at the back of the temple courtyard. Their numbers had to be near one hundred today.

One hundred souls choosing to follow Yahweh. *Thank You, my Lord, for directing my path here. You have given me the desire of my heart, to serve You.*

"Shalom, Shiri, my song."

Speaking of desires of her heart.

Amram flashed her his glorious smile, then directed his attention to Ezekiel. "What did I miss?"

"Ezekiel is exhorting us to—" She frowned, trying to recall what Ezekiel had just said. Stepping into the cool shadow of the temple, her thoughts became clearer. "—to hide Yahweh's words in our hearts, to not sin against Him."

Amram rubbed his hands together. "King David's psalm."

Shiri hid a smile as Amram began humming the opening of the song. She could sense his perusal, and all attempts to focus on Ezekiel's message fled as rapidly as the heat rushing up her neck. She swallowed, hoping to replace the moisture that had left her mouth. Shyness and daring warred within her like an amateur flutist trying to make his instrument heard above the clamor of the harps and drums. She turned her head to meet Amram's intense gaze.

"We'll have to add that to our rotation." His chin tipped up and his whisper wrapped around her. "Can't you just hear us singing that together?"

Shiri's breath caught. Together.

By the time she remembered how to nod, Amram had turned his attention to the message. He crossed his arms and his foot tapped to the tune inside his head. A satisfied smile rested on his face. The thought of singing with her seemed to please him.

How had she learned his mannerisms in three weeks of working together, even with so much intermediary time? Because the months in between had been filled with continual thoughts of the handsome choirmaster, replaying his every shift and intonation. She inspected her hands before Amram could notice her silly, adoring expression.

Together.

Shiri's fingers moved in synchronization with the flute-song in her mind. The melody trilled around her like a gentle breeze through a field of flowers as though they sang it even now.

That evening Shiri exited the dining hall, halting at the sight of the man in Levitical garb leaning on the pillar, head turned toward the sky. She squinted to discern in the dim light. Ezekiel.

She glanced back into the hall where a servant swept. Another rolled up the eating mats.

A sigh drifted her way. Something troubled Ezekiel.

It had been a couple days since she'd seen him. They hadn't established a standard practice of when she would report in, and she was accountable to him. Approaching, she cleared her throat softly.

He stood unmoving.

"*Ahem.*"

Ezekiel turned and briefly smiled. "Shiriel. God is the song of my life."

She shrugged, attempting to lighten the mood. "What can I say? My *abba* lives and breathes music." What weighed Ezekiel's countenance?

A soft chuckle drifted on the cooling air. "It suits you. Is your *ima* musically gifted as well?"

"Oh, goodness, no." Shiri giggled at the memories of *Ima* joining in the musicality that filled their home. "She always quotes King David, saying to make a *joyful* noise to the Lord, 'it doesn't say it has to sound good.'"

That produced a full laugh. "I'll have to remember that."

Shiri's heart ached as Ezekiel's smile faded into discouragement. She cleared her throat. "My *abba* didn't marry until he retired from service here. Well, continual service." Ezekiel would be able to figure that out. Why couldn't she say things simply, without all the extra? "Naturally, he poured into me his love for the flute. My cousin too—my *doda* is a widow—so *Abba* stepped into Chesed's life as a second father."

"How is your *ima's* health? Any better this month?" Ezekiel tented his fingers, then fisted his hands.

Shiri rubbed the back of her neck and shifted from one

foot to the other. Though this conversation had nothing to do with temple protocol, he was thoughtful to ask. "*Ima* has always been frail. However, she seemed stable when I left."

"Does she wish you didn't come as often?" Ezekiel searched the stars.

"On the contrary. She wants me to serve Yahweh and be happy." Shiri fingered her sash.

"Are you happy here?"

The image of a man as tall as King Saul, handsome like King David, and as charming as King Solomon filtered in her thoughts. She covered her cheek. If Ezekiel turned her direction, he'd hopefully only see her silhouette and not the blush.

"Yes." Shiri mentally congratulated herself for her succinctness. "Aren't you?"

Ezekiel turned and the light from the hall illuminated the distress on his face.

"I'm sorry. I don't mean to pry." Shiri gave him some space.

"It feels like nobody cares. No matter what Yahweh says, they choose to do whatever they want."

Shiri halted. "Today there were one hundred people who hung on your every word." Was it a sin to exaggerate? She hadn't counted, but it had to be close.

"Out of how many people in Jerusalem?" Ezekiel swiped his hand across his face. "I can't help them if they don't take the time to learn."

Shiri blinked. "You don't think they apply what you teach? The time of listening and learning from you is one of my favorite parts of serving here."

"Truly? Do you feel it is equipping you to serve in famine or plenty? To follow Yahweh in whatever is expected of you?"

"Does a flute decide what song to play?"

Ezekiel's eyes crinkled. "I have to say, before I accosted you, I didn't pay attention to music."

Did he tease, or did he not follow her reasoning? "Consider the New Gate. Does it decide who can enter into the temple? Its only job is being a gate—allowing access to Yahweh's presence. Each person must decide to enter."

Ezekiel tapped a curved finger to his lips.

"You are a gate for the people. Yahweh has given you the privilege and responsibility to speak to the people's hearts. It is up to them to decide whether to listen and learn." Shiri shifted her weight to one side. Who was the priest here?

"You are very wise, Shiriel."

Internally, she squirmed under his intense scrutiny. "And that is the influence of an *ima* who was the daughter of a scribe."

The lamps from the dining hall winked out one at a time. Shivering as the evening breeze toyed with the wisps of hair poking out from her scarf, she backed away. "Good night, Ezekiel."

After the conclusion of her week, Shiri settled back into duties at home. Ezekiel's urgency pressed heavy on her chest. Hearing his admonitions day after day had opened her eyes to Judah's depravity. The gates of the temple were still open, yes, but she now saw the creeping darkness of Judah's apostacy, burgeoning in the alleyways and displayed in the casual attitudes of her countrymen. *What is one hundred compared to a backsliding nation?*

Shiri shivered and ducked her head into the dim interior of the house. "*Ima*? I'm going for water."

"Of course, dear. Take your time."

"Are you comfortable? Can I help you into the courtyard?" Shiri lowered the yoke with empty jars to the stand by the door. "The sun is warm and the birds are singing. You'd be closer to *Abba's* workshop if you needed anything."

Ima exhaled. "I don't want to be a burden."

Based on *Ima's* tone, she lingered in pain today. Shiri smiled brightly to hide her rising concern. "It will do you good." She knelt and wrapped her arms around her *ima's* waist. "Ready?" As gently as possible, she stood, lifting *Ima* to her feet.

Ima inhaled sharply and steadied herself on Shiri's shoulder.

"I'm sorry to cause you pain."

With a shake of her head, *Ima* concentrated on putting one spindly leg in front of the other. They were the same height and, at one time, the same build. Even since yesterday, *Ima* seemed weaker.

In the shade of *Abba's* workshop, Shiri lowered *Ima* to the cushions and fretted over the placement of each one.

"Go on. I'm fine." *Ima* patted her hand.

Shiri shifted one last cushion and rose. She brushed off her hands and leaned into the workshop. The lingering scent of sweet almond oil and the gritty sound of *Abba* rubbing the smoothing stone up and down his current flute spoke of the harmony in their household. "*Abba*, I'm going to draw the water. *Ima* is here in the sun."

Abba acknowledged with a smile. "Thank you, my daughter." He lifted the flute and trilled a tune to escort her.

Shiri fetched the yoke, feet as light as the notes Abba sent her way. The beauty of the early autumn afternoon swirled around her with the breeze. The plum trees lining the path boasted leaves dappled with orange. The flute's melody called out and her feet responded, crossing here, shuffling sideways, a sashay around a circle. The long jars on either side of the yoke swung crazily, and she laughed, grateful no one could see her foolishness. She concentrated on planting her feet respectably.

Not a moment too soon. Keziah stepped onto the road from her new husband's courtyard with her water jars. Of course, her friend had seen her silliness many times and would likely join in a bout of laughter. Or would have two months ago, prior to her marriage.

Shiri shut out the melancholy of growing older and lengthened her stride. "Keziah, wait for me!"

Keziah glanced over her shoulder and squealed. "Shiri! When did you return? I miss you so much!"

Shiri grinned. Keziah hadn't grown up *that* much. "Two days ago."

"I want to hear everything!"

"It's so wonderful." Shiri closed her eyes and breathed in. "I love serving in the temple. Amram says—"

"And who is Amram?" Keziah jerked Shiri to a stop.

Shiri touched the flush in her cheek. "He is the choirmaster, the worship leader—"

"Ahh." Keziah coyly rested her hand on her cheek. "Does Amram reciprocate this affection?"

Who was Shiri fooling? She had sighed with Keziah over her betrothal to Bildad just a year ago.

"I think so." She leaned close. "He calls me his song."

"That is so sweet. What else?" Keziah put a hand to her chest and quickly grabbed for her yoke again as it shifted too far to the right.

They took their place in the line at the well. Shiri glanced at the woman in front of her and whispered, "We sing together. It is the most glorious thing—worshiping Yahweh together."

Keziah clapped her hands together, drawing the attention of the woman in front of them who jiggled her head with a knowing smirk. When she faced forward again, Shiri and Keziah laughed silently behind their hands.

"What is new with you?" Shiri leaned close.

Keziah glowed and whispered, "I'm with child."

Another squeal and an amused glance from the woman before them.

They leaned their heads together and caught up with all that had happened at the temple and Keziah's two months of marriage. Long after they had filled their water jars, they lingered at Bildad's gate. The sun dipped lower, and Keziah reluctantly went inside with the promise of catching up on the morrow.

Shiri turned toward home, crossing the empty courtyard and bending at the knees to set the branches of the yoke in the frame. "I'm home!" She kneaded her shoulders and stepped into the dim interior. "I just had a delightful visit with Keziah..." Her gaze adjusted to *Abba*, standing beside *Ima's* cushions. Shiri blinked at the smile softening the lines of *Ima*'s pain.

"What is it?" Shiri knelt and kissed *Ima's* cheek. "I haven't seen you this happy for some time."

Ima glanced at *Abba*, then at the cup he held. Shiri stared at the intricately detailed cup. To her knowledge, the only time it had been used was for *Ima* and *Abba's* betrothal. Shiri sucked in a breath and rose, searching *Abba's* face.

"I have agreed to your betrothal, my daughter." *Abba* lifted his chin.

Amram had come! The music of the moment swirled around Shiri's heart. "Truly?"

Abba jerked his chin again, and *Ima* shifted her gaze beyond Shiri.

A smile spread from ear to ear as she spun around to see...*Ezekiel.*

Why was he here? Shiri scanned the room. Amram was nowhere to be found.

Ezekiel stepped forward, gaze shifting from her to *Abba*. He cleared his throat and gave a nervous smile. "Hello, Shiriel."

Did he come on behalf of Amram, like Abraham's servant on behalf of Isaac?

She turned again to *Abba*, questions unable to form.

"Blessed are You, Lord our God, King of the universe," *Abba* lifted the cup, "Who creates the fruit of the vine."

"Amen," *Ima's* soft voice cut through some of Shiri's confusion.

Shouldn't the groom be here for the ceremony?

Abba extended the cup to Ezekiel. "Blessed are You, Lord our God, King of the universe, who sanctifies this marriage through the betrothal."

The eaves of the house threatened to come crashing down.

Ezekiel was the groom.

Wait. She backed away, shaking her head, and stumbled across the courtyard and into *Abba's* workshop. Leaning over his worktable, she sucked in breaths that didn't quite fill her lungs.

Ezekiel? Was this a cruel joke?

A shadow crossed the doorway. Shiri straightened and clenched her skirt as *Abba* entered.

Abba put a gnarled hand on her shoulder. "You are ready to be married, Shiri."

"Yes, but…Ezekiel? He doesn't even like me."

"Do you think he would offer marriage if he didn't like you?" Abba chuckled.

Shiri pressed against her temples to halt the cacophony of thoughts.

"He is a good man, my daughter. He loves and serves Yahweh."

"But—" *What of Amram?*

"I am old. Your *ima* is ailing. Ezekiel will care for you and provide a godly home for you." Abba straightened, his expression and shoulders set. There would be no use asking for more time. "Come. We will finish the ceremony."

With each step, Shiri's chest tightened. Her heart thudded faster than Chesed's fingers on his drum.

Avoiding Ezekiel's gaze, she focused on the cup. Abba

repeated the blessing and Ezekiel drank. A calloused brown hand extended the wine to her. It should be smooth, artistic fingers.

Abba nudged her. "Drink."

Shiri put the cup to her lips, and the wine stung the back of her throat.

Ezekiel's sandals peaked out from under his robes.

Abba placed his arms around Shiri and her…betrothed. "After one year's time, you will come together as husband and wife."

She ducked from under *Abba's* embrace and fled from the house.

10

Her heads judge for a bribe, her priests teach for pay, And her prophets divine for money. Yet they lean on the LORD and say, "Is not the LORD among us? No harm can come upon us."
—Micah 3:11

Now what?

Ezekiel blinked at the empty doorway. That didn't play out as he had planned it. Shiriel clearly hadn't been expecting him. The other night at the temple, she hadn't been hostile toward him as she spoke of the value of serving as Yahweh had equipped.

Why had he thought she wouldn't be opposed toward him now?

He didn't doubt his affection that grew daily toward Shiriel. The depth of her character and simple zeal for Yahweh had completed a hollow place in his heart. Internally he squirmed. The timing felt—wrong, yet the burden of knowledge pressed on his shoulders.

"Shiri, come back." Ibraham crossed to the door with a pained shuffle.

Ezekiel scratched his neck. The outer gate creaked on the hinge and slapped shut.

Ibraham exhaled and rested his head against the doorframe.

"She will come around." Dvorah beckoned Ezekiel close. He knelt, and she placed a cold hand on his head. "We are proud to have you as part of the family."

Ezekiel swallowed at the ache in his throat. His own *ima* and *abba* had been gone so long. Would they have rejoiced over his choice of bride? He scrubbed his face. "I'm sorry if this seems rushed. I cannot explain the urgency I feel—"

Ibraham sat beside his wife and put his arm around her. "We know the timing is of Yahweh. We've been praying for a solution such as this. I am a worthless, old flute maker. My days are numbered."

"As are mine." Dvorah rested her sallow face against Ibraham's shoulder. "Go, speak to her. Your love for Yahweh will win her over."

Ezekiel pushed off his knees. He strode out the door, touching his fingers to the door frame, then to his lips. *Coming and going, You are my God.*

At the gate, he glanced both ways. Shiriel headed southeast toward Jerusalem at a rapid pace, already a considerable distance from him.

"Shiriel! Wait!" Ezekiel began to jog and frowned down at his Levitical garb. The day was still warm, and running would work up a forbidden sweat. He slowed to a swift stride but couldn't gain ground on Shiriel the whole way from the outlying village to the Sheep Gate at Jerusalem's northern wall.

Inside the city, she wove her way through the narrow streets towards the temple. Did she intend to pray?

Ezekiel entered the New Gate with a nod at the guard on

duty. Shiriel veered left toward the music risers. *What are you doing?* He continued his straight course and stepped into the shadows off to the side of the risers as Amram closed his hand after the last word was sung.

"Another excellent day. Yahweh is indeed pleased with your efforts." Amram crossed over to collect the coins from the official offering box.

"Amram." Shiriel stepped to his side.

"Shiri, my song." Amram straightened, and a smile spread across his face.

Ezekiel's gut twisted. Did they have an understanding?

"You're back already? Excellent! I've got a new arrangement I want you to sing." Amram poured the coins into a small pouch.

The need to see Shiriel's expression nearly drove Ezekiel from his hiding place.

"No, I wish to speak with you."

"What is it? What has happened?" Amram furrowed his brow.

"My *abba* has arranged a betrothal for me." The quiver in her voice wrecked Ezekiel.

Amram took a step back and crossed his arms. "I guess congratulations are in order."

"I can still sing." Shiriel ducked her head.

"Who is your intended?" Amram arched an eyebrow.

"Ezekiel. The scheduler."

"That do-gooder?" Amram scoffed and shook his head. "He won't allow you to sing."

A sniffle came from Shiriel. "There is still time. If you went to my *abba* today…"

"Your *abba* is not going to cancel a betrothal."

"And…um…offered instead." Her shoulders rose slightly.

Ezekiel slowly released his own pent-up breath.

Amram stepped back, and a sneer curled his lip. "Me? Why would I want to do that?"

"I thought that you…that we…" She buried her hands in the fabric of her dress and her volume dropped. "You called me your song."

The quiver in Shiriel's voice sparked a protective fire in Ezekiel, rivaling the need to defend the temple's purity. How long had Amram been leading her on?

The choirmaster's sharp laugh halted Ezekiel's approach. "You are a gifted musician. I have never given cause for you to believe differently. It was nice while it lasted. Your singing under my direction brought many generous donations."

A sniff from Shiriel. "For the temple, right?"

Amram laughed. "Sure."

Shiriel remained still as stone as Amram shook his head and stomped away.

Ezekiel narrowed his eyes. Amram's behavior had been exemplary of late, but, apparently, he still found ways to dip his hand into the offering and falsify the amount given. He must be held accountable.

Shiriel's shoulders sagged and her head dropped.

Insides twisting, Ezekiel turned away. He'd had no business listening to that exchange. But he had pledged to be Shiriel's protector in the temple—and now in life. He had a duty to shelter her. Pivoting, he dug out the cloth he used to wipe sweat from his forehead. Stepping in front of Shiriel, he cleared his throat.

Her head jerked up, revealing her red nose and tears in her eyes. The cleft in her chin quivered. Ezekiel extended the strip of linen.

She accepted it but didn't meet his gaze.

"Did he lead you on or make promises to you?" Ezekiel was too late to shelter her from hurt. But he would seek justice if necessary. "Anything inappropriate?"

She shook her head, dislodging a pent-up tear. "No, not in words. Just in my hopes. How could I be so foolish?"

"You did nothing wrong, Shiriel." Why couldn't he call

her Shiri as everyone else did? Ezekiel resisted the urge to wrap his arms around her. "He should've handled instructing you more professionally."

Shiriel pressed the cloth to her eyes.

How could he get her to smile again? "I can have him mysteriously off the schedule when you come, or give him latrine duty."

She met his gaze as the gong announced the evening meal.

"We should head back. They need to close the gates." He shifted his weight. "I'm sure you'd rather not remain all night and possibly cross paths with him. I surely wouldn't."

Shiriel gave a small smile. "Why are you being kind to me after I declared my affection for another man?"

"Because," Ezekiel ushered her out the New Gate. "I'd have felt the same way if he had agreed."

Her scrutiny sent an army of ants scurrying inside his gut. He rubbed his hand over his beard and stood tall. He did care for her.

She glanced away and hurried down the street.

Ezekiel matched her stride. "I am sorry the betrothal caught you off guard. I intended to speak to you after receiving your *abba's* blessing. He felt it best to proceed."

"He does remember you accused me of witchcraft, doesn't he?"

"Yes." Ezekiel halted and expelled a breath. "I told him you might not be in favor of the idea."

Shiriel paused but didn't turn. "*Abba* pushed this through, didn't he?"

"He only wishes to ensure your future."

With a brief shake of her head, Shiriel stomped off.

"A flute doesn't decide what song to play." Ezekiel called after her. "Nor does a gate decide who may enter."

She glanced over her shoulder. "What are you trying to say?"

"I choose to be your gate. To guard you and provide for

you." That sounded better in his thoughts, but it did produce a smile.

"My *abba* does think highly of you."

Relief pushed the trapped air from his lungs. He laughed nervously. "And your *ima* does too."

Shiriel halted and covered her face in her hands. "I'm so foolish. I offered myself to a man who never once thought of me. Ugh. I'm such a fool." Her voice wobbled.

"It isn't foolish to want to be loved," Ezekiel whispered, clasping his hands behind his back. He stepped in front of her. "Yahweh has created us with that desire, to reflect how He wishes us to love Him."

Understanding lit her eyes in the twilight. He gestured to the road, and she fell in step beside him. They walked on in silence.

He should say something. Something clever about how delighted he was to be betrothed to her and how he would care for her and be honest—unlike Amram.

How could he compare to Amram's charm? If only he'd paid attention to the music sooner, they'd have something in common. *Your love for Yahweh will win her over.* He slanted a glance at her.

Shiriel tensed as they arrived at her house. Her chin dropped.

Ezekiel's chest constricted, pained for what Shiriel would have to endure while informing her parents of her actions.

"Shiri, is that you?" Dvorah's thin voice filtered out of the house.

"Yes, *Ima,* I'm home." Shiriel's shoulders rose.

Ibraham appeared in the doorway, concern etched on his lined face.

Ezekiel acknowledged the unspoken questions. *She's safe now.* Inside the house, a meager meal was laid with the care of a grand feast before Dvorah.

Shiriel remained by the door, staring at the spread of food. "*Abba*, I…ran off because—"

"—Because she had some loose ends to tie up at the temple." Ezekiel stepped around Shiriel and clasped arms with his future father-in-law. Unless she denied him still. Sweat beaded on his forehead, and he stole a glance at his intended's down-turned head.

Ibraham cleared his throat. "Shiri, your *ima* and I have prayed for Yahweh's provision for you, and we ask you to trust us. We believe Ezekiel is the answer to our prayers. He will hold tight to you, and more importantly, to Yahweh."

Out of the corner of his eye, Ezekiel noticed Shiriel had turned toward him. "Yes, Abba. I trust you."

Ezekiel's stomach gave a funny flip.

"Then, tonight we celebrate—" Ibraham shrugged apologetically, "—on barley cakes and plums and lentils."

Shiriel buried herself in Ibraham's embrace, and Ezekiel averted his eyes.

"I wish I could honor you in a greater fashion, my daughter."

"You do honor me. You know that's not important to me."

Ezekiel glanced around the room. In this time of famine, it was unlikely people would spend money on luxury items like flutes when they could barely afford grain. It was good he could contribute to the family as part of the bridal contract.

Ibraham released his daughter, and she flung herself into Dvorah's arms as if she intended to leave that night, never to see them again. Dvorah waved Ezekiel over. He knelt on her other side across from his betrothed. In a year's time, Shiriel would be his wife.

In the midst of Ibraham's prayer, Ezekiel stole a glance at Shiriel. A single tear trickled down her face. She caught it with the knuckle of her fore-finger and lifted her eyes. A flush spread across her cheeks as she met Ezekiel's gaze.

His breath caught as the depth of her expression reached out to him, connecting her to him with the hurt he saw.

Shiriel gave a tight smile before glancing down.

Uneasiness pressed in Ezekiel's chest. Was he wrong in coming forward with this betrothal? Would Shiriel's countenance soften toward him over the course of the year? With the famine, the raids, and the inevitable promise of Nebuchadnezzar's looming invasion, would there even be cause to celebrate in a year's time?

11

Therefore thus says the LORD concerning Jehoiakim king of Judah: "He shall have no one to sit on the throne of David, and his dead body shall be cast out to the heat of the day and the frost of the night. I will punish him, his family, and his servants for their iniquity; and I will bring on them, on the inhabitants of Jerusalem, and on the men of Judah all the doom I have pronounced against them; but they did not heed."
—Jeremiah 36:30-31

B*ang!* The throne room doors flew open. "King Jehoiakim is dead!"

From the overwatch, Gilead's arrow lined up with the messenger's heaving chest. A soldier from the city wall.

The man fell to his hands and knees before co-regent Coniah's throne, gasping for air.

Coniah leaned an elbow on his knee. "Explain."

Slowly, Gilead released the tension on the bow, and the arrow flopped.

"Advisors…" The man struggled to breathe normally. "Nebuchadnezzar…"

The throne room doors flung open again, and six of King Jehoiakim's advisors strode in, their robes swishing. A collective gasp rose from those in the throne room.

Gilead once more pulled the string taut, the feather brushing his cheek.

"You haven't been granted audience." The guards blocked their advance, swords whisked out of their sheaths.

"What is the meaning of this?" Coniah jerked two fingers and the guards stepped aside.

"Oh King, live forever." Shelemiah—King Jehoiakim's representative of foreign affairs—bowed with a flourish. "We have just arrived from Riblah and a meeting with Nebuchadnezzar."

Coniah lowered an open palm beside the throne in signal.

Sweat dripped down the side of Gilead's face. *Please, Yahweh, let the command of the king be justified.*

"Why is Nebuchadnezzar's arrival in Riblah of more importance than my *abba's* death?"

Silence cast its eerie pallor.

"Soldier, you may proceed. You were telling me how my *abba's* advisors killed him."

Shelemiah stepped forward. "My apologies, oh King, I intended to give you the whole story. My priorities were out of order."

"Indeed, they are." Coniah's palm remained flat.

The advisor spread his arms wide, leaving his chest a perfect target. "I regret to inform you that King Jehoiakim is indeed dead. He fell over the wall by the north gate."

Sure, he fell. There wasn't a man amongst that lot who hadn't waited for the opportunity to push him. Gilead squeezed his eyes shut. Jehoiakim was still the chosen king.

"Why were you on the north wall, advisor?" Coniah's tone lowered.

"We had just arrived from Riblah. Nebuchadnezzar is

heading this way, and he demands that King Jehoiakim pay the tribute or die."

"And who sent you to collaborate with Nebuchadnezzar?"

"The king did, of course." Shelemiah clasped hands over his heart, a clear indicator of his own agenda. "Nebuchadnezzar's timeline had just been accelerated. He will march south as soon as he has brought Riblah to order."

Gilead adjusted his sights to Shelemiah's neck and scanned the faces of the other men. Arms crossed here, a chin lifted there. All stood in arrogant unity.

"And how did the king respond before he fell?"

Shelemiah didn't seem to register Coniah's dangerous tone. He sneered. "He boasted that King Nebuchadnezzar couldn't enforce that threat. Then he slipped. He stumbled backwards. Before we could reach out to catch his majesty, it was too late."

Coniah's hand snapped shut.

Gilead nocked his second arrow before the first buried itself into Shelemiah's throat. In less than a minute, all six treasonous advisors lay sprawled in their own blood.

"Indeed, you were too late, Shelemiah." Coniah flounced to Jehoiakim's throne and sat with a flourish, obscuring his full face from Gilead's view. "I doubt you'll make the same mistake again."

Nebat, the governor of throne room protocol, shifted and cleared his throat. "What should we do with the king?"

"I am the king!" Coniah's neck turned red and the vein on his temple bulged.

"Yes, my king." Nebat prostrated himself on the ground. The swish of robes filled the throne room as all present followed suit. "May I rise and declare the excellent news officially for the annals?"

"You may rise." Coniah leaned back and caressed the ebony work on the throne.

Nebat stood on the bottom step of the dais and faced the

room. "In accordance with the laws of the land, I present the ruler of Judah and lord of the land, King Coniah, son of Jehoiakim. May he live forever!"

"May he live forever!" The words bounced off the cedar-paneled walls.

Turning, Nebat bowed at the waist as the people rose. "What is your command regarding…your *abba's* body?"

"My *abba* was an imbecile!"

Nebat stumbled off the step.

"He squandered the opportunity Nebuchadnezzar offered." King Coniah waved for the servant with the tray of delicacies. "Jehoiakim's body will remain outside the north gate. When Nebuchadnezzar arrives, he will see the decaying body and know I do not stand by Jehoiakim's incompetence."

Gilead ground his teeth. This young whelp had no sense to run a nation.

Dread knotted in his stomach, lumping along with bitter foreboding. As terrible as this development was, the nation of Judah deserved King Coniah. *Yahweh, help us to be faithful, regardless of what comes.*

Before the servants had disposed of the ambassadors' bodies, Gilead's replacement arrived, brimming with questions. Gilead grunted a brief explanation and slipped away.

In his haste, he moved with more noise than he should have as he ducked through the labyrinth of hallways. The winter night air sent chills down Gilead's arms. He should have grabbed his cloak. Too late now, he slapped his arms and moved swiftly to the temple, hoping against hope that the gates were still open. He skidded to a halt at the looming fortress and tried the latch. Bolted.

Think. He swung around to the gatehouse on the southwest corner. Should he wait until morning?

Urgency and an unsettled feeling drove him on. He pounded his fist on the wooden door. "Open up!"

Pashur, the chief governor of the temple, pushed out the

small panel and leaned out, spilling warm yellow light into the street. "Who goes there?"

"I am Gilead. I must see Ezekiel."

"I am sorry." Like cool water on a hot day, Pashur's smooth voice poured out of the small window. "The temple complex is closed. You may come back tomorrow at the third hour to offer your sacrifices."

Gilead grabbed the closing panel. He'd climb through this window if need be. "I won't enter, but I won't leave until I have spoken with Ezekiel."

"Ezekiel is otherwise occupied."

"Where is he?" Gilead mentally mapped out the streets surrounding the temple. If Ezekiel was anywhere near the walls, Gilead could call to him.

"Pashur, what seems to be the trouble?" Ezekiel's voice filtered out.

"There is no trouble. I was telling this man to return when the temple gates open—"

Gilead's shoulders stiffened. "Ezekiel! King Jehoiakim is dead."

After a gasp and the shuffle of feet and robes, Ezekiel's face appeared at the opening. The darkness couldn't conceal the deep lines between his eyes or the unspoken question.

"It wasn't me. The story is, he fell off the north wall. King Coniah has commanded his body to remain there, just as Jeremiah prophesied."

Pashur's face vied for space beside Ezekiel's. "I suppose Coniah summons a priest for the coronation?"

A proper ceremony was the man's chief concern?

"He did not. He's already assumed the throne." Gilead rubbed his arms but couldn't warm away the dread. "Nebat has already declared him king."

"How does he expect to show loyalty to the people and Yahweh if he doesn't include the priest in the ceremony?" Pashur huffed.

The man's blindness was incredible. "I don't think he intends to include Yahweh in his reign."

Ezekiel shook his head and briefly closed his eyes.

Gilead fought back a smile. At least he wasn't stuck dealing with chosen ignorance every day. He angled his head, blocking Pashur from the conversation. "Nebuchadnezzar collects tribute in Riblah. Soon he will turn his troops toward Judah."

"We must prepare the tribute. I will begin cataloging what is in the treasury." Pashur whirled and the hurried slap of his sandals grew faint.

Gilead scrubbed at the disbelief that surely marked his countenance.

Ezekiel chuckled and shrugged. "How did Coniah react?"

"He believes Nebuchadnezzar will extend mercy because he will understand it wasn't Coniah's decision to withhold tribute."

"This is what we've been preparing for." Ezekiel pinched the bridge of his nose. "This is fulfillment of prophecy. Regardless of Coniah's motives, there is no longer hope for Judah."

The air grew heavy between them, pressing down on Gilead's spirit.

Ezekiel sighed. "We shall renew our efforts to strengthen the followers. Recruit more who will listen and learn. How long do we have?"

Gilead leaned his shoulder against the gate. "With an army marching? A month. Three months at most, depending on how cooperative the other nations are."

Time drew short. And yet here they stood, with no idea what to do. Gilead studied his friend. "What does this mean for your betrothal?"

Ezekiel pushed out a breath. "I don't know. As Yahweh wills, I will obey."

"You could move up the wedding."

"And what good would that do? Nebuchadnezzar will not show favor just because I have a wife."

Gilead indicated the shadowy forms of two men approaching.

The man on the left spoke. "There's no guarantee of the outcome. All we can be sure of is Nebuchadnezzar is Yahweh's chosen servant to chastise us."

Ezekiel leaned his head for a better view. "Jeremiah?"

Gilead turned his back to the men. It was hard to keep up with whether Jeremiah was a fugitive or a free man. The order changed day to day. Best to be cautious. Now he could honestly say he hadn't seen who the man was.

"Jehoiakim was warned countless times. Yet he continued to lead Judah into danger and allow her destruction." The grief in the man's tone swirled around Gilead like the frost of the night.

"And yet, we must have faith that Yahweh will not destroy us." The voice sounded like Baruch the scribe. "Yahweh said our offspring shall return in rest and ease."

"It seems better to submit to Yahweh's chastisement and deflect to Babylon." This from Ezekiel. "If we fight, are we not declaring our independence and ignorance as Jehoiakim did?"

Gilead restrained himself from pivoting. "Are you suggesting we willingly submit to a king more evil than our own?" He clenched his fist.

"I know it contradicts human nature, old man—" Only Jeremiah would call out Gilead's age.

Gilead snorted. "You're a fine one to talk."

"—but we must consider Nebuchadnezzar is still subservient to the God of the universe, even if he doesn't acknowledge it."

"Surrendering to the Chaldeans is submitting to Yahweh." Baruch again.

Out of Gilead's peripheral vision, Ezekiel made a move as

if to pinch the bridge of his nose. "What of Coniah? Do you think he can be influenced?"

Gilead turned slightly to see Ezekiel nod to him. "King Coniah acts as if he is the victim of his *abba's* sour grapes. He seems to think Nebuchadnezzar will forgive the offenses."

"Which might be to the benefit of the people—if the co-regent… king... grovels." Ezekiel gave a mirthless chuckle. "Although it will be a shock to our young king when Nebuchadnezzar exacts justice for *Coniah's* sins. We will pray that his heart softens—"

"No." The sharp retort that could have been from Jeremiah bounced back off the walls of the narrow street of the city. "Do not pray for him. Yahweh has cloaked Himself as with a cloud. He will not hear. Pray instead, that the followers are strong."

Silence settled.

Despite the inevitable demise of Jerusalem, Gilead found solace in the camaraderie strengthened with the bond of adversity.

Yahweh still reigned.

12

And Nebuchadnezzar king of Babylon came against the city…Then Jehoiachin king of Judah, his mother, his servants, his princes and his officers went out to the king of Babylon; and the king of Babylon, in the eighth year of his reign, took him prisoner.
—2 Kings 24:11a, 12

The mid-morning sun shone bright as Ezekiel navigated to the Tower of Hananel at the north-west corner of the temple complex, using the same route he'd taken multiple times a day throughout the three months of Coniah's reign. Each day he climbed the ladder's steps, his heart pounding in trepidation. Surely this time he'd heard the distant thunder of Nebuchadnezzar's approaching army above the sacrificial lambs bleating outside the temple walls.

Only the hills awash with spring color greeted him. He gripped the railing. "You'd think I was eagerly anticipating Nebuchadnezzar's approach and the ensuing trials."

At the base of the tower, Samuel, the water boy, lounged

in the shade. His eyes widened, and he jumped up as Ezekiel descended.

"Have you completed all your tasks for the morning?"

"Yes, Master Ezekiel." Samuel leaned back against the stonework and crossed his ankles. "Ah. The joy of a good rest."

"Indeed." Ezekiel rolled his shoulders but could not shake the apprehension pressing on his spirit. "How would you like to climb the watchtower? It's much cooler up there."

"You mean it?"

"Sure. Just alert me if you see—" How freely should he speak with a young boy?

"If I see the Chaldean army." Samuel's voice bounced down from inside the turret.

That answered that question. "That is correct." Ezekiel turned toward the musicians' risers.

"You're going to sigh at Mistress Shiri, aren't you?" Samuel leaned out of the tower with an impish grin.

"I am going to do *all* my rounds." Ezekiel didn't have to explain himself to a boy. He twirled his hand. "Watch the north."

Samuel's boyish laughter followed him.

So what if he spent extra time listening to the music? It was one week a month. Inexplicably, Ezekiel breathed a little easier whenever Shiriel served at the temple.

Despite the unknown surrounding him, he mentally surveyed the faces and numbers of the faithful. He passed by the New Gate. Everything was as it should be.

The sound of a flute—transverse or forward he still couldn't quite discern without seeing the instrument—called to him.

He pushed aside the foolishness creeping in. Even if it wasn't his beloved, it still was a piece of her world. A few steps closer and Shiriel came into view, and yes, she did play her flute—transverse flute.

He nodded at Keziah, who stood with rounded belly before the risers, and planted his feet in Shiriel's line of sight. In the months since the betrothal, Shiriel's childhood friend had become a regular fixture in Ezekiel's life—on his visits to Shiriel's home and her visits to the temple. A sweet woman with a gentle spirit, Keziah and her husband listened and learned, keeping strong in the faith of Yahweh.

The smooth, hollow melody soothed his weary muscles. His eyelids closed as he reveled in the peace and rest. Too soon, the tempo indicated the song neared its end.

He opened his eyes and found Shiriel watching him. A blush crept up her cheeks, and she smiled shyly his direction before turning her attention toward Amram. Did she still favor him?

Ezekiel narrowed his eyes. Despite his petition to Pashur, Amram had not been addressed regarding the alleged stealing. Pashur had disregarded Ezekiel's concerns, passing it off as the musician's artistic temperament, and Amram remained unchastised. Ezekiel had been allowed to post a sentinel at the official offering box. The servant had been reassigned after one week's time.

The choirmaster signaled Shiriel, who rested her flute on her stool and stood. Amram smiled generously at her. She frowned and planted her foot behind her. The straightening of her shoulders indicated she braced herself against Amram's charm.

Good for you.

The music recommenced, and Shiriel's hips swayed, keeping time. She extended her hand to the passing crowd, and the pure tones came from her throat. "*The Lord is the strength of my song*—"

Each person who paused and glanced her way she greeted with a welcoming smile. Her kindness and compassion satisfied Ezekiel's soul. Indeed, Shiriel would be an asset to his ministry before Yahweh. His eyes traced the smooth planes of her face and the dip in her chin. Was there any woman as fair as his betrothed? Even the spring flowers to the north could not compare. When he entered into the betrothal contract months prior, he had admired Shiriel's character. Now there wasn't a day that went by that he didn't long to be near her.

Samuel's cheeky assessment had been accurate. Ezekiel was besotted with her.

"Master Ezekiel!"

The small, panicked voice ripped through Ezekiel's thoughts. He whirled to find Samuel wide-eyed and dodging around worshipers. Time slowed then accelerated with dreaded certainty.

The Chaldeans drew near.

All the moisture left Ezekiel's mouth, and his chest thumped in rhythm with his swift pace. He grabbed Samuel's arm and together they ran to the north tower.

Ezekiel's foot slipped off the ladder's rung. He pressed upward, ignoring the scraping pain in his leg. He braced himself on the terrace and fixed his gaze to the north, sucking in air.

Apprehension swirled like the cloud of dust rising from the horizon. *Yahweh, be my strength and my shield!*

Clambering down the ladder, Ezekiel sprinted back to the musicians' risers. He halted in front of the trumpeters, bracing his hands on his knees. "Sound the shofars!"

The trumpeter blinked and his mouth dropped open. Some of the choir members broke off mid-word. The musicians glanced to Amram, who frowned and waved for them to resume.

"The shofars!" Ezekiel snatched the ram's horn from the stand and rotated it so the large opening pointed up.

"What are you doing?" the trumpeter hissed.

"Sound the alarm! The Chaldeans approach." Ezekiel blew in the shofar, and the air from his lips sputtered in the horn.

Amram rolled his eyes and heaved an exasperated sigh. "What is so important for you to interrupt our performance?"

"Ezekiel?" Shiriel lifted her gaze from his foot. "You're bleeding."

"The Chaldean army approaches." Ezekiel shook the shofar at the trumpeter. "We must sound the alarm."

Shiriel's eyes widened. Glancing over her shoulder at Amram's disapproval, she took the shofar from Ezekiel and shoved it into the trumpeter's hand. "Sound the alarm. Do as he commands."

Ezekiel waited long enough to see the man raise the horn to his lips before spinning around and dashing toward the New Gate. "Close the gate!"

The shofar blared out, notifying the palace guard who would alert the entire city—not that their depleted resources could withstand a siege.

Yahweh, what is the wisest course of action? He approached the gate as it ground shut.

"What is it?" The guard drew the key from his tunic and inserted it into the lock. With a twist of the wrist, the tumbler bolted into place.

"The Chaldeans approach." Ezekiel shoved the guard toward the tower. "Watch the northern horizon. Provide updates."

The soldier darted away.

Ezekiel ran around the perimeter of the temple complex. All gates must be closed. The people needed to be instructed and calmed. What of the citizens outside the temple gates? What of—?

He pressed his hands against his head to slow the thoughts pounding like hail on a stormy day. Altering his course, Ezekiel wove through panicked priests and worshipers and knelt at the steps leading to the Court of Women. He inhaled deeply. "Yahweh, You are my Sovereign. Show me what You want me to do."

Did he hear the thunder of hoofbeats? Or just his own pulse? He squeezed his eyes shut and forced calm through his stiff limbs. If only Jeremiah was here to consult. The proverb of Solomon penetrated his thoughts. *Trust in the Lord with all your heart and in all your ways. Acknowledge Him and He will make your paths straight.*

Ezekiel exhaled. Straight paths. Which were what?

He glanced up at the sound of footsteps halting nearby—Shiriel and Keziah.

Shiriel extended a water ladle. "You should drink."

There wasn't time. He shook his head.

"Drink." Shiriel's eyebrows rose. "You are the gate keeper. If you aren't coherent, how will the people listen to your instructions?"

Amusement sparked briefly in his inner tumult. He accepted the ladle and obeyed. His thoughts cleared as the cool liquid quenched the thirst he didn't realize he'd had.

Shiriel glanced over her shoulder and clenched her hand in the folds of her tunic. "What do you need us to do?"

"We need to gather the people and keep them calm." Ezekiel pushed himself up and brushed off his hands. "Tell them to gather here."

Keziah's eyes widened. She bit her bottom lip and hugged her swollen abdomen.

"Is your husband here today?" Ezekiel bent to see Keziah's face.

She shook her head, dislodging a few tears.

Oh, Yahweh! What will become of us?

Shiriel wrapped her arms around Keziah's shoulders and smiled. "Why don't you wait here, so everyone knows where to come?"

Keziah nodded and swallowed. Her eyes watered.

Shiriel gave her a squeeze and darted off. "Over here. Everyone, gather at the steps!"

Ezekiel studied Keziah as she sniffed and then climbed

three steps. Responsibility for the people in his charge knotted his shoulder muscles.

Swallowing back the doom, Ezekiel scanned the fearful faces of the gathering crowd. *Yahweh preserve us.* His thoughts and prayers mingled as he checked the remaining gates. Did he secure his people to their destruction? They didn't have the food resources to feed all these people.

The rumble of the approaching army could not be ignored any longer. Ezekiel made his way through the crowd gathered at the steps. Neither Pashur nor anyone with higher authority was present. Even the high priest, Seraiah, turned expectantly to Ezekiel.

Ezekiel set his shoulders and climbed one step higher than Shiriel and Keziah. "My people." He lifted his hands. "Do not fear. Do not panic. If you have been around the temple recently you have heard us say this day would draw near."

The pounding stopped outside the city walls, followed by the whinny of a horse.

A sob came from Ezekiel's left. He pressed on. "Yahweh has foretold this day through the prophet Jeremiah. Nebuchadnezzar, king of Babylon, will surely exile the artisans and leaders among us."

Amram's shoulders hunched forward. "We shall resist!"

"No!" Ezekiel raised his voice to still the buzz of people siding with Amram. "This is what we have been preparing for. *This* is Yahweh's plan for our nation. Fighting against Nebuchadnezzar is futile."

"What hope is there?"

"What about those who aren't important? I am just a vine-dresser."

"I don't know. In the past he has allowed some to remain behind." Ezekiel searched the anxious faces. "Those of you who have listened to my instruction and learned of Yahweh's plans, please stand at the base of the steps."

The crowd parted as men and women made their way to

the front.

Ezekiel assessed their fortitude. "These men have trained for this. Gather around one of these—"

"King Coniah has opened up the city gates! He and his entourage carry the white flag!" A runner came from the Hananel Tower. "He speaks now with Nebuchadnezzar!"

"He has doomed us all!" A wail spread from voice to voice.

"My people! Remember, Yahweh is still in control. King Coniah has been appointed by Yahweh for this time." Ezekiel's chest constricted. "We will praise and not cower. Yahweh wouldn't chastise us if He didn't love us as a son."

A woman glanced toward the New Gate and covered her moan with her hand.

"Those who reside at the temple, collect your things." Ezekiel paused. Should he gather his own belongings to prompt them, or remain and rally their courage?

"Will Nebuchadnezzar allow us to take our belongings?"

"Does that mean he will be deporting all of us?"

Ezekiel closed his eyes. People didn't think rationally in panic. "Can I read the mind of Nebuchadnezzar? I do know if he takes you and you don't carry your belongings, he won't wait around for you to fetch them. Now, go! Meet back here."

"What of the rest of us?" Keziah's voice wobbled.

"Be strong." Ezekiel strode through the dispersing crowd to the gatehouse, calculating with each step. How much time did they have? According to Nebuchadnezzar's previous purge, eight years prior, the temple would not offer special favor or sanctuary.

He had been in the countryside burying his *abba* and settling his estate and had returned to Jerusalem to find the aftermath of the Aramean, Moabite and Ammonite armies. Even now he could hear the wails of the people. The citizens and the city had been trampled over in accordance with the proclamation of the Lord to King Jehoiakim.

He bundled his robes together and surveyed his chamber. Nothing else would serve purpose if he did travel to Babylon. He turned his heart and feet back to the people, pausing at the New Gate.

It would not prevent the violent Chaldean army from entering. They'd merely destroy God's holy temple with force. Against all instinct, Ezekiel unlocked the gate and propped it open wide enough for a man to enter.

David's psalm of the great Shepherd drew him back to the Court of the Women where Shiriel led in song. The people sang together with apprehension and resolve.

Ezekiel fixed his gaze on Shiriel. Protectiveness surged within. What would barbarians do to an unmarried woman? Could he help her escape the courtyard unnoticed? What would await her if he did? Dvorah could pass on any day, and Ibraham had no income.

"*—even though I walk through the valley of the shadow of death, I will fear no evil for You are with me—*"

He clenched his fist, taking in the concern in her eyes as she bravely sang, flute and bundle at her feet. Keziah stood on the steps clutching Shiriel's hand, her own singing distorted—from tears or inability. The irony made Ezekiel smile. He wouldn't have known Keziah was off-key before he'd heard Shiriel sing.

"*—You prepare a table before me in the presence of my enemies—*"

Bang! The New Gate slammed open and fierce Chaldeans swarmed in marching, pounding across the quarried stone. Within seconds, they threw back the gates to the Women's Court with a mighty clatter. Swords were drawn and soldiers split from either side of the contingent, flowing like rivers around the perimeter of their huddled crowd.

The woman beside Ezekiel flinched and whimpered.

He made his way to the steps, needing to reassure the people. Needing to be near Shiriel as her voice cracked.

"Be at peace." Did they understand the urgency to be calm?

"Who is in charge?" A Chaldean warrior spoke in broken Hebrew. He swept the point of his sword over the crowd.

The soldiers fanned out, surrounding their group, hyenas crouching around his terrified flock.

The people pressed together, and the Chaldeans advanced, tightening the noose cubit by cubit.

Ezekiel drew in a deep breath. "I am the acting governor of the temple. We want no trouble."

He leaned toward Shiriel as the Chaldean officer plowed through the crowd, shoving against any who did not move out of his way fast enough.

"Our betrothal contract was legally binding," Ezekiel whispered, meeting her frantic gaze.

"What?"

"You are my wife."

Hesitation flickered in her eyes. She cast a glance at Keziah. "What will *Abba* say?"

"Kneel!" the Chaldean roared, "or fear the sting of our sword. Hands on your head."

Ezekiel motioned to the people and lowered himself to his knees. "Your Abba would prefer this to…"

Shiriel helped Keziah to a kneeling position.

"You are my *wife*." *Yahweh, help her understand.*

The officer's heavy footwear slapped on the quarried stone.

Shiriel shifted her anxious gaze from the soldier and met Ezekiel's stare. Her shoulders quaked, and her lips pressed in a line.

Keziah stifled a sob.

One step below Ezekiel, the officer drew his sword back.

Ezekiel squeezed his eyes shut. Something blunt slammed against his temple, sending him sprawling down the steps. Pain studded with lights flashed through his head.

13

And [Nebuchadnezzar] cut in pieces all the articles of gold which Solomon king of Israel had made in the temple of the LORD as the LORD had said. Also he carried into captivity all Jerusalem: All the captains and all the mighty men of valor. Ten thousand captives and all the craftsmen and smiths. None remained except the poorest people of the land.

—2 Kings 24:13b-14

Unconsciousness stalked Ezekiel like a ravenous lion. He forced his eyes open.

"May this be an example to you. Your leader has left your gate open for us to enter."

The darkness on the edge of Ezekiel's vision subsided enough for him to push himself to his knees. "I am Ezekiel. Apprentice to Jeremiah the prophet."

That seemed to catch the Chaldean's attention.

Ezekiel pressed on. "We understand Nebuchadnezzar is appointed by our God to pass judgment. We will comply with your requests."

The Chaldean roared with laughter and wiped his tears from his cheeks. "Very well, Jew—"

What does that mean?

"—I am Rabgar-Nebo, Captain in the army of Nebuchadnezzar, King of the World." He snapped his fingers.

A soldier snaked a hand out and dragged Samuel to his feet. His dagger leapt to the boy's neck as fast as lightning.

"No! Please." Ezekiel halted as the dagger tipped into Samuel's skin.

"This is how it will occur, Jew. You will identify which of these—" Rabgar-Nebo arced his sword over the whimpering congregation, "—are the best and brightest. Your great king, Nebuchadnezzar, permits your poor and ordinary people to remain to till his land here."

Samuel cried out as the soldier's corded muscles tightened around his neck.

"Yes of course. You have my word. Please don't harm the boy."

Rabgar-Nebo laughed again. "The Jew says he complies, but he bargains like he has something to trade."

Ezekiel studied the Chaldean's sun-browned face. He seemed to be in good humor. "I do have something to trade."

Rabgar-Nebo arched an eyebrow and gestured for Ezekiel to proceed.

"I offer cooperation and compliance. Which makes your job of shepherding Judean hostages much easier." Sweat beaded on Ezekiel's top lip.

"We accept your gift of goodwill, priest." Bowing with an exaggerated flourish, Rabgar-Nebo sheathed his sword and grabbed Samuel's hair, yanking him from the soldier's grip. "Just so you remember your motivation."

Ezekiel's pulse roared in his ears. *Be calm.* He focused his gaze on Samuel, trying to reassure him. "You have my word."

Rabgar-Nebo appraised Ezekiel, then scanned the downturned heads of the crowd. With a curt nod, he jerked his head and dragged Samuel into the courtyard. Ezekiel staggered to his feet and stumbled after Rabgar-Nebo to the New Gate. The majority of the soldiers herded the people toward the gate while the remainder marched into the inner sanctuary.

The sound of pounding against metal drowned out the grunts of effort. Ezekiel pressed his hand against his throbbing head. *Yahweh, not Your temple.*

Rabgar-Nebo swung around to face the congregation. "Those of you who the mighty priest releases will receive a mark on your wrist. You will return to your land. Those who the priest identifies as influential will make camp outside the city."

The Chaldean leaned close to Ezekiel, the aroma of sweat and garlic filtering around the threat. "I am very good at discerning lies and will swiftly lose patience. I will strip flesh from the child if I detect lies."

Samuel's eyes widened and his hand trembled.

"I will comply." Ezekiel forced a smile and eyed Samuel. *Trust me.* The weight of all the souls pressed on his shoulders. He wiped sweaty palms on his robes.

A soldier shoved a priest of the treasury forward.

Ezekiel cleared his throat. "This man is a priest. He is in charge of the treasury."

Rabgar-Nebo tipped his head and a soldier materialized. "Excellent. I'm certain he will have much to contribute to the King of the World's campaign."

The priest shifted and sent a nervous glance to Ezekiel.

Ezekiel dipped his chin to his chest. What choice did they have?

Amram was next. "I am a farmer. My harvest of wheat is ready for the great king's harvest."

Wheat wasn't even in season. Ezekiel's mouth dried like the parched land. The man's deception would cause a world of trouble. "This man is the chief musician."

The side of Rabgar-Nebo's dagger dipped to Samuel's wrist. "I warned you . . ."

"Stop!" Ezekiel reached out. "Great Captain, your stipulation was if *I* lied. I have spoken truth."

Rabgar-Nebo contemplated, not withdrawing his blade. "Is he any good?"

"One of the best musicians we have."

Amram's eyes conveyed hatred. "I will not use my talent for your evil purposes!"

Shrugging, Rabgar-Nebo jerked his head.

A soldier brushed past Ezekiel, knocking him off balance.

The metallic zing of a sword unsheathing rang out simultaneously with sound of the blade slicing Amram's throat. A woman screamed.

"No!" Ezekiel lunged forward and was shoved with the butt of a spear at his spine. The quarried stone rushed up to meet him, and he managed to position his hands to break his fall.

A scream reached his ears, and the edge of a blade pressed against his neck.

"This is not a negotiation!" Rabgar-Nebo shouted. "You *will* submit."

"My people—" a foot stomped on Ezekiel's neck, pressing his cheekbone against the stone walkway a handbreadth away from Amram's unseeing eyes. "—my people. Nebuchadnezzar is Yahweh's servant."

The pressure increased and Ezekiel coughed. *Yahweh, who will keep my people strong if I die here?* Instantly, the weight lifted, and he was jerked up by his robes.

Rabgar-Nebo's face came into focus. "It seems as though the prophet has instructed you well."

Ezekiel inhaled through his nose as the front of his tunic dug into his airway. He gasped out, "I am on the side of truth."

"You will decide if you trust your god—" Rabgar-Nebo

shook Ezekiel. "—or more importantly, if you trust this priest."

Ezekiel silently pleaded with the people, pressing against his lip where his teeth had made their mark. *Yahweh, please help them comply. Help them trust.*

Rabgar-Nebo signaled for the next in line with a hard glare. The baker's face drained of all color as he fixated on Amram's blood.

"This man is a baker in the kitchen." Ezekiel moistened his lips. *Please, no more insubordination.*

"Welcome to the service of your new king." Rabgar-Nebo flicked his wrist, indicating the fierce soldier waiting outside the gate.

The baker clutched his bundle to his chest and cautiously stepped around Amram's pale body.

The sun beat down on the enduring processional. Most were accepted into the Chaldean camps as slaves.

Samuel now sat at the soldier's feet. Ezekiel's head swam and he felt faint, but Rabgar-Nebo showed no signs of slowing. At the back of the diminishing line, Shiriel wiped tears from Keziah's cheeks.

Rabgar-Nebo followed his gaze. "How tender. Let me guess—" he nodded to Keziah's rough-spun dress, "—you are a farmer."

"Keziah's husband tends fruit trees just outside the city. Plum in the late spring." Ezekiel couldn't bear to gaze at Shiriel's despair. Should he leave her behind with her *abba*?

"I am sure you and your husband will continue to produce crops from the king's land."

A soldier yanked her from Shiriel's embrace. Keziah cried out as a hot iron pressed to the flesh of her wrist.

Shiriel sniffled—her expression one of attempted bravery—and waved as Keziah was pushed away.

Rabgar-Nebo barked out an order in Akkadian, and the soldier halted Keziah. "What of the boy?"

"Samuel? He is a ward of the temple. He is a water boy." Ezekiel motioned for Samuel to rise.

"Hmph." Rabgar-Nebo frowned. "He is now a ward of the fruit-keeper's wife."

Samuel's eyes widened.

Keziah squeezed the boy's hand tightly, turning her face away as he was branded. Hand in hand, they followed the line of those relegated to remain behind.

"And this soggy woman?" Rabgar-Nebo surveyed Shiriel's linen dress. "She is a priestess?"

A chill snaked up Ezekiel's spine. To his knowledge, priestesses for other gods did as much to serve the worshipers as their idols. "A musician." He pointed to the flute protruding from her bundle. "My wife."

Shiriel stepped close and extended a bundle. "Here are your things."

"Thank you, that was very thoughtful of you." Ezekiel tried to reassure her with his smile and felt Rabgar-Nebo's scrutiny. He coughed. "As always."

The Chaldean crossed his arms. "What makes you think you will be joining our expedition, priest?"

Ezekiel's stomach dropped. He'd never considered he'd be left behind.

"You saw how the people responded to my…husband." Shiriel kept her gaze down. "You'd have unrest if you left him behind."

Rabgar-Nebo threw back his head and laughed. "She stands in the gap for the people as you do. You are a match made by the gods."

Ezekiel drew in a breath. "She is a gift from Yahweh, yes."

"All right, mighty priest. You may accompany us on our fine journey with your wife." Rabgar-Nebo's tone conveyed humor. He gestured with a flourish and started through the soldier-lined corridor to the Sheep Gate leading to the north of the city.

Shiriel clutched her bundle to her chest, and her forehead furrowed. She glanced over her shoulder into the courtyard. The pleading in her eyes made Ezekiel's chest ache. They would likely never see the temple again. He'd never serve as priest. Never again secure these massive gates or walk these hallowed stone bricks.

The smoke from the altar rose straight to heaven. Would his people be walking away from Yahweh's favor as they had in their hearts all these years?

"Are you coming, wise priest?" Rabgar-Nebo cocked his head, and his bushy eyebrows became one.

Ezekiel swallowed at the lump in his throat and leaned toward Shiriel. "It's time."

She caressed the door frame and brushed a tear from her cheek. Stepping gingerly over Amram's stiffening legs, she pressed her hand against her mouth. Was this renewed moisture in her eyes for the grotesque display of Amram's slit throat, or did she still pine for him?

Ezekiel shook his head. It was inappropriate to be so selfish as to entertain jealousy now that Amram was dead. "May I carry your satchel? I promise not to destroy your flute."

Shiriel glanced his way, her half smile causing tears to overflow. She shook her head. "Thank you, though."

Together they stepped over the threshold of the City of David and into servitude to the Chaldeans.

Their steady stream of people was one of many being pushed and prodded from the gates of Jerusalem and directed to the north-east. Livestock herded without command of where they went.

The sun dipped towards the horizon to their left, and still they pressed onward over the hills of Judea—those hills that appeared so serene and gentle. Now with the hundreds of people trudging over them, the close view of these hills was rocky. One wrong step on these loose rocks and a person could plunge into the wadi below. Ezekiel swallowed and inched away from the edge. *How like the slippery slope of sin unaddressed.* The continual choices of kings who had not heeded the warnings of truth. The Chaldean soldier before him didn't even breathe heavily, unfazed by the trek that beleaguered the Judahites. Was every plodding footstep heavier from the shame of now acknowledging generations of sin?

How did Shiriel fare with this treacherous path? Apart from the occasional sniffle, she had trekked at his side in somber silence.

Cresting the hilltop, Ezekiel sagged in relief to discover small fires dotting the valley below.

"Take heart, my people. We shall rest soon." Ezekiel's sandals bit into the tops of his feet on the decline. Even in the gathering dusk, the shoulders of his people straightened, and their steps became quicker.

Dark forms already huddled around the cooking fires. Ezekiel glanced over his shoulder to see the rise behind him alive with the winding path of the human river, and his heart squeezed. Yes, this was just reward for Judah's wayward ways. *But it doesn't feel good watching it unfold.*

Ezekiel tripped over a mound of flesh and swung back around. "I'm sorry, I didn't see."

A groan preceded the clank of chains. "Ezekiel? Is that you?"

"Gilead?" Ezekiel peered through the dark, the campfire casting an eerie yellow glow on the archer's face, but the light was not distorted enough to hide the discoloration around his eye or the gash in his lip.

Shiriel gasped and knelt before Gilead. "What have they done to you?"

"Did you think soldiers would be allowed to be without restraints?" Gilead grimaced and raised shackled hands to his head.

"I will find water." Shiriel stepped closer to the firepit and inspected each of the pots. "Here it is."

Gilead pushed himself to a sitting position. He drank from the ladle and surrendered to Shiriel dipping her sash into the water and pressing it to his lip.

Ezekiel set his bundle beside Shiriel and navigated the nearby campfires, taking inventory of his fellow captives. For once, knowing who everyone was and where they were didn't serve him. His knowledge meant nothing.

He shuffled back toward the first campfire, where all had settled for the night.

A Chaldean soldier stood watch, glancing up as he approached.

"Good evening, my friend." Ezekiel lifted his hand and the man grunted. Did he speak Hebrew? Perhaps it would be best to try again in the morning. He stretched and began to lower himself to an empty space.

His eyes widened. He was a married man. Their ruse would not carry on if he left her unattended. He scanned but couldn't discern between the dark forms. The Chaldean faced his way with a threatening slump of his shoulders.

Ezekiel swallowed. "Shiriel?"

On the far side of the campfire a head raised.

He shuffled carefully to her and laid beside her with room for another person between. Tension poured from Shiriel. She sniffed, and Ezekiel reached to where her hand should be but only patted dirt. She sniffled again.

Rolling on his side, Ezekiel whispered, "I'm sorry we won't have a marriage ceremony."

"It's not that. It's just…" She covered a whimper with her hand.

"What is it? Are you hurt?" He peered through the darkness.

Shiriel shook her head, and her hand landed between them.

He touched her fingers, hoping to offer comfort.

She stiffened but didn't draw back.

"Your *abba* and *ima*? Keziah?"

"Will we ever see them again?"

Ezekiel exhaled, wishing he could offer her reassurance. "I don't know." Even if they did return to Judah, the chances of Shiriel's parents living that long were slim. He gently squeezed the top of her hand. Perhaps singing would make her feel better. Well, not his—he couldn't make a sheep feel comfort.

He began to chant where she had stopped earlier. "*You prepare a table for me in the presence of my enemies*—"

Voices around the campfire joined in, vastly improving the song. "—*and I will dwell in the house of the Lord forever.*"

Shiriel turned her back, her shoulders shaking from suppressed sobs.

14

You shall eat unleavened bread with it, that is the bread of affliction (for you came out of the land of Egypt in haste), that you may remember the day which you came out of the land of Egypt all the days of your life.
—Deuteronomy 16:3b

Shiri braced her hands on her lower back and stretched from grinding grain. A month's time they had dwelt on the plains north of Jerusalem. So far she'd been able to shelve her own devastation in light of the others' suffering.

Borrowing Ezekiel's faith and steady assurance, she served with the children, prepared food, played her flute. Slowly, steadily, the morale increased and the exiles united. Daily, the number of captives grew, and more men and women gathered to listen and learn from her husband. Heat warmed Shiri's cheeks, and she restrained herself from checking over her shoulder. Legally, Ezekiel *was* her husband. Why did she still blush at the thought of sleeping beside him?

Tonight was the Passover, the time her people celebrated their release from slavery. What was there to celebrate now on the brink of entering bondage? Did Yahweh consider their ways? Would they spend the rest of the days here, still on Judah's soil?

She hummed the first song of today's *Hallel. The Lord is high above all nations, His glory above the heavens.* Even the Chaldeans? Y*ahweh, I am in the dust and trash heap. Lift me up.*

A ruckus drew Shiri's steps toward the center of camp to King Coniah's white tent.

"Just because we are trapped in the wilderness does not mean I have to live like a filthy nomad! It's not my fault my father doomed Jerusalem."

Shiri peered around the tent to find the young king sitting on an open-backed bench in what he probably imagined a pose of authority.

"I want roasted meat!" King Coniah pouted. "Make it happen."

The servant bowed low. "My king, I understand your concerns. Even if there was meat available, all the people are preparing for the Passover—"

"Do not tell me you understand when you do nothing to accommodate me! How could you possibly understand me? You are nothing. I am king!"

"Spying, are we?"

Shiri jumped and covered a gasp, nearly dropping her bag of flour. Rabgar-Nebo stood beside her, glowering down at her.

"I…heard the commotion." Shiri swallowed and stepped backward.

Rabgar-Nebo shifted his gaze to the king's spectacle and snorted. "There is always a commotion with the child-king."

Did he think Coniah young or childish? Either way fit. Shiri covered a smile and began to back away.

"Where do you think you're going, Little Bird? Your child-king would find his spirit eased by your music." Rabgar-Nebo muttered, "Perhaps he will stop being a nuisance."

Shiri halted her retreat. King Coniah had a reputation of being a wolf—like his father. She shivered and dug around the bed of her thumbnail with her fingernail. "I don't have my flute."

A small prince dashed by, his arms extended for balance, and his caretaker close on his heals. The young boy chortled and dodged the opposite way, much to the woman's chagrin. She lunged and snagged his sleeve, masking her irritation with a forced smile.

"Pedaiah…" She blew her hair from her forehead. "Princes do not dart around. Princes walk with decorum."

Shiri's heart squeezed. Little boys should be free to run and play. She cast another glance around the campsite. The king's mother and wives lounged on cushions in the shade, and five of the six young princes were entertained by caretakers. The sickly cry of Coniah's infant son drew a haggard sigh from his nursemaid.

"No matter, I'm sure the child-king has some instruments." Rabgar-Nebo shoved her forward. "*Prince* Coniah, I present you a musician. She will play for your relaxation."

"I guess it's better than nothing." The king expelled air as if the very idea irritated him. "What do you play?"

"The flute, my king." Shiri cast a desperate glance at Rabgar-Nebo "I can go fetch it." *And not return.*

"My son, Assir, plays at one. You can use his." Coniah snapped his fingers at one of his wives. She dipped her head in compliance, but not before Shiri witnessed the glare of disdain.

"Who are you?" Coniah studied Shiri critically. "Not a palace musician. I haven't seen you before."

"She was in the temple of your god." Rabgar-Nebo's big voice came over her shoulder. "She is the wife of a priest."

"A priest, huh?" Coniah's voice perked up. "Send for him. I want to ask him how long before I am to return to my throne."

Rabgar-Nebo whistled between his teeth, and a soldier approached. "Prince Coniah demands audience with the priest—" He turned toward Shiri expectantly.

"Ezekiel." She gave directions to their tent.

"Yes, my commander." The soldier pounded his chest and strode away.

Before Shiri could contrast the respect given Rabgar-Nebo and not Coniah, the royal wife emerged from the tent and extended a silver forward flute.

"Thank you." She lifted her eyes to the girl not much older than her own age. The hardness in her expression made Shiri's heart ache. What this woman's life consisted of, Yahweh only knew.

Lowering her gaze, she fingered the flute. *Abba* would be appalled. Royals always wanted their instruments weighted down with metal and encrusted with jewels, despite the superior sound quality of simple reed flutes.

Should she announce that her preferred flute—and thus skill—lay with the transverse flute? If she didn't, did she open herself to the king's displeasure because she wouldn't excel?

Rabgar-Nebo shifted, and all debates paled in light of a bigger concern that the Chaldean officer would leave her alone.

"Why do you delay?" The king struck his hands together.

Shiri lowered herself and blew into the flute—inwardly cringing at the lackluster sound—and did an experimental scale. Chances were the prince, of five or six years old, who played *at* the flute, did not set a high standard. Perhaps a tune to prepare the atmosphere for Passover would be appropriate.

She breathed out strains of the Passover psalms, and soon enough the king stopped watching her and resumed sulking. The young princes sat one by one before her, enthralled.

Ezekiel strode around the tent, and Shiri winced at his set expression. He had been in the middle of preparation for the Passover and Sabbath, no doubt. Already she knew her husband didn't like to be called off task. He knelt on one knee, not noticing Shiri. "You wished to see me, King Coniah?"

Coniah leaned an elbow on his knee. "Sit."

"Majesty, it is Passover. I must—"

"Sit!"

Ezekiel sat before the king, his back still toward Shiri. From the stiff line of his shoulders, he was not happy about it.

"When will I return to my throne?"

"My king?"

Coniah waved his hand. "Jehoiakim was taken to Babylon to establish loyalty, then returned. Since it is his doing we are in this mess, once I renew fealty to Nebuchadnezzar, he will send me back. Right?"

Ezekiel cocked his head to the side. "Have you had such assurances from Nebuchadnezzar?"

The king rolled his eyes as if Ezekiel was the one speaking irrationally. "I don't need his affirmation. The prophets confirmed this…jaunt would be two years."

Two years? Surely Shiri misheard. She played softer, ears straining.

"If you trust Hananiah and the others, why do you call for me?" Ezekiel's tone sounded incredulous.

"You disagree with the royal prophets?" Coniah's eyebrows tented.

"My belief is they are misleading you." Ezekiel leaned forward. "I follow the teachings of the prophet Jeremiah."

A string of curses flew from Coniah's mouth.

Shiri's neck heated and her ears burned. The oldest prince at her knee—presumably Assir by the way he proudly watched her play—covered his ears, and fat tears rolled down his cheeks.

The vein in the middle of the king's forehead bulged. "This is not my doing! Jehoiakim cursed us with his disobedience. Why should I have to suffer?"

Shiri caught Rabgar-Nebo's sour expression and would

have laughed if she hadn't had a flute in her mouth. All doubt of the Chaldean's command of the Hebrew language fled. He'd clearly meant childish.

"Does not the proverb say 'A father eats sour grapes, and the son's teeth are set on edge'? Judah has been led astray too long. Yahweh's cup of wrath now tips toward our people." Ezekiel rose. "If that is all, I have Sabbath preparations to conclude."

Not waiting to be dismissed, Ezekiel marched back the way he had come.

Shiri's chest constricted. *Wait. Don't go without me.* She unplugged all her fingers from the holes and created a dissonant sound. Ezekiel turned her way, and his eyes widened. He pivoted slowly. After speaking so boldly, would Coniah permit them to walk away?

"Oh, there you are." Ezekiel cleared his throat. "Are you ready to return to our tent? The Sabbath and Passover begin at sunset."

Shiri rose, glancing at King Coniah thrashing around on his throne. Perhaps they could sneak away before he noticed. Two of his wives rushed to his side, coddling him. She handed the flute to Prince Assir and bowed at the waist. "Thank you for allowing me to play your flute. Do you think you could try and imitate the sounds you heard?"

The prince's eyes widened, and he blew a sour note then frowned. "Will you come back tomorrow and play for me?"

Shiri glanced to Ezekiel who dipped his chin. "I will return again, my prince. Perhaps I can teach you how to play even better?"

The boy's smile lit up his face.

Shiri felt the urge to kiss his chubby cheeks. "Until tomorrow then." She scooped up her bag of flour and followed her husband.

Ezekiel glanced at the sun's low position and led the way

toward their camp. Shiri nearly trotted to keep up with his long stride.

"Ezekiel?"

"Yes, Shiriel?" Ezekiel slowed his pace.

She studied her dusty feet. "Thank you."

Abruptly, Ezekiel planted his feet, and Shiri skidded to a halt. She lifted her eyes shyly.

"It is my pleasure. I will do my best to protect you." The sincerity in his eyes warmed Shiri like the caress of the gentle evening breeze. He opened his mouth, then closed it again. "We should return before sunset."

Shiri touched her warm cheek and fell in step with Ezekiel's slower pace. They arrived with enough time for her to scramble through the last-minute preparations.

As Shiri led her first Passover prayer as matron of the household—her cramped household of Gilead, two other soldiers and Ezekiel—a lump in her throat restricted her words. Did *Ima* still live to bless her *abba's* household? And what of Keziah? Had she communicated how Ezekiel had protected her with his name? Would they make room in their lives for Samuel now that the new child would be here soon?

The tent flap snapped open, and Shiri felt the heat of the candle on her hand. She jerked back as Rabgar-Nebo entered, filling the small tent with his presence. "We leave at sun up. You will inform the others. Anyone not ready will be left as food for the vultures."

Ezekiel and the other men acknowledged, "Yes, Commander."

Rabgar-Nebo nodded curtly and backed out again, pausing before glancing at Shiri. "You will not be needed to teach the young prince music, Little Bird."

She blinked and leaned closer, trying to discern his expression in the low light.

"The King of the World demanded a token of the child-king's allegiance."

"What token did King Coniah give?" Ezekiel scrubbed at the back of his neck, sending a chill down Shiri's spine.

Rabgar-Nebo's expression of stone did not waver. "He has sacrificed his oldest son to the gods."

If Shiri hadn't already been kneeling, her legs would have given out on her. She glanced to Ezekiel and didn't find the assurance she had come to expect.

Her husband drew in shallow, rapid breaths. He focused on the flame of the candle and cleared his throat. "Did King Nebuchadnezzar require this?"

"It was the child-king's suggestion."

The tent flap closed, and tears blurred Shiri's vision. *Have mercy on us.*

Ezekiel put his hand over hers. "Yahweh is just. We will serve Him in a new land. Hope is not lost."

Shiri blinked hard. "The Lord is my light..." The words valiantly tried to maneuver around the squeeze in her chest and the boulder in her throat. "Of whom shall I be afraid?"

She passed the first dish around to their little family. The herbs of suffering were bitter indeed.

There was no atoning for the sins of this nation.

15

The king of Babylon…gave orders to his generals to take all that were in the city captives, both the youth and the handicraftsmen, and bring them bound to him; their number was ten thousand eight hundred and thirty-two; as also Jehoiachin, and his mother and friends. And when these were brought to him, he kept them in custody, and appointed Jehoiachin's uncle, Zedekiah, to be king; and made him take an oath, that he would certainly keep the kingdom for him, and make no innovation, nor have any league of friendship with the Egyptians.

—Josephus Chapter 7 section 1

On the twenty-ninth day of the fourth month which was in the first year of King Coniah's captivity.

Nearing the fourth month of travel, vegetation became visible on the horizon, stretching from north to south as far as the eye could see. The greenery framed the silver, glistening ribbon of the Euphrates, beckoning with promises of cooler temperatures and water from the river to wash away the incessant dirt.

Surprisingly, the ten thousand men, women, and children

stolen from their homeland had maintained a generally positive outlook. Even now a band of captives sang psalms of hope, led by Shiriel.

Ezekiel's gaze lingered on his wife's compassionate face. In this new environment, he learned she possessed a tender spirit that made her approachable to women and children alike. As if she knew the nature of his musings, Shiriel reached out to a woman whose stamina waned. The woman fanned her flushed face and allowed herself to be led forward.

Shiriel leaned close to the woman and said something, eliciting a smile.

The shadows of night, however, continually crept through her bravery, and silent tears shook her shoulders as she lay beside him. She eased many burdens during the day. If only Ezekiel could alleviate her affliction when the moon rose.

Was her bravery a front? No. Compassion and strength for others did not exclude her own heart from bearing down with the heavy weight of sorrow. The nights revealed much about his wife, yet he knew so little. Did she cry as a release from being strong for the others? Was she homesick?

"You could ask her."

Ezekiel jerked his head to the right. How had he not heard the clank of Gilead's approach? "Ask her what?"

"Ask her what concerns her. You've been staring at her as if she is an elaborate mystery that will never be solved." Gilead lifted bound hands to swipe away a fly clinging to the sweat on his brow. "Women like to be understood but don't—or won't—disclose their feelings. Asking is better than guessing."

Did Shiriel *wish* to confide in him, and he hadn't given her the opportunity? She seemed so strong. Did she have needs he didn't see? Ezekiel's feet drifted into Gilead's path.

Gilead twisted his torso to allow space for Ezekiel to right his steps. "Take time to woo her."

Heat rushed up Ezekiel's neck faster than the sun rising on

the Persian plain. "Gilead! I can't…we share a tent with three men, including you."

Gilead threw back his head and guffawed. "There is more to loving a woman than a marriage bed."

Shiriel turned her head at Gilead's broad laugh.

Ezekiel squinted at the sunlight bouncing off the Euphrates River. "You are very learned, for a man without a wife."

"A little too much, too late." Gilead's jaw clenched. The shake of his head forbade further discussion. What secrets did the archer hold fast?

Before Ezekiel could ruminate, Gilead thrust his hip into Ezekiel's side, flinging him into Shiriel's path.

"Oh!" She broke off mid-song and lifted hands to catch or right him. What she could do to prevent his weight if he actually toppled escaped him, but the gesture did encourage him.

"Are you well?" Shiriel surveyed his person.

Ezekiel tossed a scowl over his shoulder as Gilead clanked by laughing. "I am fine. Gilead seems to think..." He halted the run-away words. He might be ignorant about connecting with this woman, but he was pretty sure he shouldn't do it by confessing the archer's theory. He rubbed his hand over chapped lips and tugged on his beard.

"I…um…appreciate all that you are doing to help keep the people calm and the morale up."

Shiriel's concern softened, and she dipped her head. Her gaze slanted up through lowered lashes. He should've complimented her long ago to disperse the burden she bore under the brave smile. Yet these burdens were ones he had essentially placed on her.

"I'm sorry. I should have left you behind to remain with your *ima*…to remain in Judah."

"You had no control over that. A wise priest once told me Yahweh is still sovereign despite the circumstances." Her stiff smile faltered. "As long as…"

"What is it?" What made her face falter?

"We left the temple, yet the smoke of Yahweh's presence remained." Shiriel rubbed at her leg. "Does He still see us? Does He still care about our well-being even as our feet stray?"

Ezekiel waited until she returned his gaze. "The earth is the Lord's, and all that is in it. Where can I go to hide from His presence?"

Shiriel's eyes widened as the psalmist's words took root in her mind.

"Even King David didn't have the temple to worship in."

Blinking twice, she gave a self-deprecating chuckle. "I hadn't thought of that."

The dust puffed up from their sandals as they plodded on.

"It feels like part of the temple is with us—being with you," Shiriel spoke softly amongst the bustle around them. "You bring us the words of truth, Ezekiel. It's easy to hold fast when you charge us with Yahweh's desires."

Ezekiel's chest swelled. To think they'd come this far from when he had accused her. His hand swung at his side, brushing against hers. To his utter surprise, she tucked her fingers into his and gave a soft squeeze. He whipped his head her direction.

Releasing his hand, she pressed her lips together and fixed her gaze straight ahead. Shiriel stepped to the side, putting distance between them.

Ezekiel glanced around. Nobody appeared to notice her breach in protocol. Affection was reserved for closed doors—not that they had any privacy in their tent. He frowned. With every step closer to the land of the Chaldeans, they walked into unprecedented territory. Shiriel was part of his flock. He had to keep her morale up as well. What's more, she was his wife.

With another glance around, he closed the gap between them and laced his fingers through hers. Shiriel's steps faltered, and Ezekiel could feel her gaze as he brought her fingers to his lips and edged close enough so their robes hid their entwined hands. Regardless of the unknown that lay before them, they stood together.

Shiriel's shy smile and the flush in her cheeks made his heart skip a beat.

They reached the banks of the Euphrates River by midday, and the Chaldean soldiers commanded the Judahites to bathe. Ezekiel was skeptical as he stepped into the murky water. Would they be any cleaner when they emerged? Still, the cool water was refreshing in the heat of summer. He ducked his head under and scrubbed at his scalp. Emerging, he shook his head vigorously and lifted his knees high to wade back to shore.

Ezekiel shielded his eyes against the sun off the river and peered to the south. How much farther did their journey stretch? He turned back to find Shiriel staring at him and tying her head scarf over wet hair.

Did mud from the river cling to him? He glanced down. Nothing was on his once-white tunic. He directed his questioning gaze back, and Shiriel blushed and turned away.

He pulled at his wet tunic that clung to muscular shoulders and arms—the benefit of years of hoisting oxen and rams onto the altar.

"Priest." Rabgar-Nebo summoned him with a two-fingered gesture.

"May I assist you?"

"You will divide up the captives into four groups. They will be dispersed throughout the kingdom according to skill." Rabgar-Nebo crossed his arms. "All soldiers will be trained according to Babylonian military ways. The artisans will congregate in one of the three cities—those in textiles will be in Bursippa, metal workers and jewelers will reside in Uruk. Finally, the musicians and those who are of a quick mind will dwell on the outskirts of Babylon where they will join in service at the king's palace."

Ezekiel swallowed as the reality of the imminent separation set in. He scanned the faces of those in the crowd. His people, who he might not see again.

Yahweh, give us Your favor in this land. May we do well for You as Joseph did in Egypt.

While the people made camp and prepared the evening meal, Ezekiel worked with a Chaldean scribe, breaking apart the flock under his watchful care. Long after night stilled the busy camp, he left the scribe's tent and wearily stumbled to his own.

He slipped in, pausing to adjust to the dark. Each of the three men lay in their normal positions, breathing heavily.

Shiriel pushed up on her elbow from their spot at the back. Ezekiel shuffled as quietly as possible around the three men he'd assigned to the far reaches of Babylonia. He pushed out a breath as he lowered himself to their sleeping mat.

"I saved you supper." Shiriel sat the rest of the way up.

Ezekiel caught her wrist and whispered, "No need. My stomach is too knotted."

"What did Rabgar-Nebo decide?"

Were Gilead and the others still awake? He didn't have the heart to tell them now. A snore erupted from Gilead's corner.

Ezekiel tugged Shiriel close, her wrist smooth under his calloused fingers. He rolled on his side, her face a distracting hand-breadth away. He lowered his whisper to a breath. "There are three major cities where artisans and masters-of-craft reside in Babylonia. Soldiers will be trained in the remote regions of the mountains of Media, and musicians will live outside Babylon to learn Akkadian."

Shiriel linked her fingers through his and leaned closer. "Will we ever see them again?"

Ezekiel closed his eyes, forcing himself to picture the faces of their tentmates. "I am worried. Gilead—all of them—will they be strong enough away from the congregation?"

She put a tentative hand on his shoulder and spoke directly into his ear. "We must have faith. You have prepared them for such a time as this."

"Gilead, and all our mighty men of valor, will become eunuchs." Was it wrong to be thinking about Shiriel's proximity while discussing another man's emasculation?

"No! Why?"

"I suppose it's a good tactic. They are soldiers trained for battle. This would prevent them from using their might against our captors."

"But they would give their pledge." Shiriel's fingers traveled across the definitions in Ezekiel's shoulders.

The darkness covered his satisfaction. She *had* been taking note of his form earlier. "Would you accept a pledge of that nature?"

She went still. "And you? What will you do?"

Did she ask in concern of whether he would be crushed like Gilead? "I will report to someone and supervise the scheduling of the 'Jews'—as they call us. Much as I did in the temple."

"Yahweh has prepared us for this." Shiriel rolled to the side she slept on, leaving a cavernous space between them. Before he could reason against himself, he tugged her close. She tucked against him and wove her fingers through his.

Ezekiel put his mouth to her ear. "I will still be able to give you children, if Yahweh allows."

Her shoulders sagged, and she gripped his fingers.

Now all they needed was privacy so they could work toward that goal.

16

The king spoke saying, "Is not this great Babylon, that I have built for a royal dwelling by my mighty power and for the honor of my majesty?"
—Daniel 4:30b

Shiri's mouth gaped at the opulence of the processional way leading into the city of Babylon. Each glazed tile bore the insignia of Nebuchadnezzar. To the west, the Euphrates lapped gently, sending the slight smell of fish on the occasional breeze. Inside the city, the line halted and began again with regularity. Shiri craned her neck to see beyond what must have been the palace and took in the lush garden stacked three stories high.

After the scorching heat and the dust from the road, those trees were a vision as they swayed, whispering of cool grass and peace. Splashes of yellow and purple flowers adorned the trailing vines, and their exhilarating fragrance hung heavy in the air.

The line moved forward again, and Shiri searched the line behind her. Still, the faces she saw were not ones she recognized. *Ezekiel, where are you?* As the day began, he'd been called away to settle a dispute. She suppressed the panic and clutched her flute. How would he find her?

Shiri jolted to a stop just prior to bumping into the person before her. Another palace caught her eye, but even the grandeur and beauty of the architecture did nothing to distract her from the ache inside.

"What is your occupation?" The mountainous Chaldean, wearing a wide gold collar, was now discernable as he sifted the exiles like wheat and chaff. He lurked behind a waist high workstation, hunching his shoulders forward as he determined each person's skill set and whether they went to the right or continued straight ahead.

She glanced over her shoulder. Where was Ezekiel?

"Why are they separating us?" The woman beside her moaned. Nothing in her demeanor or pack indicated her profession.

"We must trust Yahweh's plan." What choice did they have? Shiri smiled with confidence she didn't feel and scanned the exiles behind her. "My name is Shiri. I am a musician."

The woman slanted old, weathered eyes. "I am Yassah. I am nothing. I embroider. I have decorated robes for the royal court in Judah."

"That is a valuable skill."

The Chaldean jerked a woman away from the adolescent boy she clung to and shoved her to the right. Her thrashing and screams faded as she was carried down a tunnel.

"Yahweh, grant us Your perfect peace. Help us to fix our minds on You." Shiri's hand ached. She glanced down to find Yassah gripping it. One person stood between them and the towering man.

"What is your profession?" the man asked in Aramaic.

"I am a jeweler. I set jewels for the kings and nobles. Crowns, necklaces, rings and the like." The man's stooped back confirmed hours of hunching over delicate work.

The guard's eyes narrowed. "Who is your king?"

Was it a trick? Did he ask to see if the allegiance of the people would be divided?

"I will serve King Nebuchadnezzar."

The Chaldean jerked his head to the right path, already eyeing Shiri's flute. "Who are you?"

Peace flooded her soul. "I am a chosen one of Yahweh." Distance could not take that from her.

Yassah nudged her.

"I am a musician." Shiri moved her fingers over the holes in the flute, as if he couldn't see the instrument.

"Who do you serve?"

"I serve Yahweh and the great King of the World."

The man pointed to the left.

Shiri scanned the line behind her. "Please, my lord. My husband—"

The man acted as if he didn't hear, and a guard yanked her down the left corridor. Moments later, Yassah hurried to her side. They were herded like sheep into a spacious but humid bathing room, where a formidable man made slashing gestures that matched harsh words spoken in a language Shiri couldn't understand. His message was clear enough—they were meant to bathe. Exiles were stripped if they didn't voluntarily remove their clothes.

A woman sobbed, refusing to disrobe, and soldiers rushed to assist her. The woman clenched her tunic to her chest, to no avail. The guards tore her tunic from her back, their jeering transcending the language barrier as they shoved her to the deck.

"Please, Yahweh." The words escaped Shiri's lips. She exhaled shakily as the men left and returned, each to his post.

Shiri cast a glance at the soldiers and marched to the poor woman.

"What are you doing?" Yassah hissed.

"Come with us." Shiri helped the woman rise.

Yassah grunted and moved to the other side. Together they shielded the humiliated woman, averting their eyes from the men in various stages of disrobing, and walked to the far side of the pool.

The humid air dampened Shiri's skin. "Get in, nobody's watching." They'd draw less attention submerged.

The woman lowered herself into the pool, and Shiri tried to shield Yassah while she undressed and slipped into the water.

And when they were through? Shiri glanced cautiously at the men coming out of the pool on the far side. They were given tunics from a large pile. "I'll be back." She put down her meager bundle and strode with purpose toward the pile of tunics.

"Shiri, no!"

Yassah's protest took away what little courage she had, and she almost turned back. *No, it'll be worse if I don't go through with it.* She studied the tiles on the floor. A pair of bare legs walked beside her, and heat scurried up her chest and neck. *Do not look up.*

At last, the mound of clean tunics appeared in front of her. Her fingers wrapped around three, and a massive hand closed around her wrist. Her heart hammered against her chest faster than Chesed's tempo on the drum when he challenged her to a musical battle.

Perfect peace. Shiri raised her gaze up the leather-shielded chest to cold eyes. His intentions needed no translation. He said something in Akkadian and switched to broken Aramaic. "You virgin?"

Did no one see her dilemma? Would no one champion for her? She couldn't bring herself to lie. *Yahweh, give me favor like You gave David amongst his enemies.* She shrugged. "Married."

Disappointment flickered across the soldier's eyes. He released her with a fierce scowl and stepped back.

Shiri snatched the three tunics and hurried back toward

where the ladies waited. Her foot slipped on wet tiles, and she flailed, righting herself and catching a glimpse of the soldier still watching her. She swallowed and took care in her foot placement.

As she sat on the edge of the pool and unwrapped her head scarf, Yassah shook her finger and gave a fierce scowl. "Don't you ever do that again."

Shiri wiggled the hem of her tunic out from under her and began to lift. "Do you propose I wait until we had need of them?"

Yassah yanked her into the pool.

Shiriel came up sputtering.

The other woman peered beyond her. "He's still watching."

"Atta's right. We will not give these barbarians a chance." Yassah shook Shiri's arm. "Don't you ever parade around by yourself before these barbarians like a wanton woman."

She was being scolded by a woman she didn't know while fully clothed in a Babylonian bath surrounded by men. The absurdity of the situation, the humiliation and fear, sought release with a breathy laugh.

Yassah glared. "Do you think this is a laughing matter?"

Shiri tried to replace her ill-timed smile with appropriate repentance. "No, *Ima*."

Atta snorted, and she helped Shiri peel the wet tunic over her head.

"Next time, Atta or I will go. Neither of us have anything the barbarians want to ogle." Yassah crossed her arms.

"Hmph." Atta's nose lifted.

"It is a blessing." Yassah shook water from her hands as if that was the end of the discussion.

Meeting Atta's gaze, Shiri winked and ducked below the surface, the distorted sound of Yassah's scolding filtered through the warm water. Shiri closed her eyes and scrubbed vigorously at her scalp. Now what?

She poked her head up and wiped the water from her eyes. What would Ezekiel say of her venture?

Shiri glanced toward the stream of men entering. How would she find him in the midst of all these men? *Why are you watching men disrobe?* She blushed and jerked her attention back to the women forging a circle and an alliance.

Yahweh, protect Ezekiel, bring him back to me.

A gong sounded. Harsh shouts led to a mass exodus from the bath. The women put on the new tunics as discreetly as possible, and Atta and Shiri flanked Yassah, clinging tightly to the older woman's arms as they shuffled through the narrow hall. With Yahweh's help and their determined hold, they wouldn't get separated.

Shiri clenched her flute in her free hand and scanned the faces of the clothed men.

Atta leaned around Yassah. "What do you search for?"

"My husband." Shiri gave way to the unease in her belly as the other women exchanged glances. "Have you heard something?"

"About your husband? No." Atta surveyed the crowd as if she'd find Ezekiel without any description at all. "When did you last see him?"

"We walked separately when we broke camp this morning. I figured—"

Another glance between the women.

Shiri gritted her teeth. "Don't say it." Suppose their pitying glances were premonition—that she would be all alone in a foreign nation? "It's been only one day. He'll probably be waiting wherever it is we are going now."

The hallway narrowed, funneling the captives around a bend and into a room opening spaciously to arched ceilings. The men before them sat, creating rows facing the front.

Atta led the way to the corner and stood behind a pillar. Shiri's gaze swept the room only to be disappointed. She leaned around the pillar and fixed her eyes on the entrance.

The room became full—overstuffed with Hebrew men—but Ezekiel still didn't appear.

She swallowed as a Chaldean paced in tight patterns and began speaking. This was the second time she had seen that wide gold collar. Was it some indication of status? The intense words he shouted contradicted the neutral expression on his face. It sounded so angry.

"He is speaking Akkadian," Atta whispered. "He says we will learn the language of the great King of the World."

Yassah scoffed.

Shiri shushed her and leaned close to Atta while staring at the man's mouth. "Why does he wear the gold collar?"

Yassah surveyed the Chaldeans in the room. "He may be a eunuch."

"Shh. You will learn the protocol of your new station. In exchange for your…" Atta searched for the right word. "… service, you will be given rations. You are privileged to be among those who serve the King of the World and his mighty kingdom."

"Where are your husbands?" Shiri whispered.

Atta's interpretation halted, and she slashed at angry tears. "The Chaldeans killed him on the threshold of Jerusalem."

"I'm sorry." Shiri shut her eyes. How could she have been so insensitive?

Yassah cleared her throat. "Well, my husband was dead long before the Chaldeans arrived. The fool left me for another woman and found himself mysteriously ill."

Shiri's mouth dropped open. "Did you…"

Yassah snorted. "No, but it sure makes the story interesting."

Atta began translating again, but Shiri couldn't focus. How could Yassah be so flippant about her husband being unfaithful?

"Everybody will be assigned to their quarters now…report back here in the morning to learn…um…assignments."

Herded down a series of tunnels lined with doorways, the soldier signaled at each new opening. The line diminished, and finally the Chaldean pointed at their tiny band and then to the next doorway. Shiri stepped into the small chamber.

A shout in Akkadian drew her attention from an oppressively small room. The soldier had Atta by the arm, shouting harsh words in her face.

Atta sucked air through her teeth, flailing her arms at the massive soldier. "I can't do this. We have to remain together."

Shiri quelled her own panic. "What is he saying?"

Atta screamed, and Yassah scolded the guard, shaking her finger in the man's face.

"Stop." Shiri's voice caught in her throat.

The guard held up two meaty fingers and spoke rapidly, gesturing towards the room. His voice grew louder and more agitated, the commotion drawing the attention of more guards. They ploughed their way through the line, tossing the remaining Hebrews to the side. The chaos magnified through the shouts echoing off the walls.

Shiri trilled a long, high note on her flute, bringing the noise to an abrupt halt.

The Chaldean's eyebrows shot up and pinched together.

"Um…What is he saying, Atta?" Shiri shifted as all eyes honed in on her.

"He says only two in the room." Atta's nails dug into Shiri's arm, her voice rising into a wail.

Shiri peered into the room that would hardly allow one person to stretch out comfortably and squeezed her eyes shut to quell her own panic.

The Chaldean yanked at Atta, hollering louder.

Atta screamed again. The other soldier unsheathed a sword and shouldered several Hebrews aside.

"Enough!" Shiri slapped the hysterical woman in the face, stunning her into silence. Yassah gasped. Shiri pried Atta's fingers from her arms and stepped forward, her insides a quivering mass. She pressed her lips together and held up three fingers to the mountainous man. "Please."

He gestured violently and shouted.

Shiri narrowed her gaze, trying to understand his expression since the language escaped her. Contrary to the harsh sounds coming from his mouth, his expression seemed to convey mild irritation rather than anger. He reached for Atta's arm.

"Atta, what did he say?" Shiri extended a hand to halt him.

"He says he is following orders. He has to obey." Atta sniffled.

Shiri folded her hands under her chin. "Please. We do not wish trouble for you. We will not complain." She clutched at the side of her tunic. Ezekiel would know how to convince him.

The man stepped close and shook his finger in her face.

A gentle answer turns away wrath.

"He says…'Three women in that space will tear each other apart like wildcats. He will receive harm.'"

"We will be calm to each other." Shiri paused for Atta to translate. "We will be like friendly kittens."

Exasperation crossed the man's face. He threw up his hands and hollered, gesturing for the next two Hebrews into the next room. The other soldier sheathed his sword and shook his head, backing away.

Atta dashed into the room with Yassah.

"Wait!" Shiri called to the soldier's departing back.

"What are you doing?" Yassah hissed. "Get inside."

The eunuch stalked back with a menacing scowl.

Shiri's heart pounded, and Atta's hands grasped her from behind. "Thank you. Atta, how do you say 'thank you'?"

Atta squeaked out a word, and Shiri repeated what she heard.

The Chaldean's eyebrows shot up and his mouth twitched.

She had probably told him he looked like a cow. She shrugged. "How do you say 'I'm an ignorant fool'?"

She tapped her chest. "Shiri." Pointing to the eunuch's chest, she raised her eyebrows.

His expression grew skeptical, but he pounded his chest. "Duzi." He turned and strode away muttering.

Shiri turned back into the room, so small the three of them could barely stand beside each other.

"Yassah, you're taking up too much space."

Already Yassah and Atta were displaying wildcat tendencies.

Shiri lowered herself into the corner and closed her eyes. Where was the perfect peace that had surpassed the unknown fear last night with Ezekiel?

The walls crushed in with each passing moment.

A night passed.

And another.

Seven days of learning customs during the day.

Each day, rather than becoming familiar, the language grew more muddled in her mind. At night, the walls of their two-person room seemed to constrict against the ache in her heart.

Worry—and Yassah's soft snoring—kept Shiri awake, assailing her thoughts. What had happened to Ezekiel? Was she meant to navigate this foreign land and people without him?

The light of hope dimmed with each day Ezekiel didn't come for her.

17

Your word is a lamp to my feet and a light to my path.
—Psalm 119:105

O*n the tenth day of the sixth month which was in the first year of King Coniah's captivity.*

Ezekiel rose from another restless night. He rubbed blurry eyes as he followed the Chebar Canal to the east, away from the refugee camp, and into the massive shadow of the city of Babylon.

To this day, there had been no sign of Shiriel. "I shouldn't have left her," he muttered aloud as he joined the crowd of exiles being ferried across the Euphrates River in the *quffas,* round basket-like boats. For eight days he had asked every Hebrew speaking person if they had seen a woman who sang like the hoopoe bird and played the flute. They all shook their heads. It was as if she had vanished.

Each day he ate his simple ration of round bread with lentils in a different spot, hoping that he'd catch a glimpse of her. Yesterday he had come full circle.

Ezekiel blew out a breath, brushed his tunic off, and reported to the station where he and Rabgar-Nebo documented and assigned Hebrews to their Babylonian positions.

"Still no sign of your little bird?" Rabgar-Nebo shrugged. "I have put in inquiries among the quarters in the palace—"

Ezekiel whipped his head around to study the Chaldean's face.

Rabgar-Nebo displayed his palm, halting Ezekiel's question. "I have heard nothing."

How easy would it be for one Hebrew woman to slip through the cracks amidst the influx of Judahites?

Ezekiel settled onto his bench, and a sigh escaped him as he surveyed the somber line of his countrymen. Anxious eyes peered back at him from care-worn faces. All had tremendous loss, and all looked to the future with apprehension. What was there to say of the fate of his people when Yahweh had turned them over to a pagan king?

To submit to Nebuchadnezzar is to submit to Yahweh. Ezekiel busied his mind with the monotonous documentation and tried to infuse his tone with encouragement. The long hours occupied his hands, confining the desire to search every dwelling and alley in Babylon to his mind.

"Your name?" Ezekiel dipped his quill into the ink as yet another Hebrew stepped into the shaded archway.

"Birsha. I am a harpist."

Ezekiel's head jerked up as if Shiriel would be standing beside him. "Where do you sleep?"

"What?" The man shifted his weight, and his gaze slanted toward Rabgar-Nebo, who poured over this morning's scroll.

"Have you seen my wife? She is a musician. She sings and plays the flute."

Birsha glanced again at the Chaldean soldier. "I'm merely trying to register."

Rabgar-Nebo turned Ezekiel's way with a frown.

"Family status." Ezekiel's stared at the ink lines as he jotted down the man's response. After he had asked the required questions, desperation compelled him to persist. "Please, my friend. Are there any female flutists among the musicians you've seen?"

"I have one daughter nearing marrying age. What are we to do about that?" His voice lowered to a life-giving tone. "There are three women. But as I hear it, they are all widowed. And so old the guards leave them alone."

Hope temporarily dampened, then rose again. These women might know of Shiriel. "Where do these women reside?"

"The north wing of the southern palace complex, to the east."

"Thank you. May the Lord bless you and keep you." Ezekiel drew the fired clay ration token from around his neck and pressed it to the man's hand with the three allotted for his family.

Birsha bowed and was escorted away.

"I saw your wife. She sure can sing." The next man in line leaned conspiratorially over the table.

Ezekiel narrowed his eyes. Everything indicated the man had heard the exchange between him and Birsha and wanted an extra ration token. *But surely this man has seen Shiriel. He knows of her talent.*

He glanced at the basket of ration chips. Rabgar-Nebo had explicitly indicated what would happen if he gave out extra. The flesh on Ezekiel's back recoiled, anticipating the lashes Rabgar-Nebo would dole out. "What do you know?"

"Know? Oh, she sings like an exotic bird."

Wisdom that would have rivaled Solomon's infused his desperation. "And her high tones?"

"Like the trill of a morning breeze, high as the palace roof."

This couldn't be Shiriel, her voice was low and rich. Ezekiel rubbed burning eyes. Was he so desperate for news that he'd settle for false information? Why did he even consider giving the man an extra ration chip? He rubbed the back of his neck. "I don't believe we speak of the same woman. My wife sings the low notes."

"She did that too." Despair flashed across the man's face. "Low like a heartbeat."

Ezekiel fixed his attention on the marks on the scroll before him. "I'm sorry. I don't have any more to give."

"You can't even help your own countryman? Chaldean pawn." The man's face reddened. He leaned across the table and fisted Ezekiel's tunic.

In less than a breath, Rabgar-Nebo's dagger pressed at the man's neck. "Is there a problem, Jew?"

The man jerked backward, shooting daggers of his own. "Your scribe gave an extra ration chip to that last man."

Rabgar-Nebo's knife remained poised, and his gaze focused on the offender. "Is this true, priest?"

Ezekiel rose to his feet. "I gave my own. The previous man had information on my wife." He swallowed. He'd been too eager earlier. Birsha had seen *old* women.

"*I* have information on your wife."

Rabgar-Nebo struck the obstinate man's face with the back of his hand. "Quiet. Just your chip?"

"Yes, my lord."

"Move on, Jew." Rabgar-Nebo shoved the man. "If you aren't satisfied with the rations you were given, you won't receive any."

"Please…my family!"

Rabgar-Nebo jerked two fingers, and a soldier assisted the man around the corner.

Ezekiel closed his eyes as the man's pleading stopped abruptly.

"What you do in your own time is your own business, priest." Rabgar-Nebo slid three chips across the table. "As long as you are at your post at the appropriate time."

The enormity of the trust Rabgar-Nebo offered stunned Ezekiel. He fingered the clay coins. "Thank you." *Thank You, Yahweh.*

Shiriel didn't appear in his line, but hope bolstered Ezekiel's spirits. This went deeper than wanting to honor his promise to her abba. Deeper even than the need to protect her. He missed her beside him, missed her singing and the smooth sound of her flute. He missed her compassionate personality and her ability to lift the spirits of those around them.

In the heat of the afternoon, Rabgar-Nebo stretched his arms over his head, signaled a nearby slave, and dismissed the people still in line. "We will resume tomorrow at the third hour."

Ezekiel blotted the ink and rolled the last parchment as the servant tucked the scrolls in a satchel.

The men in line shuffled away with shoulders stooped. Where did they sleep until they were assigned livelihoods and living quarters?

The uncertainty gnawed at his insides, yet there was nothing he could do. Ezekiel closed his eyes, but already the memories of the order he maintained among the temple's pillared halls faded as if he stared through a sandstorm.

Ezekiel turned to Rabgar-Nebo. "With your permission, Great Captain, I'd like to assist this man to the archives."

The Chaldean cocked his head. "To be useful, or to gain access to the palace complex?"

"Both, my lord."

Rabgar-Nebo shrugged a shoulder and strode away.

Ezekiel hurried behind the slave, thanking Yahweh with each step.

The slave grunted out directions with gestures as he put the day's scrolls on the shelves.

"Thank you." Ezekiel bowed at the waist.

The slave raised an eyebrow and gestured for Ezekiel to leave the massive library.

Trust from the captain extended only so far. Ezekiel complied and strode north with purpose, hoping no one would question his presence. His confidence grew as he passed people of many races in the halls to the north of the palace.

He ducked into the barracks only to halt at the sheer size. Three halls—tunnels rather—with door after door stretched before him. He could search six months and never cross paths with her. *Please, Yahweh, give me a sign.*

In the Scriptures, Yahweh gave directions through tangible ways. A burning bush? Ideal, but unlikely. No bushes grew in these windowless halls. He could bring a fleece like Gilead of old.

"Watch it." A man in linen trousers brushed his shoulder.

"My apologies." Ezekiel stepped back and absently watched the man strike a flint stone and light the torch at the entrance.

A pillar of fire by night and a cloud by day? Ezekiel stiffened.

The man lit the torches down the center passage. *Your word is a lamp unto my feet and a light to my path.* Was this for him?

If it were Ezekiel lighting the torches, he would have begun from one of the side passage-ways and worked logically toward the other side. The torch-lighter's erratic pattern, though strange, could mean nothing at all.

Or it could be a sign.

Common sense warred with faith as the corridor grew brighter with each torch the man lit. After a long while, he returned to where Ezekiel lurked and began again in the tunnel to the left.

Squaring his shoulders, Ezekiel slipped into the center aisle, heart pounding fast. The first few rooms were empty. He heard stirring in the fifth room and knocked. "Shiriel?"

The door opened, revealing a Hebrew man. Ezekiel

pushed down disappointment. "I'm searching for my wife. Are there any women in this hall? Musicians?"

The man's gaze traveled up and down Ezekiel. He jerked his head. "Down the hall, three or four doors down."

She was close! It would be foolish to claim he could sense her, but he couldn't convince himself otherwise. He counted and recounted the three doors and knocked.

Nothing. Frustration rose up like a turbulent wind. He pounded his fist against the door. "Hello?"

He could bypass her altogether and not know it because of bad timing. Would the room have evidence of her? A garment? A scent? He had to know. He tugged on the string and lifted the latch.

"What do you think you're doing?" A woman's voice accosted him.

Ezekiel turned to find an older woman with arms crossed. The torch cast shadows on her face, giving her an irritable air. "I am seeking a musician." He held up his hands as if holding a flute. *Fool! She can understand Hebrew.* "She has a cleft in her chin."

The hand jammed on her hip, coupled with the expression that indicated the woman's urge to attack him, reminded Ezekiel of a skunk that puffed itself up in the pretense of danger, larger than it was.

"You're in the wrong place." She skirted him, slid into the room, and slammed the door behind her.

"Wait!" The rope for the latch slid through the hole in the door before he could grab it. He pressed his ear to the door and heard a muffled whisper.

"Shiriel? Are you in there?"

Silence met him. Ezekiel's gaze darted over the solid door, and he slammed his palm against it. Who was in there with the old woman? What did they know? He had to see that other woman's face.

He rubbed his temples, trying to use reason. That other

woman wasn't his wife. Would her tongue be any looser than the old woman's?

Shoulders sagging, Ezekiel weighed his options. He could come back tomorrow. *No, tonight.* He had to know if they'd seen Shiriel. He stepped into the shadows and pressed himself against the wall to wait.

Men passed by him in clusters, oblivious to his position. Still Ezekiel trained his gaze on the door. Would it weaken if he took a running start and rammed it with his shoulder?

He froze. Soft footsteps approached. Shaking slumber out of his eyes, Ezekiel appraised the shadowed figure approaching. Did he peer through drowsiness, or was it—?

Moving into the circle of light Ezekiel waited, his lungs screaming from trapped air.

The figure half-stepped to a halt.

"Ezekiel?" With a shriek, Shiriel flung herself into him, knocking him back.

He held her tight, lifting her to her toes. Hang the customs. "Thank You, Yahweh."

Shiriel's arms tightened around his neck, and her cheek was wet against his. "You came for me."

"Of course I did."

She stood back to survey him, a shy smile shining through her tears.

For that smile, he would have searched the far reaches of Babylon's empire.

18

Build houses and dwell in them; plant gardens and eat their fruit. Take wives and beget sons and daughters…that you may be increased there, and not diminished.
—Jeremiah 29:5-6a,c

After assuring Yassah and Atta that Ezekiel truly was her husband, and procuring promises that they would visit each other often, Shiri left the cramped quarters. Tears stung the back of her eyes. Even though it had only been a short time, the unusual circumstances had forged a bond of family.

Ezekiel seemed to sense her somberness as they walked down the poorly-lit hall in silence. He halted abruptly and tugged her into a deep shadow. Apprehension crept along Shiri's shoulders. "Will there be trouble for me going with you?"

"No. I have permission from Rabgar-Nebo, in a manner of speaking."

Shiri peered into the empty entryway. "Then why—"

Ezekiel shifted close and rested his hand on her waist. "I missed you, Shiriel."

Her heart and thoughts stuttered as he pulled her close.

"I know you cared for Amram, and I am nothing like him. I hope, one day, you can come to think of me with as much fondness as I think of you."

Shiri blinked. He still believed she favored Amram? Any affection for the choirmaster had diminished long before their journey to Babylon. Truly, any thought of him that lingered would vanish completely if Ezekiel kept holding her so.

"I *am* fond of you, Ezekiel. When Amram rejected me… my proposal of…my feelings for him rapidly faded. I understood how foolish I was. Now…" His breath caressed her cheeks to the point of distraction. "Now I have thoughts only for you."

Time stretched in silence. Ezekiel didn't move.

Shiri pressed her lips together and traced her fingers up the defined muscles on his arms.

He tipped her face and leaned close, brushing her mouth with a kiss that ended too soon. A delicious shiver spread through Shiri's belly, and her eyes fluttered open.

Ezekiel traced her cheek with the back of his hand. "Let's go home."

The following days blurred together.

They'd walk together to the palace complex where they sat through language classes that baffled her. Ezekiel picked up the language with a speed that confounded Shiri even more than Akkadian. Eventually, she could pick up the gist of the conversation—if she stared improperly at the speaker's mouth and they spoke at a speed a snail could best. Hopefully Ezekiel and his quick mind would always be around to translate for her.

He would then escort her to the music hall where she could at least understand that language—although, like Akkadian, the music seemed nasally. Harsh. Angry. Unlike the music of Yahweh's temple, that flowed like the wind through a wheat field and moved with depth and conviction.

After seven long days—the Chaldeans didn't honor the Sabbath—the week would begin again, and the endless cycle of straining to understand the world around her. The bright spot came on the Sabbath nights when the Hebrews who dwelled on the west side of the city gathered at their campsite after the workday concluded.

Shiri surveyed their growing congregation as she concluded the psalm of thanksgiving. She made her way to where Yassah and Atta sat. The water in the canal lapped at the banks, easing away the tension behind her eyes. Yassah patted her hand and nodded her appreciation.

Ezekiel rose and covered his head with his prayer shawl. "Blessed are You, oh Lord, God of Israel."

A man on the left side stood. "Before you begin, I'd like to say something."

Shiri's eyes widened, and she glanced to Ezekiel's slight frown. He would not be happy about the interruption. Before he could object, the man plowed on.

"I am Ahab, from the tribe of Manasseh."

A murmur rippled through the crowd. Shiri's mouth dropped open, and she stared at him. She had never seen an Israelite. His dark hair and olive skin resembled the Judahites. They were, after all, descendants of the same man.

"We of the houses of Judah and Israel are many. If we band together, we will be a mighty army. We can fight for our freedom and reestablish our nation."

"How have you come to this conclusion?" Ezekiel's brow furrowed, and the expression he wore was one reserved for people he thought foolish or deluded.

The Israelite faced the congregation, spreading his arms wide. "My good people, what could Yahweh intend by depositing us all in this location but to unite our nations once more? We are rallied and strong. We can break the yoke Nebuchadnezzar uses to oppress us."

Shiri locked her gaze on Ezekiel's face as an excited murmur spread through the seated crowd like the guttural Babylonian throat singing.

"Have you not heard?" Ezekiel's voice surpassed the chatter. "This time of exile is designed by Yahweh so that we would return to Him."

"And that is just what I propose. We will return to our nations." Ahab put his hand on Ezekiel's shoulder. "You work with the numbers; you know better than I the strength we have. Our people are scattered through the nation but the network is strong. We can rally within three months and be back home."

Back to Jerusalem? Back to the temple and *Ima* and *Abba*?

"No!"

Shiri jumped as Ezekiel slammed his fist against his hand.

"He should hear the man out." Yassah clicked her tongue and shook her head.

Shiri pressed her mouth closed against agreement. "I am sure Ezekiel has good reason for what he says."

"Hmph." Yassah crossed her arms.

Please have a good reason.

"Are you not aware we are in the same land where our father Abraham was called? Yahweh has brought us here in His great mercy." Ezekiel planted his imposing frame directly in front of Ahab. "You will not fill these people's minds with your disobedient talk. Our nations rejected the ways of truth. This is our due. Until we get our hearts right before the Lord our God, we are in exile."

A smooth smile spread across Ahab's face. "And as Abraham was called forth from this very land, so are we to the promised land."

Shiri shuddered at the man's smooth tones. He seemed sincere, but she had been fooled by charm once before.

"To the south the Tower of Babel stands abandoned." Ezekiel advanced on Ahab. "A cursed memorial to man's attempt to tread their own path, rather than follow Yahweh's commands."

Ahab's expression hardened, and he addressed the man who had established himself as an elder in their congregation. "What became of them?"

The elder rose. "You are expecting me to say they spread out away from this place. But you overlook the pain and division they endured."

"That's the one," Atta whispered. "That is Dumah. He is the one I've been telling you about."

Shiri peered with interest at the elder who Atta said seemed to favor her. "He stands for what is right. That is admirable."

"He is making a name for himself amongst the wise men who work figures." Atta fluttered her hand before her face. "Dumah is so respected he receives a double ration."

Well off and wise. What a combination. Would Dumah treat Atta well? Atta had mentioned her previous husband had been quarrelsome and a constant source of shame. She deserved someone who would take care of her. Shiri patted Atta's hand as she turned her attention back to the Israelite.

Ahab spread his arms. "I offer you the chance to reunite with family in our homeland—"

"Would you escape Yahweh's chastisement elsewhere? Indeed, you would only make your lot worse." Dumah aligned his shoulder with Ezekiel's. "I stand with the priest."

Ezekiel acknowledged Dumah and stepped forward. "You have presented your case, and we will not join you. Please leave."

"Why don't you allow the people to choose for themselves?" Ahab smiled at the congregation and reached to the man in the front. "Would you like—"

Ezekiel pushed his hand away. "I am the leader. I am looking out for the best interest of this flock."

The man shot to his feet. "We are capable of making our own choices."

Another man stood, and another.

Atta dug her fingers into Shiri's arm and peered toward the city, eyes wide. "Look!"

Shiri turned to see a troop of men approaching. Did the Israelites already have an army assembled? Her gaze latched onto the Chaldean soldiers flanking the ranks.

A man broke formation and quickened his stride. "Ezekiel!"

Her husband cast a wary glance toward Ahab, who seemed just as distracted.

"I am Ezekiel." He struggled through the crowd, and they all twisted around to observe this latest development.

The man, adorned in Hebrew clothing, opened his arms. "I'm Gemariah…my chambers overlook the temple courtyard."

Ezekiel broke into a smile and embraced the man. "My brother! What news do you bring of Jerusalem?"

"I bring word from Jeremiah concerning you."

"Me?" Ezekiel's eyebrows rose.

Gemariah indicated the congregation. "All that the Lord has caused to be carried away from Jerusalem."

"How timely is your arrival." Ezekiel cast a smirk over his shoulder. "Ahab and I were just now debating the merits of our exile in Babylon."

Gemariah's face drained of color. "Ahab, son of Kolaiah?"

Ahab leaned back. "Do I know you?"

"Uh…no, but the Lord does." Gemariah blinked as if seeing a spirit.

The whole congregation glanced, spellbound, between the two men.

"What is your message, friend?" Ezekiel put his hand on the man's shoulder.

Gemariah flicked his gaze across the crowd and ran his tongue over his lips. He shifted his weight and cleared his throat twice. Shaking himself, he unfurled a scroll. "Thus, says the Lord of hosts, the God of Israel, to all who are carried away from Jerusalem to Babylon. 'Build houses and dwell in them. Plant gardens. Continue in the ways of families so you'—we—'may increase.'"

One of those who'd sided with Ahab called out, "What are you saying?"

Gemariah lifted his gaze from the parchment. "The Lord is saying 'get comfortable.' You will be here seventy years."

A collective gasp spread on the wafting breeze.

Seventy years? Her parents would likely sleep with their fathers before this year's end.

"Seek the peace of Babylon." Gemariah swept his arm to the soldiers who had accompanied his entourage. "Pray to the Lord, for in their peace, you will have peace."

Shiri glanced toward the smug expression on the Chaldeans' faces. What they must think about people who not only submitted to exile but were commanded to pray for their captors' well-being.

A soldier raised his hand in a signal, and before Shiri could take a breath, the Chaldeans formed a perimeter around the people and bound Ahab and Ezekiel with chains.

Chaos broke out. Women screamed, men stood shoulder to shoulder with raised fists, and soldiers drew swords. The soldiers plowed through the crowd, shoving and pounding the exiles on the head with sword hilts.

Shiri pried Atta's fingers from her arm and scrambled to her feet. She couldn't be separated from Ezekiel again.

Ducking between soldiers and exiles, Shiri stumbled as a man in front of her toppled from a blow to the temple. She pressed her hand to her mouth and picked her way around men who had submission chosen for them. At last, Ezekiel was within reach.

The soldier guarding her husband shoved her away, and she bounced off a Hebrew. Her impact sent him into the waiting fist of a soldier. "I'm so sorry!" She ducked as the man came reeling backward into Ezekiel's guard.

"Enough!" Ezekiel's broad voice carried across the crowd in Hebrew, then Akkadian, but did nothing to calm the riot. He turned to his captor. "We were meeting peaceably, officer. We do not conspire against Babylon."

The guard pounded his fist on the back of a Hebrew's head, sending him swiftly to the ground.

Shiri took advantage of the distraction, ducked under Ezekiel's arm, and clung to him. The shackles clanked as he put himself between her and the soldier. At the front of the congregation, Ahab twisted and lunged, slamming his head against the nose of the soldier guarding him. Blood spurted and other soldiers pounced on Ahab, pounding him and tackling him to the ground.

Shiri whimpered, "What do we do?"

Ezekiel shielded her from a flailing fist, sucking in a breath as it connected with his shoulder. "Once this is contained, they will see we mean no harm."

"How? They think you are siding with Ahab."

"We have truth on our side. They will see we are compliant."

"What if they don't?" Shiri closed her eyes to the chaos.

Ezekiel lifted his hand to cradle her head, and the weight of the chains hung heavy on her shoulders. He searched her face with a tenderness that made time slow. "Shiriel?"

Her breath caught in her chest. "Yes?"

"If I am taken, you must remain strong. Faithful like Abraham."

19

For I know the thoughts that I think toward you, says the LORD, thoughts of peace and not of evil, to give you a future and a hope. Then you will call upon Me and go and pray to Me, and I will listen to you. And you will seek Me and find Me, when you search for Me with all your heart. I will be found by You, says the LORD, and I will bring you back from your captivity.
—Jeremiah 29:11-14a

Air deflated from Shiri's lungs as surely as they had been pricked with a needle. She blinked and lowered her gaze to hide her disappointment. Ezekiel began speaking Akkadian, and she couldn't concentrate well enough to understand.

Why had she expected, in the midst of a riot, he would confess his love for her? He hadn't said as much in the dark of their tent. She mentally gave herself a shake.

The man called Gemariah waved his hands and spoke rapidly. Those with him tried to pull Chaldeans off Hebrews, only to be bounced back like small pups contending with full grown hunting dogs for scraps. Atta and Yassah wailed and wrung their hands. Ahab's shouting ceased, and a soldier straddled him, pulling his hands behind his back. His bruised and bloody face pressed into the rocky soil, but he didn't move. Was he dead?

"Your rebellion will not go unnoticed, Jews. Nebuchadnezzar will surely punish this uprising."

Gemariah's colleague knelt before Ezekiel's captor. "General Vakhtang, you know Gemariah and I are ambassadors of peace. These people do not all stand on the side of one rebel."

The captain contemplated this and scanned the faces nearby. He grabbed the man who wore scorn like a garment to his feet. "Are you peaceful, Jew?"

The man glanced toward Ahab's still form. "I am peaceful."

Shiri shivered at the hatred in her countryman's eyes.

"Will you pray for us?" the captain mocked.

The man's lips formed a line, and his chin tipped up in defiance.

The captain struck his temple, sending him sprawling.

Shiri jumped and stifled a cry against Ezekiel's chest.

The Hebrew pushed himself to his knees and lifted insolent eyes. "I will pray for you—pray that you are struck down by an agonizing plague and that your family is ravished before your eyes and your livestock—"

Ezekiel wrapped his arms around Shiri's head, blocking her view of the soldier thrusting his sword, but he couldn't obstruct the sickening sound of flesh being sliced and the thud of a man's body against the ground.

"Make your choice. You will seek the best for the King of the World, or you will join this rotten fig in judgment." The captain kicked Ahab's side, eliciting a groan.

"My people, you have heard the confirmation of Jeremiah. We will live at peace here. Join me in the way of Abraham. Not the independence of the Tower of Babel." Ezekiel's voice vibrated from his chest.

The captain scrutinized Ezekiel. "An influencer. Perhaps we should leave you bound so the others don't forget." He wrenched Shiri from Ezekiel's hold and thrust her to her hands and knees. She yelped as her head snapped back and her scarf was yanked off along with a few hairs. Her eyes smarted.

"What is your objective, General?" Gemariah's robes swirled beside Shiri. "The man and his wife are not opposed to you. The people have heeded your warning. If you plan on executing all these people, then do so. Do not say one thing and act in an opposing way."

The general threw back his head in laughter that set Shiri's flesh to crawling.

Did human life only hold value as sport to this man? How could she pray peace for him?

The captain stepped toe-to-toe with Gemariah.

Shiri sucked in her breath, but the Hebrew ambassador did not flinch. "Do you bring harm to the messenger of the mighty prophet Jeremiah? The king will not be pleased."

Vakhtang jerked his head. "It is dark. This gathering is disbanded."

The soldiers stepped back and prodded the families away.

Ezekiel called after the shaken congregation, "Until next Sabbath. Remember, faith like Abraham."

A soldier grabbed Ahab's chains and dragged him, face down. Another Chaldean kicked then urinated on the dead man—disgrace in any language.

Shiri sucked air through her teeth and turned her face from Ahab's distorted form and horrific moan.

General Vakhtang swung around. "Come, *favored of the king*. Your royal palace awaits."

Gemariah didn't heed the tone in the captain's voice. "I

will stay and deliver the remainder of Jeremiah's message, as King Nebuchadnezzar has commanded."

"Suit yourself, filthy Jew." Vakhtang left, mercifully taking Ahab's cries of agony with him.

Shiri pushed herself to her feet, brushed off her knees and hands, and flung her arms around her still shackled husband.

He patted her stiffly, attention on Gemariah's entourage, who had busied themselves by dragging the dissenter's body away from the assembly, kicking dirt over the swath of blood left, and digging a trench for his final resting place.

"You shouldn't do that."

Shiri inspected the shackles for any breach. "You are my husband. I am with you no matter what happens. If we can find a small piece of metal, we should be able to jar the lock—"

"It isn't appropriate. Affection isn't for the public to see. We both are bound by propriety." Ezekiel scowled. "You could have been beaten or killed."

She glanced over her shoulder. No one gave them heed. Swallowing, she searched Ezekiel's expression, and her heart sank. He spoke in seriousness. "I'm sorry. I did not mean to violate customs."

Ezekiel crossed his arms with a clank of chains.

Humiliation shrouded Shiri's thoughts. She cast her gaze to her sandals. "I will prepare food to serve our guests."

"Don't light a fire. It's the sabbath," Ezekiel instructed as he opened his arms as wide as the bonds allowed and embraced Gemariah.

Gemariah set about examining the shackles. "Perhaps a mallet? We could smash the bonds?"

"As long as you do not smash my hands in the process." Ezekiel laughed.

A metal worker produced a hammer with an iron head and led Ezekiel to a large stone.

Shiri winced as the man began pounding on the chain in

the center. *You will still need to disengage the locks.*

Clang! The shackles sprang free.

Shiri inhaled and shook aside the feeling of failure. She had thrown herself into Ezekiel's arms in a blatant display of affection in public. Brushing off her hands, she strode to their tent and busied herself preparing their waning supplies. She would need to stop by the marketplace tomorrow. *Yahweh, draw out this food to feed all these men.*

She rolled her shoulders back, spirit still disquieted. *Help me be an asset to my husband and not hinder him because I make thoughtless mistakes.* The sound of the men's voices outside brought Shiri's attention to the meager furnishings of the tent. She scooped up the coverings from the sleeping mat, stepped out in the dusk, and formed a circle on the ground. Fruitlessly, she tried to count the men milling around, all engaged in animated conversations.

Numbering the men would not do any miracle for the food supply. Either there was enough, or there wasn't.

Slipping into the tent, Shiri knelt to lift the platter. Would the scribe know of her parents? How could he? Scribes wouldn't concern themselves with villagers, and the chances of *Abba* socializing in the temple were slim.

She ducked out and served the men. Each one ripped large fistfuls of bread rounds and passed around the cold lentils and the dates. The lentils reached Gemariah and Shiri saw the bottom of the bowl. She pressed her lips together. There were still three men to serve—none of them seemed any less hungry. The last man scraped the sides of the bowl, barely seasoning the bread, and turned expectantly toward Shiri.

"I am sorry. That's all I have. I wasn't planning—" She stopped. It would be rude to say they weren't prepared.

The man shrugged and scarfed the bread. She sat off to the side, ready to serve—not that there was anything left to offer—and tuned into the conversation.

"Seventy years?" Her husband shook his head. "Indeed, I have heard Jeremiah say it, but now it has such certainty. It is a long time."

Gemariah put his hand on Ezekiel's shoulder. "Take heart. After seventy years, Yahweh will perform His good word toward you and cause you to return."

"Are you saying Yahweh will extend our lives? That He will bring a ninety-five-year-old man out of captivity?" Ezekiel's skeptical tone was not lost on Shiri.

Gemariah sat silently. "No. I have no guarantee of that. It seems unimaginable. Perhaps it is the generations to follow. At any rate, Yahweh knows the thoughts He has for you. He declares thoughts of peace and not of evil. He will give our nation a future. Hope."

Shiri absorbed the words and hope mingled with despair. Although the history of their people was sprinkled liberally with elderly women making life-changing journeys—Sarah, Miriam, Naomi—the likelihood of her returning with the remnant were slim.

Yahweh, do You really see our people in this foreign land, away from the temple where You dwell?

Hope. The God whose word produced worlds declared peace. A future.

Surely goodness and mercy will follow me all the days of my life—even here. *Yahweh, help my doubt. I want to serve You. Use me as You see fit.*

Later, when all the men rested in the open and Ezekiel lay beside her on the bare sleeping mat, tears blurred her vision and her throat closed up. Until now, she had hoped—believed even—that she'd see her little home again. *Abba's* eyes would crinkle when he saw her, and *Ima* would reach out for an embrace.

Never again.

Finality clogged her throat, and the darkness shrouded the tears dripping down her cheeks.

20

Thus, says the LORD of hosts, the God of Israel concerning Ahab the son of Kolaiah, and Zedekiah the son of Maaseiah, who prophesy a lie to you in My name: "Behold I will deliver them into the hand of Nebuchadnezzar, king of Babylon, and he shall slay them before your eyes."
—Jeremiah 29:21

O*n the twentieth day of the seventh month which was in the first year of King Coniah's captivity.*

The predawn lightened the first day of the week with muted colors, and Ezekiel rubbed blurry eyes as he and Shiriel made their way through the city. As much needed as the fellowship with Gemariah and others had been, his back missed the bedding they had borrowed. He'd have to seek extra provisions for tonight.

Those blankets had been folded neatly by the tent when Ezekiel had risen, and the men had gone.

"I'll have to go to the market." Shiriel must have been thinking the same thing.

Ezekiel shifted his gaze toward her down cast shoulders. "I'm sorry they put you out. Of course, I didn't know any sooner."

"Don't be. I'm glad we were able to serve them in their need."

What had subdued her cheerful morning dialogue and humming? Then again, seventy years would damper any spirit. "In a way, it's good to have closure. Don't you think?"

"In a fashion. We can invest our energy into here rather than hoping—" Shiriel's voice grew thick. She brushed a fly away from her face. "Do you suppose you could obtain more rations?"

Ezekiel shrugged as they approached the music hall. If she wanted to share, she would of her own accord. "I should be able to. Wait for me at the market."

Shiriel squinted toward the rising sun. "I will."

"I'll be praying you are able to understand the language lessons today." Ezekiel turned to the north.

"Ezekiel?"

He glanced over his shoulder. "Was there something you needed?"

Shiriel blushed and averted her eyes. "I will be praying for you too."

He stepped close and rubbed away a smudge on her cheek. She followed his every move, letting out a breath as he stepped back. Something flickered in her eyes. Probably missing her family. He gave an encouraging smile. "Take heart. This is part of Yahweh's plan."

A group of Hebrews strode past them into the tunnel, jabbering away.

"I should go." Shiriel waved and followed after.

Ezekiel whistled the tune Shiriel normally hummed as he strode to his station. The sound stuck in his throat at the sight of fierce Chaldean soldiers by his table.

Before he could think of any errors he had made, a captain stepped forward. "Come with us."

The brief thought to run crossed his mind.

He set his shoulders and fell into formation behind the captain. Defying Chaldean warriors was suicide.

He couldn't have switched yesterday's figures. Impossible.

They marched to the throne room and directly to the raised throne. Ezekiel's eyes widened. *This* was the man said to ride a male lion with a snake as a bridle? The imposing crown and stately curled beard couldn't disguise King Nebuchadnezzar's height—or lack thereof. Yet, the cold, calculating expression on his face declared he lived up to the ruthless stories.

The guards halted, and a strong hand pushed Ezekiel to his knees on the marble tile. He braced his hands and bowed his head. The ominous feeling grew, overtaking his common sense. What had he done to warrant this audience? He closed his eyes and inhaled the perfumed air. *Yahweh, fight for me, so I can continue to serve Your people.*

"This is the one organizing gatherings of the Jews?" King Nebuchadnezzar's accusatory tones raised defensive prickles on the back of Ezekiel's neck. "You can see, Jew, what measures I take against insurrection."

A coughing moan drew Ezekiel's attention to the side of the throne room where Ahab was restrained, arms chained above his head. His belly was flayed open and flies buzzed on and around the wound like they would a rotten fig.

Vomit pressed up Ezekiel's throat. He averted his eyes and breathed in through his nose.

Nebuchadnezzar leaned forward. "Are you Zedekiah, son of Maaseiah?"

"No, great King of the World." Ezekiel blessed his *ima* for not naming him Zedekiah. "I am of the same school of thought as the prophet Jeremiah. I pray for the peace of Babylon."

"Hmm…" King Nebuchadnezzar crossed his arms.

An idea came, and Ezekiel forged ahead before he lost nerve. "How can I pray for you, my king?"

"You are a bold one, aren't you?" Nebuchadnezzar's tone hardened. "The prophecy declares I shall roast this man in the fire for the disgraceful things he has done to your countrymen. What say you?"

Sweat beaded on Ezekiel's brow. "I would have you pardon him in your great mercy, my king."

"Even though he has prophesied lies in the name of your god?"

Ezekiel swallowed and saw Ahab's shape in his mind's eye. As horrendous as it was, accepting Yahweh's judgment was right—even when the judge was a vicious pagan. *Yahweh, strengthen Your people that they can repent of their ways.*

"I granted you audience for another reason. I am giving you a house in Tel-Abib. Your people will see the reward in pledging their loyalty to my kingdom."

A house? What was the catch? Ezekiel's thoughts swirled. "My king is most generous."

"You will continue to bolster the Jews in my service, and you will host any ambassadors who come to this land. They will be served from the king's finest, and you will tell how great and generous my provisions are."

"Your generosity and kindness are unheard of, my king." Ezekiel warred with himself. "I will gladly declare your deeds as long…as long as what you ask does not contradict my God."

Mirth came through Nebuchadnezzar's words. "I am, after all, *appointed by your God* to rule your nation."

"Yes, my king." For now.

"You are dismissed. Rabgar-Nebo will settle you in your new house."

Ezekiel pushed himself to his feet, keeping his torso bowed. "Oh King, live forever. Your kindness surpasses—" his own king's, certainly "—all expectations."

Rabgar-Nebo stepped in front of Ezekiel and strode toward the entrance.

"Jew."

Ezekiel's foot hovered mid stride. Had it all been a ruse? He turned back and bowed at the waist. "Yes, oh King of the World?"

The pause seemed infinite. "You may pray for my health and prosperity."

Was there more under the hesitation? "Yes, my king." Ezekiel remained bent until Rabgar-Nebo prodded him on.

Was this possible? A house?

The captain veered into a hallway that sloped downward.

Ezekiel's heart pounded against his chest as each step led further into the bowels of the palace. They emerged into a room with a blessedly higher ceiling. A torch lit the basic room where a soldier stood before an iron gate. A massive ring of keys weighed his sash down.

This was his house? A prison cell? A lump rose in his throat.

Rabgar-Nebo exchanged words with the guard, and the creak of the gate resounded down the tunnel, even smaller than the one they had just left.

Think logically. Ezekiel wasn't bound. Rabgar-Nebo took no key. Unless there was more than he could see, he wouldn't be imprisoned. Their footsteps slapped against the cold floor as the torch lit the path directly in front of them. The dark corridor led ever down.

Another turn. Would he be able to retrace his steps if necessary?

A glow of steady light drew Ezekiel's attention. "Whose cell is that?"

"That is where your child-king resides." Rabgar-Nebo stepped aside to make room for Ezekiel to pass. "Your first assignment is to inform him of the length of time your people will remain in Babylon."

Ezekiel grinned. Translation, *Tell Coniah to quit whining.*

"Who's there?" Coniah's nasally whine drifted out of the cell.

Rabgar-Nebo said nothing.

"It is Ezekiel." He stepped into the ring of light that illuminated the stark walls.

"The priest?" Coniah's face appeared between the bars. His gaze latched onto Rabgar-Nebo. "I'd like to lodge a complaint. Your guard refuses to accommodate my demands. I am only receiving one meal a day, and I am reduced to using the same waste pot each day. My—"

Rabgar-Nebo slammed his metal wrist guard against the bars and the noise filled the space.

Coniah crossed his arms with a glare.

Ezekiel took in the king's surprisingly luxurious accommodations. "We are not here as guests, my king."

"I willingly surrendered. I deserve to be treated as an ally."

Ezekiel's eyebrows shot up.

Coniah's eyes narrowed. "Don't flash that disrespect to me. I am your king."

"With all the respect due to you, our nation is being judged on account of the hardness of our hearts and our refusal to put Yahweh in His rightful place in our lives."

"That's not my fault." Coniah sulked over to a silk covered pillow as if he expected Ezekiel to grovel for favor. "My *abba* destroyed all chance of peace."

"You had your chance to reign two separate times. You did nothing to change the course of our nation."

"I was a *child*. Besides, everyone knew my *abba* would return soon—as I will."

Rabgar-Nebo cleared his throat and jerked his head to the side.

Ezekiel honed in on the deposed king. "You will not be released soon. I have received a message from the prophet Jeremiah. We are bound here seventy years. You'd better grow accustomed to your silks and meals from Nebuchadnezzar's table. Your people suffer far worse."

Turning on his heel, Ezekiel stalked into the dark. If he delayed, he would likely say something that wouldn't be honorable.

Rabgar-Nebo caught up, and by the light of his torch, Ezekiel could see the hint of a smile.

"I can't survive like this for seventy years!" Coniah's scream chased after them.

Ezekiel shook his head. Nothing to hint at concern for his subjects' well-being. How could a man in the king's position not give a second thought to his people? He lived in luxury, and his people shared two rations between a crowd.

All the way to the Chebar Canal, anger fueled Ezekiel's steps. Tel-Abib lay just beyond the exiles' impoverished camp, where the people slept on the ground. And their king complained about his plush cushions.

Ezekiel skidded to a halt as Rabgar-Nebo turned into the small courtyard of a two-level house. A modest door opened into a long common room, already laden with bedding and a bountiful feast—food that complied with Hebrew laws. A steady stream of servants brought more bundles and cushions and baskets. The sun stretched afternoon shadows deep across the courtyard before the servants disbanded and Gemariah and his entourage arrived.

"The Lord has blessed your faithfulness abundantly." Gemariah's eyes sparkled with his approval.

The responsibility to shepherd wisely settled comfortably around Ezekiel like a mantle. It would be an honor to serve the exiles in this capacity.

21

I will visit you and perform My good word toward you, and cause you to return to this place.
—Jeremiah 29:10b

Shiri waited at the market stall closest to the ferry's dock. A glance toward the horizon revealed the sun sitting in the same position it had been a moment before, if not lower.

The vendor behind her backed a hand cart to the baskets of lentils.

Chewing the inside of her cheek, Shiri scanned the dwindling crowd once more. Still no sign of Ezekiel. She stepped forward.

"I'd like two—" She held up two fingers and raised the ration chips around her neck.

The vendor rolled his eyes, speaking rapidly.

Shiri shook her head and searched for Ezekiel. "Please. Two."

The man heaved an inconvenienced sigh and scooped

lentils into a sack. He shoved it at her and dug around for his ledger.

What about their guests? Shiri's stomach clenched and imbued determination. "Pardon, please."

Propping a straight arm on his shelf, the round man raised scowling eyes.

"Please…I have guests. I need nine more servings." Shiri switched to Hebrew, counting out her fingers.

He jutted out his chin and rattled off a string of words.

Shiri's chest itched. She lifted her shoulder and shook her head. "I don't know."

Advancing toward her, and speaking as to a child, the vendor pointed to her chest.

Yahweh, protect me. She fixated on his exaggerated lip movement.

"Rations. Rations." He jabbed his finger at the clay chips.

Oh. She shifted her weight. "My husband..." She gestured towards the palace and brought her hand above her head. "Husband."

Move on. Say something else. All Akkadian words she had managed to retain took their leave. Tears burned the back of her eyes. She held up nine fingers and moved a hand as if tapping each man's head, then presented the two ration chips. "Husband."

The vendor shook his head and swatted his hand as if she were a fly. He turned his back and resumed loading the cart.

Ezekiel would be able to communicate. Shiri glanced dismally at the meager pile of lentils, certain the vendor had not used a fair scoop.

Where could Ezekiel be?

Shiri waited until no vendors remained and the sun touched the river. She clutched her flute and the sack of lentils and fell into step with a straggling group of Hebrews heading up the Chebar Canal.

It wasn't like Ezekiel to forget an appointment. Where

would she even begin to search for him? He always continued north after depositing her at the music hall, but where his station was, she didn't know.

She curbed her thoughts. He probably waited now at their fire with their guests. They'd have a good laugh over her inadequate language abilities. She must have misunderstood. *He* probably had already picked up the extra rations.

"I should have given him these ration chips, and only one of us would have had to go to the marketplace."

Engrossed in searching the blazing cooking fires, Shiri nearly passed her own tent. The fire had not been lit, and the tent stood dark.

Ezekiel had not come home.

Sweat trickled down Shiri's back, contrasting the breeze coming off the canal. "What do I do?"

Could she even light the fire in the cooking pit? Ezekiel always gave direction, but he wasn't here. In a land of harsh soldiers, the absence of her husband didn't bode well.

"Little Bird."

Shiri wiped away the moisture dripping from her nose and turned to see Rabgar-Nebo materializing in the twilight. "Do you know where my husband is?"

The Chaldean's stoic face strangely comforted her. "He sent me to fetch you."

Her shoulders sagged, and she gulped in air to prevent the tears of relief from springing forth. "I will just put my flute in the tent."

"No. Everything you want, you will take." Rabgar-Nebo gestured to the tent.

Shiri ducked inside and felt her way through the shadowy dwelling. "Even Ezekiel's things?"

"Everything."

Bundling all their worldly possessions in a large swath of fabric, Shiri wrapped together an unwieldy bundle. Though there was nothing of great substance, it was bulky and loose.

She clutched it tight, wedged today's rations to her chest, and gripped her flute. The whole affair slipped as she ducked outside. Shifting everything still felt precarious, but at Rabgar-Nebo's impatient crossing and uncrossing arms, she hefted the whole lot close and followed him, trotting to keep up with his long strides.

Rabgar-Nebo led her to the lights of the establishment to the east—too small to be a town, and too large to be a sole estate. Why was Ezekiel here? Did his appointment documenting their countrymen change location?

Shiri's fingers cramped around the flute. Loosening her grip caused the makeshift baggage to slip, and the lentils rattled against each other as they spilled. She squeezed her eyes shut momentarily. How many had she lost? Perhaps she could retrieve them in the light and brush them off; she couldn't afford to waste the food.

"Do you know if the scribes from Jerusalem are still here?" She called out to her guide.

Rabgar-Nebo grunted, and Shiri pictured his displeasure.

She bit back the questions that continued to present themselves. Rabgar-Nebo thought talking a waste when a job had to be done.

The Chaldean took an abrupt turn to the right and pushed open the door to a two-story villa.

Noise burst into the night.

"Whose house is this?" Shiri stepped into the well-lit room, surveying the people reclining before a sumptuous feast. The tantalizing aroma of the variety of foods made her stomach cramp with hunger.

Shiri's threadbare sleeves wrapped around the bundle of equally scant clothing. She glanced over her shoulder, hoping for reassurance from Rabgar-Nebo, but he had left without a farewell.

"Shiriel! You're here!" A man rose from his mat and strode towards her.

"Ezekiel?" Shiri blinked. Her husband was adorned in billowing linen trousers, a tunic of fine colors, and turban wound upon his head. All the men enjoying the festivities wore the same style—the Hebrew ambassadors. "What…why?"

Ezekiel laughed.

At her? Probably at the answer he had yet to share, right?

"This—" he swept his arm to include the room, "is our house."

Shiri's mouth dropped open.

"The king has rewarded my loyalty and has given me—us—this house."

How could that be?

"Ezekiel, come. The food grows cold." Shiri recognized Gemariah.

Her husband laughed again and half-turned. "Do you like it? We've been here all afternoon."

Did he not remember his promise to meet her?

"Where should I put—"

Ezekiel strode back to the banquet, already rejoining the conversation.

Shiri's gaze darted around the spacious common room. A set of stairs raised her eyes to the arches supporting the roof—rounded wood, curving up to a graceful point. She deposited her bundle in the corner by the clay oven.

The lentils gave a pitiful rattle. *You feel out of place, too?* She surveyed the guests. Each man seemed content, so Shiri turned to the food preparation area in search of food for herself. Apparently, all had been set out.

Her stomach clenched and demanded that she consider breaking tradition and sit with the men to eat.

"Pass the—" The man on the left indicated the half-full platter of roasted meat.

Shiri bent to retrieve the tray and delivered it to eager hands. Hesitating a brief moment, she scooped up the dish of pureed eggplant and walked around the perimeter under the pretense of offering it to others, but in fact planning all the while how she could connect the mouth-watering concoction with the rounds of soft wheat bread on the other side.

Gemariah swung his arm back as she passed behind him. "—Mattaniah sticks up his nose and says 'I am Zedekiah, now. I am king.' As if he'd allow anyone to forget that."

The men were still laughing as Shiri knelt for the bread. She didn't even make an excuse for taking it, not that anyone would have noticed, they were all caught up in Mattaniah's selfish ways.

Shiri settled into a corner, ripped off a piece of a bread round, and scooped up some paste. The garlic and turmeric united together in a delicious swirl of texture and flavor. Leaning her head against the wall and closing her eyes, she hoped her groan was inaudible.

Hunger may indeed be the most skilled cook, but there was something to be said for the delicacies of the aristocrats. When the edge to her hunger dulled, Shiri forced herself to slow her ravenous consumption. She nibbled and studied Ezekiel.

How different he appeared in Chaldean garb. *Abba* would be proud of Ezekiel's achievement, *Ima* would gush over the house, and Keziah would giggle over how stately Ezekiel was.

Shiri's eyes burned and a lump formed in her chest. *Yahweh, You have given us abundant blessings in this strange land.*

The tune to *The Joy of the Lord is My Strength* played in her thoughts. Her life was here in Babylon, now. Her husband, a decorated man, a house large enough to host their flock for Sabbath instruction, food. Despite her deep loss, Yahweh had not abandoned His people in this city.

When the men had eaten their fill, they began spreading pallets of blankets around the room.

Shiri cleared away—and sampled—the food, discovering a small dug out under a large plank. She stepped down the one stair and situated the remainder of the food into the cool of the packed dirt cellar. Securing the plank, Shiri spread the rug back over it.

She tiptoed past where Gemariah knelt on his pallet with eyes closed and lips moving. With one last glance to be sure everything was set to rights, Shiri turned to the stairs.

"Sleep well, mistress." Gemariah yawned and stretched.

"You as well, my lord." Shiri hesitated. "Forgive the intrusion. I wonder, do you know… how the villagers fare?"

"As a whole they carry on." Gemariah ran ink-darkened fingertips through his beard. "Is there someone in particular your concern leans toward?"

Shiri swallowed. "My *abba*, Ibraham, was the choirmaster before Amram. They live in the village north of Jerusalem. Perhaps you knew him?"

"I did. I can't say that I've seen him since he retired."

"He rarely left the house. Most of the time he is caring for my *ima*." Shiri forced a smile and pivoted. "Thank you anyway."

"I can check on their welfare when I return."

Somehow that calmed her anxious thoughts. "Thank you, I'd be truly grateful." They'd be able to know what had transpired, at least.

She trudged up the stairs and could almost hear *Ima's* words—*Choose joy, Shiri*—even as her illness confined her to a cushion.

Oh, to have *Ima's* arms and wisdom embracing her once more.

22

The word which Jeremiah the prophet commanded Seraiah the son of Neriah, the son of Mahseiah, when he went with Zedekiah the king of Judah to Babylon in the fourth year of his reign. And Seraiah was the quartermaster. So Jeremiah wrote in a book all the evil that would come upon Babylon.

—Jeremiah 51:59-60a

594 BC

Three years later.

Gilead adjusted the wide gold collar of his shame. After three years, the glances—from collar to face, to trousers, then away—still affected him. It wasn't as though he'd had much of a choice in the matter.

He marched through the streets of Babylon behind General Vakhtang, always aware of the shifting shadows and movement in high places. After his training, he had risen in rank to Vakhtang's personal bodyguard.

The general, a cold and ruthless butcher, regrettably found

value in Gilead's skill and loyalty, though he was liberally abused and derided.

Gilead scanned the processional behind him. At the rear of the party, Seraiah, the Judahite quartermaster, gawked at the sites of the city's finery. In front, King Mattaniah—or Zedekiah, as Nebuchadnezzar had renamed him—rode in a litter on the backs of burly men with the air of a visiting dignitary, rather than a vassal about to be reprimanded.

Gilead had served as an archer since the days of King Josiah. How could a godly man spawn such wicked offspring? First Jehoahaz—his reign of terror had only been three months before Pharaoh Neco had deposed him—then Jehoiakim had been evil in the flesh. Coniah had been incompetent and spineless, his life characterized by pouting. And Zedekiah, Josiah's youngest son, who schemed with determination to buck all authority.

Shaking his head, Gilead scanned the high places. Who was he to judge a man whose offspring strayed? Though in his case, when he devoted himself to the teachings of the law, he was the one who had turned away from his son. How many things had he done since the exile that would sustain his son's belief that he was a hypocrite? Many things that conflicted with the scriptures. *Yahweh, if I haven't drifted too far from Your care and reach, forgive me for thinking myself better than these men. You appoint men to their position, not me.*

At the marble steps leading to the palace, the slaves knelt, and Zedekiah climbed down from the litter, caring not that he stepped on a slave's hand in the process.

Gilead tracked Zedekiah's calculating stare to Seraiah. The tension between the two had been palpable the whole trip. Zedekiah had summoned Seraiah many a night in attempts to dissuade his allegiance from Jeremiah's task.

Something passed across the quartermaster's expression before he guarded his thoughts. Did Zedekiah suppose he had

Seraiah's loyalty? Whatever message had been drilled into Seraiah would be brought to light.

Their company entered the throne room, and Gilead broke away from Vakhtang's side, blending in the shadows.

Zedekiah strode forward without invitation, his surprisingly pristine robes sweeping behind him on the tile.

Bow, you fool! Gilead could see Nebuchadnezzar's archer targeting Zedekiah.

Nebuchadnezzar dismissed the scribe presenting the day's transactions. "Do you presume to come before me as an equal? You will bow your knee and your will to me!"

Chaldean swords clanged, and General Vakhtang shoved Zedekiah to his hands and knees. With a lift of his powerful leg, Vakhtang stomped on Zedekiah's lower back, unfurling him on the floor.

Zedekiah's cry of pain muffled against the tiles.

"What is this I hear of you inciting revolt amongst my provinces?" Nebuchadnezzar leaned forward with narrowed eyes.

Zedekiah lifted his head and shoulders. "Your reign is short lived, *oh Mighty King*." He gestured to the properly kneeling Seraiah. "I have word here from the God of the world that you will be overthrown, and Babylon shall become a heap, a dwelling place for jackals—"

"According to whom?" Nebuchadnezzar brushed off his shoulder.

"Jeremiah, prophet of the Most High God," Zedekiah spoke as if he and Yahweh were on good terms. "Your time to rule over my nation is ending in two years. Then we will overtake the 'Praise of the Whole Earth.'"

"Two years?" Nebuchadnezzar tented his fingers with an amused expression on his face. "Did Jeremiah tell you this?"

Zedekiah pushed his hands off the floor, rising to his knees. "Yes."

Seraiah's glare to Zedekiah did not go unnoticed.

Nebuchadnezzar honed in on the quartermaster. "You have something to say…against your prince?"

Seraiah bowed his forehead to the ground. "I am Seraiah. Brother to Baruch, the personal scribe of the prophet Jeremiah. King Zedekiah is…distorting the message entrusted to me."

"Ah." King Nebuchadnezzar folded his hands. "Distorting how?"

"If it pleases the king?" Seraiah reached into his satchel and unrolled a thick scroll.

"Proceed."

"The word that Yahweh spoke against Babylon and against the land of the Chaldeans by Jeremiah the prophet. 'Declare among the nations—'"

Nebuchadnezzar pinched the bridge of his nose. "As enthralling as Jeremiah's lengthy missives are, you will speak the whole of the matter first. Then I will consider if you shall continue with the minutia."

Seraiah's tongue ran over his lips. "Yes, great King of the World."

"Did Jeremiah say two years and go back on his earlier number?"

Slanting a glance at Zedekiah, Seraiah winced. "No, my King. That was given by the prophet Hananiah…who is now dead."

"Shut your mouth!" Zedekiah hissed.

"Silence!" Nebuchadnezzar jerked two fingers, and Vakhtang kicked Zedekiah in the ribs. "Your messenger speaks, not you. Your words are drivel and your thoughts your downfall. You, Zedekiah, hold position in Judah because I put you there. If you knew this God you speak of with such familiarity, you would not be justifying yourself before me."

Nebuchadnezzar flicked two fingers toward Vakhtang. "Remind this howling puff of empty wind why he is really here. Then take him to Coniah's cell. Whoever impresses me most will return to Judah on my behalf."

Zedekiah's screams echoed off the walls as Vakhtang dragged him out.

Gilead shook his head. *Wait until the actual torture begins.*

King Nebuchadnezzar rose. "The destruction Jeremiah speaks of, when will it occur? Did he mention me?"

Seraiah fiddled with the parchment. "No, Great King. There is no time frame."

"If it doesn't concern me, I don't wish to hear it." Nebuchadnezzar strode down the steps of the dais.

"May I throw it in the river, Great King?" Seraiah's timid request halted the king's departure.

"What?"

Seraiah braced his hands on the floor. "I have been instructed to read this book in the city of Babylon and cast it into the Euphrates."

Nebuchadnezzar considered and released Seraiah with a wave of his hand and brusquely strode out of the throne room.

After receiving dismissal orders from Vakhtang—two days respite after he delivered Seraiah and his attendees to the Jewish quarter in Tel-Abib—Gilead loosened his march and escorted Seraiah to the bridge spanning the Euphrates.

Seraiah read from the scroll, and Gilead clasped his hands behind him. He surveyed the dwelling places that would someday be burned and could picture the passageways blocked as Jeremiah foretold. All the riches and glittering idols would be winnowed in the day of Yahweh's harvest of doom.

"—The Lord has opened His armory and brought out the weapons of His indignation—" As quartermaster, Seraiah had the ability to cast his voice so all nearby could hear. It rose and fell with great feeling. "—put yourself in array against Babylon all around, all you who bend the bow. Shoot at her and spare no arrows for she has sinned against the Lord—"

Gilead's warrior heart swelled at the thought of the Portion of Jacob wielding a battle ax and weapons of war.

"—their Redeemer is strong. The Lord of Hosts is His name, He will thoroughly plead their case."

The word of the Lord, read aloud, bold and strong, breeched the callousness of what he'd been exposed to for so long and pierced deep into his soul. He stood ever aware, weeping inside. *Yahweh, plead my case for I don't deserve to come before You. Renew a right heart in me again. Guide me to who You would have me be.*

Seraiah completed the reading, and the weight of future judgment was as tangible as the bridge beneath their feet. Like Judah, Babylon would not repent of their wicked ways.

"May I have that rock?" Seraiah pointed by Gilead's feet. Gilead hefted the stone with both hands and held it while Seraiah tied it to the scroll with a somber expression.

A chariot clattered across the bridge. The mighty charioteer held the reins of powerful steeds, adorned with crimson fringe and fire in their eyes. Inside, a Magus in his silk robes studied a scroll.

The Hebrews exchanged glances.

"Oh, Lord, You have spoken against this place to cut it off, so that none shall remain in it, neither man nor beast, but it shall be desolate forever." Seraiah dropped the judgment of Babylon into the river that gave her life.

Plunk! The water swallowed up the coming fate of the proud city.

Gilead turned and led the seven men along the east bank of the Euphrates, through the marketplace and east on the Chebar Canal. In his comings and goings with Vakhtang, he'd never been to the Jewish quarter in Tel-Abib. Curiosity fueled his steps. Did the Hebrew people live their faith unfettered here in the shadow of Babylon?

Two days amongst his people. A craving for fellowship rose in his belly stronger than his weariness.

Seraiah stepped beside Gilead. "Was Nebuchadnezzar serious about pitting Coniah and Zedekiah against each other for the throne?"

Gilead scanned his surroundings. "King Nebuchadnezzar's actions are…unprecedented. Yet, I have no reason to doubt his words."

"Who will comply?" Seraiah discerned the need for caution and lowered his voice.

"I haven't seen Coniah for years." Gilead shrugged. "I have no idea his current disposition, yet, he hasn't blatantly opposed Nebuchadnezzar—as I can tell."

Seraiah tapped a finger to his lips and shrugged.

Once in Tel-Abib, Gilead stepped up to a man inside his gate. "Can you point us in the direction of the house where visiting dignitaries take up residence?"

The man's gaze shifted from Gilead's bearded face to his collar, below his waistband and away. He addressed Seraiah, "The second house on the right." The man glanced Gilead over again, shaking his head.

Gilead leveled him with a glare. *As if you uphold every aspect of the commandments.* Pivoting, he quickened his stride. Perhaps it would be more restful by himself. Who needed the company of judges?

The door of the second house stood open, inviting—if one was whole. He glanced over his shoulder where Seraiah lagged.

Seraiah's eyes widened. "Look out!"

Gilead whipped his head around, hand on his bow, and almost tripped over a small child toddling like a drunken soldier. He step-hopped to the side, narrowly missing the baby's bare toes.

Through no fault of Gilead's, the baby flailed her arms and went down on her padded bottom.

Tears filled the child's eyes, and she released a piercing wail.

23

The work of righteousness will be peace, And the effect of righteousness, quietness and assurance forever. My people will dwell in a peaceful habitation, In secure dwellings, and in quiet resting places.
—Isaiah 32:17-18

Shiri's heart stopped at the sound of Kelila's distress, then pounded a pulsing beat. She whirled around, searching in all the normal places—under the preparation table, the pile of rugs in the corner that beckoned her adventurous daughter like a mountain called to an explorer. The corner behind the door Kelila had yet to figure out how to back out of.

"Keli?" Shiri called up the stairs. *Oh Lord, please let her not have discovered the stairs yet.*

The cries teetered towards screams. Outside! How? Shiri had blockaded the door. She tore away the cushions that had failed to keep her daughter confined and skidded to a halt at the sight of an archer holding Keli and gingerly patting her back.

Instinct conquered timidity, and she plowed ahead with fisted hands. "Give me my child!"

The soldier's eyes widened as Shiri snatched Keli from him. Clutching her sweet babe close, Shiri kissed her plump cheeks. "There, there, it's all right. *Ima's* here." She backed up. No matter how stuffy the house grew, the door would remain shut and bolted.

A swarm of Hebrews she didn't recognize converged on her. "Mistress, it's not how it seems. Your daughter fell…We were only trying to help."

The toddler fussed and squirmed. Shiri twisted to shield Keli.

"Shiri?" The soldier took two steps.

She glanced at his face for the first time. "Gilead?" The years had added more gray to his temples and lines to his face, but his eyes were as intense as always.

"*You* are the host for ambassadors?" Gilead scanned the house behind her. "I didn't know. All this time I didn't know."

"What are you doing here?" Shiri halted her flood of questions at the faces of the weary travelers—her guests. She dipped her head. "Forgive me, my lords. My husband and I welcome you to our home."

"Is Ezekiel here?" Gilead's eagerness made her smile.

"Soon. Please come—" She couldn't invite the men in without her husband present. All other times, Ezekiel had escorted the ambassadors to the house.

Gilead reached for the strewn cushions in the doorway. "We will wait out here until he arrives."

Shiri distributed cushions, and a breath of relief pushed out of her lips. "Of course, make yourself comfortable in the shade."

With the escapee tightly on her hip, she bustled inside the dim kitchen, blessing Nebuchadnezzar and the messenger who had arrived earlier with provisions for the imperial guests.

Keli squirmed and fussed. Her back stiffened, and she grunted.

"I don't think so, little bear." Shiri plopped Keli on the preparation counter and buried her face in Keli's belly. "You are too swift for *Ima* to keep up."

Shiri reached for the basket of raisin cakes, gave one to Keli and spread the rest on a platter. Happy babbling filled the kitchen and Shiri's heart. Taking advantage of busy hands and still feet, Shiri steadied the babe with a hand and plucked mint leaves from the plant on the small window sill, crushing them into a pitcher of water.

"Well, little one, that's the best I can do with you helping. What do you say? Shall we take the men some refreshments?" Keli kicked her legs when Shiri scooped her up. "I know, you'd much rather walk."

The water jar and the ladle mocked her full hands. This would have to be done in stages. Balancing the tray on her arm, she emerged into the afternoon sun.

A slave pushed himself up.

"No, allow me to serve you." Shiri held out Keli to Gilead. "Do you mind?"

Gilead's eyes brightened and a sheen of moisture covered them. "Come here, sweetheart. Why don't you sit with *Saba* Gilead and give your *ima* a break?"

She served the raisin cakes, her chest swelling at the enthralled expression on Gilead's face as he carried on a conversation in Keli's language.

With speed—and two hands—as her allies, Shiri brought out the cold water to drink and a basin to wash the feet of her weary guests. She knelt before the slaves. "Thank you for your service. You are seen. We welcome you to reside here in peace. You are secure, and we offer you quiet rest in our home." She repeated the blessing over each of the eight pairs of dusty feet and tossed the grungy water at the base of the lavender bush beside the door. Rubbing her finger and her thumb over a stalk, she brought the aroma to her nose.

The men leaned back against the wall. One reclined on the ground, eyes drowsy. Keli lay in the crook of Gilead's elbow, her arm flung back and her little mouth open in sleep. Gilead spoke quietly to the Hebrew beside him.

Shiri bent to rescue Gilead from Keli's sweaty deadweight.

"She favors Ezekiel." Gilead seemed reluctant to release her. "And yet, she's beautiful."

"Do you have any children, Gilead?" Shiri hefted Keli to her shoulder, catching a glimpse of his gold collar. How could she be so insensitive? "Forgive me."

Regret passed across his eyes and he scanned the canal. "I do. Or did. I don't even know what has become of him. Before I committed my way to Yahweh, my son—both of us—lived loosely. He had gotten a married woman pregnant, and I came unhinged on him. I had just started following the law, and I knew he had violated Yahweh's standards. Even a non-follower knew that."

Shiri's heart ached. "What happened?"

"The woman's husband divorced her. Cainan, my son, came home one day furious. Apparently, she had seen a midwife and forced the pregnancy to drop. She went back to her husband, and Cainan left that day." Gilead's jaw tightened. "I lost my son and my grandchild in one week all because I preached and lectured what I hadn't practiced."

Shiri shifted. The weight of Gilead's revelation lay as heavy as Keli on her shoulders.

"I know I am a different man now, but…"

Words wouldn't come. Her wobbly smile wouldn't convey Gilead's value like she intended. He smiled tightly in return, put his arms behind his head, and closed his eyes.

Depositing Keli in a nest of cushions, Shiri set to preparing a meal fit for her weary guests. Not long after she put the leg-of-lamb on the spit to roast, Ezekiel's voice traveled inside. She smiled at the excited male voices talking over each other. Ezekiel would be able to encourage Gilead.

"Welcome to our home." Ezekiel strode into the house followed by Gilead and the others.

Keli began to cry as the men's loud, unmodified voices filled the room.

Shiri turned to the nest that no longer would contain the headstrong child. "There's my sweet girl! Did you have a good rest?"

With a smile, Keli lifted dimpled arms and clung to Shiri's neck with sticky raisin-cake fingers. Changing the soiled linens, Shiri swung her head back and forth with silly faces. Soon they were both giggling.

"Keli-Keli-Kelila!"

Keli's mouth formed a circle and her head tilted. "Baba. Baba."

"Do you hear *Abba*?" Shiri glanced to where Ezekiel sat engrossed in conversation.

Babbling, Keli reached her arms toward him, opening and closing her hands.

"*Abba* is busy. Why don't you help *Ima* prepare the meal?"

Keli lunged as they walked past, throwing Shiri off balance.

Gilead reached up for Keli with a smile. "Synagogue. Is that Greek?"

"Yes, it describes the purpose perfectly. It means 'to bring together' or 'a place of assembly.' We are able to raise up our people in the ways of our fathers." Ezekiel grew animated, as he always did when speaking of his flock. "We do a selection from the law and words of Isaiah. Shiriel leads us in the psalms."

Gilead turned toward her, and a smile crinkled his eyes. He nudged Seraiah. "Perhaps we should have waited to toss Jeremiah's prophecy. We could have shared it with the assembly."

"We call ourselves The Remnant." Ezekiel's expression spoke of his wariness to accept untested words. He didn't want any false teaching poisoning the minds. He shrugged, and Shiri knew he had found peace in the idea since it was from Jeremiah. "If you recall the words, we'd be happy to have you share this Sabbath."

A savory aroma wafted Shiri's way, indicating the lamb was ready. She carved the meat in hearty slices and turned out the meal before the guests. Humming about David's ten-thousands, she made sure all the men were satisfied before sitting cross legged before Keli. Tearing bite-sized pieces of soft bread, Shiri half-listened to the explanation of how they had implemented the Sabbath.

"Sabbath is just in the evenings for now. I'm working on obtaining permission to have the whole of the seventh day as a day of rest." Ezekiel fairly glowed with a spark Shiri hadn't seen in a while.

Though he denied any change, a restlessness had taken ahold of him. Hopefully this visit would lift her husband's spirits. A discontent seemed to grow in him daily, as if he was built for grander things. Shiri knew in her mind his shortness of late wasn't directed at her. It was another thing to convince her heart.

Later that evening, she pondered the little things that brought fulfillment—keeping house, caring for Kelila, encouraging The Remnant on Sabbath. Tel-Abib had expanded into a peaceful hub of Hebrew dwellings. Soon after Ezekiel and Shiri had moved into their house, Atta and Dumah had married and settled two doors down. Their world was established. Comfortable.

"That was good. It is good to have someone wanting to learn again." Ezekiel's voice tugged Shiri from the verge of sleep.

She pushed her eyes open. "Did you know Gilead has a son?"

"The elders are getting complacent. I see them through the week, and it's as if they haven't even been to the synagogue on the Sabbath. They have unfair prices; they give their word and aren't genuine." Ezekiel threw the bedding off. "Even Gilead doesn't give his all. He's holding back thorough commitment."

Shiri rolled on her side and tugged the covers to her chin. "He doesn't feel he can be forgiven of his past."

"That's foolishness!" Ezekiel sat up. "Where is it in the law that indicates God will forgive only sins of the righteous?"

"Shh." Shiri glanced at Keli's still form on the pallet in the corner.

"You can't agree with him?"

"No, of course not. I'm just sharing what I observed."

Ezekiel flopped back on the sleeping mat, exhaling noisily. "I just feel…seven months."

Shiri drew him close. "Hmm?"

"In seven months, I would have been ordained as a priest." He propped his hands behind his head.

Ah. This explained the restlessness. Shiri draped her arm across his middle and rested her head on his shoulder. "Yahweh is still using you. You are respected by Hebrews and Chaldeans alike. You have the opportunity to speak to listening ears every Sabbath."

His chest deflated under her cheek, and air from his lungs stirred her hair. "I just feel… I'm not living up to my potential. I was made for more than this."

Shiri's hand clenched. She was a simple woman, content with serving their flock as they had for the last three years. If Ezekiel aspired for greater things, what would be expected of her?

24

The word of the LORD came expressly to Ezekiel the priest, the son of Buzi, in the land of the Chaldeans by the River Chebar; and the hand of the LORD was upon him there.
—Ezekiel 1:3

593 BC

On the fifth day of the fourth month which was in the fifth year of King Coniah's captivity.

Ezekiel constructed his booth from palm fronds. The gentle lapping of the canal conveyed a message of peace while the heat from the sun indicated despair. Unrest. Indecision. Just like the warring factions in his soul.

He tied off the last palm, lowered himself into the shade, and surveyed the desert plain beyond the grand canal. "All right, Yahweh. It's time You and I had a talk." Not that he had the right to demand audience with the Most High.

He roughed his hands through his hair and expelled a breath. "You know what I mean, Lord. What purpose do You have for me?" Crawling out of the booth, he dipped his hand into the water and tried to imagine the flowing current sweeping away his anxiousness.

Ezekiel bowed toward the direction of Jerusalem. "Search my heart and my thoughts. Try me." If he were in the Holy City, he would enter into the fast for the priesthood. Today, the thirtieth anniversary of his birth, and he served not in the temple but the faraway land where the people grew more acclimated to Babylonian culture by the day.

Shiriel's concerned expression floated to his mind's eye. How could he reassure her when he didn't know what plagued him? Now that Kelila was weaned, Shiriel had returned to playing her flute in the palace gardens in the mornings, dropping Kelila off with Atta, two doors down, each day. Gilead came as often as he passed through Babylon.

All things that anchored Ezekiel when his faith longed for more.

"Yahweh, my soul desires Your presence. Like a deer pants for water. You've seen my unrest. What purpose do You have for me?" Ezekiel had every intention of fasting for the whole week, yet already his body sought distraction. *I'm only hungry because I know I'm not supposed to be.*

Wind from the north whipped up, pelting sand at him with such heated intensity that Ezekiel nearly fell into the canal. He shielded his eyes and turned to behold a great cloud thrashing around in a frenzied circle.

"What…?"

The air—oppressively hot for the third hour—crackled, and the cloud was devoured by a raging fire. The flame licked higher and higher, engulfing itself. The inferno passed over Tel-Abib in the distance and lowered as it drew closer. Ezekiel put his hand on his pounding chest. He stood in its path!

He spun around. The booth would be consumed within seconds. An explosion of light arrested his feet before he could jump into the canal. Amber pulsed out of the midst of the fire, revealing four creatures.

The creatures drew near, sparkling like burnished bronze. Hands of men were tucked under four wings, Ezekiel recoiled and shielded his eyes, uncovering them just as quickly. He couldn't peel his eyes away from the grotesque sight of four faces—an eagle, a lion, an ox, and a man—on each man's body.

He stumbled to the right, and the creatures followed his movement.

Without turning or adjusting course.

They just…tracked him, like a wolf intent on its prey.

Ezekiel tripped over a rock and fell on his backside. Hooves of calves dashed to-and-fro, coming straight towards him. Fire and lightning flashed between the creatures. He scrambled backward but couldn't escape the feeling of being watched. He shuddered and passed a hand over his face.

Instead of dissolving, the creatures grew more defined. Beside the hooves, wheels of beryl intertwined together, rims as high as he was tall, with a multitude of eyes all watching. The wheels moved as one when the creatures did, closer, surrounding Ezekiel.

"Yahweh! What madness is this?"

The creatures halted without warning. All the eyes in the wheels lifted to the firmament above. Air on both sides pressed on Ezekiel's chest. He sucked a breath through his teeth, staring at the crystal firmament, so brilliant and clear. What color had the sky been?

The sound of mighty waters rushed in conjuncture with the movement of the creatures' mouths. Ezekiel pressed his hands over his ears but couldn't deafen the volume of the creatures' wings snapping, or the pounding of their fists to their bronze chests—the tumult of a massive marching army clattering to a halt.

The droning of the deafening buzz clarified into a chant that his ears couldn't fathom, but his spirit could. "Holy, holy,

holy is the Lord God Almighty, who was and is and is to come."

Son of Man.

The sound resonated above the crystal firmament, through the earth, and into every fiber of Ezekiel's being. Indeed, the Voice that created the heavens from nothing now addressed him, strengthening and humbling him.

A sapphire throne materialized with the likeness of a man high above it. Ezekiel's gaze traveled up the fire of the legs, bright as the sky after a storm. The prism of color seared his eyes. Still, he couldn't turn away. He had to see. To know.

The Almighty's chest of amber glowed from fire within. Power and grace exuded from the glory of El Shaddai, God Most High.

Falling on his face, Ezekiel covered his head. Oh, that the dirt would swallow him, and the earth bury him. "Oh God! I am unworthy."

Son of Man, stand on your feet and I will speak to you.

He should obey, should take heed, but he couldn't move his limbs.

A breath of air imbued him with honor and strength, lifting him to his feet. "Speak, my King. Your servant listens."

I am sending you to rebellious Judea. Even now, they transgress against me.

"To Judah, my Lord?" The exquisite pattern intricately carved in the rich blue of the sapphire throne mesmerized Ezekiel.

Whether they hear or refuse, they will know a prophet has been in their midst.

"Will they not choose Your ways?" Despair rose within Ezekiel's breast, as if it was *him* the people turned against.

Do not be afraid of their words or dismayed by their looks. You shall speak My words to them whether they listen or not.

Sweat poured down Ezekiel's back as a hand descended from the heavens, unfurling a scroll. Lamentations, mourning, and woe covered the massive scroll front and back.

"No, my Lord. The people have endured much suffering already. Why should I speak if they won't listen?" The thought slipped uncensored through his lips.

You will not be rebellious like the house of Israel. Open your mouth and eat what I give you.

Ezekiel's mouth opened at the command of the Creator. He grimaced and turned his face, unable to close his lips. The judgements that should have soured his insides filled his stomach with the sweetness of honey. The words of unspeakable devastation through destruction filled Ezekiel with knowledge. Each word meant to bring harm warmed his insides with hope in the glory of the Almighty.

If I had sent you to the those who spoke another tongue, they would have repented. Not that impudent, hard-hearted house of Israel. They haven't listened to Me nor you.

I have made your face harder than flint against their anger toward you.

Hardness spread across Ezekiel's cheekbones. He ran a hand across his face, expecting to find granite. He pushed out a jagged breath as his fingers touched flesh.

Son of man, you are My mouthpiece. Receive into your heart all My words. Speak also to the captives whether they hear or not.

The blue from the throne poured into the sky, restoring the color—pale by comparison. The thunder of great waters flowed from the mouths of the creatures. "Blessed is the glory of the Lord from His place." All wings unfurled, touching the one beside it.

A gust of wind lifted Ezekiel in the air. *Wait.* He tumbled along with the current carved away by a river of air, yet his body sat in the booth by the Chebar Canal. A surge of power deposited him in a heap on packed dirt.

Ezekiel shook his head to awake from the trance, and slowly the glittering haziness subsided. *Tel-Abib.* The modest houses created an unofficial courtyard around a gnarled poplar tree. People would congregate under its shade to escape the blistering desert heat. At this time of day, the square was empty but for two elders from the congregation.

"Dumah! Perez. You will not believe what I have seen!" Ezekiel's feet were weighted down as if he dragged them through silt and water. No matter how many steps he took, he made no progress. Had the constitution of his body been transformed? Was this a normal after effect of being in the presence of the One who had formed him then being returned to the sinful world? "My brothers!"

"—Their god, Shamash, is the same. He rides through the sky in his sun-chariot and sees all. He sheds light on the world and rules with justice. Gods and men fear him. Just like Yahweh. It is the same god. Merely a different name."

Ezekiel's skin grew hot, and fury burned in his chest. He raised sluggish hands. "Stop! Yahweh is nothing like Shamash. I forbid you to say that."

Neither man acknowledged Ezekiel. Had they not heard his shout? The conversation unfolded, a grotesque tableau presented before him, but he could not influence how it played out.

Perez shook his head. "I am not sure. Yahweh says there are no other gods beside Him."

"Who is supreme like You in the whole pantheon of gods." Dumah crossed his arms over his chest with exaggerated casualness. "Shamash gave the law to Hammurabi. Yahweh gave the law to Moses."

"But some say that Shamash transforms into Nergal at night and judges the dead with violence, death, and decay. Yahweh wouldn't take a consort, especially not the goddess of the underworld." Perez lowered his voice to a whisper and glanced over his shoulder around the square, yet seemed to stare right through Ezekiel.

Dumah threw back his head and chuckled. "Who alone can judge? Yahweh. Though the Chaldeans have adapted His ways to fit their understanding, He alone judges the living and the dead."

He reached into his sash and withdrew a round amulet with a symbol of a sun on it and tied it around Perez's neck. "Wear this by your heart. It will ward off the evil spirits that plague you with uncertainty. Yahweh brings light to all."

"No!" Ezekiel lunged for Dumah and slammed into an invisible wall.

Dumah drew Perez away, changing the subject to the pattern of the stars.

Bitterness and heat singed through Ezekiel. How could they compare the shining presence of Yahweh to a god of the underworld?

Shiriel and Kelila walked by. Kelila yanked at her hand in attempt to pry herself free from her *ima's* grip and watchful guidance. Just as Israel and Judah had with Yahweh. Again, he could not gather them to himself or draw their attention.

Despair soured Ezekiel's spirit.

The weight of a hand pressed on his shoulder. Who had seen him? Who was aware of his presence? None but the One who knew him in his *ima's* womb.

The hand of the Lord lay strong upon Ezekiel, sustaining him for seven days as he sat unseen amongst the people who put on false pretenses in his presence and now showed their apathy and apostasy in the square of Tel-Abib.

On the seventh day, Yahweh's voice permeated Ezekiel's being.

Son of man, I have made you a watchman for My people. If you give no warning when I speak, he shall die, and I will require his blood at your hand to the

wicked or to the righteous. If you warn him and he doesn't heed. You will deliver your soul.

Monumental pressure and pride warred in Ezekiel's chest. Would the people heed his words?

Arise, go into the plain, and there I shall talk with you.

The hand of the Lord lifted Ezekiel, and in a flash the square of Tel-Abib had transformed into the plain to the east of Babylon. The glory of the Lord shone down like it had at the Chebar Canal.

Ezekiel fell to the ground and again was lifted to stand before Yahweh. What should have been his ordination as a priest was a call to prophecy, placed on him by the glory of God. Like all the prophets before him, the message would not be received.

Ezekiel wept bitterly at the instructions that emerged from his core. He and the message of God's wrath were one.

25

And you, O son of man, surely they will put ropes on you and bind you with them, so that you cannot go out among them, I will make your tongue cling to the roof of your mouth, so that you shall be mute and not be one to rebuke them, for they are a rebellious house. But when I speak with you, I will open your mouth, and you shall speak with them, 'Thus says the LORD God.' He who hears, let him hear; and he who refuses, let him refuse.

—Ezekiel 3:25-27a

O*n the twelfth day of the fourth month which was in the fifth year of King Coniah's captivity.*

Ezekiel tumbled in darkness, unaware of the passage of time. He reached his hands out to break his fall, but they refused to obey, and his face absorbed the impact, hardening like granite. Vileness permeated his thoughts and coursed through his veins. He cried out for salvation, yet his tongue clung to the roof of his mouth.

No! He refused to give in. He had been called by the Most High. Truth brightened at the edge of despair, pulsing faintly, sending flashes of glory and purpose through the dense cloud of doubt.

He who hears let him hear.

A hand pressed on Ezekiel's shoulder. Reassurance of the Lord's presence in spite of the heaviness and immovability of the rest of his body. Cold seeped through his side. Pressure on his left hip and his ribs. His fall ceased.

He opened sluggish eyes to close them against the light. Cool, packed earth beneath him. The heaviness in his body dissipated as the realm of the unseen gave way to the familiar. Prying his eyes open, Ezekiel blinked and the blurry object before his focus became a hand. His—though he had no command over it.

Beyond lay the sunken space that had seated many an ambassador. His house. He searched the room. *Shiriel.* The house lay quiet. With much effort, he trained sensitive eyes on the window beside the door. The sun seemed to be midway across the sky.

Soon the door creaked open, flooding the room with light. Kelila darted in, pulling free from Shiriel. The girl's happy dance consisted of shuffling around in a circle. "Ha. Ha. Ha. Ha."

Shiriel, I am here.

"I'm glad to be home too." Shiriel shut the door against the heat of the sun and scooped up their daughter with smiles and kisses. They spun in a circle, and Shiriel amused Kelila with mouth exercises for the flute.

Kelila blew out her lips in imitation and laughed.

Depositing Kelila on the floor, Shiriel patted the child's bottom. "*Ima's* going to prepare supper. Where is your chariot?"

"Char-i-ot?" Kelila lifted her hands and shoulders.

"Go find it." Shiriel turned to the kitchen, humming.

Drool formed at the corner of Ezekiel's mouth. *Come over here, Kelila. Abba needs help.*

The chariot lay on its side in the middle of the gathering area.

Kelila wandered into the kitchen and scrunched up her little shoulders. "Char-i-ot?"

"I don't know, sweetheart. Go look." Shiriel continued measuring out lentils.

"Help me." Kelila fussed and tugged on Shiriel's skirts.

"Just a moment, Keli. *Ima's* hands are busy." She added water to the mix and pushed the pot over the fire, then replaced the sack in the cellar. "Shall we find it?"

Shiriel offered her hand and wiggled her fingers.

Kelila squawked her refusal.

Exasperation spread across Shiriel's face. She closed her eyes briefly, shook her head, and began searching high and low. "Chariot, where are you?"

Kelila shielded her eyes too. "Where are you?"

Look this way. I am right here.

Shiriel bent to the babe's level with fake surprise. "I think I see something."

Their daughter followed the direction of Shiriel's pointing finger and gasped. "Char-i-ot!" Kelila ran with open arms to the seating area, already making her chariot noise.

Shiriel put her hands on her lower back and stretched, facing Ezekiel.

Look up, Shiriel. I need you.

She turned without a glance his direction.

Oh God, am I still merely an observer? A specter? I can't do this alone.

The hand of Yahweh's presence rested on Ezekiel's shoulder.

I am with you.

I know, Lord, but all the prophets had support. Jeremiah has Baruch. Elisha attended Elijah. Moses had Aaron and Joshua.

At the moment the Hand lifted, Kelila glanced toward him.

"Baba, Baba!" She rushed to him, shoulders leading the way.

Thank You, Yahweh.

She squatted and stroked his beard, babbling and leaning in with noisy and wet kisses.

His hands wouldn't embrace his daughter. *Kelila, get Ima.* He tried to smile, tried to gesture, but only succeeded in slightly shifting his face.

Kelila plopped against Ezekiel's chest and whispered secrets only she understood in his ear. She burrowed under his arm and covered her face, as if they shared a grand hiding spot.

How long would he lie there if she grew bored and found something else to do? He concentrated on his fingers, straining against the confines of his body.

Shiriel still had her back to them, humming, oblivious.

Kelila sat up, and Ezekiel's head thudded to the ground. Concern filled the child's eyes, and she squeezed his face. "Baba?"

I need Ima. His fingers extended in a curve.

Grabbing hold, Kelila nodded and wagged her finger, sternly scolding much like Shiriel did. She braced her hands on the ground, pushed her bottom in the air, grunted, and righted herself. "Baba, Baba, Baba!" She ran with blessed focus and collided with Shiriel's leg. "Baba, Baba."

Shiriel continued needing the dough. "*Abba* should be home soon."

Kelila tugged on Shiriel's skirt. "Baba come."

"I know, love." She scooped up the girl. "I miss *Abba*, too. Soon."

Her back rigid, Kelila flung herself back with a shriek, forcing Shiriel to release her.

Ezekiel wished he could laugh, for once glad of his daughter's willful spirit.

"Keli, you must show respect to *Ima*," Shiriel's voice carried a warning.

With a gasp, Kelila clapped hands over her cheeks. "Baba! There he is. Come see."

"*Abba's* not here. Soon." Mercifully, Shiriel allowed herself to be yanked along.

Well done, Kelila!

Shiriel came his direction, peering over her shoulder toward the door. "Sweetheart, *Abba* will come from outside when—" She broke off as she noticed him. Her eyes widened, and she covered her mouth. "Ezekiel! What has happened?"

She flung herself beside him, her hands hovering over him.

Ezekiel strained to loose his tongue.

Shiriel framed his face with her hands and tears pooled in her eyes. "Shh."

"There he is!" Kelila clapped her hands and patted Shiriel's arm.

"I am so sorry! You were trying to tell me the whole time, weren't you?" She dashed tears from her cheek and scanned Ezekiel. "Can you move? Kelila, go fetch *Abba* a cushion for his head."

"A cushion?" Kelila showed no indication she intended to rise.

"Now." Shiriel's voice rose, and her chin quivered. She leaned up. "*Ima* is going to get it first."

Kelila shrieked and engaged, rushing to the piled cushions. She selected her favorite—the one with blue silk tassels on each corner—and dragged it backwards.

Shiriel cradled Ezekiel's head on her lap. "Have you been stung by a scorpion? A snake? Oh, Yahweh, he can't move!"

Ezekiel closed his eyes while Shiriel gently lowered his head to the cushion. *Thank You for granting my petition.*

A kiss pressed against his temple, this one moist from tears. "I'm going to get help. Stay here."

His fingers curled at the touch of her hand. *Don't leave me.*

"You squeezed my hand!" Shiriel's smile dislodged more worried tears. She pressed his hand against her cheek. "I'll be back as soon as I can with the physician. Keli, let's go. We have to go see Atta."

"Atta?" Poor girl. What went through her little mind?

The house grew as silent as his voice. *How am I to get Your message to the people if my words don't come?*

The shadows had lengthened before Shiriel rushed in, followed by the physician from the corner booth in the marketplace.

"— I found him on his side, unable to move. In this same position." She knelt beside him.

Ezekiel would have welcomed the kiss she held back.

The physician poked and prodded Ezekiel, stretching out each of his limbs. "Hmm. He's paralyzed, all right. I would venture a guess he's been struck by the sun. The gods are showing their disfavor and have taken away his thoughts and abilities."

Shiriel pinched the bridge of her nose and shook her head. "I believe he can still think. I'm sure of it. I can see it in his eyes."

"He can't move or speak. Your husband isn't in control of himself."

Her hands came around Ezekiel's face. "You can hear me, can't you?"

Ezekiel strained to nod. The sound of sucking through straw came from his throat.

Shiriel turned hopeful eyes to the physician. "He can move his fingers. Ezekiel, do you think you can write on a tablet?"

Air sucked through that straw in his throat.

Darting to the jars that held his writing supplies, Shiriel grabbed a tablet, missing the physician's raised eyebrows and skeptical expression. She pressed Ezekiel's fingers around the stylus and steadied the moist clay tablet.

Ezekiel closed his eyes and drew in a prayer. *Please, Yahweh, be with my hand.* His hand strengthened, and he could hold the stylus naturally. His chest heaved and tears sprang to his eyes. He pressed in the clay, thinking through each word. There wasn't space enough or time to convey his whole week.

"Yahweh came to me. I am bound one day for each year Israel and Judah strayed."

Shiriel covered a sob. "How long?"

"Three hundred ninety days Israel. Forty days." His hand cramped, and he squeezed his eyes shut.

Shiriel's gentle touch removed the stylus from his grip and straightened his fingers. "What do I do?"

The physician heaved a sigh. "He would be better off if you surrendered him to the sanatorium with all the other cripples."

"That is not…That is not the way of our people. He says he will be restored from this."

"You asked for my opinion." The man muttered in Akkadian.

"Forgive me. I mean no disrespect." Shiriel rubbed Ezekiel's hand as she responded in Hebrew. "He would be better with family. We can care for him without violating the laws of our God."

Throwing up his hands, the physician turned toward the door.

"I meant to say, what I can do to make him comfortable? To care for him."

The man heaved a bothered sigh and studied Shiriel. He shook his head with another sigh and brusquely yanked Ezekiel's legs this way and that. His arms were next, as the physician showed Shiriel how to exercise his stiff limbs. Most humiliating of all—the physician slit his trousers and roughly girded his loins just as they had done to Kelila. He stared at the pile of pallets in humiliation.

"You will need to rotate and raise him up." The physician

gestured and demonstrated. "So he can relieve himself. You will rub salve on his hip and side. Or he will develop sores. Put a cushion between his knees. Are you sure about this? The strain on you will be monumental."

Shiriel's squeeze brought Ezekiel's gaze to her pale but determined expression. "Yes, my lord. He belongs with me."

Tears leaked from Ezekiel's eyes. Shiriel wiped his cheek and gave a wobbly smile.

The physician rolled his eyes and stood. "Come to my booth tomorrow. I will give you a salve to rub on the skin that presses on the ground."

"Yes, my lord. Thank you for your time." Shiriel followed him to the door and pressed something in his hand.

The man's countenance lit up. "I will prepare the salve."

Nodding, Shiriel leaned her head on the door frame for a long moment. "I must retrieve Keli. I'll return shortly."

Shiriel returned and finished the food preparation silently. Kelila's cheerful disposition deteriorated as the evening grew later than her young body was accustomed to. After Shiriel hand-fed Ezekiel, and monitored Kelila's intake, she scooped up their daughter.

"Let's get you to bed, shall we?" Shiriel waived Kelila's arm to him and left the room.

Ezekiel's knees pressed together, and his hip ground into the floor. His ribs were crushed with his weight.

Yahweh, how? Even now, my body will fall backward. Pain intensified in his joints and shoulders. Three-hundred ninety days on this side?

26

Son of man, I have made you a watchman for the house of Israel.
—Ezekiel 3:17a

When Shiri came down into the main room, Ezekiel's face was red, and the vein in his forehead bulged. He strained against himself, eyes closed, fingers moving to form a claw.

Her heart squeezed. Ezekiel was in prime physical condition, yet had been reduced to being cared for like an infant. She drew in a fortifying breath against the emotions and lay at his back, slipping her arm around his waist. The tension in his body eased, then heightened, his claw-like hand twitching.

Shiri leaned on her elbow and rubbed his arm and shoulder. "It's all right. I'm here." When his tense muscles eased, she peered around at his face. "What do you need?"

Ezekiel's eyes darted wildly side to side.

"Do you want a drink?" She pushed herself to a sitting position.

Immediately, his hand thrashed, and he opened his mouth, but no words came.

Tears blurred Shiri's vision. "I'm sorry, I don't know how I can help you." She reached over him and caught his twitching hand.

His fingers curled slightly over hers, and a rasping sound came from his throat.

She stroked his cheek with her other hand and smiled with braveness she didn't feel. "It will be all right. We'll figure it out."

Ezekiel's eyebrows jerked and his fingers tightened.

"Did you want my hand?"

A slight squeeze.

Shiri smiled and brushed a kiss to his forehead. "Allow me to adjust."

Ezekiel rasped when her hand slipped from his.

"Give me a moment—" Shiri lay on her left side, folded his grasping fingers through hers, and raised their joined hands to his chest. "Does it hurt to move like this?"

He brushed her thumb.

She pressed a kiss to his back and held him tight. His breathing evened in sleep, but worry plagued her. More than four hundred days? What would become of them? Would Ezekiel be able to carry on his overseer duties? Did Yahweh tell Ezekiel what was to come?

Her joints ached. *If my husband has to endure four hundred days, I can manage one night.*

Ezekiel's breathing centered her thoughts. If this was of Yahweh, He would equip them to fulfill His call.

The next morning, Shiri awakened to the smell of urine. Ezekiel's arm lay across his eyes.

"Did you move your arm? That's wonderful!" Of course, he did. Who else would move it? Shiri rubbed the muscles in her neck. Guilt arrested her stretching. Ezekiel couldn't ease his aching muscles. Her foot tingled as she rose and fetched a new robe and clean clothes from upstairs.

She returned and touched his arm. "Ezekiel? I'm sorry. We should do this before Keli awakens."

No response.

Shiri drew back his robe, nearly gagging with the stench. *Yahweh, help me.*

The work indeed was strenuous, more so than Shiri had anticipated. Perspiration traveled her spine by the time she managed to wriggle the bedclothes from beneath her husband, change, and clean him. Muscles aching, she wiped her forehead on her sleeve, rearranged Ezekiel's robe, and carried the soiled linens outside to the large laundry cauldron and poured water over it.

A glance at the sun's position sped her movements. "Keli, *Ima's* coming to prepare you for the day." She darted up the stairs and into the bedroom. Perhaps she could get Dumah and the other men to transfer Ezekiel onto the bed.

Keli stirred and stretched. She fussed as Shiri lifted her and tugged away from the comb.

"Sweetheart, *Ima's* in a hurry. We must move faster."

"No. My do it."

The sun climbed higher. "Fine." Shiri scooped her up and carried the comb and her independent daughter down the stairs.

"My do it. My do it."

Shiri deposited Keli near Ezekiel and retrieved bread and cheese from the cellar, groaning at the sight of her own crumpled tunic. "Can I leave Keli with you? I need to dress myself."

She plopped the food next to them as Keli's comb snagged on a tangle.

Keli squawked. "*Ima* do it."

"I have to prepare for the day." Shiri took the stairs two at a time, guilt pouring over her as Keli's fussing turned into full-on crying. She donned a fresh linen dress and retied her sash on the way down. "Come, Keli, time to go see Atta."

"Atta?" Smears of soggy bread adorned Keli's tunic and hair.

Shiri hung her head. "Yes, dear. Ezekiel, I have to play today." How could she leave as her husband lay on his side with only movement in his arms?

But if she didn't report for duty, there'd be no rations, no further employment, or worse. She knelt beside Ezekiel and rubbed at the ache in her chest. "I can stay."

Comprehension flashed across Ezekiel's face, and he moved his face slightly to the side, mouthing 'no.'

"I'd rather stay to care for you. You know that, right?" Shiri rested her hand on Ezekiel's face.

He patted her knee, then pointed to the door.

Her flute was still upstairs. She rubbed her temples. "Do you need anything? Can you eat this alright?"

Ezekiel picked up a round of bread and pressed it into her hand.

"Thank you, I'll be back after the seventh hour."

One more trip upstairs, a fussing toddler on her hip reaching for her bread, and they made it out of the house. *I am going to be late.* She deposited Keli two houses down with a hurried explanation. Shiri glanced at the sun, abandoned all decorum, and began to run. As she careened down the street by the river, the *quffa* began to pull away from the dock.

"Wait! Please!"

The ferry man looked back, and a smile spread across his animated face. He shouted in Akkadian, cheering her on with his flailing arm. He reached out for her hand and propelled her into the boat.

Shiri clutched the side of the basket-like *quffa*, as it jostled with her momentum. "Thank you." She nodded to the other passengers as the pilot plunked his oar into the water. Ezekiel had not ridden the ferry with her for a whole week, yet today, loneliness overwhelmed her. Her husband was paralyzed at home. Had he been suffering this whole week? What had he seen? *Yahweh came to me.* Ezekiel's words scratched on the tablet brought odd comfort.

The shadow of the southern palace fell over Shiri as the *quffa* jostled against the dock. The other passengers disembarked, and Shiri scrambled out behind them, thanking the pilot as he shoved off.

The brassy sound of the gong marking the hour spurred Shiri into motion. She ran all the way to the palace complex, then slowed her stride and regulated her breathing as she slipped into the hanging garden just as the harpist entered from the far gate.

Bless the man's tendency to be late. She hurried to the bench where the musician with the *oud* waited. Pressing against the stitch in her side, she breathed in through her nose while the harpist took the last few strides.

The *oud* player plucked out a melody, and Shiri began to play the Babylonian tune. Her thoughts wandered around the simple song. *Yahweh, I am so unprepared for this.*

I will uphold you with My righteous right hand. The truth Isaiah documented from Yahweh strengthened her like an intricate melody.

At the midday break, the harpist and the *oud* player seemed to take forever, tugging at Shiri's patience. *Hurry up.* She closed her eyes and trained her thoughts on the gentle cascading of the waterfall across the way and breathed in the heady fragrance of roses. The rose, with its soft petals and vibrant colors, was carefully tended and cultivated. The nurturing care given each plant did not cease when the blooms fell in the winter. Indeed, the dormant months were more dependent on the gardener's caring touch.

This is only a season.

What if Ezekiel needed her? She rubbed her bruised hip.

If she was stiff and sore, how much more would he be? Could she alleviate his pressure in any way?

The harpist whistled, indicating the royal women entering the garden. The unspoken rule amongst the three musicians—unspoken because she didn't fully understand what they said — one of them would always be at the ready for times like now. She lifted her flute and trilled out a tune befitting a bird's song and a stroll in the lush gardens.

When the replacement musicians finally appeared, Shiri made her way back to Tel-Abib with haste. She strained her neck to look at her house as she knocked on Atta's door. *Please let Keli be ready to go.*

The door opened, and Atta flung her arms around Shiri.

Impatience stirred inside Shiri like boiling stew. She patted Atta's back. "Is Keli ready? I am anxious to be with Ezekiel."

"Keli, *Ima's* here." Concern edged Atta's eyes. "So, what happened exactly?"

"I returned home yesterday and..." Shiri glanced toward her silent house, and emotion clogged her throat. "And… Ezekiel lay there. He can't speak or move. Except his arms."

"I'm so sorry." Atta put her hand on Shiri's arm.

The door frame blurred as tears formed. "Um... he said—wrote—he had seen Yahweh, and he was meant to be like this because of Israel's and Judah's sins."

"Is he a prophet?"

"He went on that fast to seek Yahweh's will." Shiri laughed despite herself. "Wouldn't it be nice if Yahweh always responded with such promptness?"

Atta chuckled. "What an honor. A prophetess in our midst."

Shiri blinked. "Yahweh hasn't called me. I'm just the wife of the prophet."

"How do you suppose your husband's message will be heard if he can't speak or move?" Atta raised an eyebrow.

At that moment, Keli came full speed around the corner, saving Shiri from responding.

"There's my sweet girl! I missed you!" Shiri knelt to intercept the wild tumbleweed.

"*Ima. Ima.*" Keli rushed with open arms, babbling about how Atta did something Shiri couldn't make out.

Keli put her hands on Shiri's cheeks with a serious whisper.

Shiri exchanged amused glances with Atta. "Is that right? Sounds like you had an exciting day. Shall we go see *Abba*?"

"Yes. Baba." Keli grabbed Shiri's hand without a backward glance.

"Thank you, Atta. We will see you tomorrow."

"Oh, Shiri, Keli and I made a meal for you. I took the liberty of putting it in your house."

Tears blurred Shiri's vision. "That is so thoughtful of you. Thank you."

Atta squeezed her hand with an expression of sympathy. "Yassah is coming over today. We will be carding wool in the cool of the garden. Come join us."

"That sounds lovely." Shiri smiled. "Let me see how the day unfolds."

Ducking out Atta's door, Shiri kept a firm grip on Keli's wrist so the little escape artist wouldn't get trampled on the short distance home. "Did you help Atta prepare food?"

Keli ignored her and rushed inside to rediscover where she had last put her chariot.

"Ezekiel? We are home." Shiri glanced toward the kitchen, sure enough a pot simmered over the fire. She turned to find Ezekiel reclining on all the pallets and blankets, his back against the wall. "Did Atta arrange this?"

His hands constricted, closing into fists.

"Your hands! That's wonderful!" Shiri knelt on the mountain of pallets and kissed his hand.

Ezekiel squinted with a look of determination.

"Have you given any thought to how you will share Yahweh's words?" She bent Ezekiel's leg as the physician had shown. "Can you press against me?"

He strained but couldn't counter the pressure Shiri applied.

"You can write it out, and I can get Dumah to speak it at the Sabbath gathering."

Agitation tensed the muscles Shiri massaged.

Ezekiel dug his stylus deep into the clay. "No."

He wrote again, and Shiri leaned to see his words.

"Yahweh will put the words in my mouth."

"Should I see if Dumah can lead a prayer?"

Ezekiel dismissed the conversation with a wave of his hand, and with great effort, he draped his arm over his face.

27

Therefore you shall set your face toward the siege of Jerusalem; your arm shall be uncovered, and you shall prophesy against it. And surely I will restrain you so that you cannot turn from one side to another till you have ended the days of your siege.
—*Ezekiel 4:7-8*

The heavy iron plate clattered to the ground, more cacophonic than an ill-timed cymbal. Shiri shifted the clay tablets under her arm. Surely, all those assembling for Sabbath synagogue stared as she disrupted their pleasantries, but she couldn't bring herself to check.

"Allow me help you with that." A man's arms clad in leather cuffs stretched into view.

"Thank you." Shiri straightened as Gilead did. Tears—never far these days—stung in the back of her eyes.

"I came as soon as I could." Concern lined Gilead's face.

"Ezekiel will be glad to see you." Would he? He grew agitated with all the attention. Shiri amended her thought. "I am glad to see you. How are you doing in General Vakhtang's service?"

Gilead's broad shoulders lifted. "He seems to take pleasure in singling me out, but he hasn't reassigned me or had me killed."

"He sees your loyalty and your value." Shiri's heart ached. Gilead's assignment would wear away at the strongest faith. "Yahweh will use you as you honor Him."

Her anxious glances toward the crowd and her hand pressed against her jittery insides probably did not escape his intuitive scrutiny.

"What's going on with you?"

Apart from the expected concern for Ezekiel? Shiri tried—and failed—to pass off her anxiety. "Um…I…There's a lot to do, and it is past time for the meeting to begin."

Gilead scanned the overfull room. Another family entered, the women and children going to the left and the husband joining the men on the right. He took the tablets from Shiri. "They'll be fine. Curiosity is an extender of patience. Where do you want these?"

Shiri briefly closed her eyes. Why was accepting help so difficult? She forced a smile. "Thank you. Over by Ezekiel. He needs them for an illustration."

Gilead's eyes widened as his gaze landed on her husband. Unlike the others, Gilead managed to suppress the mortification in favor of genuine concern.

Please don't let Ezekiel see this as charity. Shiri rolled her shoulders back and shot a grateful smile at Atta who occupied Keli. She collected her flute and the scroll Ezekiel had meticulously written as the latest family deposited a bulging cloth bag on the preparation table.

"Thank you so much," Shiri mouthed.

Pity cloaked the woman's eyes. She nodded and smiled too brightly.

Upon hearing of Ezekiel's condition, all the neighbors had given generously from their supplies. There had been many odd looks as Shiri explained countless times they could only accept the lentils, millet, wheat, barley, spelt and beans. She came to recognize the glazed-over look that followed her explanation of Yahweh's command. But their gifts freed her up from going to the market this week, and she spent the time learning how to combine these ingredients into a palatable bread.

"Thank You, Yahweh, for Your generous provision," Shiri murmured and made her way to the east wall where Ezekiel lay. "And thank You for relenting on us using human waste for fuel as I make this bread." She shuddered as she knelt in Ezekiel's line of sight on the women's side. Collecting the cow dung made her nearly wretch as it was.

Dumah rose and extended his arms to embrace the congregation. "Shabbat shalom."

"Sabbath peace to you," they echoed back.

"Before we begin," Dumah glanced at Shiri for confirmation. "Ezekiel and Shiri would like to thank all of you for your kindness and generosity. You have displayed Yahweh's provision in giving food supplies."

Shiri moistened her lips as curious and compassionate gazes turned her direction.

"As you have heard, Ezekiel has been struck down by Yahweh." Dumah raised his hands to quiet the murmur spreading across the room. "We have faith that this condition is only temporary."

The teacher from one of the synagogues in the city of Babylon called out, "How can you be sure?"

Shiri straightened. "Because the God of our fathers gave His word to my husband." Ezekiel's expression didn't change, but Gilead's nod encouraged her.

Dumah stepped to Shiri's side. "Yahweh has appointed Ezekiel to the role of prophet. As with all the prophets who have gone before, Yahweh has a reason for what He requires of His chosen ones. Let us begin."

Shiri exhaled gratefully as Dumah began the Shema.

"Hear, oh Israel, the Lord our God is one—"

The congregation joined in, their voices filling the room. "You shall love the Lord your God with all your heart and with all your soul and with all your strength."

Dumah bowed his head and raised his hands. "Prepare our hearts, oh Lord, for the wisdom that will be imparted. Look upon us and be merciful to us, as is Your custom to those who love Your name."

"Amen. Let it be so," Shiri whispered.

Huz, the musician who played the kinnor, created a soulful tune, and his fingers danced over the strings. Shiri's flute traveled the melody like a prayer.

An atmosphere of worship descended upon the congregation. Shiri lowered her instrument, closed her eyes, and lifted her heart's desire in song. "*Create in me a clean heart, oh God, and renew a right spirit within me*—"

Huz halted his strumming and lent his voice to hers.

At the end of the song, Shiri opened her eyes to the reverent crowd. Gilead lifted one hand in surrender, and his mouth moved silently.

Dumah called on someone to recite from the law of Moses, and the people intoned together, "Blessed are You, Lord God of our fathers."

Shiri passed the scroll to Dumah. Ezekiel had grown agitated each time she brought Dumah up, but what choice did she have? Dumah read more clearly than Perez, and there weren't any other elders appointed at the time.

The people leaned forward with bated breath as Dumah unfurled the words Yahweh had pressed upon Ezekiel.

"By the hand of Ezekiel, being of sound mind—"

Shiri scanned the enraptured faces in the crowd as Dumah read of the creatures. Some shivered, some raised their hands in worship, some crossed their arms, yet all sat spell-bound.

"—And above the firmament over their heads was the likeness of a throne in appearance like a sapphire stone; on the likeness of the throne was a likeness with the appearance of a man high above it—"

Wonder sent a shiver down Shiri's arms, as had done each time she had read the scroll. What would it be like to be in the presence of God Almighty? She glanced at Ezekiel's stiff form. Would the crippling glory be worth coming before God?

"—His waist upward I saw, as it were, the color of amber with the appearance of fire all around within it—" Dumah lowered the scroll and glared at Shiri. "What have you given me to read?"

Shiri's gaze darted to Ezekiel and back. "What do you mean?"

Dumah gripped the top of the parchment and tugged as if it would tear like papyrus. "You can't read this. To have it written, indeed, is blasphemous."

Her mouth dropped open.

"No one can see the form of God and live."

The crowd gasped.

"We will hear the prophecy of the Lord but will not hear this trash." Dumah thrust the scroll to Shiri and stalked to his place.

Heat rushed up Shiri's face. She glanced to Ezekiel. *What should I do?*

Ezekiel brushed his hands off, and his head tipped slightly side to side.

But Yahweh came to you. Surely, He was meant to be shared.

Ezekiel motioned for the tablets, and Shiri knelt by his side, cradling the precious words of life beside her. She handed her husband the first tablet. *Please, Lord, let them hear.*

With speed and quality that would shame Chaldean relief sculptors, Ezekiel scratched out a realistic depiction of the temple and the north-eastern wall of Jerusalem. He reached for the next tablet.

Shiri stood the tablet against the prepared ledge.

"What is it?" A loud whisper traveled from the back of the room.

"Is that the temple?"

"He has captured it brilliantly."

Ezekiel reached for the third tablet, and on it went until Jerusalem stretched across five tablets.

A smattering of applause filled the room.

"It signifies the steadfastness of the Holy City and how we shall return to all its splendor!"

But Ezekiel wasn't through. He directed Shiri and Gilead to place the pre-formed, hardened clay siege mounds against the tablets and battering rams up against the bottom of the ledge in front of Jerusalem.

Each piece Shiri situated felt like a spike against her heart. She placed the replicas of tents to the north-west of the temple.

The murmurs of the congregation grew louder. "Why are they making war against Jerusalem?"

"It's showing how Yahweh will deliver us from our enemies, as He delivered Hezekiah from the Assyrian army."

Ezekiel shook his head and grabbed at the iron plate. His white-knuckled fingers slipped off the smooth surface as he tried to move it.

Gilead picked the iron up with two hands. "Where would you like it to go?" Ezekiel patted the pallet beside him. Gilead leaned the plate against Ezekiel's side. "Like this?"

Nodding, Ezekiel lifted his arm with great concentration and pushed at his sleeve, sliding it up to his shoulder.

"What does it mean?" Dumah glanced from the scenes to the terrible expression of hardness on Ezekiel's face.

Gilead blinked, coming out of a stupor. "It is a military

gesture. To uncover your arm means the certainty of the event —the siege of Jerusalem in this case."

Ezekiel dipped his chin in acknowledgement.

"Jerusalem's destruction is set. It cannot be changed or redirected." Gilead pressed his hands to the side of his head.

Shiri covered her gasp.

Dumah crossed his arms and tapped his sandalled foot. "What of the iron plate?"

"Thus, says the Lord God—"

Shiri whirled around. Ezekiel's voice transcended his previous vocal excellence.

"—This iron plate is a wall between Me and the city of Jerusalem. My face is set against My people because they have set their hearts against Me."

Ezekiel fell silent, and a buzz of whispers spread over the congregation. He met Shiri's gaze, the determination on his face reiterating what he had instructed her earlier.

A lump formed in Shiri's throat, and the back of her eyes burned. Before she could convince herself to resist, she knelt at Ezekiel's side and reached over him for the rope she had previously deposited. The hemp fibers slivered into the sensitive skin on her fingers as she tucked the end under his thumb and loosely wrapped it around his extended wrists.

He brushed her hand and mouthed, "Do it."

Shiri blinked rapidly, sending tears down her face. She tugged the stiff rope tighter, until the pressure left white bands on his flesh. Gulping back a sob, she wiped her arm across her eyes. Her hands shook and refused to form a proper knot.

Ezekiel's face contorted with pain, yet she had to continue.

Again, leather clad wrists reached in at her time of desperation, cinching the rope with efficiency.

Shiri sat back on her heels as Gilead tied Ezekiel's ankles, trussing him like a lamb for slaughter. Her husband's body, a symbolic offering of the role of prophet. Shiri's chest shook with suppressed sobs, and she felt the weight of the people's stares.

Glancing from Dumah's skeptical expression to Gilead's pale face, Shiri pressed her lips together. Who would expound on the meaning?

She stood, and, against her capabilities, her mouth opened and she spoke. "The job of a priest is to intercede on behalf of the nation." Shiri swept her arm toward Ezekiel, and her throat threatened to close. "Yahweh has hardened His face like stone to our pleas of deliverance. This is the time of His judgment. And as such, your priest has been bound. Forbidden to plead on your behalf."

"There are other priests." Dumah scowled at her.

"Are there other priests who have heard a direct word from Yahweh? Or seen Him?"

Dumah strode toward her with hands fisted at his sides. "Yahweh will have mercy. It isn't in His character to destroy His Holy City. You are out of line. Who are you—a woman—to instruct the congregation?"

In a flash of gold, Gilead stepped in front of Shiri, guarding her from Dumah's advance.

The elder hesitated.

"She is like the prophetess, Deborah. Stepping up when the men around her refuse to obey the call of the Lord." Gilead's charge strengthened and frightened Shiri.

She pressed on her middle, and her mouth went dry.

Gilead turned his head toward her. "Carry on, Shiri. What else would Yahweh have us know?"

Shiri buried her hands in the folds of her tunic to keep from chewing on her nails. Sweat beaded on her back, and she drew air in through her nose.

She cast a glance at the disgruntled Dumah. At Gilead's encouraging nod, she gazed upon the faces hungry for direction and cleared her throat. "The iniquity of Israel and Judah has been laid upon my husband. He will remain this way, one day for each year our fathers rebelled against God."

"You are happy about this?" Dumah scoffed.

"My husband is suffering. What do you think?" Shiri's voice cracked. "I would have you turn your hearts to Yahweh with all that is in you, so Ezekiel won't have to bear *your* iniquity."

The bold words flew from her mouth before she could censor them. *What have I done?* She could feel the disapproval rolling in waves from the women's side.

Dumah shoved his nose in the air and pivoted. The elders from the other synagogues followed piously, and the congregation rose as one.

"May the Lord bless and keep you." Gilead's voice carried across the room, halting the mass exodus.

Dumah—the elder who should have led the Aaronic blessing—glared with narrowed eyes at Gilead. At the conclusion, he turned on his heel and led the retreat.

Would they return next week? Did they not see the indications of Yahweh's judgment? They had been enslaved by a pagan people and deported from the Holy City. Their circumstances would continue to unravel unless they turned their hearts once again to Yahweh.

Shiri exhaled. She had broken protocol to a massive degree. Would Ezekiel be unhappy with her?

If she hadn't spoken up, who would have defended the name of the Lord?

28

Surely I will cut off the supply of bread in Jerusalem; they shall eat bread by weight and with anxiety, and shall drink water by measure and with dread.
—*Ezekiel 4:16b*

Gilead glowered at the backs of the departing people. His fingers itched. What he wouldn't give to fashion arrows of truth to pierce through their indifference and calloused attitudes. He slanted a glance at Shiri's sagging shoulders. Nobody should be attacked in their own house.

She passed her hand over her eyes, and Gilead noticed dark circles. Stepping over a clay siege mound, she paused before the tablet bearing the temple. "I'm sorry."

"There's nothing to apologize for." Gilead couldn't read Ezekiel's expression. "They need to see their sin does affect people."

Shiri shifted the iron plate off Ezekiel's side, jumping back as it crashed to the floor. She lay her hand on his arm. "Can I get you anything?"

Keli toddled up, fussing and pulling at Shiri's sleeve.

Gilead squatted beside them. "Why don't you and Keli get some rest. I can straighten up down here."

She glanced at Ezekiel. "Oh, I couldn't."

"I can do whatever Ezekiel needs." Gilead offered his hand.

Keli's squawk tipped Shiri's scale of indecision. She leaned in Ezekiel's line of vision. "I will be back as soon as Keli falls asleep."

"You'll do no such thing." Gilead held her elbow as she struggled to her feet. "You'll be back when *you* have slept. Ezekiel will be fine. It'll give us a chance to catch up."

Shiri's expression remained doubtful, but she did scoop up the cranky child and trudged to the stairs. "Oh, Gilead, if he needs—"

"We will be fine."

"But—"

Gilead crossed his arms. "Shiri. I can handle it. Go." He waited until he heard her footsteps above him. He turned to Ezekiel. "You should encourage her to get help."

Ezekiel glowered at him with an indecipherable intensity. Was this the man's common countenance, or did he resent the suggestion? Perhaps both.

"What do you need?"

Ezekiel brushed his hand away.

"Do you and Shiri have signals or anything?"

The priest pointed to the tablets still displayed like the mosaic walls of Nebuchadnezzar's throne room.

"You write everything? Sounds tedious."

This time Ezekiel gave a definitive glare.

Gilead smudged out the southern corner of Jerusalem and didn't hide his grin. Ezekiel would be better off if he kept his humor up. "What was it like in the presence of God?"

Ezekiel gestured to the rolled scroll and wrapped his fingers in a fist.

"I'd love to read it." Gilead pushed the clay tablet under Ezekiel's hand. "What was He like?"

A long, slow blink.

Gilead crossed his arms. "You'd be better off engaging than moping."

Ezekiel glared and picked up the stylus. "Terrible. Unfettered." He rubbed it out with the side of his hand. "Free. Yet a burden for the people."

"Is there more of the message?" Gilead planted his hand on his knee. "Was it meant for the exiles only?"

Ezekiel rotated the tablet. "Jerusalem."

They would receive it less favorably than those in Babylon. "Any idea how to get the message out?"

The stylus dug through the clay aggressively, and Gilead repositioned himself so he could read as Ezekiel wrote.

"Imprisoned in Babylon. In my body. I'm appointed prophet. Can't act on behalf of people. Here or Jerusalem. How am I supposed to do this?" He flung the stylus away and covered his face in the crook of his arm.

Gilead raised his eyebrows. Though justified, discouragement wasn't what he had come to expect from his mentor. He pushed Ezekiel's arm. "You ask and accept help. I leave for Jerusalem next week. I can deliver the message to Seraiah. Possibly Jeremiah."

The arm came off Ezekiel's face. He pointed at the stylus.

"You need a stack of styli beside you." Gilead stretched for the writing utensil, barely nicking it. Grunting, he extended on his side and slid it to Ezekiel and pushed himself upright.

Ezekiel scribbled on the tablet. "Easier to just get up."

"Ha, ha. Aren't you the funny one?" Gilead smudged out the marks and waited for the new inscription.

"Vakhtang?"

That would be a hindrance. General Vakhtang personally searched everything Gilead brought along. "We'll think of something. It wouldn't be the first time Yahweh has hidden something for His purpose."

After a moment the stylus scratched into the clay. "What's new with you?"

Gilead scanned the words again. This would normally be where he shared his woes and Ezekiel would set him on the right path. He blew out a breath. What right had he to complain about Vakhtang's mistreatment in light of Ezekiel's ailments? "Talk for another day."

How could he transport the message without arousing the suspicion of his Hebrew-hating master? He could memorize it. The thickness of the scroll halted that thought. His mind couldn't retain information with the clarity of a younger man.

He studied the pallet of blankets. His bones ached from just a short time. Was there anything he could do to relieve the pressure Ezekiel must be feeling even through the stack of blankets? Something like the frame of the loom with a suspended blanket or leather straps? Could he obtain wood for the frame?

He was still at work when Shiri descended the stairs appearing more rested. She smiled at him before sitting beside Ezekiel and leaning close to whisper something in his ear.

Ezekiel covered his face with his arm.

Shiri straightened her shoulders and crossed to Gilead. "What are you working on?"

"Trying to come up with a frame that will relieve the pressure." He scanned her face. "You wouldn't happen to know how we can sneak a scroll to Jerusalem, would you?"

"I could sew it into—" She scanned his short tunic and wrapped trousers. "Hmm… The inside of your satchel?"

"You don't think the stitches would show through?"

Shiri pursed her lips. "You're probably right." She propped her hands on her hips and scanned the room.

Gilead kept his gaze on the peg he pounded, coupling two corners. "Is he able to work?"

"Yes. I deliver his reports in the morning and collect his duties and assignments in the afternoon." Shiri's smile didn't hide the worry behind her eyes. "What about under a saddle blanket?"

"The scroll? How big is it unfurled?"

They walked together to Ezekiel's side, and Shiri spread it wide with a questioning glance. "What do you think?"

Ezekiel grunted low and guttural.

"We're thinking under a saddle blanket." She turned to Ezekiel, who swatted his hand in dismissal.

Gilead's gaze narrowed. He carried the parchment to the floor of the common room.

Shiri followed, folding a blanket. "He's disappointed. He'd prefer to be taking the message himself. He feels useless."

"He doesn't need to be a grouch," Gilead muttered.

"I'm sure he doesn't feel well. Hopefully this bed will help." Shiri held up the quartered blanket. "How is this?"

"It should be about right." Gilead stepped back while she spread the blanket over the parchment. "You're doing well, Shiri."

She flashed an unconvinced smile. "It doesn't seem that way to me."

"I'm going to petition the men in the congregation to help with Ezekiel's exercises and such."

"That would be very helpful. Thank you." Shiri inspected the layers. "I think I can add a third layer to envelop the scroll. Will you be able to bring me a camel blanket?"

Gilead studied the young woman. The steadfastness in her smile would serve her well in the arduous days to come. "Shiri?"

She glanced up. "What can I help you with?"

"I wanted to tell you—" Gilead smoothed the blanket. "—We'll probably need a lining to protect the document from the sweat and grime."

"Good point." Shiri flipped the cloth over and smoothed the creases out.

Gilead cleared his throat. "Your singing is lovely."

"Thank you, Gilead, that's kind of you to say."

"I mean it. Whenever you sing, my soul…I'm prepared to worship. My shortcomings and sins fade away, and I feel Yahweh's forgiveness and grace."

A sheen of moisture filled Shiri's eyes. "I'm glad."

Ezekiel tapped, drawing her attention.

She set down the scroll and pushed herself up.

"I'll go." Gilead stopped her. "What does he need?"

"I'm not sure. He'll have it written down on the tablet." She chewed on her cheek and her eyebrows tented. "I can just—"

"Let me help you." Gilead put his hand on her arm. "I'm here today."

He felt her gaze as he knelt by Ezekiel. *Yahweh, strengthen my friends—my family.*

A similar prayer crossed his thoughts constantly as he accompanied General Vakhtang to Jerusalem over the following weeks. Each day he personally placed Vakhtang's saddle over the discreetly hidden parchment.

Though the captain would derive pleasure from bringing the message of Jerusalem's destruction to fulfillment, Gilead didn't want to give Vakhtang any fuel in advance.

The late summer heat dried the Judean hills, leaving behind a swath of brush and dust, but the familiar terrain still produced the standard ache in Gilead's chest.

Outside of Jerusalem, Vakhtang ordered the entourage to set up camp. "Jew." He grabbed Gilead's beard.

"Yes, mighty Captain?"

"You will remain in camp, as is our custom." He challenged Gilead to disobey. "I hate to have you inciting a riot."

"Yes, my lord." Gilead accepted the shackles' bite on his wrists and ankles without protest.

"Hmph." General Vakhtang frowned and attached the chain loosely to a stake.

Believe me, I'd rather not be kneeling before you. Gilead kept his eyes trained forward as the captain mounted a stallion, flaunting his position and authority as he rode into Jerusalem's gates.

The campsite rose around Gilead in the same position it had been in Ezekiel's tableau. He could imagine the siege mounds and the battering ram in place against the city. *Yahweh, I know it's too late for the city, but strengthen those who are faithful to You. May more follow Your ways, despite the coming judgment.*

Before long, the servant Abell, wearing King Zedekiah's insignia on his arm, came up the rise, leading donkeys laden with baskets. He dipped his head. "Greetings and peace to the camp of the mighty general. I bring means for a feast."

Gilead gave him a cursory glance, aware of the Chaldeans raising Vakhtang's tent to his left. "The great general thanks you for your hospitality. I trust King Zedekiah is well?"

The servant's grimace wasn't well hidden. "King Zedekiah continues in as good of health as ever."

Meaning he continued in his own path and flaunted his disobedience to Nebuchadnezzar.

"The captain and his camp wishes to remind Zedekiah that his loyalties toward Babylon should be strengthened." Gilead kept his tone militant and carefully crafted his words. Nothing he said could be used against him.

The servant chatted about seemingly insignificant decrees and events in the surrounding area. His veiled message indicated the priests and leaders continued to direct the people in false belief that Yahweh would defend the city.

Gilead battled the deep grief threatening his stalwart expression. He couldn't give the Chaldeans any reason to question this interaction.

The servants completed the unloading and stood behind Abell.

"May your stay in Judea be fruitful." The faithful man bowed at the waist and turned to leave.

"I wonder, Abell." Gilead's pulse sped. He twisted his wrists and the chains clanked. "It was exceptionally hot on our journey. Would you recommend a trustworthy launderer for the various blankets?"

A Chaldean soldier stepped forward, hand on his short sword.

"My apologies, Ifra, was that your duty?" Gilead's rapid pulse threatened to disclose his secret.

Ifra's beady eyes honed in on Gilead's sweaty brow. "We've never washed the blankets before."

"Exactly why they need it now." Gilead wrinkled his nose. "I should send you, too. You reek as bad as the linens."

Ifra growled and began to pull his sword.

"I believe the quartermaster of Judah's army would know who can take such a sizable load," Abell interjected.

"Seraiah? That would be excellent. Please send him my greetings." Gilead turned his head sharply to Ifra. "On second thought, Ifra here will do it to demonstrate his loyalty to the mighty captain."

Gilead rubbed sweat off his brow with the back of his hand.

"I will not do laundry like a woman," Ifra snarled. He snapped his fingers and addressed a slave. "Collect the saddle blankets off all the beasts."

"I will be sure to tell the mighty general of your initiative." Gilead brought his chained fist to the heart that served Yahweh.

Abell responded in kind.

29

Indeed you are to them as a very lovely song of one who has a pleasant voice and can play well on an instrument; for they hear your words but do not do them.

—Ezekiel 33:32

"Unacceptable." Ezekiel's supervisor swept the side of his hand across the marks on the tablet.

Shiri swallowed, aware of the sun creeping higher. "If it pleases my lord, I can have him redo the figures and calculations."

"This information is outdated before I even read it," the man bellowed and flung the tablet at Shiri's feet.

"I can bring it earlier." Could she? Already she was stretched thin getting Keli out of the door on time. Her chest clenched at the thought of starting their day earlier. The mornings consisted of preparing an increasingly stubborn daughter. Keli responded to her rushing by going all the slower, then clinging and sobbing when Shiri deposited her and her heart with Atta.

"I have scribes who reside at the palace and can keep track of the Jews more efficiently." The man dismissed Shiri with a wave.

"It will only be for a short time more." They needed Ezekiel's rations to pay Atta for caring for Keli.

"Your husband's services are no longer needed."

Shiri blinked at the man's back as he left the room, not even reimbursing her for the work Ezekiel had done. She collected the tablet and trudged into the open, then broke into a run to the gardens. She couldn't afford to lose her position, too.

To her relief and Yahweh's favor, the garden was free of all but the groundskeeper and her fellow musicians.

"A thousand apologies. It won't happen again." The one Chaldean phrase she could say with clarity, and rarely with any substantial meaning. It always happened again. She puffed air in her cheeks and began warming up, blowing out long notes from low to high and back again.

Yahweh, I need a miracle. What will we do without Ezekiel's income? In the weeks since Gilead had recruited help from people to sit with her husband, the volunteers had dwindled. As had their donations of food.

Shiri held the highest note as long as her breath sustained it, releasing none of the tension within.

At least she wouldn't need to divert to Ezekiel's supervisor any longer. That would save precious time.

The harem gates opened, and Shiri held the heavy weariness at bay as three royal concubines emerged for their daily stroll.

She caught the tune the *oud* player strummed out and joined in. Today, her flute's offering was somber, bringing a haunting tone to the melody. The harpist scowled at her, and Shiri concentrated on commanding her fingers to play the expected frivolous notes.

At the end of her shift, she trudged home, her feet heavier

than a funeral dirge. She tapped at Atta's door and leaned her head against the frame. The sound of women's voices drew her around to the back of the house.

Atta waved. "We're out here."

Yassah turned. "Shalom, Shiri."

An extra cushion beside the women beckoned Shiri with seductive danger. If she sat, she wouldn't be able to rise for a week.

"See, didn't I tell you? Right as Keli has fallen asleep." Atta raised her eyebrows to Yassah as she offered Shiri watered wine.

Shiri held up her hand. "No, thank you."

"Right. Only water." Atta rolled her eyes.

Yassah tsked. "That explains why Keli is a terror and antagonizes you so in the morning. The poor child isn't getting enough sleep."

Shiri stared at the ground and moistened her lips. She couldn't even make the right choices for her child.

"Won't you stay a while, dear?" Atta patted the cushion. "Give the baby a few more minutes to sleep, or she'll take it out on me tomorrow." The women tittered as if that was the most profound statement.

The cool breeze and promise of fellowship drew her and warred against duty. "Some other time. Ezekiel will expect me."

Atta and Yassah exchanged glances.

"Ezekiel's duties were assigned to a scribe today." The dust that coated Shiri's sandals blocked her throat.

Yassah opened her arms. "You poor dear."

"What will you do?" Atta clucked her tongue.

Shiri allowed herself a moment against Yassah's shoulder. "I don't know."

Could she obtain more hours playing her flute? Find other work in the kitchen or cleaning? What of Keli? She drew in a breath. "I don't have a plan yet, but would you be willing to watch Kelila for longer?"

An unfamiliar expression crossed Atta's face.

"I can reimburse you more," Shiri mumbled.

Atta's gaze shifted to the house and back. "I'll think about it."

"Thank you." Shiri couldn't look at her friend's face. She fled into the house to rouse Keli, who squawked and flailed like a pied crow fighting for territory. They were both in tears by the time they arrived two doors down. There'd be no convincing Keli to return to sleep now. Inevitably, she'd slumber right as Shiri would set the evening meal.

"Up, up." Keli fussed as Shiri set her down.

"Sweetheart, *Ima* has to check on *Abba*."

"*Ima, Ima, Ima*!" Keli sobbed, opening and closing her little hands.

Relenting, Shiri tried to smile as she scooped up her daughter. "Let's help *Abba* together, shall we?"

How would Ezekiel take the news?

"How are you feeling today?" She scanned the tablet. No message for her, but the parchment had fresh markings. "You've been busy. That's good."

His hand clenched and unclenched, and his eyes shifted restlessly.

Keli screamed, "My want down!"

Ezekiel pressed his hand over his ear and gestured with his elbow.

Tears stung the back of her eyes. *He's irritable. It isn't personal.*

Shiri deposited Keli and knelt before Ezekiel. He put his hands on her shoulders as she shifted him to a sitting position. When he had relieved himself, and she'd cleaned him, she applied salve to his side and propped cushions behind him to support him while his side got a temporary reprieve.

Collecting the waste pot, she tempered her steps. Her irritation would only cause more frustration if she spilled. Breathing into her shoulder, she cleaned the pot outside the line of houses and rubbed it with sand.

What will happen to us? The afternoon sun baked her concerns and her fears with the unpleasant aroma, eliciting a gag.

She returned home to find Keli playing contentedly with her chariot. She should tell Ezekiel about the scribe, but irritation still lined his eyes. *Later.*

She struggled to find her song as she ground together the lentils, spelt, wheat, barley, millet, and beans. The moisture in her mouth dried up as she added water, just enough to bind the coarse flour together. *Yahweh, though I'm grateful for Your provision, I can't deny that I'm looking forward to not eating this bread already.* She didn't even want to count the days remaining.

When the bread was cooked thoroughly, Shiri pried the crumbling rounds off the sides of the clay oven and onto one plate—wrestling multiple dishes and a cranky toddler was a battle she didn't want to fight tonight.

"Keli, supper is ready." She turned to find her daughter sprawled on her back, mouth parted in sleep.

Shiri's head sagged forward. A good *ima* would wake her child so she could eat. A good *ima* would ensure her child received enough sleep in the first place. She crossed the room, nudging Keli with her foot as she passed.

Keli flung her arm over her face.

Shiri didn't have the fortitude for this. She hovered above her sleeping daughter long enough that she almost fell asleep herself. Shaking her head, she continued to Ezekiel's side and deposited the platter between them.

"Blessed are You, Lord our God, Ruler of the universe, who brings forth bread from the earth."

Ezekiel scooted the tablet to her.

Shiri squinted against the darkening room to read the message aloud. "Don't sing tomorrow."

She glanced at her husband. "A message from Yahweh?"

Ezekiel etched more.

"No songs at all? Or…" Shiri leaned close.

"People come only to hear you sing. It distracts from the word of the prophecy."

The bread of anxiety stuck in her throat. She took a sip of her portion of water and the heaviness in her chest increased. Not sing?

He scratched on the tablet. "Huz can lead."

Shiri traced a water drop down the side of her cup. "Can I still play the flute?" She slanted her gaze to see Ezekiel dip his chin. The band tightened around her chest. She rubbed at a wrinkle in her skirt. "I never meant…"

Yahweh, I never wanted to lead others away from You. But not sing? Her vision blurred with tears threatening to overflow.

He patted her hand, wiped crumbs from his mouth, placed his arm beneath his head and closed his eyes.

Shiri pushed the dish away, leaving half of her portion untouched. She should feed Keli.

Ezekiel pulled her hand up to his shoulder.

"Is your neck tight?" Shiri repositioned and began massaging his tense muscles. "Ezekiel?"

He opened one eye.

"Um…the supervisor has given your assignments to someone else. He didn't give me rations for the work today. What should I do? Should I search for more work?"

Blowing out a long breath, Ezekiel did not glance back.

"I think Atta will watch Keli more, if I increase her supplies."

Ezekiel covered his face with his elbow, signaling the end of the conversation.

Another glimpse at Keli and Shiri crept around to Ezekiel's front. "Will you be all right a little longer in the day?"

He swatted his hand.

She lowered herself in front of him, scooted close, and laid her head against his chest, desperate for the comfort of his arms.

A startled grunt scratched from his throat. He stiffened, pushing her back, not meeting her gaze, his hands guarding his loins.

"I wasn't… I just…" *I just wanted you to reassure me.* She rolled over so he wouldn't see the tears slip down her cheek. *Yahweh, I'm so alone. I know Ezekiel is going through a lot, but he doesn't see how it affects me. That I need his support. Sustain me, Lord. I don't know what to do.*

The next morning Shiri forced a cheerful smile as she welcomed the congregation. She informed Huz of the change and lifted her flute. Several times she tripped over the melody. *Get ahold of yourself.*

Huz led the chanted psalm, then sat with the men.

Dumah—and all the congregation—turned expectantly toward Shiri.

She pressed her lips together and rose. "We have decided to forgo the additional singing in order to focus on the message of the Lord." Could they tell she didn't agree with the decision?

Atta's husband faced the congregation with disapproval all across his sour face. "The words of the law of Moses—"

Shiri felt the people staring at her the remainder of the time. When the service blessedly drew to a close, she took her leave and reported to the music hall for her afternoon assignment—the banquet hall today. Bowing at the waist, Shiri turned.

"Flute player." The chief musician's voice drew her back.

"Yes, my lord." Shiri concentrated hard. Thankfully, he always spoke to her as if to a child.

"I need a flute. Another flute in the afternoon…" He pointed to her with raised eyebrows.

"Yes, yes. I'll do it. Thank you."

"Each afternoon." He jabbed the ration chip around her neck and held up two meat-like fingers.

More work equaled more rations. *Stop nodding so hard. He will think there is something wrong with you.* "Many thanks, my lord."

Shiri floated to the banquet hall. *Thank You, Yahweh!*

30

I will bring you back from your captivity; I will gather you from all the nations, and from all the places where I have driven you, says the LORD, and I will bring you to the place from which I cause you to be carried away captive.
—Jeremiah 29:14b

The thrashing of the drums and the high whine of bows drawn across the tight strings of the kemenche swirled around Shiri. The dancers and their sheer fabrics swayed and twirled on the other side of the screen. Here in the throne room, the music was always rapid—as if to rile the blood within to the frenzy of war.

Each night she departed the throne room with a pounding head and racing heart. Thankfully, the distance to Atta's house dispelled the stirred anger.

It took a mere two days of Shiri's new schedule before Keli—well rested—was pleasant in the evenings and two weeks more before she began to throw fits when Shiri came for her, demanding Atta. Each passing month solidified Atta's place in

Kelila's affection, while shifting Shiri to a second thought. Tonight was no different. Keli sobbed and clung to Atta's neck.

"Come along, Kelila." Shiri dislodged her daughter. "*Ima* missed you. Let's go home and see *Abba*."

"Why don't you leave her here tonight?" Atta raised her voice over Keli's wails.

Shiri squeezed her eyes shut, her body tensing. "That is kind of you to offer, but no thank you."

Atta crossed her arms and raised her eyebrows.

"We'll see you in the morning." Shiri pried Keli's fingers from the door post. "Thank you."

"My… want… Atta," Keli sobbed.

Of course you do, Atta accommodates your every whim. "We'll see Atta in the morning. Now it is time for *Ima* and *Abba*."

"No!" Keli clenched Shiri's cheeks, digging her nails in. "My want Atta!"

Anger roiled inside Shiri. She ducked into their house, barely managing to refrain from screaming back. She plopped Keli beside Ezekiel, answering the question in his expression. "She's screaming at me and scratching me."

Ezekiel caught Keli's arm as she tried to wriggle away. He shook his finger at her and lightly swatted her bottom.

If he were able to verbally admonish her, his placid display might have worked, but instead it only fueled their willful daughter's steam. Keli shook her finger in his face. "No, *Abba*, no. No hit."

Shiri's mouth dropped open. "Kelila. You do *not* speak to *Abba* that way. We are to honor *Abba*."

"No, *Ima*." Keli shook her little finger again.

Red fringed Shiri's vision. She swatted her daughter's bottom. Keli dissolved into wails and tears of her great injustice.

Shiri stared at her shaking hand, then to her sobbing daughter and immobile husband. She hadn't struck hard enough to cause damage, and certainly Keli needed the correction. "I'm sorry, Keli, *Ima* shouldn't have struck you in anger."

Keli ducked under Ezekiel's arm, crying.

Cold permeated Shiri's arms and legs. She shivered and turned woodenly to light the lamps and grind the grains for the bread. Enough for the next day as well. A tear splashed onto the millstone, and she wiped her nose on her sleeve. What right had she to strike her child?

Keli *shouldn't* have acted that way.

Shiri hung her head. She *did* have the duty to correct her daughter's disobedience. If left to her own devices, Keli would bring harm to herself, much like the land of Judah had. *Oh God of my fathers, please soften Keli's heart to Your ways.*

At Keli's giggle, Shiri turned to see the girl pulling Ezekiel's hands away from his face to reveal a silly expression. She giggled with Ezekiel, clung to Atta, and screamed at Shiri.

It's only for a time. Shiri squared her shoulders and patted the bread rounds to the sides of the clay oven. She measured out the rations of water and flipped the bread over. When their meager meal had browned, she set the platter before her family with a quick prayer.

Keli made a game of offering Ezekiel her bread then snatching it back with a shriek, usually with a bite missing.

Shiri nudged her. "Keli, eat. *Abba* has his own."

Keli took a big bite, grimaced, and stuck out her tongue. The soggy bread threatened to tumble out despite Shiri's warning look.

"Keep it in your mouth." Tears blurred her view of her own bread—overcooked on the edges, not cooked thoroughly on the inside. She set it down and rose to her feet. Would she never get the hang of this dough? Out of Ezekiel's line of sight, she slid down the wall and hugged her knees.

Small hands patted her face, and with a knee to the bladder and an elbow to the inside of the arm, Keli wriggled onto Shiri's lap with a grunt. "There's *Ima*!" The small girl leaned against Shiri's legs and propped her feet on the wall, with no residue of the previous storm.

Unworthiness warred with gratefulness as Keli now took the role of forgiveness and sins forgotten. Shiri managed a smile and dislodged more tears. "I'm sorry the bread wasn't cooked well."

"Blah." Keli rubbed her tongue with little fingers.

"You know you shouldn't treat *Ima* like that." Shiri cleared her throat. "You can't grab *Ima's* cheeks and scream. You can't say 'no' to *Ima* and *Abba*."

Did the child understand anything Shiri said? She pressed against her heart. "You hurt *Ima*."

Keli's face crumpled. She patted Shiri's cheeks.

"You hurt *Ima's* face, too." The life lesson was lost on Keli. "Yahweh wants us to be kind."

"Be kind?"

"That's right." Shiri kissed the babe's chubby cheeks. "I love you, Keli."

"My love *Ima*." Keli submitted to Shiri's embrace for a brief moment, then wriggled free and twirled in circles. "My is dancing."

"Beautiful." Shiri leaned her head against the wall, smiling as Keli fell on her bottom and pushed herself up, resuming her passionate dance.

Shiri should prepare everything for the next day, but all her energy drained into the floor. Keli's dancing and singing lingered at the front of Shiri's mind as her eyes closed. Awareness of a crick in her neck woke her.

She rubbed bleary eyes. How much time had passed? She steadied herself on the wall and stretched stiff legs. Keli lay sprawled across Shiri's side of the sleeping mat, and Ezekiel's chest expanded in sleep. She stumbled around the room extinguishing lamps and setting the room to rights. Keli should sleep in her own bed, but Shiri couldn't muster the energy.

She climbed over her sweet girl to shield Ezekiel from reckless thrashing. Even in sleep Keli resisted Shiri's embrace, flopping the other direction. *I'm going to regret this.* Shiri's thoughts faded into black, only to be jolted awake by Keli's wild sleep habits —many times.

Far too soon, Ezekiel stirred behind her. He allowed her to pretend to sleep a while longer, then tapped her shoulder.

Blowing out a breath, she opened her eyes as Ezekiel gestured to the pale light of dawn peeking in the window. She groaned and rubbed her throbbing temple. "A minute more." The heaviness in her body gave a discouraging inventory. Sleep once again had denied her its restorative properties. Worse still, she had no motivation or desire to rise and serve Babylon, or her family. Her soul was a parched clay cup—empty, with nothing to give.

Already she felt like weeping.

Yahweh, sustain me today. How can I continue for— how many more days was it? She'd lost count.

Keli was sluggish rising and clung to Shiri's neck when they arrived at Atta's. Shiri's heart simultaneously rejoiced and constricted at the unusual display of affection. She plodded to the gardens for the morning and the throne room in the afternoon. Weariness plagued her steps to the marketplace—grains for her and Ezekiel and candied dates for Atta. The treats Atta requested cost the entire amount of Shiri's second ration chip. Why did she overwork for this? She should be home in the afternoon.

She shook her head. What Atta would ask for mornings alone, plus the grains they needed—meager though it was—exceeded the allowance of one ration chip.

"It's only for a season." What good was the harvest of this season if it broke her down before it came to pass?

Keli came without a protest, and Shiri exhaled in relief as they entered the still air of their home. "Shall we get some fresh air in here?" Shiri rolled the half-gate she had crafted from a discarded chariot wheel across the door. She'd woven fabric through the spokes with the hope Keli would see it as a solid barrier. So far it had been successful.

She set to assisting with Ezekiel's needs and exercised his legs. Normally she gave a commentary of her day as she massaged salve onto his skin, but nothing came to mind. She had performed all her duties, hadn't she?

"Shalom, the house!" A shadow fell across the doorway.

Shiri's head jerked up. She'd know that voice anywhere. She straightened Ezekiel's garments and ran to the door, wiping her hands on a cloth. "Chesed!"

Rolling back the gate, she flung her arms around her cousin's neck. "What are you doing here? Are you just arriving in Babylon? What of Reumah and my nephew?"

Chesed laughed. "It's good to see you, too. I was taken in the same wave as King Coniah."

Shiri covered her mouth. "All this time? Come in. How long are you here for?"

Repositioning the chariot wheel, Chesed stepped in and surveyed the room. "Just until dusk. My master is passing through. I am in Al-Yahudu, to the south." His gaze landed on Ezekiel.

"You remember my husband, Ezekiel?" She led Chesed by the arm. "He can hear and will respond by writing on the tablet."

Chesed glanced back to Shiri. "I had heard…" He extended his hand.

Ezekiel clasped Chesed's arm and shot an intense look at Shiri.

Her cheeks heated. She had flung herself into the arms of another man in plain view of the town.

"It's good to see you. I'm sorry for your…" Chesed stuttered and shifted to the side.

Keli's thin, wayward hair popped over Ezekiel's shoulder, followed by her wide eyes.

Shiri laughed. "This is our daughter Kelila."

A shadow crossed Chesed's expression and he stiffened. "You are fortunate."

"What is it?" Shiri followed after him to the doorway and searched his face. Time had not changed her ability to read his thoughts. "Reumah and Ocran?"

Chesed shook his head.

"What happened?"

"I was taken from the marketplace. I don't know if they're even alive. I search every Jewish community, hoping—"

Shiri's heart ached. She resisted the urge to comfort him as she had when they were children. "I'm so sorry."

"I don't know what is worse, not knowing, or seeing your spouse deteriorate before your eyes." Her cousin shifted his gaze to Ezekiel.

Conviction pricked Shiri's heart. Her trial was temporary.

Chesed squeezed her shoulder. "Enough about things we can't control. Tell me about your singing. I need some encouragement."

Shiri lowered her gaze to Chesed's dusty sandals and forced a laugh he would see right through. "Who has time?"

He tipped his head to see her face. "Even in your synagogue?"

"It was—we felt—too much distraction. The congregation didn't pay attention to the words of the Lord." Not that they applied it without her singing. "But I still play *Abba's* flute. I play in the gardens and in the throne room."

Chesed grimaced. "If you could call that Chaldean dissonance playing."

"I won't argue with that." Shiri offered a cushion.

"What has become of us?" He sank down and rested his head in his hand. "Life looks nothing as we planned it as children. We are supposed to be the chosen people."

Shiri dampened a rag from their carefully portioned water and knelt to wipe dirt from her cousin's feet. "We are still

Yahweh's people. He didn't abandon us but allows us to prosper."

"Says the woman eating rations of war." Bitterness transformed his face.

How he knew didn't matter. "Yahweh wouldn't be a good God if He didn't carry out judgment. There is still hope. Surely, you've also seen the remnant of our people. The reunification of our nations."

Chesed's acknowledgment didn't convey belief. "I'm so tired, Shiri. When is it our time? Our people are slaves. We are bound by the whim of our pagan masters. Torn from those we love. Or watching them deteriorate. When will Yahweh avenge us?"

Shiri's chest ached. "Stay strong. Serve in your position with all that you have. Remain faithful and Yahweh will be with you. He will direct your path."

"How can you say that? You who have the worst lot of all? Your husband is a prophet for God, yet he has been struck down. An example that wields no influence on the people whatsoever."

Shiri frowned. Chesed's words dangerously resonated with her feelings. She fixed her thoughts on Yahweh's goodness and truths. "Yahweh is still good. Here in Babylon as much as in Jerusalem. I don't know what His plan is, but He is not found off-guard by our trials. You must hold fast to that. He is with us in the midst of our hardships."

Too soon, Chesed rose to leave. The edge of his frustration seemed to have receded. Could it be merely the interaction and companionship?

An ache consumed Shiri as he departed. Was she that desperate for human contact? Who else had expressed concern for her in the past six months?

He drew her close and moved his chin back and forth on the top of her head like he always did to annoy her. "Take care of yourself, Shiri."

Tears spilled over. "Go with God, cousin. I shall pray for your peace."

"And I yours." He smiled down at her, lifted a hand toward Ezekiel, and wiggled his fingers to Kelila. Turning his face toward Babylon, he departed with shoulders drooping.

Shiri's throat closed around a lump. There was no guarantee she would see him again. She stood with the spring evening before her and a stale air of burden behind her. Another gate to her old life slammed shut.

Chesed could no more help her through this taxing season than she could him.

31

When you pass through the waters, I will be with you; And through the rivers, they shall not overflow you.
—Isaiah 43:2a

The next day, after serving in the throne room, Shiri took the long way home and stood on the Nabu-Polassor Bridge spanning the Euphrates.

Behind her, the spring waters raged and swirled over the banks of the Chebar, diverting disaster from Babylon. The levees spread the wealth of inundation to the different parts of the kingdom.

Yahweh, I know You are with me through deep waters, but I'm barely staying afloat.

A surge of water rushed toward the bridge. She closed her eyes and tipped her face up as the tumultuous current relentlessly splashing against her soul threatened to sweep her under.

There's no one to share this burden with. I know You are good and I praise You, but… She glanced at the still-light sky. Why did she feel guilty for lingering? She needed time to rest, didn't she?

What right had she to steal moments to herself? Her husband needed her. Atta grew agitated if Shiri didn't come before supper.

Trudging off the bridge, she turned her steps to Tel-Abib. Her hands shook, and her head was in a constant state of fog from malnutrition. She pressed her shaking hands against the ache in her belly, temporarily relieving the pressure.

Nothing relieved the pressure in her heart.

At Atta's house, Shiri tapped on the door frame and considered resting her head against the wall.

"Come." Atta called over the scrape of dishes and serving mats.

Shiri pressed on a smile and stepped in to face Atta's disapproval. "I'm sorry I'm late."

"Hmph." Atta continued scraping the puréed eggplant onto Dumah's fluffy wheat bread rounds. Heavenly garlic aromas wafted toward her, making her mouth water.

Poor Keli. Shiri's selfishness resulted in her daughter suffering through the torture of watching others eat food she didn't eat at home.

But Keli didn't fuss or fidget. She lay listlessly on her cushion.

"She's feverish," Atta accused.

Shiri sprung to her child's side. "*Ima's* here, sweetheart."

Heat radiated from Keli's skin. Her bottom lip stuck out, and she opened glassy eyes. "*Ima*?"

"She fell ill around the sixth hour." Atta didn't turn.

"Oh, sweetheart. I'm so sorry you don't feel well." Shiri's ache intensified as fat tears rolled down Keli's furnace-like cheeks. She drew a shaky breath. Tomorrow was the Sabbath—Shiri would be able to remain with her daughter longer.

She dismissed the urge to apologize. She couldn't control a fever.

Dumah leaned close to Atta, whispering with an intense expression.

Atta caught a drip of eggplant with her finger. "Dumah doesn't want her here until she is well."

Shiri glanced at the ceiling, seconds away from joining Keli in sobbing. "What am I supposed to do?"

Atta popped a piece of bread in her mouth with a satisfied smack of her lips.

"I'll figure it out. Thank you." Shiri stomped out. By the time she'd walked the length of two houses, Keli's heat radiated through Shiri. Leaning back, she balanced her daughter's weight with one hand and opened the door with the other.

Keli slipped lower, and Shiri barely reached the cushions before dropping her. She smoothed her hair and kissed her cheek.

"*Ima, Ima.*" Keli clung tight to Shiri's arm.

"I know, sweetie. *Ima* will be right back. I'm going to find something to help you feel better." What that was, Shiri didn't know. There wasn't much food in their siege pantry. "Oh, Yahweh, help my child."

Ezekiel clapped his cup on the ground across the room. She turned to see him pointing to Keli, questions in his eyes.

"She has a fever." Shiri dipped a rag in the water jar and spread it across Keli's face. "Dumah doesn't want her over until she is well."

Did they have any frankincense from pre-siege days? The poor mothers of Jerusalem whose children had sickness in the days of actual siege. Shiri added water to the pot of lentils. Perhaps a warm broth would speed Keli's recovery.

Ezekiel pounded his tablet, and Keli's sobs ripped a hole in Shiri's heart.

When the lentils had cooked, she divided the stew into two bowls and plopped one before Ezekiel, turning to Keli without looking at the message scrawled on his tablet.

She sat beside Kelila, lifted the girl to a seated position, and blew on the broth. "Here, sweetheart, sip on this."

Keli sagged against Shiri and opened her mouth slightly. Immediately, she began to cry.

"What is it? Is it too hot?" Shiri tested a bite of the lukewarm liquid. She offered another spoonful. "You have to eat something."

Thrashing, Keli cried all the harder, upsetting the spoon's contents down her front.

Ezekiel signaled for her, and Kelila clung tighter.

Another clop of the cup.

"Lay down, sweetheart. You don't have to eat if you don't feel like it."

Keli sobbed and clutched Shiri's tunic.

Shiri lowered her down, trapped by unrelenting little hands.

"*Ima*, my needs you."

Two taps.

"I can't come right now. Keli needs me." Hysteria threatened Shiri at knife-point.

Three swift taps. I. Need. You.

She pushed up from the pallet only to be tugged back down. "Keli, let go. I must see what *Abba* needs."

"*My* needs *Ima*."

Shiri pried herself free. "Yes, dear, I know, but *Abba* needs me too."

Keli wailed and knocked over the bowl of soup as Shiri dodged her grasp. The stew pooled, the puddle spreading. Shiri's emotions teetered dangerously—soon they too would spill.

Attempting to block out Keli's cries, Shiri bent over Ezekiel's tablet.

"Eat with me."

Eat what? Her portion had been spilled by their ill daughter.

He thrashed his arm and began scratching the stylus in the clay.

Shiri turned away and dashed her tears away with her sleeve. Despite her attempts to care for everyone, no one was satisfied. She couldn't come out ahead. An ugly sob pressed up her throat, and she slid down the wall behind Ezekiel and out of reach of her daughter.

They could get along without her all day long. Why did they both demand her attention now, at the same time? She curled on her side on the floor, unable to restrain the flood of emotions. *Oh, Yahweh! I need You. Sustain me.*

Slam! A fist pounded on the door.

Shiri started and pushed off the floor. Who would be here at this hour? She straightened her skirts, swiped her sleeve across her face, and stepped around the invalids to the door.

"Can I help you?" Shiri opened the door to reveal a Chaldean soldier. A pulse pounded in her ears.

"Are you the musician?" His eyes narrowed at the noise inside.

"I am."

"Your presence is requested in the throne room."

Shiri glanced out at the winter night's darkness. "Now?"

The soldier sneered. "Yes, now."

"*Ima*, my needs you!" Keli sobbed.

Shiri rubbed her gritty eyes. "I'm not able to leave now. My daughter is ill and my husband—" she gestured to Ezekiel.

Wrath clouded the soldier's expression. He shouldered the door open and strode across the room to Keli's cushion, drawing his short sword. "I can eliminate those distractions."

"No! Please!" Shiri dove between the blade and her daughter.

The soldier leaned back smugly. "The King of the World will not be so favorable if you deny his request."

"Yes, my lord." Shiri hung her weary head, catching a

glimpse of her rumpled tunic. "May I take a moment to make myself presentable for service?"

Pristine appearance was expected in the throne room.

He stared at her critically and gave a curt nod. "Be quick."

Shiri rose. "Forgive my boldness, my lord. My daughter screams because she is frightened. Would you please stand by the door?"

The soldier seemed to weigh the value of obeying a slave against the possible benefit of less noise. He backed to the door and crossed his arms. "Hurry."

Shiri darted up the stairs two at a time. What kind of fool left their defenseless family in the same room as a Chaldean soldier on a mission? Throwing on a fresh linen dress, she rewrapped her hair as she trotted down the stairs. She scooped up the make-shift sheath she had created for *Abba's* flute and tied the leather strap around her waist.

The Chaldean gave a nod of approval and turned on his heel.

Ezekiel's agitation and Keli's despair smote her soul. What could she do? Shiri rammed into the soldier's back. "A thousand apologies. I didn't realize you weren't moving."

"Put the child with your husband."

Shiri blinked. "Pardon?"

"I have children," came the only reply.

She scrambled to obey, lest he should lose his good temper. She hoisted Keli and murmured against her ear, "Here, sweetheart, you can sleep with *Abba*."

Mercifully, Keli stretched out her arms to Ezekiel.

Shiri swallowed hard. "I'm sorry."

Ezekiel rubbed Keli's back and mouthed, "I can handle it."

She swallowed and pressed a kiss to both of their foreheads and tried to keep stride with her thoughtful benefactor.

Upon arriving at the throne room, Shiri snuck behind the screen and untied her flute. She heard two hushed voices and nothing else. Nebuchadnezzar didn't hold audiences at this time. Just her, and the soldiers that likely lurked in the shadows. Something must be troubling the king.

Shiri began to play tranquil garden tunes. She played until her mouth dried, then sipped from the dipper of water from the ever-present bucket and picked up the *oud* from the stand beside her. She loved to listen to its crooning and had watched the musicians enough to know she could play it.

She cradled the large, pear-shaped soundboard and held the bent neck. The strings all were doubled, except the thickest string at the top. Its low, soulful note stood alone. Shiri strummed and tickled the strings as the musicians had, and the rich tones surrounded her heart.

Closing her eyes, she could imagine the plaintive tune swirling up and down the hills in Judea. In her mind's eye, sheep scattered through the pastures, content.

Oh, that King David would've had an instrument this fine!

The Lord is my Shepherd, I shall not want. He leads me beside still pastures. He restores my soul. Please, Yahweh, restore my soul. I'm so drained.

Peace that had eluded her now washed over her heart. *Surely, goodness and mercy shall follow me all the days of my life and I will dwell in the house of the Lord—*

A shadow loomed beside her. Before she could lift her eyes, a hand struck her in the mouth, sending her sprawling off the stool.

"What are you doing?" A guard hissed at her and began rapidly speaking. His words escaped her, but his meaning did not.

Had she been singing aloud? She flinched as the soldier drew back his leg.

From beyond the divider a commanding, deep voice barked, "What is going on? Why did the music stop?"

32

And in the matters of wisdom and understanding about which the king examined them he found them [Daniel] ten times better than all the magicians and astrologers who were in all his realm.
—Daniel 1:20

Shiri flung a desperate glance at the guard's face and found no sympathy. He dragged her by the back of her tunic and thrust her around the screen to her knees.

Prostrating herself before the dais, Shiri whimpered. Her heart's pounding amplified on the cold marble tile.

The soldier spoke from his kneeling position beside her. "… Protocol… Jew…"

Since she hadn't caught the beginning of his rapid report, catching up now was impossible. *Yahweh! Who will care for my daughter and husband?*

Silence fell.

The soldier rose to his feet and kicked her side.

Had Nebuchadnezzar given permission for her to speak? Why wasn't she able to retain the language? She stole a glance up at the soldier, who gestured forward with an annoyed expression.

"A thousand apologies, Great King of the World." And thus concluded the only words she could lend to a complete sentence in Akkadian. "I did not…speak aloud."

Shiri squeezed her eyes shut and pressed her fingers against her forehead, but the words did not appear. "I did not…" The Hebrew word for "intend" slipped out. "… My heart is heavy and I didn't…"

The king repeated her words and rattled on in Akkadian.

At his pause, Shiri lifted her head and gaped at his jeweled sandals as if they would interpret. "Yes, my King."

Out of the corner of her eye she saw the soldier raise his whip arm. Shiri whimpered and braced herself.

"Wait." A new voice halted the soldier's movement. "King Nebuchadnezzar, I believe there is an explanation." The man spoke slowly, with a Hebrew accent.

The whip remained suspended.

"Do you understand protocol, woman?" the man asked in Hebrew.

Shiri shifted her eyes to the set of sandals to the right. "Yes, my lord. I understand protocol but not Akkadian."

The Hebrew laughed. He spoke quickly in Akkadian. Back to Hebrew, "The king asked if playing music for him made your heart heavy."

"No! It is my honor to serve the king." Shiri swallowed. "My child is ill, and my husband also. I confess my mind drifted. I did not realize I sang aloud."

It wouldn't matter that she had a countryman translating for her, she had still broken protocol. She closed her eyes, waiting for the sting of the whip. "A thousand apologies. I did not mean to insult the king."

The congregation would arrive at the third hour. Atta would care for Keli—hadn't she hinted numerous times that she would rather raise Keli as her own? Her heart clenched.

Nebuchadnezzar spoke, and the Hebrew cleared his throat. "The king says your voice—the heaviness of your heart—matches his spirits tonight."

Tears sprang to her eyes. "I'm sorry the king is weighed down."

Another exchange. "For tonight alone, you may sing if your heart escapes your voice."

"Thank you for your great mercy, my King." What favor Yahweh had languished upon her! Shiri exhaled, then squeezed her eyes shut. Should she say anything? Did they understand what she sang? The Hebrew would have, but would he turn her over?

It didn't matter. He knew and Yahweh knew.

"A thousand pardons, my king." She addressed the jeweled sandals and switched into Hebrew. "I did not merely *speak* out of protocol. I prayed to my God—the God of the Jews."

She could feel the weight of the Hebrew's gaze as he translated.

The king replied, and her translator laughed. "Nebuchadnezzar says 'Belteshazzar'—that's me—'has been trying to convert me to his God. Perhaps it is a sign.'"

Shiri's eyes widened.

"I believe he meant that humorously," Belteshazzar's voice carried sadness. "I thank you for your integrity, dear sister. You may continue your music."

Pushing off the tile, Shiri backed away, head lowered appropriately. Her spirit checked and she hesitated. She lifted her eyes to the heavy silk covering the king's knees. "I will pray that you also will find peace, my King."

Behind the screen, she righted her stool and selected her flute. Better to keep her mouth occupied. Her hands shook as she drew the reed to her bruised mouth. Wincing, she blew out a breath. She centered her thoughts on Yahweh, King of the Universe, and played the psalms of David, praying they would bring Nebuchadnezzar comfort.

Yahweh, I've lost my joy. Please restore it to me at times when I am overwhelmed. Your ways are true, and it is my joy to serve You. May I serve my husband with as much joy as I have serving this king with my music.

Peace knit her soul to the One who knew her before she was born.

At the first hour, musicians arrived, and Shiri headed home, spirit light.

Yahweh would sustain her, and their marriage would be revived. She opened the door slowly and crept over to Ezekiel's pallet. Keli's hair lay in damp strings across her face, and her forehead was cool to the touch.

"Thank you, Yahweh." Shiri glanced up to see Ezekiel watching her. Renewed thankfulness overwhelmed her. She almost didn't make it home.

"Ezekiel?" She shifted Keli and sat between them. "I wanted to apologize. I haven't been serving you with honor. I have been overwhelmed and allowed that to cloud my behavior. I'm sorry."

Shiri stroked Keli's hair while Ezekiel began to write.

He handed her the tablet. "I need a barber."

She had sought his forgiveness and all he wrote were those four words? Shiri blinked at the marks in the clay.

He took back the tablet and scratched more.

Anxiously, she waited to read the words of encouragement he would offer.

"Before synagogue. Message from Yahweh."

There was no message of unification, no apology for being irritable, only demands.

Shiri couldn't convince her heart of what her mind knew—it *would* be hard to write all those words and emotions.

He didn't acknowledge her apology, didn't respond in kind, only covered a yawn and closed his eyes. Between the feverish Keli and the prophetic message, he probably hadn't slept.

She rose and bleakly headed to the market for a barber. She gave the man instructions, sent him in, and waited outside.

How foolish she had been to assume that he would have a transformation because she did.

She sat beside the door and drew her cloak tightly around her. Weariness weighed heavy on her eyes. The birds chirped in the early morning sunshine, lulling her mind to dulled awareness of the sounds around her. Minutes passed. Perhaps hours.

"Shiri?" The voice came insistently with the shake of her shoulder.

Slowly, she climbed the rungs of consciousness.

"Shiri? Are you alright?"

Opening her eyes, she found Gilead squatting beside her with eyebrows furrowed.

"Shabbat shalom." She smiled and rubbed her eyes.

"What is going on?" Gilead surveyed her.

"I am well." She tipped her head to the house. "Ezekiel has a barber inside. Another message from Yahweh."

Gilead glanced inside and quickly back to Shiri. "Why are you sleeping outside?"

Shiri stretched her neck from side to side. "I was summoned to play last night. I just returned."

With a sympathetic grimace, Gilead lowered himself with a grunt and stretched out his legs.

"It turned out to be a good thing." Shiri smoothed her tunic. "I felt the presence of Yahweh in the way I did in the temple. Although I don't know why. I fail Him in so many ways."

"How so?"

Shiri shrugged and rubbed her neck. "I had this amazing experience, I come home, and nothing has changed. I had dreams of serving Yahweh together and I'm—not. Anything I do and still I feel not enough."

Heat surged up Shiri's spine. Gilead served a pagan master and *she* complained? "Forgive me. I have no reason to gripe."

Gilead patted her hand. "You can't compare my situation with yours. Your frustration and loneliness is valid—are valid."

Shiri studied the warrior. "How do you keep your focus true?"

"I try to remember I have been placed in this position by Yahweh. To remind myself that our nation will be blessed because of my efforts." He turned a compassionate glance her way. "You *are* serving the Lord. Just because it is different than you envisioned, doesn't make it any less important. Yahweh is not taken by surprise."

Shiri blinked. Circumstances *were* different, and she'd attempted to retain the way it had been in Jerusalem. *Yahweh, I see I've been trying to serve You in my own way. What way would You have for me?* "I just feel like I'm doing nothing—"

"Shiri, taking care of Ezekiel is massive. Because of you, he can continue to do his ministry—" Gilead broke off as the barber came through the door, muttering under his breath.

They both stood, and the Chaldean glanced between them. "It is done. He wouldn't permit me to dispose of the hair." He extended a hand.

Shame purled through Shiri. She squirmed as a child caught in a falsehood. Last night's ration chip would supply a small portion of broth to help her daughter heal, to say nothing of Gilead's extra mouth. She had nothing else of value to offer the barber. She pressed her lips together and forced her hand to the ration chip around her neck.

Gilead put his hand on her arm, reached into his side pouch, and pressed a coin into the man's hand. "We thank you for your service."

The man eyed Gilead's fat pouch and bowed at the waist. "I am glad to serve. Of course, I *did* make a trip out of my way. *Very* early in the morning."

"And still, the whole day stretches before you. You are free to rake in more profit." Gilead tightened the pouch and plucked the bowstring across his chest.

The barber scowled and sulked away. "Crazy Jews."

Shiri shifted her weight and cleared her throat. "I'll reimburse you." *Somehow.*

Gilead lifted Shiri's wrist and closed her fingers around a handful of coins. "Consider it my tithe."

Her hand instinctively cupped around the currency. "I can't accept this. This is more than half—"

"This is for the Lord's work. Don't deny me the blessing of giving." He held up his hands, refusing to take the coins, and backed into the house, leaving Shiri staring through tears at Yahweh's provision.

She followed Gilead inside and tucked the treasure into the dugout behind the nearly empty sack of beans. Replacing the plank, she turned to the chatter across the room.

Back to where her efforts might not be appreciated. One foot in front of the other. *Yahweh, restore Your joy to me as I serve how You decide.*

Her feet refused to take more ground, and her mouth dropped open. Ezekiel's head and face were completely shorn, like a sheep ready for summer heat.

33

And you, son of man, take a sharp sword, take it as a barber's razor and pass it over your head and your beard; then take scales to weigh and divide the hair.
—Ezekiel 5:1

Deep loss curled in Shiri's chest. The lack of hair accentuated the weight Ezekiel had lost and his frail stature. The set of his lips indicated a message far more devastating. His bare face truly resembled Keli's.

She glanced at the blank tablet.

Gilead already assisted in sorting the hair into three piles around the still-sleeping Keli.

Shiri reached for her sweet girl and paused. When was the last time she reached out for her husband? She put her hand on Ezekiel's shoulder and waited until he turned toward her. "I love you."

Ezekiel's eyes narrowed. He slanted a glance to where Gilead continued his sorting and gave a brief nod.

Shiri swallowed and lowered her gaze. She still loved him

even if he didn't respond. Shifting Kelila out of the way, she began setting the house to rights for the sabbath gathering.

Soon the cushions were set—and filled. Shiri struggled to keep her eyes open through the prayer, the songs, and the reading of the law. If only she could ignore all the people around her and rest as Keli did.

"—'therefore as I live' says the Lord, God. 'Surely, because you have defiled my sanctuary with all your detestable things, and with all of your abominations,'" Ezekiel's voice rang strong, despite his weak appearance. "'Therefore, I will also diminish you.'"

Shiri shivered as the warning fell on deaf ears.

"'—My eye will not spare, nor will I have pity.'" Ezekiel indicated the three piles of hair, equally weighed. "'One third of you shall die of pestilence and be consumed with famine in your midst.'" He brought a sword among the piles.

Someone to Shiri's right gasped as the hair flew up and fluttered to the ground.

"'One third of Jerusalem shall fall by the sword, and I will send the other third to the wind.'"

Gilead leaned forward at Ezekiel's gesture, selected a handful of hair and bound it to the edge of Ezekiel's garment. He cleared his throat. "This represents us—the remnant—saved from destruction by Yahweh's hand."

His archer's eye scanned the crowd. "Take heed to the words of the Lord, lest He send His destruction against you. The day approaches when Jerusalem will be no more."

"What does it have to do with us?"

Shiri blinked at the woman beside her. Was she that calloused? On the other side of the room the men crossed their arms over their chests and hearts and shook their heads.

Did they believe they were out of Yahweh's reach?

"'Oh, mountains of Israel. Hear the word of the Lord.'" Ezekiel's voice rose above the murmur as he turned his face to the west. "'Indeed, I, even I will bring a sword against you—'"

"Why did he shave his head? You said he was a priest. Doesn't he know that makes him unclean?"

Shiri resisted the urge to turn and identify which newcomer it was that spoke so boldly.

"Shh. That's his wife."

"Poor thing. I wouldn't put up with my husband defiling himself."

"You should hear her sing. Her voice is divine."

The urge to defend her husband warred with sadness of at the state of their souls and the apathy in their hearts. Shiri turned and fixed her gaze on the women.

The speakers had the decency to turn away and still their tongues.

Yahweh, why do they not see what lies before them?

"'—I was crushed by their adulterous heart, which has departed from me, and by their eyes which play the harlot after their idols.'" Ezekiel pounded his fists together and stamped his foot.

The woman next to Shiri jumped.

"'They will loathe themselves for the evils which they have committed in all their abominations, and they shall know that I am the Lord. I have not said in vain that I would bring this calamity upon them.'" Ezekiel spelled out disaster upon disaster for Jerusalem, yet shame did not take residence on the faces in the congregation.

Dumah rose as the prophecy ceased. The elder cast a disapproving glance upon his shorn shepherd. He turned a magnanimous smile to the congregation. "May the Lord bless you and keep you. May He make His face shine upon you and lift up His face to you and grant you peace."

Shiri didn't have the capacity to greet people as they departed. Instead, she held Keli close. After all, it wasn't often her daughter was content to be still in her arms. When only Gilead remained and Keli tired of sitting, Shiri pressed off the mat and straightened her skirts.

As she knelt beside Ezekiel, he covered his face, but not before Shiri caught sight of his watery eyes. "I'm sorry, love. They seem to lose interest quickly."

Gently, she tugged his arm down and framed her hands to his cheeks—smooth, yet rough with stubble. "I am here with you. You are not alone in this."

Ezekiel closed his eyes and leaned against her hand.

She glanced over her shoulder. Gilead occupied himself on the other side of the room, and Keli wandered into the kitchen. What she wouldn't give to lie against his chest and feel his arms around her.

Instead, she crawled to his feet and began manipulating his legs. His eyes squeezed shut, and Shiri studied his face freely. His chin was better suited without whiskers—not that the knowledge would console him now. The weariness returned with the force of a ravenous beast.

"Gilead, how long are you here for?" She should probably rest before her shift.

"Until sunset," Gilead called across the room. "Do you need to leave Kelila here?"

"Yes, please. Atta didn't want her coming ill. She'll probably sleep most of the time." Shiri ducked to see the sun's position through the door. No time to rest. "Do you mind?"

"Of course not." Gilead patted Keli's head.

"When do you head to Jerusalem next?" Shiri's eyes burned. "Should we come up with a new technique, or…?"

"Two days. We travel first to Nineveh, then south." Gilead scratched his bearded jaw with his thumb. "I don't believe Vakhtang has any idea what transpired. But the other slaves… Do you think it would be less suspicious to do the same laundering act? Or more so to try to make another contact?"

Shiri's thoughts muddied. "I will think on it." She covered a yawn and pressed her fingers to her lips then to Keli's head. She waved to Ezekiel, strapped her flute to her waist, and trudged to receive her afternoon assignment.

She stood in line, half asleep, creeping forward as one by one the musicians headed to their duties. At last, she stood at the table.

The supervising musician stacked his scrolls and spoke in broken Hebrew that was furlongs better than her Akkadian. "All the positions have been filled today. You are free to go."

Shiri blinked.

"Report to your normally assigned duties tomorrow." The Chaldean turned to leave.

He glanced over his shoulder, caught her dumbfounded stare, and reached into his pouch.

"Fine. Here is a ration chip. For your effort. I suppose it's not your fault your services aren't needed."

The hazy thoughts cleared enough for her to thread the chip onto the strap around her neck. "Many thanks, my lord. I shall report to my normal duties tomorrow."

"See that you do. Don't think this will happen again," he growled.

"No, my lord."

Shiri detoured to the market to replenish her supplies and rushed home, yawning all the way. She explained her return to Gilead and climbed the stairs where she could rest. Collapsing on a comfortable pallet used for ambassadors and guests, she fought to think clearly.

Mentally, she skipped over the scroll's safe passage to Jerusalem—she'd need more capacity for that. Ezekiel would need olive oil or salve rubbed into his head as the hair would begin to grow back.

Would Gilead be around when she needed to place Ezekiel on the other side? They were still months away from the end of Israel's confinement—that could wait too.

If Keli remained ill beyond today, who would care for her? Would Atta relent if she saw Keli was on the mend?

What has become of us? We're supposed to be the chosen people. Chesed's words seemed logical to her weary thoughts.

No. Shiri forced her eyes open. "Yahweh is good. He is not surprised. He is refining my love for Him." She allowed her eyes to close—not that she had much choice. Music swirled around her insides like an all-encompassing breeze. *Thank You, Yahweh, for meeting me where I am—I was—restoring my soul.*

The faces of her dear ones came before her mind's eye—the only prayer she could muster. Ezekiel. Keli. Gilead. *Abba* and *Ima.* Keziah. Samuel.

Restlessness rumbled her spirit. Why did she seek Ezekiel to meet her needs when Yahweh was the only One who could? *Yahweh, if my husband never loves me as I think he should, help me to meet his needs anyway. Those that are mine to meet.* Yahweh didn't need her explanation. *May I love him as You do and be an encouragement to him in this challenging time.*

The cushion beneath her head drew away coherent thoughts. She eased into sleep. Deep peace rolled over her.

What overwhelmed and crushed, provided life. Beauty promised from the destruction. Music swelled gently around, over, and through her. The pain of this season was only temporary in comparison to an abundant harvest.

She could persevere. She would cling to hope.

For Your glory, Lord. Shiri surrendered.

34

"As I live," says the Lord God, "I have no pleasure in the death of the wicked, but that the wicked turn from his way and live. Turn, turn from your evil ways! For why should you die, O house of Israel?"
—Ezekiel 33:11b

Shiri continued to surrender daily over the months. At times she fought exhaustion and feelings of incompetence. At times Ezekiel was irritable and uncomfortable. She sang more when putting Keli to bed and preparing the bread of sorrows, training herself to use those times to connect with Yahweh's heart.

She needn't have worried about turning Ezekiel over—she came home on the three-hundred, ninety-first day and already he lay on his right side to carry the weight of Judah's sin. Forty days more. Shiri's hope buoyed; the end of this trial drew ever closer.

Ten days prior to the end of Judah's symbolic bondage, the congregation gathered once again in their house. Dumah led them through the reading of the law of Moses, and Huz and Shiri directed the chanting of the psalms with their instruments.

Perez stood and read from the scroll of Isaiah's words. "The wolf shall dwell with the lamb, the leopard shall lie down with the young goat. The calf and the young lion and the fatling together; and a little child shall lead them—"

Ezekiel sucked in a gasping breath, his rigid body stiffening. His eyes darted to and fro, seeing the unseen.

Perez droned on, unaware of the spectacle arresting the congregation's attention.

Shiri pressed her hand to her mouth, her feet frozen to the ground as if she stood in the mud pits. Two women, whispering their gossip, leaned together and bumped against her. The jolt awakened her, and she darted forward, only to be blocked by another woman who stood to get a better view of the sight. *Oh, Yahweh, please don't take him.* Scrambling over the feet and legs of the worshippers, she finally reached her husband and cradled his head on her lap.

Perez followed her movement and halted the reading. "What is it? Shall I fetch a physician?"

"I don't know." Shiri surveyed her husband. "Ezekiel? Can you hear me?"

"Let us pray for our brother and lay on hands." Perez placed his hand on Ezekiel's leg. "Oh God of our fathers. We ask that You comfort Ezekiel. If this is of You, give him the strength to learn what You would have him know."

A guttural moan came from Ezekiel's throat. He flung his arm above his head, and Shiri dodged his flailing hand.

"Shh."

The people hovered, shock worrying their faces.

Yassah pressed a wet cloth into Shiri's hand.

"Thank you." She gently moved Ezekiel's arm and draped the cloth across his brow.

His eyes twitched and his mouth opened, emitting a gasping groan. He strained, trying to form words.

"Ezekiel? I'm here." Tears blurred Shiri's view of his unseeing eyes. "Please, Yahweh."

Keli ducked through the forest of legs and straddled Shiri's lap, almost sitting on Ezekiel's head. "What happened?"

A lump grew in Shiri's throat. No child should have to see their *abba* experiencing an episode like this. She drew Keli's head to her shoulder. "It's all right, sweetheart."

Keli grabbed Shiri's cheeks. "Why is *Ima* sad?"

Shiri's smile couldn't convince a blind person. She swallowed. "I am concerned for *Abba*. He doesn't feel well."

Yassah reached for Keli, but Shiri held the girl close. "It's all right."

Keli wriggled around and patted Ezekiel's face.

"Be gentle." Shiri captured rough hands.

"'S'alright, *Ima*." Keli settled back against Shiri's chest. "Yahweh's talking to *Abba*."

A twitter of nervous laughter spread through the crowd.

"Sweet child."

"Such faith."

Shiri leaned around to see her daughter's satisfied expression. Did the child know something? Could one so small hear from Yahweh? *And a child shall lead them.*

"What do you mean, Keli? Do you think *Abba* is praying?"

Keli huffed. "*Ima. Abba* watches and listens. *Yahweh* talks." She climbed off, using Shiri's arms for support, and wandered away.

Perez cleared his throat, waiting on Shiri's direction.

What should she do? If it was a vision from Yahweh, Ezekiel would want the people to hear. How long would it take? She blew out a breath. "I believe Ezekiel is experiencing a vision from Yahweh. You are welcome to wait, or I'm sure he'll share with us next Sabbath."

Dumah rose and spread his arms. "Until then, let us proceed with the service. Shall we face the door to give Ezekiel some privacy?"

The crowd resumed their seats, facing away from Ezekiel's distress.

Shiri shifted her legs to the side.

Perez resumed reading from Isaiah's scroll. "He will set up a banner for the nations—"

Ezekiel's brow furrowed, and a tear slipped down his cheek. What did he see that caused such agony? Finally, his countenance eased and his chest swelled. His eyes closed and he rested.

Yahweh, continue to go before us as we bear Your standard.

Shiri ignored the curious glances as the service continued. A handful of people rose and whispered their farewells and exited.

The afternoon shift. Shiri closed her eyes. Only ten more days of walking away and leaving her husband helpless. A few days more of this haggard pace. She expelled the pent-up air in her lungs. Positioning a cushion under Ezekiel's head, she stood, and waited for her leg to stop tingling.

Ezekiel's breathing evened out, his shoulders shuddering now and again. Arranging parchment and the ink horn within reach, Shiri stepped sideways around the perimeter of the room to where Keli occupied herself with scraps of fabric. She knelt and whispered, "*Ima* has to go now. You'll be going home with Atta and Dumah today."

Together they sought out Atta, who smiled in their direction.

Keli wrinkled her nose and flashed a toothy grin. "My go with Atta."

"I love you." Shiri paused. "Keli, do you know what *Abba's* thinking all the time? Can you tell when Yahweh speaks to him?"

"*Abba* looks." Keli threw her arms around Shiri's neck, knocking her backward.

Shiri braced herself as Keli planted a hard kiss on her cheek.

"*Ima* go now." She resumed separating the fabrics.

"My wise girl." Shiri rose and rested her hand on Keli's hair.

When she returned with Keli in the evening, Ezekiel's eyes were open and alert.

Shiri squeezed Keli's hand. "*Abba* is awake. Shall we race?"

Keli shrieked and darted across the room.

"Be gentle." Shiri followed.

"—Atta says 'no, no, Keli' and my wanted to go outside." Keli huffed and clenched her hands.

Shiri lowered herself and tousled Keli's hair. "This little one knew you were having a vision."

Ezekiel raised his eyebrows and touched Keli's cheek. Precise markings nearly filled the parchment at his side.

"May I read it?"

He slid it towards her, still listening intently to Keli's prattle.

Shiri skimmed past the introduction. Chills rose the flesh on her arms at the description of Yahweh. "He stretched out the form of a hand and brought me—in visions of God—to Jerusalem."

Her breath hitched. "You saw Jerusalem?"

Ezekiel dipped his chin, sadness lining his eyes.

A lump pressed on Shiri's throat as Ezekiel shrugged his shoulders. He probably didn't see anyone she knew. She cradled the memories of her family to her heart and read again of Jerusalem and the temple.

"Furthermore, He said to me, 'Son of man, do you see what they are doing, the great abominations that the house of Israel commits here to make Me go far away from My sanctuary?" Shiri gulped but couldn't staunch the sobs from her throat and belly.

How had they gotten so callous to Yahweh's temple? The next section depicted idols, creeping things, abominable beasts, and priests and elders worshipping stone and metal with dark clouds of incense.

"Oh, God!" Shiri thrust the parchment away from her. "Why, Lord? Why do they mock You so?"

Ezekiel stretched for the parchment, scanned it, and tapped a section.

"I can't read about the idolatry." Already her heart crushed against her ribs. She cupped her hands over her wet cheeks.

Ezekiel tugged her hand down and tapped the scroll. The expression on his face made her want to run away.

A whimper escaped Shiri's throat.

He rubbed the back of her hand and laced his fingers through hers, lifting their hands as one.

Shiri studied his hand on top of hers, refusing to see the message underneath. He squeezed her hand—the most intimate gesture he had made in months. "I don't want to know."

The pain of sorrow in his eyes pierced her. Ezekiel gripped his chest with his other hand, pleading. If she didn't read it, he'd have to bear the burden alone. He swiped at the moisture building in his eyes.

"Will you..." Shiri squirmed. Ezekiel hadn't seemed to think she needed anything from him during the past year. "Will you help me?"

His mouth formed the word "yes."

"All right." She sat on the pallet, resting against his middle.

He stiffened.

"Please. I need to be close to you."

His chest expanded against her back, and his arm came around her.

Shiri drew in air through her nose and peered at the section he had pointed out. She wouldn't ever be ready for what she was about to read, might as well get it over with. Dashing the tears away, she wiped the moisture on her dress so she wouldn't smear the ink. Picking up the parchment, she found her voice, "The glory of the Lord departed—" her voice cracked. She lifted her face to the ceiling and blinked away tears. "—Departed from the threshold of the temple—"

Grief rolled over her like the darkness of the Chaldean rituals. She drew her knees to her chest, covered her face, and wept. Even Keli's presence could not temper the sound rushing forth from her belly.

How could they survive this crippling blow? Their people *wanted* the other gods, and Yahweh had turned them over to their base desires.

Ezekiel's arms tightened around her and tugged her down. She buried her face in his shoulder, muffling the sound of her sobs. *Yahweh, You are justified. Your love and kindness has extended far beyond what we deserve.*

When her eyes were puffy and her nose clogged, Shiri lifted her gaze to her husband's face. "What do we do? We are people without a land and without...without a God."

Ezekiel brushed her cheek and reached for the parchment.

Shiri pushed herself up. *Please don't abandon those who seek You.* She followed the path his finger made. "I will give them one heart, and I will put a new spirit in them, and take the stony heart out of their flesh, and give them a heart of flesh, that they may walk in My statutes and keep My judgments and do them."

She searched Ezekiel's face for answers he couldn't vocalize, then turned once again to the words. "They shall be My people and I will be their God."

He patted her back.

"When?"

The troubled expression returned. He shrugged his shoulders.

"How long, oh Lord, will You turn Your face from us?"

Ezekiel clasped his hands together and pointed up, eyebrows raised.

Keli wandered over and plopped in Shiri's lap. "*Abba* says 'Yah-weh.'"

Shiri simultaneously laughed and sniffled. How had she become so wise? "That's right, Keli. *Abba* says we will still praise Yahweh."

A sassy head bob accentuated Keli's impatience. "No, *Ima.* My say that."

This child. "I know, sweetheart, *Ima* was agreeing with you." She exchanged a look with Ezekiel in silent pact.

We will still praise Him. No matter what.

35

Three hundred and ninety days; so you shall bear the iniquity of the house of Israel. And when you have completed them, lie again on your right side; then you shall bear the iniquity of the house of Judah forty days. I have laid on you a day for each year.
—Ezekiel 4:5b-6

Shiri's heart skittered against her chest, matching the birds' erratic wing-flaps against the wooden cage she carried. Their nervousness was justified. Shiri had splurged today for a feast.

Today was the fortieth day since Ezekiel lay on his right side.

"I'm sorry. And I'm not." Shiri laughed at herself for apologizing to quails. Her feet and heart were light as clouds flung across the late-summer sky.

She skipped past Atta's house, blessing her friend's generous offer to keep Keli a bit later than normal. Bursting through the door, Shiri paused while her eyes adjusted. "I'm home!"

Ezekiel sat—upright—with Gilead in the center of the room, surrounded by scrolls and parchments.

Thank You, Yahweh! Shiri lowered the cage to the floor and launched onto Ezekiel's lap. "You are sitting!" Shiri laughed and wiped away tears. She wrapped her arms around Ezekiel's neck. "Hi, Gilead," she said between kisses to her husband's cheeks.

"Hi, Shiri." Gilead chuckled softly. "I'll give you some time together."

Ezekiel held up his hand and mouthed, "Wait." He turned a disapproving glare to Shiri.

Her heart sank and her cheeks heated. How quickly she'd abandoned all sense of propriety. "Your pardon." She lowered herself to the floor.

Gilead's eyes crinkled. "Nothing to apologize for. I understand your excitement."

Shiri glanced over the scrolls—ones she hadn't read before. "Would you like me to sew this into the saddle blanket?"

Gilead glanced at Ezekiel. "He feels we should take a different approach this time."

"Oh. Of course." Shiri smiled. "Tell me how I can help."

Ezekiel picked up a tablet and began to write.

"Where did you travel to this time, Gilead?"

"Egypt."

"I bet it was exquisite!" To see the legendary pyramids and the lush fertile land of the Nile!

"The place is beautiful—"

Ezekiel put the tablet on Shiri's lap.

"—But so heavy. Dark. I can't explain it."

Shiri drew her eyebrows in and offered a small smile before reading Ezekiel's words.

"We are fine. Quail." Ezekiel rubbed his stomach and smacked his lips.

"It won't take long. I've got time." Shiri's heart swelled as she surveyed his upright form.

He wrote again. "No need. Not your job."

Shiri blinked at the abrupt words. *Don't take offense. It's time consuming to write full sentences.* "I am willing—"

Ezekiel shooed her with his hand. He didn't want her help? Shiri pressed her lips together, and the words etched in the tablet blurred. She cleared her throat and pushed herself up.

Touching her leg to get her attention, Ezekiel held his hand about Keli-high and raised his eyebrows.

Did he think she'd forgotten their daughter? "Atta offered to watch her longer for today. Would you like me to fetch her?"

Ezekiel's eyes narrowed, and he gestured to the spread parchments.

Defensive words sprang to her tongue. Shiri restrained them before they humiliated her more. She pivoted on her heel and escaped to the sun-baked outside.

"I can come back later." Gilead's voice filtered outside.

Shiri leaned to the door and shook her head at herself. She wouldn't hear Ezekiel's response.

After a pause, Gilead spoke, "She's eager to see you. She has worked hard—"

Silence.

Gilead sighed. "I think your idea of grain jars—"

Shiri's vision blurred with tears. Did her contribution over the last year and two months not matter? She trudged to the palm tree at the edge of the canal. *Yahweh, I feel foolish for taking offense, but it feels like he is pushing me away.* "I just want—"

What *did* she want?

A cloud covered the sun and she shivered. Why did she struggle so with being affected by every minute change in temperature? Why couldn't she be consistent? The sun didn't change its message—it was constant despite the cloud across its path.

The gray water of the Chebar offered no perspective. Pushing out the air from her lungs, she returned to the house and began preparing the quail for the feast.

Later, when Keli slept and Gilead had gone, Shiri straightened the living area. Ezekiel leaned against the wall, resting against a sturdy staff.

Gilead had joked he probably would sleep standing up tonight if his muscles would support him.

Why had she expected an instant recovery? "Do you want help?"

Ezekiel's shoulders slumped, and Shiri held onto his waist while he slid down the wall on a fresh pallet of blankets. He used his hands to shift on his back and spread his arms wide with a sigh.

"I bet it's nice to be on your back?" Shiri extinguished the lamps and lay beside him. He shifted and she held her breath, anticipating a touch that didn't come.

His breath evened out in sleep.

Sleep that eluded Shiri. Assailed by disappointment and doubt, she lay still, trying to pray. Her heart shrank inside her chest. If supporting her husband wasn't her job, what was? *I shouldn't have thrown myself at him like that. Not with Gilead there.* Even if Gilead hadn't been there, Ezekiel would not have received her display of affection. These past fourteen months had surely put a strain on them.

What should I have done? What choice did I have? Shiri rolled away from Ezekiel and curled on her side.

Each day he gained more strength and walked a little longer.

And needed Shiri less.

On the sabbath after the synagogue meeting, people crowded around as Ezekiel displayed his re-found mobility.

Shiri stood by the door with a smile plastered on, but no one wanted to leave the fellowship.

Even Keli was surrounded by admirers. "What a big help you were when your Abba couldn't walk."

Shiri picked up her flute and slipped out unnoticed. "What is wrong with me? I don't need praise and adoration."

She marched briskly to report for duty, pressing down the growing ache in her chest. Why had she worked herself to the bone over the last fourteen months? What contribution had she made to further Ezekiel's ministry?

None, apparently. She had been stretched so thin between all the responsibilities, and nothing had been done well.

"That's self-pity." Shiri glanced around as she climbed into the *quffa*. Nobody acknowledged her speaking to herself.

Today marked the highest attendance since Ezekiel's first day being ill. *I don't know why I'm struggling with this. Why did my emotions get so swirled around?*

The scheduler assigned her to the gardens, and she spent the afternoon communicating with her fellow musicians, watching and hearing the cues, creating seamless music.

The best musician was not the one noticed, rather the one not realized. If she did her job right, the people in the garden wouldn't be able to distinguish the music apart from the general ambience of the garden.

When she returned home, the house was suspiciously quiet. "Hello?"

Ezekiel lifted his chin in greeting from where he sat engrossed in scrolls.

Shiri began straightening the disheveled cushions. "Where is Keli?"

He pointed in the direction of Atta's house.

"I thought, now that you are well…"

Ezekiel did not divert his attention from the scrolls.

Pressure built behind her eyes, and she pinched the bridge of her nose. "I guess I'll go retrieve her." Did he not realize how much Atta required for reimbursement? Was it too much to ask him to care for his daughter for a few hours?

He lowered the scroll and beckoned for her.

"I have to fetch Kelila. Dumah gets impatient." Especially since Shiri had said they didn't need care for Keli today.

Outside Atta's door, Shiri unwrinkled her brow and plastered on a smile. "Thank you for taking her, I'm sorry if it was an inconvenience."

"No inconvenience." Atta gave a tight smile that communicated the opposite. "We had been planning to take a stroll. I wasn't aware I was caring for her today."

"I'm sorry, Atta. I thought Ezekiel would—" Shiri closed her eyes. Anything she said would not reflect on her husband well. "I'm sorry."

Atta uncrossed her arms and blew out a breath. "I'm sorry for being irritable. Dumah was anticipating the time together."

Shiri rubbed her neck and lowered her eyes. "I will try to be more consistent with communicating."

"What's going on?" Atta reached out for Shiri's arm.

"I thought it would be different," Shiri mumbled. "But I didn't get Ezekiel's opinion. I just assumed."

"Atta!" Dumah called from inside.

"I suppose we both assumed." Atta stepped aside as Keli came barreling out.

"*Ima*!" Keli flung her arms around Shiri's knees.

Shiri patted her daughter's head and steadied herself on the door frame. She surveyed the emotion on Atta's face. "What is troubling you?"

Atta's gaze darted into the house. She lowered her voice to a whisper. "Dumah is… frustrated with Ezekiel. He thinks that Ezekiel is putting on a show."

"You know he isn't, right, Atta?" Heat rose in Shiri's chest.

"There's more than his opinion that weighs heavy." Atta reached out to Keli and drew her hand back. She cleared her throat. "I knew the possibility of having a child at my age was slim when we married, but I assumed…I didn't figure that Dumah would be…inconvenienced by children."

"Oh, Atta." Shiri squeezed her friend's hand. "I'm so sorry that I have put you in this position. Shall I look for other arrangements for Keli?"

"No!" Atta dabbed a tear from the corner of her eye. "We've come to an agreement. I can care for Keli, and I don't bring up children. Most of the time, Dumah is gone when Keli is here. She is such a sweet child. Aren't you, Keli?'

Keli grabbed Atta's hand and planted noisy kisses on it. "My love Atta."

"I love you, too." Atta's smile was bittersweet.

"Thank you, Atta. Please share my apology with Dumah." What else was there to say? Shiri shifted her weight. "Shall we go see *Abba*?"

"What's the plan for tomorrow?" Atta rubbed Keli's shoulder.

"I don't know. I have to check with Ezekiel." Shiri closed her eyes. "Are you available?"

"Of course. You know I love Keli…as if she were my own."

"I'm sorry." Shiri's chest itched. "I know you prefer to have it planned better. I'll inform you as I know."

Shiri directed her bouncing daughter toward home. All this time and Keli had been a strain on Atta's relationship with Dumah. Was there someone else who could care for Keli? She couldn't pull Keli away when Atta had no other children.

I can't keep on at this pace. I'm worn thin.

Not that deliberating mattered, she had brought this upon herself. What had she expected? That Ezekiel would take over her role as a housekeeper, caregiver, and cook as she worked? When she hadn't asked him to do any of it? If only he were able to provide a source of income.

Ezekiel lowered his scroll as they entered and summoned Shiri.

She glanced at the cushions strewn around the room and into the cold kitchen. "Keli, would you like to make a cushion-cave?"

"Yes, my make a cave." Keli clapped her hands and set to dragging cushions to the center of the room. At least the mess would be restrained in one area.

Ezekiel's gaze made her squirm as she sat before him. She twisted her fingers. Setting aside the scroll, he lifted her chin and studied her face. He scowled simultaneously while pointing from her to him and mouthed, "Why are you mad at me?"

Shiri turned her face. This conversation wouldn't be easy. Ezekiel grew impatient when conversations required him to write on the tablet extensively. "It's hard for me to do everything. I feel…overwhelmed. I had hoped we could rely on Atta less. Keli spends more time with Atta than with us."

Ezekiel frowned and picked up a tablet.

Shiri scooted around to the side to see as he wrote.

"I have my ministry."

"I know." She had carried that load too.

"You think you can do it better."

"No, of course not. I've never wanted to…I merely want to support you. I want to serve together."

Ezekiel scowled as he wrote.

"Atta wanted to know the plan for tomorrow. I guess I just tell her the same as normal?" Shiri winced. This attitude was not helping solve the problem.

He shoved the second tablet at her. It always bothered him when she carried on two conversations at once.

"Sorry."

"Why are you mad at me? You don't want my position—I think you would be happy."

"I am happy. It's just..." Shiri blew out a breath. "What am I meant to do now? I'm not saying my way is better or that I am right."

Was it wrong to take advantage that he couldn't interrupt? Were her needs and feelings not important enough to be heard?

"I want to be your helpmate. To be evenly matched like stallions pulling a chariot. When you took over the ministry again, I felt like nothing I did mattered." If she looked at his reaction, she wouldn't say the whole thing. "I know I haven't done a good job on any of the things I've set my hand to. The house—"

Keli's cave of cushions toppled as if to prove her point.

"Atta is more Keli's *Ima* than I am, but I work so much."

She glanced at Ezekiel's message. "What do you want?"

"I want—" She twisted her fingers. "—In a perfect situation, I would work in the mornings again and be home for you and Keli in the afternoon."

A dream that proved elusive if they only had one income. How would Ezekiel react to working again? What could he do with limited mobility and no words?

"Or if you cared for Keli part of the day." Who did she fool? Neither was a realistic option. She shouldn't even have brought it up. Her emotions pushed against the back of her eyes. Predictable. "I don't know what to do. I'm sorry."

Ezekiel scribbled with a thoughtful expression. "I can't watch Kelila now." He gestured to his staff and his mouth.

"I know." Shiri blinked tears back and tried to smile.

"Until I find a position, you will need to work. Will pray. Maybe one afternoon. God's will." Ezekiel clasped his hands.

Hope surged through her burden as Ezekiel closed his eyes and lifted his hands, his mouth moving in prayer.

Thank You, Yahweh, that I don't have to do this on my own. She opened her eyes as Ezekiel scratched a stylus across the clay.

"I appreciate your—" he rubbed out work, "—everything." Ezekiel swept his arm around the room and reached behind her. Shiri leaned forward, turning where he gestured. "Do you need something?" Her eyes widened as his hand rested on her waist.

He tipped his head and tugged at her.

Hesitantly, she scooted close to his side. He drew her head to his shoulder and rubbed her arm.

Her chest swelled with joy as she wrapped her arms around her husband's middle.

Ezekiel leaned back and searched her face. "I do love you, Shiriel," he mouthed.

Shiri drew in a shaky breath and smiled. "I love you, too."

Truly, she could do a great number of things when he supported her so.

36

"By day you shall bring out your belongings in their sight, as though going into captivity; and at evening you shall go in their sight, like those who go into captivity. Dig through the wall in their sight and carry your belongings out through it…for I have made you a sign to the house of Israel."
—Ezekiel 12:4-5, 6b

O*n the twenty-ninth day of the seventh month which was in the sixth year of King Coniah's captivity.*

Ezekiel studied Shiriel closely over the next couple of weeks. He'd been such a burden to her, yet when he attempted to take back his responsibilities, she felt he pushed her away. He shifted restlessly as she mingled among the congregation. *I can't help it. The Lord has hardened my face to the people.*

Did she have visions of grandeur doing the job he should be doing as if she would be another Deborah?

Yet something nagged at his spirit. He had been calloused against the people's complaints that the Lord would not divert from His necessary judgment. What about that could be softened toward his wife? Was that even something he could do? He couldn't change who he was. Before the thought even finished forming, the extent of change he had undergone in the last fourteen months flashed before his eyes.

He had changed by the Lord's doing. Could the Lord do a work in him through his marriage too? *Yahweh, there is a rift between us. Bind us together once again. Show me how to make my wife feel valued and special.*

She turned his way and waved.

He smiled back and rolled his shoulders, shaking free the insecurity. She said she wanted to support his ministry. He'd have to trust. Ezekiel braced himself on his staff and hobbled along the side of the room to meet her. Pain—his constant companion—shot down his left side.

"I think everyone is here." Shiriel brushed his shoulder. "Is that everything?"

He scanned the supplies, and his mouth formed the word "yes."

"I'm sorry I can't be here for the whole thing. I'll be back as soon as I can."

They'd be fine. He nodded.

Her brow furrowed and she worried her lip. The shadows under her eyes and the slight slump in her shoulders spoke more to her permanent state of exhaustion than today's concern.

What position would accept a cripple and a mute? Would taking on a job for the king conflict with his calling from Yahweh?

Ezekiel ruefully shook his head. His calling also included being a provider for his wife and daughter. He was a gatekeeper for the whole nation, yet too long he hadn't tended his home and his wife. Was there a way they could ease each other's burdens and accomplish the goal more efficiently? He squeezed Shiriel's fingers and formed the words, "It will be alright."

Hobbling up to the front, he was intercepted by Perez.

"I know you are about to begin, but I wished to speak with you about the children." Perez put his hand on Ezekiel's shoulder and smiled as his gaze traveled around the room and landed on each child. "The elders and I have discussed the possibility of you training them up in ways of the law and the prophets."

How could I train up these children without a voice? Ezekiel touched his mouth and cocked his head.

Perez folded his hands. "Yes, of course, there would be some challenges. We haven't worked through all situations. Perhaps Shiri or someone could be your voice and supervise the children while you share your knowledge. I feel the parents would be willing to take a tithe from their supplies as payment."

Ezekiel blinked and felt his mouth drop open.

"Think of the children." Perez hurried on. "If we do nothing, what is to stop them from assimilating into the Chaldean ways?"

What of Kelila? Ezekiel mouthed, "Boys and girls?"

Perez's glance followed Ezekiel's pointing finger. "Of course. These are different circumstances. Girls would be most welcome."

Would the supplies tithed be enough to carry them through with only one salary? Confidence settled in Ezekiel's gut. This was right.

Turning back to Perez, he mouthed, "Thank you," then continued to where all the tools lay as Dumah completed the reading of the law, rolled up the scroll, and sat.

Ezekiel searched the faces of the crowd, ready to be entertained.

Son of man, you dwell in a rebellious house which

has eyes to see but does not see and ears to hear but does not hear, for they are a rebellious house.

Shiriel came up behind him as they had rehearsed. "What did Perez have to say?"

Ezekiel beamed and mouthed, "I'll tell you later." He pressed his lips together and gestured broadly toward the stairs.

Kelila wandered up and clutched Ezekiel's trousers. The congregation chuckled.

Ezekiel shook his head. Kelila had to be involved with everything.

Shiriel reached for their daughter's hand with an apologetic glance. "I shall prepare our belongings for captivity." She whispered something to Kelila, who yanked her hand away.

"No. My stay here. My dig with *Abba*."

The congregation laughed and Ezekiel shrugged. He couldn't be deterred because of Kelila's antics. He staggered like an old man to the wall as Kelila darted back and forth underfoot.

Atta half rose from her cushion. "Keli, come sit with me."

"No!" Kelila jerked into Ezekiel, jarring his weight to his left side.

His eyes watered and he sucked in a breath. He waved Atta back with a grimace. At the wall he tapped his daughter's head and pointed to the pickax.

"My will help *Abba*." Kelila bent over and gripped the tool with both hands, growling as she tugged the handle up.

He angled her and swung her arms so the pick-ax connected with the wall.

Kelila chortled. "My did it, *Abba*!"

Ezekiel leaned heavily on his staff and swung the mattock one-handed against the wall.

"What is he doing?"

"Why is he busting down his house?"

Ezekiel frowned and swung again. If only he could growl

like Kelila—it seemed to help her leverage. This time a crack appeared in the plaster.

Shiriel deposited a load of bundles beside him. "Would you like a bench?"

He wiped the sweat from his brow on his shoulder and mouthed, "Yes, please."

Crack! The point lodged in the hardened mud. Ezekiel swiveled it around and yanked it free as Shiriel dragged over a bench.

Her hand on his back as he lowered himself was just the support he needed.

When she came downstairs again, the cracked plaster was a hole the size of Kelila's hand.

Ezekiel blocked out the sounds of the people, as they had blocked out the voice of Yahweh, and continued to chip away at the wall in his house. With each blow, his countenance grew harder.

Sweat dripped down the sides of his face and his back. Yahweh would have to break down the people called by His name, as well as the Holy City. Would they listen after Jerusalem's destruction? Would they then bend their wills to His?

Shiriel stood by the door, tears streaming down her face. She waved her fingers and pressed them to her lips as she headed out the door.

Ezekiel glanced from the pile of all their earthly possessions to the remaining congregation. Those who served afternoon shifts had left, and all others sat in clusters chatting like women at a well.

It was a good thing Shiriel had compassion on these half-hearted individuals. They wouldn't get any concern from him. But what could he say? Nothing. His wife worked on the Sabbath.

He squeezed his temples with one hand. *Yahweh, You told me there would be a remnant.*

Chink. Chink.

Ezekiel opened his eyes to Kelila pounding at the wall with a small awl.

"My helping, *Abba*."

Atta would be all over him for allowing Kelila to play with a sharp tool. He hunkered down at her side and picked up a flat-edged chisel. Instead of offering to trade—she'd hold all the tighter—he wedged the chisel into the growing crevice and popped out a large chunk of wall. The dried mud crumbled as it hit the floor. He dug out another chunk.

Kelila gaped at her small indent and over to his hole. She reached for the chisel. "We trade, *Abba*?"

Ezekiel raised his eyebrows.

Her thoughts played out across her face. "Please?"

Nodding, Ezekiel traded and squeezed her shoulder.

By the time Shiriel returned, the congregation had long dispersed, and Kelila had abandoned her digging. Evening's coolness seeped through the hole. Ezekiel's shoulders and lower back burned, and still he scooped out dirt with his hand.

Now the people had returned with their curiosity and wagging tongues and set up vigilant guard outside the house.

"See, he's made a hole big enough for a person to squeeze through."

"And why the luggage?"

They'd be front and center for the spectacle, but heaven forbid they permit the message to change their hearts.

Shiriel packed a few things at the food area and brought Kelila over. "Ready?"

Ezekiel lowered himself and shimmied through the hole—not quite as big as it could be. Shiriel and Kelila handed out their bundles and crawled out.

Kelila laughed and clapped. "Again." She pushed a satchel back inside and crawled in then out. "Here my am!"

Ezekiel lifted a shoulder. The people would get the point.

Shiriel gave a wry smile, then pulled a sash free and bound

it over Ezekiel's eyes.

He steadied himself against the wall and felt her turn toward the crowd.

"Come back at first light for the word of the Lord."

Grumbling and questions from the people nearly masked Shiriel's movement beside Ezekiel. He concentrated on her rummaging through their belongings.

Panic built in Ezekiel's chest, and he groped the smooth surface of the plastered wall for a hold. His breathing magnified in his ears. *This is foolish. I'm directly next to the house, why does it seem the ground is tipping?*

"Ezekiel?" Shiriel's gentle touch grounded the irrational disorientation. "I've spread out a blanket. Shall I help you down?"

Walking his hand down the wall, the floor to Ezekiel's stomach dropped as if he stood on the pinnacle of a building. *Oh, Yahweh! I can't see!* Every handbreadth down the wall was accompanied by intense shaking and dread. Finally, his fingers jammed into the ground, and he drew in a gasping breath.

"There we are." Shiriel guided his hand to the stack of their belongings.

Ezekiel crawled forward, patting the bundles, and rested his back against them.

Shiriel draped a blanket around him, and Kelila sprawled between them, breathing deeply in the carefree slumber of innocence.

Ezekiel shivered despite the security of his house behind his back. It would not end well for those who continued to resist the Lord's chastisement.

At first light Ezekiel awoke to the sound of his neighbors approaching. He stretched and adjusted the sash so he could not see.

Shiriel stirred and squeezed his hand. "Ready?"

Ezekiel found his staff and struggled to his feet as Shiriel greeted the congregants. He needed her not just for her eyes and her voice. She supported him in so many ways—emotionally, physically. Groping around, he caught her hand and gave it a squeeze.

She pressed a round of bread into his hand and whispered, "Be mindful of Keli to your side."

He bit into the heavy, dry bread, and violent quaking overcame him. All the moisture in his mouth leeched into the bread. He coughed as a piece lodged in his throat.

Shiriel handed him a dipper of water.

His hands trembled, splashing tepid liquid down his tunic. Anxiety pressed on him from all sides, competing with the dry bread to steal his breath.

"What is he doing?"

"Is he having another spell?"

Ezekiel latched onto Shiriel's steadiness beside him.

Shiriel righted the ladle and lifted his hand so he could drink.

He downed the remaining water, and the presence of God Most High pushed out the worry. For in the presence of God Almighty, anxiety has no place.

"Thus says the Lord, 'This burden concerns the prince and Jerusalem and all the house of Israel with him.'" Strength filled his voice and his legs. "'I am a sign to you. They shall be carried away into captivity and the prince shall bear his belongings on his shoulder. He shall cover his face so that he cannot see the ground with his eyes.'"

"Do you mean *King* Zedekiah?"

Ezekiel dipped his chin toward the sound of the voice. "'I shall spread My net over him and he will be caught in My snare. I will bring him to Babylon, to the land of the Chaldeans yet he will not see it.'"

"Why the shaking with the bread?" Dumah's voice came closer. "Did that have meaning?"

At least today, they were asking the right questions. "'They shall eat their bread with anxiety and drink their water with dread so that land may be emptied of all who are in it, because of the violence of all those who dwell in it. The cities shall be laid waste. The land made desolate. You shall know that I am the Lord.'"

From the back of the crowd, someone spoke up. "The days are prolonged. Every vision fails. Yahweh wouldn't make desolate His Holy City."

"'The days are at hand and the fulfillment of every vision.'" Ezekiel ripped the sash from his eyes as fury burned white-hot in his chest. "'I am the Lord. I speak and the word will come to pass. It will no more be postponed. In your days, you rebellious house, I will say the word and perform it.'"

Dumah leaned toward the man beside him, not attempting to lower his voice. "He prophesies of times far off."

Concern etched Shiriel's face and worried her eyes. She pushed her hands on her hips. "How can you still say that?"

Ezekiel pointed his staff at Dumah's chest. "Thus says the Lord God, 'none of My words will be postponed anymore. The word which I speak will be done.'"

"Well, you're the prophet," Dumah's tone dripped with sarcasm. "The scriptures only say the Lord will leave His peace upon Jerusalem. They are merely the words of *God*, what value could they hold?"

Shiriel gasped beside Ezekiel.

"'You who seduce My people saying 'peace' when there is no peace. You build a wall and plaster it with un-tempered mortar.'" Ezekiel closed his eyes. Calling out Dumah amongst the crowd could have ramifications for Kelila's care, but he couldn't close his mouth. "There will be flooding rain, great hail stones, and stormy wind. This false wall of peace will crumble down to the foundation."

Dumah strode forward, slightly bent at the waist with his chest leading. "You're the one who has broken down. Have you seen yourself lately? You have destroyed your own house in the name of what? A message from Yahweh?"

"Dumah!" Atta covered her mouth with both hands.

The crowd shifted.

"You put on this show week after week. But who's to say your dramatics aren't the thing leading our people astray?" Dumah spat beside Ezekiel's sandals. He turned to the wide-eyed crowd. "You don't have to put up with a man affected by spells of the moon. I am not going to. Next week I'll be going to a synagogue where the truth is preached."

Nobody spoke as Dumah stomped toward his house.

"Atta?" Shiriel stepped to her friend. "You don't believe that, do you?"

"I don't know. What am I supposed to do, Shiri? He is my husband."

"Atta!" Dumah bellowed from their door.

"Bring Keli by as normal." Atta spoke quickly, "I'll talk to him."

Shiriel returned to Ezekiel's side, and they watched the crowd exchange shocked glances. Would any of them return next Sabbath? He exhaled, legs once again weak. Each family group turned away unaffected. *Will they not listen to You?*

"It needed to be said." Shiriel tipped her face to the side. "Perhaps Yahweh is pruning the apathy out of the congregation."

Ezekiel's shoulders sagged, and he turned to the house. It might be easier to crawl back through the hole again, rather than to make the trek around to the front door. With Shiriel's steady hand on his back, he lowered to the ground and wriggled inside, avoiding his daughter's prone form.

Shiriel passed in the bundles and their small daughter and crawled in. They blockaded the hole with the bundles, and Ezekiel leaned against the wall and closed his eyes.

His wife scooted close and rested her head on his aching shoulder. "I like serving with you. Helping you."

He squeezed her arm. They were a good team.

37

The word of the LORD came to me saying, "Son of man, write down the name of the day, this very day—the king of Babylon started his siege against Jerusalem this very day.
—Ezekiel 24:1b-2

On the eighth day of the tenth month which was in the ninth year of King Coniah's captivity.

True to his word, Dumah and Atta didn't attend Ezekiel's synagogue the next Sabbath. Word had it they had walked to the congregation in Babylon, taking along a handful of families. According to Shiriel, their friendship was stilted, though Atta still cared for Kelila in the mornings. Combined with Shiriel's half-day income and the donations from the parents, Ezekiel had been able to focus on the work of the ministry and the schooling of the children four days a week. For that, he was grateful to God.

And so their days passed. Months had passed into years. Yahweh still delivered thoughts to be written and words to be said. Ezekiel continued to send messages back to Jerusalem with Gilead's assistance.

Most noticeable was the change between him and Shiriel. More often than not, they understood each other and took time to pay attention.

Ezekiel had come to realize Shiriel *was* better at some things. Yahweh showed him how to rely on her strengths in the ministry. In turn, she gave way to his gifts and leadership.

Shiriel played a quick scale on the flute, drawing his attention—and that of the class of children. Why he had agreed to teach children to read and write the scripture while he still could not speak was beyond him. At least his strength had all but returned, except for the occasional sharp pains in his left hip and leg.

That was why they were an asset together. Over the three years since he had been released from paralysis, Yahweh had healed their relationship, smoothed over their rough spots, and blended them together seamlessly.

"All right, children, gather round." Shiriel corralled the children with kindness and patience, smiling warmly as the girls stood before her and the boys clustered in front of Ezekiel.

He raised his eyebrows as they stood respectfully at attention. Miracles still happened. Ezekiel scanned the boys' faces, searching for one to lead. He rested his hand on Rushack's head.

Rushak turned his face to his classmates and removed his small turban. The boys followed suit, and the girls lifted their scarves to cover their heads.

"Hear, oh Israel, the Lord our God is One—"

The children's voices lifted, unified in devotion to Yahweh. These were the ones who listened and learned. The next generation. An unexpected career turn, for sure, but so much more pliable than their parents. These were the remnant who would be restored into the homeland.

Losing Dumah, along with several other families, three years prior was an unfortunate casualty, but necessary. Since then, their smaller congregation seemed to dig their roots deeper. These children were the proof.

Yahweh, shape these children into men and women after Your heart.

Rushack read from the selected scripture, and the children recited after him line by line.

Ezekiel held up his hand and shook his head. A couple of groans floated up—including one from his own daughter. Kelila had held onto her stubborn independence as she grew in stature and mind.

Rushack followed Ezekiel's stern gaze to the girls' side. "I can help you."

Kelila crossed her arms. "I don't need help." Her passionate, unwavering confidence—the combination of his and Shiriel's strengths and flaws—sparked from her eyes.

Ezekiel lifted his gaze to the blue sky outside the open door. *Lord, may she hold onto the truth with as much tenacity.*

"I know you can do it."

This young man could handle her well. Ezekiel glanced at Shiriel, who smiled at the pair knowingly.

What are you thinking? Dismissing the thought, he turned his attention to his miniature congregation. He walked among them, correcting the hand form of one writing, listening to the recitation of each small group.

At the end of their time together, Ezekiel lifted his hands in benediction, Shiriel vocalized the Aaronic blessing, and the children sang the benediction psalm.

The children burst through the door like floodwaters over the banks of the Euphrates.

"Until tomorrow, Master Ezekiel." Rushack bowed his head.

Ezekiel held up three fingers.

"Oh, right. The first day of the week." Rushack walked off. Even his stride was serious.

"He is sweet. Very respectful." Shiriel stood at Ezekiel's side. "I like him."

Ezekiel blinked. Had he missed part of the conversation?

"He deals with Keli gently and encourages her to be a better student." She waved as children went their separate ways. "Is he a Levite?"

Where had that come from? Ezekiel shrugged.

"Something to consider. I think he's what—nearly ten years old?"

Ezekiel lifted his palms up and mouthed, "What are you speaking of?"

She took in his still-confused expression. "A husband for Keli. We have less than ten years."

Turning, Ezekiel glanced from his daughter as she balanced on the low wall, sleeves rolled up in fierce determination, to the calm young man whose little brother had just tripped. Rushack lifted his brother and brushed off his knees. With a word from Rushack, the small boy lifted his chin and swiped his sleeve across his eyes.

Ezekiel contemplated with fresh sight. Rushak loved the ways of Yahweh and called out the bravery in his fellow classmates. Could his steadiness call out Kelila's gentle side?

Things to consider, indeed.

The next day at midday, Shiriel and Kelila swung the door open with a bang.

"—And Atta said it was un-conven-shunnal. What's 'un-conven-shunnal,' *Ima*?"

"It means not the typical way of doing things." Shiriel glanced behind her and closed the door firmly. "Did you argue with Atta?"

"Well…" Kelila balanced on one foot.

"Keli. Atta is your elder. You must show respect." Shiriel's warning didn't carry its normal weight. She tipped her ear to the door.

"But *Ima*, she's wrong!" Kelila stomped her foot as Ezekiel approached. She glanced up. "I didn't mean to stomp. I was off-balance."

Ezekiel narrowed his eyes. Little imp. He jerked his head towards Shiriel and mouthed, "Apologize."

Kelila lowered her chin. "I'm sorry, *Ima*. I really didn't mean to stomp."

He tapped his chest.

"I know. My heart overflowed and wanted to…even though I *was* off balance." Kelila dragged out a dramatic sigh. "May I go?"

"Mm-hmm." Shiriel shifted aside the drapery from the window and peered through the slit.

What had her so distracted? Ezekiel touched her arm, and her hand flew to her mouth.

"You startled me." She gave a nervous laugh and snapped the drape closed.

Ezekiel tipped his head and mouthed, "What is it?"

"I don't know." Shiriel inhaled shakily. "I think someone followed me."

Ezekiel's eyebrows shot up. He jerked open the door and searched the streets. A child ran after a ball, and women talked over a courtyard wall. He turned back and shook his head. He didn't see anyone unusual.

"I was in the garden playing." Shiriel ran her hands over her face. "Two soldiers were talking behind the draping tree."

Ezekiel whipped his gaze back outside.

"They came around the tree, saw me, and stopped. Then they walked away."

"What did they talk about?" He tapped his mouth.

"I don't know what they said. I don't pay attention. Plus, it was Akkadian." Shiriel twisted her hands. "It felt like someone was watching me the rest of the morning."

"Where were the other musicians? Did they see it too?" Ezekiel mouthed, strumming a poor imitation of a harp.

"They were in different parts of the garden. Many people

decided to stroll today." Shiriel wrapped her arms around her waist and laughed nervously. "Perhaps I just imagined it."

Ezekiel glanced up and down the street again, then shut the door. He scanned the room with new perspective. If a Chaldean soldier wanted to cause harm, what would stop him? The house wasn't fortified in any way. The law of the land placed the Hebrews at the mercy of Babylonian whim. They had no status, no rights.

He enveloped Shiriel in his arms and rubbed her back.

She rested her head against his chest and eventually relaxed. "Thank you. I don't know why I was so jittery." She smiled up at him, her eyes at peace.

Peace that Ezekiel didn't feel. How likely was it they stopped talking out of surprise, rather than harboring ill intent?

How could he protect his family?

Apprehension nagged at his thoughts all evening and ushered him into worried dreams. The hand of the Lord aroused him before the dawn with a message of increasing intensity and urgency.

A word that chilled Ezekiel to the bones.

When the first rays of morning light shone through the windows, he read back over what he had written by lamplight. "The ninth year and tenth month, this very day the King of Babylon started his siege against Jerusalem this very day. Thus says the Lord, put on a pot, set it on and also pour water into it. Gather pieces of meat in it—every good piece—"

Every jot, every tittle in place. His time of confinement had been a mighty trainer for his handwriting—perfection the first time. He skimmed over the words.

"Then set the pot empty on the coals, that it may become hot and its bronze may burn. That its filthiness may be melted in it, that its scum may be consumed."

The smell of charred meat was so tangible, Ezekiel gagged and glanced again to the quiet kitchen.

Soft footsteps on the stairs announced Shiriel's approach.

"Good morning." She pressed a kiss to his head and scanned the parchment. "Is there anything I need to prepare for synagogue?"

Yahweh had said this was a parable, not an illustration. Ezekiel shook his head and tapped his mouth. "Yahweh will give me words."

Shiriel's expressive face crumpled into a frown. She must've noticed the part of the siege. Or that Yahweh wouldn't relent. She blew out a breath. "What God has done is rightly done. It's what Jerusalem deserves."

She rolled her shoulders and moved into the kitchen to prepare the wheat bread to break their fast. Humming interspersed with words from a song—her way of processing Yahweh's judgment and intentionally shifting her focus to the Lord instead of the circumstances—filtered from her workspace.

Ezekiel blotted dry the ink on the last paragraph, and a warm breeze heightened his senses. He bowed to the ground and rested his forehead on clasped hands. *Speak, Lord, your servant listens.*

Son of man, behold, I take away from you the desire of your eyes with one stroke, yet you shall neither mourn, nor weep, nor shall your tears run down. You will sigh in silence and make no mourning for the dead.

Your temple, Lord? Zion?

Bind your turban on your head and put your sandals on your feet, do not cover your lips and do not eat man's bread of sorrow.

The breeze lifted Ezekiel to a sitting position, but the hand of the Lord still pressed heavy on his shoulder. Shall not mourn? The message seemed simple enough, yet lingered with cryptic meaning.

Over the years, he had come to terms with Jerusalem's

impending doom. No longer did it destroy him. He stroked his beard, and his gaze landed on Shiriel.

The pressure on his shoulder smote his heart and spirit.

The one thing he loved more than any other.

38

So I spoke to the people in the morning, and at evening my wife died; and the next morning I did as I was commanded.
—Ezekiel 24:18

O*n the tenth day of the tenth month which was in the ninth year of King Coniah's captivity.*

The blood roared in Ezekiel's ears and black spotted his vision. *No! It is too much. I can't continue the ministry without my wife.*

"Kelila!" Shiriel sang at the base of the stairs. She flashed a knowing smile toward Ezekiel. "Do you think she heard me?"

No, God, don't take her from me!

Shiriel ran lightly up the stairs. "Time to rise, my darling. It is a beautiful day to serve Yahweh."

Ezekiel propped himself up with his staff and clambered halfway up the stairs before he met Shiriel, descending with six-year-old Kelila in tow.

"Did you need something?" She stood above him, beside him now.

He reached for her, straining against his throat.

Shiriel sniffed the air. "Oh no! The bread!" She dashed down the stairs.

"Morning, *Abba*."

Ezekiel patted Kelila's wild hair and maneuvered to descend again. His sleepy daughter plodded down the steps in front of him with a speed that would make a sluggard jealous.

Shiriel deposited still-steaming wheat bread on their eating mat as they made it to the common room. She smiled as they sat and bowed her head. "Blessed are You, Oh Lord our God, King of the Universe, who brings forth bread from the earth—delicious wheat bread that is soft and light—"

Kelila giggled.

"—May we be strong with what You have set before us."

Ezekiel snatched up her hand. *No! Take that prayer back.*

"What is it?" Shiriel glanced at the blank tablet for a message he couldn't write. She brushed his cheek with the back of her hand. "Is it from Yahweh's message?"

Nodding, Ezekiel swallowed at the boulder in his throat.

She searched his face, her own eyes adapting to the depth of sadness he exuded as if she could read the message. "It's all right. What God does is just and right."

How could it be just for Yahweh to take his wife from him? Several times Ezekiel attempted to etch a warning into the clay. Each time he smashed it out with his fist. Sweat beaded on his forehead and dripped down the side of his face.

Shiriel continued about her normal business, humming, straightening up the cushions, wiping down the surfaces, and sweeping the packed dirt floor.

Each move she made, he tracked with the accuracy of a hawk sighting a rodent. She didn't seem unwell.

Together, they greeted their flock filtering in.

"How are you doing today, Master Ezekiel?" Perez didn't wait for a reply.

In his mind, Ezekiel shouted against the confines of his body, raging to take his wife and daughter and run. Hide.

The gatekeeper of Israel opened his mouth and proclaimed the message of Yahweh's cooking pot. No differentiation or favoritism between the people. All fell under judgment. He glanced at the sun's shadow creeping in the doorway.

Shiriel would be leaving soon. Death stalked his wife, and he had done nothing different than normal.

Shiriel strapped on her flute and slipped out the door.

Ezekiel rushed to the end of the message.

Perez rose to lead the closing prayer as Ezekiel dodged around the seated congregation and limped after her. His staff smacked on the packed dirt.

She turned the corner, buzzing scales with her lips.

Shiriel! Wait. Ezekiel broke into a run.

Her face appeared at the corner of the house. "Ezekiel? What is it? What is wrong?"

Pain stitched his side.

"Did something happen to Keli?" She reached her arms out to him.

He shook his head. *Not to Kelila, to you.* He crushed her to his chest. Never mind the breach in protocol.

"You're shaking." Her voice muffled against his shoulder. She drew back, eyes filling with concern.

Ezekiel dislodged the tablet hanging around his neck and held the stylus poised to write. How did one tell his wife she would soon die? He ran a hand over his face and mouthed, "Stay. Don't go."

"But I have to report for duty." Shiriel glanced at him, incredulous.

"Not today. Stay. Please. With me."

"I don't understand."

"Send messenger." Or not. It didn't matter.

Shiriel no longer watched his tablet, instead she searched his face. "This is really important to you."

Ezekiel clutched her arm. He *had* to keep her with him.

"All right. If you're sure it will be fine."

It wouldn't be fine. Abandoning a post was a serious offense, but what could they do to her? Reality, surreal but sure, slammed into Ezekiel's gut. She wouldn't be around to punish or reprimand.

"Did you have something in mind?"

Besides not leaving her side? Ezekiel would suffocate if they went back into the house. He swung his hand toward the first thing he saw. "The canal?"

A smile bloomed on Shiriel's face. "Sounds lovely." She peeled his fingers from her arm.

Panic pounded Ezekiel's chest. He grasped at her with both hands.

"I'm going to fetch Keli. She'd love to go."

Oh God! Will you leave our child motherless? He shook his head vigorously and pointed to Shiriel and to himself. "Just you and me."

The smile returned. She rose to her tiptoes and pressed a kiss to his cheek. "I will make arrangements."

Unwilling to let her from his sight, Ezekiel followed. Simple arrangements were never simple, and Shiriel got trapped in conversation as the congregation dispersed. He shifted his weight off his left side and glared at the sun's path. *Yahweh, give me time.*

At last, Shiriel closed the door behind her and the last guest.

Kelila hopped with four-year-old Mikal. "We can play synagogue school. I'll be the teacher."

"Thank you, we sure appreciate it." Shiriel embraced Mikal's *ima*. "We will repay the favor sometime."

Mikal and Kelila giggled and hopped away.

Kelila, come back. You won't see your ima again.

Shiriel called softly, "Keli."

Skipping back, Kelila flung her arms around Shiriel's waist. "Yes, *Ima*?"

"Remember who you belong to." Shiriel smoothed their daughter's wayward hair.

"I will."

They touched foreheads for the last time.

Kelila waved at Ezekiel and skipped off with Mikal. Shiriel didn't even watch. Instead, she smiled up at Ezekiel. "Shall we?"

They turned west and followed the Chebar away from Tel-Abib, strolling to a grove of poplar trees. The winter breeze brushed off the water and swirled through the draping branches as they sat facing the water.

"You know what I miss?" Shiriel shivered.

Ezekiel put his arm around her, pulling her to his aching heart. A grunt found its way through his body's defenses.

"Your voice. I mean, it's…miraculous to hear Yahweh speaking through you." She encircled his middle with her arms. "But I remember your voice carrying to the corners of the temple. Even then Yahweh used you."

His throat squeezed.

Shiriel gazed at him with adoration. "I'm so proud of you."

He traced the curve of her cheek and the indent in her chin. Pressure built up inside with no outlet.

No words.

He couldn't even weep.

"It has to happen this way." Sadness lined her eyes.

Did she know?

"Jerusalem must fall. The sins of our fathers are too great. No partiality."

No partiality.

Ezekiel laid his head on Shiriel's lap and held tight to her back.

Oh God, I cannot stand in the gap for Israel and Judah—their blood has filled Your Holy City. But my wife serves You and loves Your laws.

"We'll get through this." She stroked his hair. "Do you recall the word of the Lord to Isaiah? There will come a day when the remnant will depend on Yahweh and will return to Almighty God."

But not soon enough. Ezekiel's airway closed. He touched Shiriel's throat and formed the word "sing."

"What do you want to hear?"

All of it, if it would slow down time. He shook his head.

Shiriel curved over him and kissed his hair. "*Hear my cry, Oh Lord, attend to my prayer. From the end of the earth, I will cry to You. When my heart is overwhelmed lead me to the rock that is higher than I.*"

Her voice rolled over him, low and rich like the sound of her flute. "*For You, oh God, have heard my vows. You have given me the heritage of those who fear Your name. You will prolong the king's life*—well maybe not *this king*."

Ezekiel tried to smile, but emotion choked him, drowning him as surely as if he'd plunged his head in the Euphrates.

"*—so will I sing praise to Your name forever, that I may daily perform my vows.*"

Who will teach our child Your ways? Who will pass on the heritage?

Shiriel transitioned into a love song—probably one of Solomon's.

Ezekiel could no longer hear over the rushing in his ears and the pressure in his head. His arm tingled and grew heavy. She shifted her legs, and he sat up.

He clenched and unclenched his hand and wiggled his fingers. What was the point of reviving them when he was dying inside?

Shiriel pushed herself up and brushed off her skirts, extending a hand to Ezekiel. "Shall we walk more?"

Heaviness in his spirit told him the time grew short. He allowed her to assist him and tugged her off balance, catching her against his chest.

She laughed and linked her fingers behind his back.

Don't let go. Hold on to me. He willed his voice to work, but sound did not breach the barrier. Framing her face with his hands, he gave a stilted smile and pressed on his heart. "I love you."

"I love you too." Shiriel twisted and drew his arms around her from behind.

The afternoon sun touched the top of a towering ziggurat, casting a dagger-like shadow across the plain.

"Are we allowed to go up in the tower? Do you suppose that's the one from the days of Nimrod?" Shiriel turned her head to study his mouth.

Ezekiel glanced upward at the looming tower with a shudder. It wasn't Nimrod's tower—that was said to be in the plain south of the city—but something about the tower made his skin crawl. He tightened his arms around her shoulders and shook his head. "No. Stay with me."

"It will be all right." Shiriel's compassionate smile compressed his stifled emotions with a fist of iron. "Yahweh will make a way. His words will come to pass."

Ezekiel's throat closed as Shiriel pressed a kiss to his hand and ducked under his arm.

"It's such a beautiful sunset! Look how soft and pleasant the desert looks!" Shiriel gestured toward the horizon where the sun dipped low, shadowing the desert sand with a soft purple hue. The poplar trees reflected off the still water of the canal, their shadows growing long.

Ezekiel ground to a halt, sending sand into his sandal. Something wasn't right. *Shiriel!*

But Shiriel kept strolling. "Don't you just feel the presence of the Lord when the day is winding to a close?" She breathed in deeply and lifted her arms.

Wait. Ezekiel reached for her hand and missed. The distance between them grew, but his feet were lead-filled.

Shiriel twirled around, backing away with a smile spreading across her face.

Thwack! Her smile dropped and her eyes widened. Her body went stiff. Ezekiel dropped his staff and stumbled into a run, catching Shiriel as she toppled forward. He cushioned her fall with his body.

An arrow protruded from her back.

No! Ezekiel searched the trees and shadows, finding no one. He stared down at his wife's vacant gaze.

A wail rent his soul but didn't sound.

Rage filled his body but couldn't escape.

Cradling Shiriel's lifeless body to his chest, he rocked back and forth. *God, would that I could die too.*

The sky went red as the sun lowered into the west, and the temperature dropped, plunging him into despair. Chills wracked his body, sinking into his bones.

His wife was dead.

The song of his life died and love along with her.

39

How long, O LORD? Will You forget me forever? How long will You hide Your face from me? How long shall I take counsel in my soul, having sorrow in my heart daily? How long will my enemy be exalted over me?
—Psalm 13:1-2

The rivers of the Euphrates swelled on the outskirts of Babylon, marking the beginning of the flood season as Gilead surveyed the walled cities with fresh eyes. Tomorrow, they'd be home after two grueling months of getting reports from Elam to the southeast.

How long had he been thinking of Babylon as home? Perhaps not Babylon, but the congregation, Ezekiel's messages, and Shiri's singing.

Gilead stood alert as General Vakhtang conferred with Kha-Hea, a messenger from the city.

Around him, the slaves prepared the campsite, shooting dirty glares his way. The talk was that Gilead thought himself better than them. In truth, he'd rather lend a hand than stand sentinel for the general. His back twinged with the scars from the one time he had helped set up camp.

"—The Jewess was taken care of." Arrogance laced Kha-Hea's low tone.

Coldness twanged around Gilead's spine.

"Any witnesses?" Vakhtang's teeth tore into the roasted lamb.

"Her husband was there, but he didn't see anything."

Juice dripped off Vakhtang's chin. "Why is the husband still alive? We can't have anything jeopardizing the plan."

Kha-Hea snorted. "The husband is that imbecile. You know, the mute, mad one who claims his god binds him. He is no threat."

Ezekiel. Gilead's stomach churned. Meaning Shiri was the one 'taken care of.' He gripped the fabric of his wrapped trousers to keep from lunging at the messenger.

Vakhtang leaned back with a sneer at Gilead. "Aren't you friends with the one who calls himself a priest, dog?"

Gilead's fingers itched to nock an arrow. He schooled the fierce rage. *No expression.* "Yes, Master."

"Wouldn't it be ironic to have *you* silence the husband?"

The general delighted in goading a reaction. Any display of opposition fueled his sadistic streak. Gilead inhaled slowly through the nose.

Yahweh, my heart is bent on anger. Help me control myself. He was no good to Ezekiel or the cause if he was dead.

Vakhtang waved his hand. "You are dismissed, Jew."

Gilead snapped his heels together and backed away. His thoughts whizzed around like arrows in battle. One lodged tight. *What had Shiri done to draw Vakhtang's evil attention?*

Had she overheard some intrigue? She hadn't played in the throne room for years now.

Captain Vakhtang carried an air of false subservience to King Nebuchadnezzar. Did he plan a revolt and Shiri walked in on him? Who else, besides Kha-Hea, was involved?

He had to get Ezekiel out of Tel-Abib. If Shiri had been imprisoned—

Gilead's thoughts halted and reared back on powerful legs. Chaldeans didn't silence people by locking them in jail. He ducked behind a tent and pounded a fist to his forehead. *Yahweh!* Would he endanger Ezekiel by going to him?

Lead me in the path of righteousness, for Your name's sake. Gilead peeled his fingers from the bowstring slung across his chest and lowered his arm. *I know vengeance is Yours, but I'd really like to be involved in this.*

He growled and mentally bowed his knee and whispered, "You are the Potter. I am but the clay. What You decide I will obey. I might need Your help, but I *will* follow Your leading." The unknown battled against submission.

Footsteps drew near to the tent.

Gilead sank into the shadows as Kha-Hea strode by.

Follow him.

Now? Or when we get to the city? Gilead followed the messenger silently to where his stallion stood being groomed by a slave.

"Why is my horse unsaddled? Incompetent fool! You knew I was in a hurry." Kha-Hea flicked his wrist and a whip snaked onto the slave's forearm with a crack.

The stallion whinnied, the whites of his eyes showing, apparently familiar with the man's hot temper. Kha-Hea jerked the whip back, and the slave screamed as his flesh tore away.

Though no one stood near, Gilead was thrust forward. He raised his hands to calm the beast—and the horse. "Perhaps I can help, my lord."

"Very well." Kha-Hea appraised him. "Move quickly."

Gilead blocked the messenger's view of the cowering, bleeding man. He reached for the stallion's lead and murmured, "Would you please tell Master Vakhtang that Kha-Hea requires my service?"

Needing no other prompting, the slave darted off.

The agitated horse sidestepped, and Gilead shoved Kha-Hea out of the way. "Apologies, my lord. The horse nearly stepped on your foot."

Kha-Hea blanched and stepped clear, alternating between grumbling and cocky arrogance. What kindled his entitlement? His rank was not much higher than Gilead's.

Gilead approached the weaving steed with palms raised. The horse reared, wild eyes still trained on Kha-Hea's whip.

"Whoa." Gilead stepped in the animal's line of sight and slowly reached again for the lead rope.

The stallion snorted but allowed Gilead to stroke his neck. As Gilead calmed the horse and readied him for travel, he covertly studied Kha-Hea's erratic patterns. The messenger puffed his chest out and strutted back and forth, muttering under his breath. What scheme elevated the man in his own esteem? What had Shiri to do with it all?

Gilead ran his fingers along whip scars on the horse's haunches and inhaled through his nose. *If he has done something to Shiri, I'll…* He'd what? Make the haughty Chaldean pay? And then what? Gilead's life was nothing if he attacked a Chaldean. To bring justice for Shiri was worth the cost of whatever torturous death he would be dealt, but what was the right thing to do?

Pray to the Lord for the peace of the city. Clenching his jaw, Gilead looked squarely at Kha-Hea. "Will that be all?"

Mounting the spirited animal, Kha-Hea dismissed him with a wave.

The slave reappeared with linen wrapped around his arm and spoke to Gilead. "Master Vakhtang commands you to accompany Kha-Hea to Babylon, alert the king of his arrival, and arrange for a banquet."

"As my master wishes." Gilead bowed his head and readied his own swift stead.

"Arrows." Kha-Hea extended his hand. "I don't trust a dirty Jew with weapons, despite what General Vakhtang says."

You'd be surprised what I can do with the bowstring. Gilead tamped his response down and surrendered his quiver. He reined back and matched the pace of the flighty, untried stallion.

Riding ahead would build distrust, and Kha-Hea was a deadly archer. His danger lay in his accuracy, yes, but the true threat was his whim.

Riding hard, they reached the palace stable as the dusk settled against the sands.

Kha-Hea flung himself from his horse and strode away as if he owned the palace.

Gilead smiled to the stable boy as he dismounted. "Thank you."

The retribution that would come for not prioritizing his assignment held no weight against the urgency in his spirit to get to Ezekiel.

Follow. The same still voice.

He clenched his fist. *Fortify my friend, Yahweh.*

A mighty man of valor didn't reach his rank by disobeying orders from his commanding officer.

Gilead snapped his heels together and marched through the courtyard. Approaching the governor of the throne room's affairs, he slapped two fingers on Vakhtang's insignia on his left arm. "General Vakhtang has returned, bringing news from Elam, and requests audience with the Crown Prince of Babylon."

"Very good." The governor scanned his tablet. "How far out?"

"The general has made camp on the outskirts of the city and will arrive tomorrow."

Kha-Hea slunk into the view down the corridor, no longer swaggering.

"Captain Vakhtang requested a feast upon arrival."

The governor's head snapped up. "It is good news, then?"

"Yes, my lord." Gilead kept his gaze on Kha-Hea's shifting stance. *What are you up to?*

"I have it on the agenda for tomorrow. The general will bring a report." The governor waved his hand.

Dismissed, Gilead slipped into the shadows. The purposeful stride of a nobleman coming from the other direction masked Gilead's soft footsteps.

The newcomer's stride faltered for less than a breath at the sight of Kha-Hea pushing off the wall. As if unaware of Kha-Hea's presence, the nobleman examined the mosaic of blue and gold tiles.

Gilead crept closer, one with the lengthening shadows.

A troop of entertainers exited the throne room by the governor's station with a swish of sheer fabrics and the tinkle of brass ankle charms.

"Tomorrow." Kha-Hea's hushed tone was nearly lost amongst the footsteps and chatter echoing down the hall.

Gilead blocked out the sounds, straining closer, pressing against the pillar.

Kha-Hea spoke again, his voice barely audible. "Vakhtang brings an army. He'll give an account of the nation, Elam's treason."

Gilead tipped his head. Elam had complied and paid the tribute in full.

"—The news will shock him so, that the crown prince's heart will fail." Footsteps echoed on the marble floor away from Gilead's hiding place.

Would it be so bad to have Nebuchadnezzar replaced?

But by Vakhtang? That would be far worse. He would offer no favor for the Jews.

Was this what Shiri had gotten involved with? The ache dug deep into his chest. *How long, oh Lord, will You delay justice for Your people?*

Stopping an assassination attempt on the king who'd

enslaved his people didn't top his list of priorities. Who would heed his warning? "What would You have me do?"

The question had barely formed before truth came to light in his consciousness.

Stand still and watch the Lord fight for you.

Gilead opened his eyes to find the general who had escorted them from Judea all those years ago approaching the governor's station.

I'm standing here, waiting on You.

Rabgar-Nebo glanced up at Gilead, eyes narrowing in recognition.

Anticipation resolved Gilead's helplessness.

The Chaldean officer beckoned Gilead with the jerk of his chin. "I know you."

Gilead bowed his head. "Yes, my lord."

Rabgar-Nebo snapped his fingers. "You were a friend of the priest."

"Yes, my lord."

The governor of the throne room glanced up at Gilead.

"How is our funny friend?" Rabgar-Nebo stood tall and clasped his hands behind his back.

Gilead lifted his eyes and kept his head down. "I'm not sure, my lord. I've heard some disturbing news and haven't had time to validate it." Not that there was much hope for disproving it.

He wiped his hand over his mouth and his beard and rolled his shoulders. "There is something else I've just now overheard that troubles me."

Rabgar-Nebo arched his eyebrows, waiting.

Inhibitions of speaking out of turn gave Gilead pause. How to get the message across? "Have you heard anything about my service that would give you any reason to doubt my character?"

The governor exchanged an amused glance with Rabgar-Nebo.

Gilead knelt before Rabgar-Nebo. "Is there anything you saw when we traveled across the land that gave you reason to doubt my word?"

"What are you saying, man?" Rabgar-Nebo's expression grew serious.

"I've overheard what sounds to be a threat to the crown prince—and thus to the kingdom of Nebuchadnezzar." Gilead glanced around the hall and lowered his voice. "Indeed, it seems I am a player in this wicked game."

Rabgar-Nebo crossed his arms. "Go on."

"My master, General Vakhtang, sent me to announce his arrival and Elam's insurrection. Only they did not riot." Gilead turned his attention to the governor. "Just now Kha-Hea spoke to someone—a nobleman—that tomorrow was the banquet, and 'it' would happen then."

The Chaldeans exchanged skeptical glances.

"You think you've heard an assassination plan? General Vakhtang makes no qualms about his dislike for Jews." Rabgar-Nebo scratched his neck. "How do I know this isn't just vindication for his ill treatment?"

"That is why I beseech you to consider what you know of me." Time stretched. Gilead's knees ached against the cool tile, and his chest squeezed with thoughts of Ezekiel's fate.

"Guard." Rabgar-Nebo's voice blasted down the corridor. "Shackle this man. Detain him."

Sandals slapped from behind Gilead and chains clanked.

"You realize I need to restrain you, in case you are involved?" Rabgar-Nebo's stoic expression gave no indication of his thoughts.

"You believe me?" Gilead willingly lifted his wrists for the shackles.

Rabgar-Nebo gave a brief nod as Gilead was led away.

Down in the bowels of the palace, Gilead was deposited in a dark cell. The brief glance allotted before the soldiers took away the torch revealed walls of stone and a pot in the corner.

The darkness pressed on his eyes like the stench of human waste.

Chains clanking, Gilead lowered himself to his knees and leaned his forearms on the moist stone floor. *Yahweh, deliver me in my innocence.*

What right had he to ask favors of Yahweh? "God, my heart is burdened for Ezekiel."

Though he couldn't bring himself to voice it, he had no expectation for Shiri's life.

Loss and regret burned his eyes.

40

Son of man, behold, I take away from you the desire of your eyes with one stroke; yet you shall neither mourn nor weep, nor shall your tears run down. Sigh in silence, make no mourning for the dead.
—Ezekiel 24:16-17a

The darkness gave no indication of time passing. Hours? Days?

Gilead paced and prayed, pouring his soul out before the Lord until all words ran dry.

Still, the burden for Ezekiel pressed against his shoulders.

Weak from lack of food, Gilead slumped against the wall. He summoned memories of Shiri singing, ushering his heart into the proper attitude for worship. Her encouraging words and smile.

She understood the struggle of life. She *saw* him.

No more. Despair surfaced from carefully buried depths.

Now every word he'd spoken in the heat of the last argument with his son paraded through his thoughts. *Worthless.*

Failure. You call yourself a changed man, yet you destroyed your son and didn't extend grace.

"No!" Gilead pushed himself off the wall. "I am changed by the grace of God."

Victory. Not defeat. He commanded his mouth to sing a song of Yahweh's goodness, to remind himself.

Somewhere down the isolated hall, a heavy door creaked open, clanging against the wall and reverberating down the tunnel.

Gilead traced his hand along the wall to the iron bars and strained his neck. Light pooled, dispelling the darkness.

Shielding his eyes, he waited.

"It turns out you were right." Rabgar-Nebo's voice accompanied the faceless form. "The crown prince is alive, thanks to you. All who were involved in this uprising have been executed."

"I'm glad." The words scratched against Gilead's throat.

Clank! The key turned in the lock.

"The prince is prepared to reward you." Rabgar-Nebo removed the shackles.

"If it is all the same, I wish no reward. I'd like to go to Ezekiel." Gilead rubbed the tender flesh on his wrist as they strode down the corridor.

"You risk your life for the prince, yet seek no recognition?" Wonder lined Rabgar-Nebo's voice. "Why?"

"I wish him no harm. He is the son of the one my God appointed over us." The tunnel grew light as they turned a curve. Day.

"There is the matter of transferring your service." Rabgar-Nebo slanted a sharp glance his way.

"I don't suppose you have need of a bodyguard skilled in archery?"

A laugh rumbled from Rabgar-Nebo's chest. "The matter will have to go before the governor of the Jews. You are free to visit your friend. I pray to the gods that your disturbing news is false. Report back to me at the first hour."

"Thank you, my lord." Gilead bowed.

Rabgar-Nebo lowered a large pendant over Gilead's head. "I'd be honored to have your allegiance." The general snapped his heels together and strode away.

As he was being ferried across the Euphrates, Gilead lifted the plaque. "Favored of the King." Frowning, he yanked it free. Recognition meant nothing when he only did his duty. He wound his arm back to send the praise of men to the depth of the swollen river.

Could this be useful for the cause? He glanced over his shoulder at the two other passengers—one had eyes closed and his chest rose and fell, the other quickly averted his gaze. The pilots dug their paddles into the churning river with synchronized efficiency.

Gilead clenched the trinket and the edge bit into his palm. Why did he debate with himself? The *quffa* bumped into the dock, jostling the sleeping man awake. He grunted and climbed out of the vessel and around the waiting passengers with admirable agility. The other passenger followed with a curious glance toward Gilead's fisted hand.

Tucking the ivory into the pouch at his waist with a scowl, Gilead hoisted himself up on the dock before the new passengers swarmed onboard.

While he lingered over an irrelevant decision, Ezekiel and Keli needed him. Grief slammed into him. Had he already disregarded the possibility that Shiri still lived? *Oh, Yahweh! Please let me be wrong in my assumption.* Gilead lengthened his stride toward Tel-Abib, unable to expect Shiri to great him at the door.

Dread tempered each step. What would he find at Ezekiel's house?

"Gilead?" Atta popped up from her garden plot.

His shoulders tightened. He couldn't very well ignore the woman, despite the urgency in his spirit.

Atta glanced down the street and back again, beckoning him close.

Squelching a growl, Gilead rested his arms on Atta's chest-high wall. "I am in a hurry."

"So, you've heard? About—" She glanced over her shoulder. "About Shiri?"

It *was* true. Gilead's gut clenched. His shoulders sagged. "What happened?"

Atta's eyes watered. "It was the oddest thing. After synagogue—about two months ago—Ezekiel and Shiri went on a stroll—I would've watched Keli, if I had known—Dumah and I have been attending the synagogue in Babylon."

Gilead rubbed his temples. "Forgive me, Atta. What happened? After the stroll?"

"I saw him come home late. He had blood on his tunic, and his hands were dirty." Atta glanced toward Ezekiel's house. "All that week *he* brought Keli to me. Never Shiri. Keli said her *ima*...I only found out when I went to borrow—"

"*Saba* Gilead!" The door flung open, and the little girl flew out.

Atta lowered her voice. "He never mourned for her. The next Sabbath, the congregation asked why, and he spouted off about our people not grieving if Jerusalem fell."

Gilead side-stepped to the gate and knelt to intercept the blur that was Keli. "There is my granddaughter."

"Where have you been? *Abba* needed you." The small girl's accusing glare blurred behind a sheen of moisture.

"I'm sorry, sweetheart. I wish I had been...I just found out."

"Are you taking me home?" Keli glanced between him and Atta.

"If you'd like." Gilead pushed off the ground with a groan

that was only partially playful. "Thank you, Atta. I will investigate the matter."

Atta clutched her chest as her eyes filled with tears. She bent to kiss Keli's cheek. "I'll see you tomorrow, dear."

When they left the courtyard, Keli tugged her hand free from Gilead's and scrubbed her cheek. "She always kisses me and asks how I am."

"I think she is sad for you but doesn't know what to say." How much would a child understand? "What would you like her to do—or ask?"

Keli contemplated with her lips tightly tucked behind her teeth. "Nobody ever talks about *Ima* with me. But I know they do before I get there because they go all quiet and sad. They think I'm a baby."

Gilead swallowed hard. "People never know what to say at times like this."

She tugged him to a stop outside her house.

Squatting before her, Gilead studied her while she shifted from one foot to the other.

She lifted teary eyes to him. "*Abba* doesn't write to me anymore. I try to be helpful and good, but I don't think he loves me any longer."

"Listen to me, little one." Gilead held her close, despite desperately needing to bathe. "Your *abba* loves you very much. He's just hurting. Grieving."

"What about me?" Keli's chin quivered. "My belly hurts."

"Are you ill?"

"No." Keli dragged the word out with an exasperated sigh. She rubbed her middle and her chest. "It's just…"

Gilead wiped at his mouth. "It is difficult for adults to express, too. All I can tell you for certain is, Yahweh is still good. This didn't surprise Him, and we are still going to praise Him. Right?"

Keli fiddled with his gold collar. "I miss her singing."

Gilead cleared his throat and pinched the moisture from his nose. He cleared his throat again. "Me too."

Her little face turned up, desperate for reassurance.

"Would you like to sing something now?"

"With you?" Keli patted his shoulder.

Gilead closed his eyes and tried to find the tune. "*How long, till You reign in Zion*—"

Keli's small voice wobbled alongside his.

Movement at the door drew Gilead's attention to Ezekiel watching with dead eyes.

Keli squeezed Gilead's hand tight and pressed close.

Leaning heavily on his staff, Ezekiel turned and hobbled inside.

"Do you have afternoon chores?" Gilead patted Kelila's shoulder. "Best get on it."

He stepped into the dark in the room and waited till his eyes adjusted. Ezekiel stood three paces away. Keli ducked around him and bustled around the kitchen.

Gilead's chest constricted. He threw his arms around Ezekiel's stiff shoulders. "I am so sorry, my brother. How are you doing?"

Ezekiel shoved him away.

Gilead winced. He'd done the same thing Keli had said didn't help.

Ezekiel wrinkled his nose and mouthed, "You stink."

"I know. I've just come from the prison."

Ezekiel plodded to the large jar of water by the door and begin ladling water into the vat over the outside fire pit.

"You're not going to ask what I was in prison for?" Gilead followed him outside.

Turning with a tolerant expression, Ezekiel didn't seem to care that water trickled down his foot.

Was this a good idea? Would he be glad of the news? Perhaps he could now grieve.

"Shiri got caught up in an assassination plot against the

crown prince. All plotters have been executed." Gilead put his hand on Ezekiel's shoulder. "I thought you'd like to know. Yahweh has vindicated her."

The muscle in Ezekiel's jaw twitched. His eyes narrowed and a coldness settled over his face. He shook his head and shuffled inside.

Gilead mashed his eyes shut. That had not gone well. He resumed the water transfer.

Ezekiel reappeared with a scroll and pushed it at Gilead's chest.

He fumbled and almost dropped it into the vat. "Sorry."

Shrugging, Ezekiel ripped the parchment from Gilead's hand and plunged it into the water.

"What are you doing?" Gilead reached into the heating water and retrieved the parchment. The ink did not run. Was it coated in oil? He examined it. Incredible.

Ezekiel pointed to the fire, eyebrows raised in challenge and mouthed. "Try burning it."

Gilead backed away, keeping the scroll out of reach. "All right, I get it. The message can't be destroyed or altered."

Hand outstretched, Ezekiel approached.

"Are you going to—?"

Ezekiel waved his hand in dismissal and jerked the scroll away. He spread the parchment wide and jabbed a section.

Gilead read aloud. "Son of man, behold I take away from you the desire of your eyes with one stroke—." He scanned the message with growing horror. Yahweh may have vindicated Shiri's murder, but He had also ordered the assassination.

He searched the words for answers. "So, I spoke to the people in the morning and that evening my wife died, and the next morning I did as I was commanded."

Gilead sank to the ground. "I don't understand." He had just told that little girl Yahweh was good. *And You took away her* ima. No wonder she stared at him like she knew better.

Ezekiel transferred the water to the bathing tub and sent a look of dejected acceptance toward Gilead.

Oh God. My brother's faith is shattered. Mine is teetering. Guide him through this trial and deliver him for Your name's sake.

Alone, behind the privacy screen, Gilead sank into the warm water and silently wept, mourning for the man who couldn't and the girl who didn't know how.

41

"To you it is commanded, O peoples, nations, and languages, that at the time you hear the sound of the horn, flute, harp, lyre, and psaltery, in symphony with all kinds of music, you shall fall down and worship the gold image that King Nebuchadnezzar has set up; and whoever does not fall down and worship shall be cast into the midst of a burning fiery furnace."
—Daniel 3:4b-6

"It's been two years."

Gilead squeezed his temples. Atta's persistence chipped away at him till he hardly knew why he stood by his position. "He lost his wife, Atta."

"Yes, he did, and it has destroyed him." Atta threw up her hands "Keli will become a woman soon. She needs guidance he can't give."

Age had turned its attention to Gilead. He rolled stiff shoulders back. "We can't separate them. They need each other."

"Ezekiel isn't in the right frame of mind to care for a young woman. He still maintains teaching the children, yet it's Keli who does all the work." The pitch of Atta's voice lowered. "Please. She carries a burden no child should bear. With your insistence, the elders will see that I am the best one to raise that motherless girl."

Was Keli better off with a woman? Gilead rubbed his hand over his face. Atta was right about one thing—Ezekiel wandered around like the dead walking, bearing permanent dark circles and lines etched from despair on his face. Two years after Shiri's death and he made no effort to heal.

Gilead was at the end of his rope. No attempt he had made to help had been received. He had been reassigned as Rabgar-Nebo's bodyguard and had been able to reside in Babylon, enabling him to check in frequently. A lot of good it did. "We can't take the child away from her father. She has lost too much already." He swung around, attempting to end the conversation.

"He's not mentally capable of caring for her." Atta's voice hitched, and she covered her mouth. "I am sorry to say it. You *know* this, Gilead. We all know this. He spends more time with hallucinations—"

Gilead glared at Atta. "Do you doubt his messages come from Yahweh?"

Atta chose her words carefully. "I care about Ezekiel. It breaks my heart to see how hard he's taking Shiri's death. What can we do? The man is a broken vessel. But look at Keli! She cannot thrive in that environment. She never comes to stay with me anymore—"

"Enough." Gilead threw up his hands and gentled his tone. "Atta, I hear your concern, but this doesn't feel right."

Atta's eyebrows furrowed. "He lost his wife. Nothing is going to make it favorable. But surely you see the poor girl's struggle."

Hanging his head, Gilead blew out a long breath. "I need to think it through. It does appear suspicious that you are the one pushing this, though."

Atta opened her mouth.

Gilead held up his hand and indicated the three men walking up the street. "Do you know these people?"

Atta shook her head and adjusted her head scarf. "They appear Jewish. What do they want?"

Signs of the time—his people dressed as Chaldeans and referred to themselves as Jews. "We are about to find out."

"Excuse me, my good man."

Gilead tipped his head. There was something familiar in the young man's eyes. He bowed. The men's silk cloaks and turbans bespoke status. Each wore a signet ring of different provinces. "How may I be of assistance, my lord?"

"I am Shadrach." The spokesman gestured to his companions. "These are my brothers, Meshach and Abednego. We understand a prophet of the living God lives in Tel-Abib."

Gilead refrained from wincing at the Chaldean names. He shot a warning glance to Atta. "What is your business with him?"

Shadrach rubbed the side of his eyebrows with two fingers, bringing memories of years past to Gilead's mind. "It is a matter of spiritual importance."

"What is your given name?" Gilead leaned on Atta's wall.

After exchanging glances with his brothers, Shadrach surveyed Gilead's leather breast plate.

What had they become? Each distrusting their fellow countrymen because of the clothes they wore.

"I am Gilead. I was an archer in the throne room in Jerusalem. I ask because you seem familiar."

Meshach leaned toward Abednego. "I knew it. I told you they had archers on the upper balcony."

Shadrach shook his head at his brother's exuberant whisper. "I am Hananiah. We were brought here eighteen years ago. My brothers are Mishael and Azariah."

The years melted away, and Gilead saw Hananiah as a boy, sitting in the throne room with the various princes on policy training days. Gilead scrutinized Mishael and Azariah but didn't recognize their faces.

"Welcome to Tel-Abib, my princes. I will take you to Ezekiel." Nodding farewell to Atta, Gilead stepped abreast of the satraps.

"I feel compelled to tell you, Ezekiel is not able to speak any words unless it's a direct revelation from Yahweh." Should he mention the prophet's state of mind?

"Perhaps he won't be able to help us then." Azariah blew out a breath.

"Ezekiel writes out answers." Sometimes. If they could capture his attention.

"He was a priest, correct?" Hananiah rubbed his eyebrow.

"Ezekiel was in the priestly service when we were exiled." Gilead rapped on the door.

Keli answered.

"Is your *abba* around?" Foolish question. Ezekiel was always around. "These men would like to inquire of him."

Peering into the house, Keli bit the corner of her lip. "Perhaps tomorrow."

An excuse offered frequently, without the promise there would be a better time. Gilead's chest constricted at the solemn expression in her eyes. Perhaps Atta was right—a child shouldn't have to care for her father.

"Tomorrow will be too late."

Gilead followed Hananiah's gaze to the south. They must be in town for the dedication of Nebuchadnezzar's golden image.

Before Keli could offer another apology, Ezekiel appeared at the door, patted Keli's shoulder, and smiled at her.

She beamed radiantly up at him and skipped inside.

Gilead made introductions and evaluated his friend with new perspective. Did those once-sharp eyes, that never missed a detail, see anything these days, or had they grown as disheveled and uncaring as the rest of the man?

Ezekiel turned back into the house without so much as an invitation. Gilead smiled regardless and directed the men into the house. Once they rested on cushions still set out for synagogue, Keli served them cool water.

Ezekiel turned toward his cup, tipping it front and back, as if testing how far he could tip it without water spilling. Liquid splashed onto his trousers, but he didn't react.

Hananiah glanced at Gilead, his intelligent gaze seeming to gauge the situation.

Clearing his throat, Gilead indicated for them to begin. If they waited for Ezekiel's go-ahead, they would be waiting till the Messiah came.

"My lord, we seek Yahweh's will with earnest hearts." Hananiah set his cup to the side and leaned forward, clasping his hands before him. "As satraps of provinces of this nation, we were invited—"

"Threatened," Azariah interjected.

Gilead covered a grin. Hopefully the man was more discreet with his Chaldean employers.

"Azariah." Hananiah turned a glare to his younger brother. "We *must* attend the dedication of King Nebuchadnezzar's…statue…idol. All who attend will be expected to bow and worship this idol. My question is this—will Yahweh excuse our actions, as our hearts will still be true to Him?"

"Like He did when Naaman converted in the days of Elisha?" Mishael fidgeted with his turban. "And had to support the Aramean King in the temple?"

Ezekiel made no acknowledgment of the inquiry.

Gilead put his hand on Ezekiel's shoulder and cleared his throat.

Blinking once, Ezekiel picked up the stylus as if it weighed a talent and sluggishly dragged it through the moist clay.

The men respectfully waited, not giving away their thoughts.

Ezekiel dropped the tablet with a clatter and folded his arms.

Gilead picked up the tablet and read aloud. "Why would Yahweh spare you if you bow before an idol?"

Mishael's turban started to unwind as a result of his fiddling. "But if we don't, we will be cast into a furnace."

Gilead's stomach sank. *Oh, Yahweh, preserve Your remnant.*

Ezekiel shrugged a shoulder.

Hananiah's brow furrowed. "Will the Lord deliver us if we stand for Him? The prophet Isaiah said 'when you walk through the fire you shall not be burned.'"

Begrudgingly, Ezekiel held his hand out for the tablet.

Gilead watched resolve settle on Hananiah's face. Azariah drew in a deep breath and set his jaw. Mishael's gaze darted between his brothers.

Ezekiel handed Gilead the tablet. "Is our God able to deliver you? Yes. Nothing is impossible. Does it mean this protection is guaranteed to His followers? No. The Lord gives, and the Lord takes away."

"Blessed be His name," the three brothers murmured in unison.

Did each man count the cost?

Gilead bowed his head briefly before scrutinizing Ezekiel. "Would it be wrong to pray for deliverance?"

Ezekiel's scowl crushed Gilead. Did he think because the Lord chose not to deliver Shiri, that all prayers would be denied? Because he had lost faith, he condemned others for having it?

He wrote with haste and smeared it out with the side of his fist, then decided on another message. "Is it worth it?"

Mishael rewound his turban. "No one would know…except us."

"We cannot follow Yahweh only when it is convenient. When privilege is lavished upon us," Hananiah reasoned. "We cannot ignore that everything we have was given to us from Him."

Azariah drew his shoulders back, and the two of them turned toward Mishael.

Mishael inhaled deeply, hesitated, then nodded once. "I will stand with Yahweh."

The brothers rose, each bowing at the waist to Ezekiel.

"Thank you for your wisdom." Resolve set Hananiah's expression. "Please pray we remain strong and do not waver."

Azariah was last. "We will see you on the other shore of the great hope."

Ezekiel's eyes narrowed.

Gilead walked the somber men to the door. "God is worthy to be praised." He embraced each man and released them to Yahweh.

They strode to the city, arms around each other's shoulders.

In this hostile land, how long would it be before Gilead was forced to make the same choice?

Fortify Your servants, Lord, as they stand for You. Deliver them from this evil plan if this is in Your will.

Heaviness weighed on his spirit as he returned to the darkened interior.

Crash!

Gilead whirled around, hand flying to his bow.

Ezekiel tore at his beard, and a feral growl scratched the air.

In five strides, Gilead had crossed the room, assessing for danger. Everything appeared as before. "What is it?"

"He has heard from Yahweh." Keli's matter-of-fact tone contrasted the way she ducked behind the preparation table.

Ezekiel, why are you acting like this? You are feeding Atta's accusations of being unfit. Gilead bent to retrieve the tablet at the base of the wall. The frame was cracked down the middle.

The same message from earlier.

"Something about Hananiah and his brothers?"

Ezekiel turned his back.

"Something bad? They will give in and bow?" Gilead strode around to face the prophet. "Write it down."

Ezekiel's face reddened and his eyes grew flinty. He jammed a stylus into the clay. "Yahweh will deliver them through the fire. For His glory."

If he clenched the stylus any tighter, it would snap in two.

"That's wonderful!" Gilead blinked. He must be missing something. "Why does that disturb you?"

Ezekiel shook his head. He smeared the words with fierce strength.

Realization dawned. "You're upset because Yahweh will deliver them, when He does nothing for your situation?"

The prophet's glare answered that question.

Gilead blew out a breath. "I don't know what to say that you don't already know. It is not ours to decide how Yahweh should act. Mercy is His to give."

Ezekiel turned his face.

When had Gilead become the spiritually sound one? He wasn't the one trained in the ways of Yahweh. "Would you rather they suffered because you are miserable?"

No answer.

Assurance filled Gilead's mind. "I know this. As Yahweh will walk these men through the fire, so He is with *you*. The flame will not scorch you either."

Ezekiel pressed his fists to his ears.

Anger surged through Gilead. He ripped Ezekiel's hands away. "Yahweh is with you. You are precious in His sight. You have been chosen for this crucible. It is an honor to serve Him."

Ezekiel shoved him away, his glare hot enough to ignite the furnace the brothers faced tomorrow. He pushed himself to his feet and limped up the stairs.

Gilead lowered his head to his hands. How could Yahweh use him if Ezekiel would not accept his help?

42

So they come to you as people do, they sit before you as My people, and they hear your words, but they do not do them; for with their mouth they show much love, but their hearts pursue their own gain. Indeed, you are to them as a very lovely song of one who has a pleasant voice and can play well on an instrument; for they hear your words but they do not do them. And when this comes to pass—surely it will come—then they will know that a prophet has been among them.
—Ezekiel 33:31-33

On the fifth day of the tenth month which was in the twelfth year of King Coniah's captivity.

"Jerusalem has been captured!" The ragged man burst into the Sabbath gathering as the congregation milled around. His face and eyes reflected the horrors he had seen.

Ezekiel's jaw popped and his tongue loosened.

Five days shy of three years since Shiriel's death.

The scene before him blurred into his grey vision.

Someone offered the traveler water.

Another washed his feet.

The elders tsked pretentiously about the fate of Jerusalem.

Now that Jerusalem's judgment was meted, he could speak on behalf of the people, but what was there to say? The congregation was hospitable and entirely missed the point.

The woman serving the messenger candied dates gestured toward Ezekiel. "That's our rabbi. He's a prophet. Wait until you hear the words he brings from Yahweh."

"His voice is so rich, when he speaks the heavens listen." A second woman hovered with golden rounds of bread.

Yet they didn't obey the words. Ezekiel should feel sorrow at their misplaced values but couldn't bring himself to care.

"You should've heard his wife sing." Both women exhaled breathy sighs and clutched their chests. "A life cut short too soon."

"Yahweh needed her more than we did."

The traveler locked a challenging gaze on Ezekiel. "We destroyed all our harps by the rivers of Babylon. If anyone performs the music of our homeland in this pit of evil, they are merely conforming to the culture around them."

A wave of darkness pressed against Ezekiel's throat. His capacity for regarding these irresponsible imposters had been exceeded. He pushed a path through the congregation to the door.

Their mouths moved, but he heard no sound. They pressed close on all sides, sucking all the air from the room. He squeezed through the door and drew in a breath that did nothing to dispel the pressure in his lungs. Rubbing the leaves of Shiriel's lavender plant, Ezekiel pounded his fingers against his forehead.

A muffled voice. A small hand slipped into his. Kelila's face came into focus. The one thing through which color still attempted to reach him.

He touched her cheek.

"It's time to start, *Abba*."

I can't. Ezekiel managed to shake his head, refusing to speak the words. *Not today. Never again.*

"Can I come with you?" Her brow furrowed, the constant expression she gave him. "*Abba*? I love you."

"I love you, too." He forced himself to form the words. How many times had he missed the opportunity with Shiriel? He touched her cheek again.

Ezekiel had to get away, regardless of Kelila's pleading look. He fled, scrambling through crowds, men, women. Despair stalked him, echoing his every step, every pound of his staff to the dirt. Still, he ran. Blackness caught up with him, slamming him to his knees.

Ezekiel drew in upon himself, covering his face from those passing by. The market? The palace grounds?

The scent of lavender breached his senses. He'd told Shiriel to stop singing because the people viewed it as entertainment. Yet that was how they saw *him.*

Shiriel. God is the song of my life. Ezekiel scoffed, the sound from his unfettered throat surprising him. Why had he never shortened her name like everyone else did? Why couldn't he have told her *she* was the song of his life?

What did he have left but hard-hearted sheep and irresponsible shepherds?

The word of the Lord pressed in his chest.

"No." His voice was foreign to his ears. "I'm not bound to You anymore!"

Resist as he might, Ezekiel found himself lifted to his feet, and his legs moved swiftly toward the palace prison. The guard on duty was vacant from his post, and before he knew it, Ezekiel stood before Coniah's cell.

This man who lounged against silk cushions and drank from a silver goblet.

A moan shattered the silence from the neighboring cell, echoing the cry of a wounded animal.

"Shut up!" Coniah hurled his goblet against the iron bars with a clatter.

Wine splashed on Ezekiel's face. Against his will he glanced at the man whose pain resonated his own.

The torch in the corridor cast light onto a man staring blankly his way, eyes gouged out. "Who's there?"

Zedekiah. Unseeing, just as the Lord had revealed.

Coniah lunged for the bars, rattling them with an intensity that would deafen a man who cared about his hearing. "Do not speak again!"

Noticing Ezekiel, Coniah ceased his ruckus. "Do you bring good news, man of God? Such as me being restored to my throne?"

Zedekiah crept forward with hand extended. "Fool! There's nothing left. Jerusalem has been razed. Which man of God?"

Coniah's arm snaked through the bars, bending and reaching for Zedekiah. "This is all your fault. You misused my throne. *You* ruined our treaty with Babylon."

"You had your opportunity." Zedekiah sneered as he groped forward. "You rolled over like a dog."

"My teeth are set on edge because of your brother's sour grapes!"

Always passing the blame. Always the victim. Disgust wormed its way through Ezekiel's apathy.

Yahweh's words opened Ezekiel's mouth. "'As I live,' says the Lord God, 'you shall no longer use this proverb.'"

Coniah whipped around to Ezekiel. "What?"

"'Behold. All souls are Mine. The soul of the father as well as the soul of the son are mine. The soul who sins shall die.'" Ezekiel had both kings' pretenses of attention. "'You are here because you have *each* sinned against the Lord.'"

Uncle and nephew sprang to the bars. Zedekiah flailed, and Coniah's hands gripped Ezekiel's throat, thumbs pressing against his airway.

Black spots dully flashed. Ezekiel spread his hands, anticipating the end. *Do it. I'm so tired.*

Death's welcome grasp weakened too soon. Ezekiel's body coughed, floundering weak and weary.

He spoke before he could fully breathe. "'Woe to you both, shepherds of Israel. You care for your own needs turning a blind eye—'" Ezekiel leaned toward the frothing Zedekiah. Did no one else appreciate Yahweh's humorous choice of words? "'—to the needs and suffering of the people you have been entrusted.'"

A cough, another gasp at extending his miserable life. "'You have not bound what was broken, nor healed those who were sick. When did you feed the flock? Or seek the lost? Yet with force and cruelty, you have ruled them.'"

Rage pressed mildly against the blanket of Ezekiel's darkness. "'Your failure has brought this calamity upon yourself and our people. Yet you wait for Yahweh's favor? You have both destroyed our nation!'" His chest heaved. Shiriel's life was too great a price for these irresponsible leaders' disobedience.

Zedekiah's grasping hands found Ezekiel's tunic. "That land is ours. Our inheritance. Yahweh gave it to us. We. Deserve. It."

Ezekiel barked out a laugh. Such misplaced faith. "Who is left to tend it? The only throne you'll ever sit on is the pot of refuse! Which is far more honor than you deserve."

Fingers tangled in Ezekiel's beard, and a jagged thumb nail scratched toward his eye. Instinct turned his face away. "Yahweh told me you'd run. I didn't expect it to be this…hideous."

A howl flared up from Zedekiah's throat. He flailed his arms into a bar, and a new scream erupted.

"Inquire of Yahweh for us. Tell Him we repent." Coniah's tone indicated anything but repentance.

Ezekiel sneered. "Would Yahweh allow Himself to be inquired of by *you*?"

"You have a special connection, right?" Coniah gripped the bars. "Ask Him how long."

"Have you not been listening? You will *die* in this land. Yahweh will not reason with either of you." Ezekiel whirled away. If he could feel, he wished it would be satisfaction.

Instead, the unending emptiness grew. When would this ache subside? He wandered aimlessly until the cooling air brought darkness. Coldness saturated him, and he sank to the packed dirt.

"I shouldn't have asked you to stop singing. That wasn't fair of me. I see now how hurtful that must've been. I didn't want to distract from the Lord's message. I'm sorry."

Lavender curled around his face, and he nestled into Shiriel's lap. She hummed and stroked his hair.

"I should've loved you better. *You* were the song of my life. I miss you."

"I know, *Abba*."

"Everything is dark without you. Come back to me."

Shiriel patted his shoulder. "*Abba*, you're talking!"

Abba? The softness of Shiriel's lap vanished. *No. Don't leave me.*

Little hands tugged on his arm, and his eyes opened to the stars in the cold night. The lapping of water nearby.

"Kelila? What are you doing here?"

"I came to find you." She grunted as she helped him sit up.

Ezekiel rubbed heavy eyes. His lashes were wet. "How did you know where I was?"

"This is where you always are." His nine-year-old daughter helped him rise and wrapped one arm around his waist. She tugged his hand over her shoulder. "Let's go home."

How many times had she toted him home? He had failed.

As a husband and a father. He mumbled, "I'm sorry. I'm so sorry."

"It's alright, *Abba.*" Kelila's arm squeezed around his middle. "I like hearing you talk."

His throat clogged. He stumbled, leaning heavily on her shoulder. Another failure. A child should gain support from her father.

Before long they staggered up the stairs, and Kelila tucked his bed clothes to his chin and kissed his forehead. "Sleep well."

Ezekiel's eyes drooped. Everything weighed bushels of grain. His hand struggled to be released from the sheets. He reached out, but Kelila had already left.

"I'm sorry." His head flopped back. Did he sleep? Was he awake? Nothing varied inside or outside him.

Dark.

Heavy.

He curled into himself, shriveling like a raisin in the heat of summer's sun.

43

Come, and let us return to the LORD; For He has torn, but He will heal us. He has stricken, but He will bind us up.
—Hosea 6:1

"She needs a mother!"

Gilead drew in a breath through his nose at Atta's familiar argument.

How he managed to stave her off for over a year was a mystery to him. This time, she had raised the question with Rabgar-Nebo present.

"Gilead, he's not able to care for even himself. Surely you see that?"

"I see it." Gilead's admission felt like sinking an arrow into Ezekiel's back.

Across the marketplace, Ezekiel—dark shadows under his eyes, shoulders hunched and muttering— sat on the half wall near the stalls while Keli browsed.

"It won't be easy." Rabgar-Nebo crossed his arms. "A child is the father's property. Hammurabi's Code gives the father precedence. Unless…"

"Unless what?" Atta pounced on the word.

"If he claims incompetence and agrees to an adoption, it would speed up the process. We could draw up a contract."

Gilead gripped his bowstring. "He's not going to admit—"

"Nonsense. Deep down, he will know he's not doing right by his daughter." Atta brushed off her hands.

Rabgar-Nebo scrutinized Gilead. "Are you sure you want to proceed? This will surely devastate your friend."

Gilead exhaled. "At this point, anything we do will result in pain. Perhaps it will wake him out of his stupor. If that is the outcome, he revives and cares for Keli. Otherwise, he acknowledges he's not well and surrenders her care to Atta."

The woman's lips twitched.

"We have to consider what is best for the girl might be remaining with her *abba*." Gilead shot a fierce glare to Atta.

She nodded reluctantly. "Fine. How do we do it?"

Gilead scrubbed his hand over his face with a growl. "Ezekiel is my closest friend. I've agreed something must be done. Give me time."

"Go home to your husband, woman." The set of Rabgar-Nebo's eyebrows indicated amusement. Compassion lay beneath his efficient persona, making him a joy to serve compared to Gilead's last master. "We will tell you when you may fret over something."

She huffed and crossed her arms but did head toward Tel-Abib.

"Don't be long." Rabgar-Nebo tipped his head to Gilead.

"Yes, master." Gilead snapped his heels. "I'll only be a moment more."

His gaze returned to Ezekiel.

Now he had a parchment spread out and an ink horn beside it.

Gilead muttered, "What are you doing?" Anything written

on his lap would not be the quality needed to preserve for posterity.

Ezekiel rolled up the parchment without blotting it and scooped up two similar scrolls.

Gilead ducked behind the hanging herbs as his friend plodded past, each footstep speaking of raw pain.

Yahweh, I hate this plotting, but I don't know what else to do. He needs restoration but isn't open to Your healing work right now. Use me to help heal my friend. Gilead ducked into an alley-way as Ezekiel stepped onto Nabo-polaaser's bridge.

Ezekiel halted in the middle and peered over the railing, staring transfixed at the murky water.

Did he contemplate flinging himself over? The water was at its lowest cycle. If he jumped, he would injure himself.

Before Gilead could act, Keli walked past his hiding place, a sack of vegetables in her arms. "*Abba*? I'm ready."

Ezekiel turned toward the sound of her voice.

She reached for his hand. "Shall we go home?"

He released his grip on the railing and dropped a scroll into the water. The second and third plunked after it. Brushing off his hands, Ezekiel allowed himself to be led back the way they had come.

Gilead pretended to examine the crate of straw beside him as they passed by. What would Ezekiel say if he knew Gilead's intrigue?

He slipped out of the alley and down the riverbank. One of the scrolls bobbed to the surface. *What have you written?*

Curiosity—and guilt—plagued him. Throwing scrolls into the river wasn't evidence for incompetence. The other two scrolls stuck on a sandbar in the middle as Gilead made it down the riverbank. Did this mean he intended to read his friend's private thoughts?

Casting a glance to the people overhead, Gilead waded into the cold water. He snagged the first scroll and tossed it to shore.

The current tugged his feet sideways, and he nearly lost his footing. The water rose above his waist and his teeth chattered by the time he reached the sand bar. He tucked the two scrolls in his wide belt.

Each step to shore dragged his feet a little off course. "I feel like I look like Ezekiel." The words lingered. Was this what his friend went through every day—each step being hauled down, not making a difference, as life's cold river dragged him off course?

"And when at last you make it to the riverbank, you don't care because you're down-trodden."

The ink had probably smeared. Whatever Ezekiel intended to discard might not even be worth Gilead's effort. He wiped his hands across his chest and unrolled each scroll. The ink smeared on the upper corner of one, but the message inscribed chilled Gilead to the core.

"Dear Love, you are supposed to outlast all things and cover all sins, but you mock me with your hollow claims. You leave a void in me that cannot be justified. All that is good and fair you destroy."

———

"That is so sad." Atta sniffed.

Gilead envied her feminine ability to express emotions. He rubbed his chest but couldn't erase his guilt. He had spied on his mentor and friend.

"Dear Hope, you've let me down for the last time." Rabgar-Nebo read again the scroll he held. "Do you suppose he's going to end his life?"

Gilead ran his hand over his face. "I don't know what to think."

"Here's the letter to Faith." Atta cleared her throat twice. "'You say Israel and Judah will be restored, but what is the point? It won't happen in our lifetime. The people don't deserve any more chances. They will only rebel.'"

"This sounds like a man who has given up." Rabgar-Nebo shook his head. "But it won't stand. He knows he wrote the missives. Your goal is to prove to him his grasp on reality is slipping."

Gilead gathered the scrolls. "Perhaps we should forget this."

Atta extended her hand. "These are a cry for help, Gilead. Ezekiel is hurting. We must help him."

"Not to mention you want to adopt his child." Gilead narrowed his eyes.

"This is more than that." Atta held up both hands. "This is about helping Ezekiel."

Helping. Right. Then why did he feel so guilty?

The rest of the day Gilead and Rabgar-Nebo oversaw housing and assigning positions to the influx of newly-arrived Hebrews.

"Please, we must remain together." The man at the front of the line stepped protectively in front of the two women. "My cousin and my sister are my responsibility."

"What are your skills? What did you do back in Jerusalem?" Rabgar-Nebo drummed his fingers on the high table.

"In Jerusalem? Nobody did much besides hope for a miracle."

Gilead stepped forward. "You will find your stride again. There is a Hebrew community already established here. Yahweh has met us in Babylon."

"What is your name?" Rabgar-Nebo dipped his stylus into the ink.

"I am Chislon. My sister, Datyah, and our *ima's* cousin, Eissa."

Datyah stared up at Gilead with innocent, simple trust, and Eissa turned a shy gaze to him.

"My training was in making anchors for the ships in Port Jaffa," Chislon gestured broadly. "But I can pretend to be whatever you want."

Gilead blinked as the idea formed. Would it be the jolt Ezekiel needed to rouse him from his stupor, or a shove over the edge? He shook his head. There was no way it would even work.

"—There is a district along the Chebar canal. You will have to reside in tents until accommodations are made." Rabgar-Nebo made a mark on his parchment. "Until then—"

"Your pardon, my lord." Gilead cleared his throat. How to articulate this off-kilter plan without sounding mad himself?

Rabgar-Nebo swiveled to face him. "Yes, what is it?"

"I had a thought I'd like to run by you, regarding how these three could serve immediately. In regards to…the case we discussed earlier."

Instructing the small family to step aside, Rabgar-Nebo turned expectantly. "What is it? Have you found a solution?"

Gilead coughed. "There are three of them. They could appear to Ezekiel as Hope, Love and Faith."

Rabgar-Nebo's eyebrows shot up faster than an arrow leaving the bow.

Gilead held up his hand. "I don't have it thought through. Perhaps it's the push Ezekiel needs. If they—those concepts—replied to his correspondence…made a persuasive petition concerning why he *shouldn't* abandon Love, Hope and Faith, it might bring him back to the living."

"Or, send him over to the edge into the realm of the mad." Rabgar-Nebo looked back, drumming his fingers on his thigh. "Do you think these Jews would play along?"

Gilead studied the new arrivals. "Look at that woman—she appears to have been around since the foundation of the world."

As if hearing his words, Eissa turned her gentle gaze

toward them. White hair fluttered beneath her head scarf, and she touched her time-lined face with a bent hand.

"You didn't answer my question." Rabgar-Nebo elbowed Gilead.

"Couldn't you see her as Love?" Gilead tore his gaze away from Eissa's compelling presence. "They'd do what you command them to do."

"True, but will they do it convincingly?"

What would You have me do, Yahweh? If the Hebrews didn't carry it off well, it was a fool's errand. They would have to personify a character trait, become that identity.

Datyah's smile lit up her simple face. She laughed at something Chislon had said.

Gilead smiled. Datyah would be Faith. He closed his eyes and waited for the nudge of conviction. "We can speak to them more, to get a feel for their ability."

"Hmmm." Rabgar-Nebo tipped his head. "Go fetch Atta. Bring her abreast. If she doesn't agree, we don't present the idea to the Jews."

"Yes, master." Gilead snapped his heels together and strode away. Such a difference in masters! A chant of gratitude accompanied his steps toward Tel-Abib. He grew more confident in the plan as he informed Atta. She agreed wholeheartedly and retrieved the scrolls from the hiding place behind her tapestry.

Together they returned to Rabgar-Nebo's station as the afternoon sun dipped low. At their approach, he waved off the remaining line. "Return tomorrow."

As others filtered away, Gilead nodded confirmation, and Rabgar-Nebo joined them as they approached the small family.

Gilead introduced Atta and made their unusual request.

"You are saying you wish your friend to believe he is mad?" Chislon crossed his arms.

"Well…" Atta squeezed her eyes shut. "It sounds terrible when you say it that way."

Gilead rubbed his fingers against his temple. "No. We wish only to draw him back, so he will engage in life again."

"Why do you think he would believe he actually speaks to Faith, and Love, and Hope?" Datyah's eyebrows furrowed. "No one speaks to…qualities. Or at least doesn't expect an answer."

Rabgar-Nebo threw up his hands. "The man hallucinates already, what is the difference?"

"You make it sound as if Ezekiel is already mad." Gilead clamped his mouth shut. Rabgar-Nebo was still his master.

"How can you do this spiteful trick to a man you claim is your friend?" Eissa's voice carried a passion that belied her frail body.

Atta clasped her hands beneath her chin. "He has a child who would be better off—"

Gilead shot a glare at Atta.

She shifted her weight and averted her eyes. "He is our friend. We don't know what else to do."

Gilead closed his eyes. If only he could go back to before these ideas came to him. "We are fully aware how foolish this is. We had hoped—" There was that word again.

Datyah clasped her hands. "We will pray that Yahweh will restore your friend."

"There is something you should know." Guilt thrust the words from Gilead's mouth. The sooner they denied the task, the sooner he could forget he'd even brought it up. "Ezekiel is a…has been appointed as a prophet."

"I think we should lend our aid."

Gilead snapped his face up and gawked at Chislon. "Pardon?"

"*And* we will pray for restoration."

Eissa frowned at her cousin. "They intend us to deceive their friend. A man of God. How can we be a part of that?"

"Even prophets need encouragement. Remember Elijah after the Lord smote the prophets of Baal on Mount Carmel. He grew discouraged. Yahweh tends to work with unconventional methods." Chislon patted Eissa's hand. "What's to say He won't use our efforts to assist in a man's rebuilding? It won't be deception if we speak truth of these qualities. We will be their ambassadors. What do you say, sister?"

Datyah's head bobbed, indicating unwavering devotion to her brother. They both turned to Eissa and waited.

Gilead shifted his weight and moistened his lips. Beside him, Atta held her breath.

Eissa exhaled and dipped her chin. "But as soon as it becomes unethical, I will no longer participate."

44

The LORD has appeared of old to me saying: "Yes, I have loved you with an everlasting love; Therefore with lovingkindness I have drawn you. Again I will build you, and you shall be rebuilt.
—Jeremiah 31:3-4a

O*n the twelfth day of the tenth month which was in the twelfth year of King Coniah's captivity.*

"—therefore, thus says the Lord God. I do not do this for your sake, oh house of Israel, but for My holy name's sake, which you have profaned. I *will* sanctify."

Bitterness knocked at Ezekiel's dead heart as he stood before the congregation. He'd much rather the Lord dwell on how Israel had profaned His holy name, not promises of renewal. A shadow darkened the doorway, and an elderly woman he hadn't seen before stepped inside. He shifted his attention back to the scroll. Had he read all this way? He couldn't recall hearing the words, yet his mouth continued to produce sound.

Not that it mattered. Who received his instruction? "—I

will give you a new heart and put a new spirit within you. I will take the heart of stone out of your flesh and give you a heart of flesh."

Ezekiel rubbed his chest. Though his own heart sat as an unfeeling rock inside, excruciating pain surely accompanied the replacement. Because that's what Yahweh gave— pain.

He rolled up the scroll and glanced to Perez to carry on with the service.

The newcomer's gaze burdened him all the way to the final song. The people dispersed and Kelila bounced up.

"May I go to Mikal's?" Her voice came from a distant land.

Ezekiel closed heavy eyes in agreement. An afternoon of not being worried over.

The last congregants took their noise and their frivolity, and he exhaled in their wake. Alone at last.

"Your pardon, priest. I wonder if you might explain something?" The voice came from where the newcomer sat.

"Not a priest." Never was. Never would be. He didn't care about this woman's problem. He indicated the scroll. "If you can read, you can see for yourself, though I doubt you'd understand."

"Yes. Eyes to see, and ears to hear, and all that." The woman pulled a scroll from her sash. "But I ask about *this* scroll—not from Yahweh's hand."

She knew of Isaiah's prophecy. Mildly impressed—no, a mild impression shrouded by indifference—Ezekiel lifted a shoulder. "Haven't you heard I speak only Yahweh's words?"

"Perhaps you did at one time, young man, but this certainly isn't from the pen of Yahweh."

Ezekiel's hand lay too heavy against his side for him to pinch the bridge of his nose.

The woman extended an open scroll.

Righting it, Ezekiel read the sloppy writing. "You were supposed to outlast all things and cover all sins—"

A chill breached his stone heart. "Where did you get this? Who are you?"

"Who did you write the missive to, not-a-priest?"

Ezekiel glared at the woman. "I wrote it to Love, as you'd know since you've read it."

"There you are." The woman spread her hands with a flourish.

Fatigue clouded his thoughts.

"You speak before the Most High God, surely you, of all people, can recognize His messengers."

Love was a messenger of God? That much he could understand. What he couldn't accept was why this woman appeared to him, pretending to *be* Love. He rubbed his beard. "What do you want from me?"

Compassion he didn't want to see poured from her eyes, her demeanor, the tilt of her chin. Ezekiel braced himself for the platitudes that were sure to follow.

"Let us reason together. You said—" she read from the scroll, "—I 'leave a void in you that can't be justified.' I think you desired a discourse with me. A debate even. You wrote me so that I'd come."

"I wrote you—Love—to say you don't exist to me any longer."

"Is that why you push your daughter away?"

Ezekiel's vision blurred. "How dare you! You leave my daughter out of this, woman."

"As you have done." The woman's eyes crinkled, and her mouth turned down. "How can you gaze upon her little face and not see the love intertwining with the pain? You call me hollow and mocking—"

Fatigue blurred the lines of established truth. Ezekiel's breath shortened into gasps. "What would you call stealing away my wife? You call her being brutally murdered 'compassionate'? Or what about not being able to grieve?"

The woman's countenance crumpled.

"Now you are going to tell me how Yahweh has grieved over His Love. That it's the same thing." The walls pressed in on him, and the air grew stifling. He sucked in a breath that lodged in his throat.

The diminutive woman's presence invaded his personal space. He had to get away. He clenched his staff and squeezed his eyes shut.

"Can you not see the love in your message?"

"I have to speak the words. I don't have to agree with them." Ezekiel's neck itched. "Please leave."

The woman gave a sad smile. "I can't leave. Love is woven together into the fabric of life through the joy and through the pain. Through a child's laughter. Love is the foundation. Yahweh is love."

Ezekiel whirled around, blocking the ear he could, and pushed his legs faster than his pain level could tolerate. Still, he strode—if a cripple's hobble could be considered a stride. His feet turned toward the west out of habit. He couldn't go to where he buried Shiriel. If that woman found him, she'd violate the sacred spot. North? Where could he go where love couldn't find him?

Ezekiel immersed himself in the marketplace and ducked into an alley. Sliding down behind a pile of crates, his labored breathing filled his ears. He pressed on the stitch in his side and tried to seal up the cocoon around his spirit so he wouldn't have to feel.

"*Abba*? Let's go home." Kelila's voice came through a tunnel.

Ezekiel rolled his head back to stare at the sky. Night. His stiff joints indicated he hadn't changed positions all afternoon.

His child scooped up his hands and leaned back to counter his weight.

Kelila grunted and sweat beaded on her forehead. "You need to try, *Abba*. I need you to try."

Ezekiel bent his knees and pushed up. She propped him

on a crate and scooped up his staff. He didn't envy her ease anymore.

Kelila led him home—that woman was gone—up the stairs and onto his pallet. Pulling bedclothes under his chin, she patted his cheeks with hands smelling of lavender.

Did he shut her out? Remorse tugged on the edge of his girded-up heart. "I'm sorry, Kelila."

She turned a soulful gaze toward him. When did she become so grown up? "It's all right, *Abba.* I know you're sad."

How can you gaze upon her little face and not see the love intertwining with the pain? Ezekiel's brow furrowed, and he studied her serious countenance. "You shouldn't have to care for me—"

"It's okay, *Abba.*" Kelila smoothed the sheet. "It's only for a season."

He pondered her confidence through night's pall of darkness. Would he ever recover from this paralyzing despair?

On the first day of the week, Ezekiel followed Kelila to the marketplace. She propped him on a half-wall by the apricot vendor.

"Stay here."

He thought about having remorse as his child dodged to avoid a matronly woman not watching her path. Did he push his daughter away? He depended on her more than he should, that was sure. The back of his neck prickled as if someone watched him.

Had the woman who called herself Love come to harass him again?

No matter, he'd just ignore her, as love ignored him.

He met Kelila's gaze. Her shoulders lowered slightly, and she reassured him with a smile. "Wait for me," she mouthed.

Ezekiel attempted a smile.

"The innocent trust of a child." A woman stood off to the side. "She expects you to be here and you are. Simple as that. Your daughter?"

Ezekiel evaluated how the newcomer's joyful smile crinkled her nose underneath dark, thick brows.

"What is her name?" The woman clasped her hands under her chin.

Why did she care? Ezekiel shrugged. Seven years ago, he would have relished starting up a conversation with a stranger. "Look what God has done," he would have said—when he could see God's plan unfolding. Apparently, part of him missed the human interaction, for he opened his mouth and responded. "Kelila."

"Lovely." The woman clapped her hands. "And so fitting for this season of expectation. The perfection of beauty. The joy of the whole earth."

With effort, Ezekiel tipped his head to face her. "My wife and I believed in the restoration of our people—at the time."

The woman rested her hand on the thin parchment rolled in her sash. "And now?"

Ezekiel's eyes narrowed. "Now it doesn't matter what I believe or do. Yahweh does what He pleases."

Her joyous smile spread across her face, missing Ezekiel's bitterness entirely. "An excellent attitude to have."

"What do you want?" Ezekiel growled. "Who are you supposed to be?"

A sheen of tears formed in her eyes. "Why have you turned your back on Faith—on me?"

Not again. "If you were Faith, I wouldn't be able to see you, now would I?"

Faith raised her hands to cover her ears. "You can see the fruits faith bears."

Ezekiel scoffed. "So what fruit are you?"

"You wrote to me. Surely you expected an answer."

Had he expected an answer? Hadn't he imagined what he would say the next time Yahweh required something from him? "Faith is useless. It serves no purpose."

"You sat on this wall, didn't you?" Faith brushed away

some dirt before sitting as well. "Did you check if the mortar had been tempered so the wall would not crumble?"

Ezekiel rolled his eyes. "Knowledge. I've sat here before."

"You were appointed watchman over our people. How can you build their faith if your own waivers?"

"I did not ask for that position." Ezekiel's knuckles turned white around his staff.

Faith jammed her fist on her hip and tilted her chin. "You asked to be a priest. It is the same thing."

Agitation stirred inside him. He shifted, regretting his vow to do better by Kelila and remain in the same spot.

"Where were you when *I* obeyed everything Yahweh asked of me, and still, He did what *He* wanted? Where are you when His remnant refuses to care?" Ezekiel wiped saliva from the corner of his mouth. "I sacrificed blindly in the name of faith. What has faith done for me?"

"You are angry at me." The woman hugged herself tightly. "Why?"

Ezekiel pushed off the wall and paced in a tight arc. "Because you count this rebellious people's future redeemable but took away mine."

Faith pointed toward Kelila's approach. "What of hers?"

"What future does a little girl have if a god kills her mother?" Ezekiel pushed himself up and went to Kelila. His chest heaved, and he fought the urge to look back.

"Who were you talking to, *Abba*?" Kelila adjusted the two sacks in her arms.

"Nothing." He felt his daughter's curious glance. "I mean, no one of consequence."

He did Kelila a favor. If she expected nothing, she wouldn't be disappointed. Right? He exhaled and lowered his gaze to his daughter. She seemed well-adjusted. What did she know that he didn't?

"Kelila?" He reached for one of the sacks. Millet. Ugh.

"Yes, *Abba*?" She wrapped her free arm behind his back.

"How are you doing so…well, with…you know, *Ima's* death, her not being here? Aren't you sad?"

She sniffled. "I am sad, but I know Yahweh is still with us, helping."

Ezekiel halted while he tempered his bitter response. "How? How does Yahweh help you?"

Kelila tipped her chin to the side and chewed on her cheek. "I don't know. I just pray and He gives me peace."

Something niggled closer to his core. Envy? Resentment? It was hard to discern a difference. "What do you pray, Kelila?"

"Mostly the psalm of David. The Lord-is-my-shepherd one." Her shoulder jostled against him as she hopped. "How come you never call me Keli like *Ima* and Atta?"

How could she be carefree? She had lost, same as him.

"Because names have meanings." And he had regrets. "To shorten the name seems to take away from who you are."

Did he still believe that? Hadn't he come to see it also could be an endearment?

"Besides, can you think of a way to shorten Ezekiel? Zeke? Eze?"

Kelila's giggle almost turned his own mouth up.

They turned to their house and paused by the lavender plant. Kelila rubbed the leaves between her fingers and inhaled.

Pain roiled over Ezekiel. He swallowed twice. "Would you like me to call you Keli?"

She tapped her fingers on her cheek. "If you think you can change. It doesn't matter if you don't. I was just curious." Kelila took the millet from Ezekiel and skipped inside.

He rubbed the lavender and breathed in Shiriel's scent.

Ezekiel's chin dropped to his chest. *I'm not ready to change. I'm still mad.*

45

For I know the thoughts that I think toward you, says the LORD, thoughts of peace and not of evil, to give you a future and a hope. Then you will call upon Me and go and pray to Me, and I will listen to you. And you will seek Me and you will find Me, when you search for Me with all your heart.
—Jeremiah 29:11-13

O*n the fourteenth day of the tenth month which was in the twelfth year of King Coniah's captivity.*

The wind tore at Ezekiel's turban and tossed him to-and-fro as he sat outside his house staring at the canal. Just as his body needed a safe haven now, his soul craved shelter from the tumult within. He gritted his teeth and closed his eyes, imagining drifting with the gentle lapping of the canal. Soon he'd weaken, and the water would pull him down; he'd not fight the current. It was better this way. He'd been disappointed too many times to count.

A shadow fell across his face. He squinted one eye open to see a man silhouetted against the morning sun.

The shadow slapped a scroll against his hand. "This is unacceptable."

Ezekiel didn't even have to ask. He covered his face with his arm and groaned. Couldn't a man rebel against God in peace? "Go away."

"I demand a rematch." Hope threw the scroll at Ezekiel's feet. "You can't discard me as if I were soiled linens."

"That's what you are to me." Ezekiel turned away. "I have no use for rubbish."

"Coward." Hope bent over him with fists clenched. "Get up! Face me like a man."

Anger couldn't penetrate Ezekiel's hardened shell of grief and pain. He couldn't be riled in this state. "Was it manly to take a defenseless woman, my wife?"

"It had to be done to show the depth of Yahweh's sorrow and pain."

"There were others." Ezekiel pushed himself up with the wall and his staff. "Yahweh could've made His point with those three men—Shadrach and the others—who had conformed to this pagan culture."

The wind tugged his turban free with ironic timing. He watched it tangle and catch on the neighbor's palm tree.

"So that's it?" Hope shoved Ezekiel's shoulder.

"That's right." Ezekiel stepped around the man. Jewish.

"And what of your wife's confident expectation? Are you denying her belief?"

A lot of good that did her. Ezekiel retrieved the strip of cloth and leaned on the palm's rough bark.

"She'd be disappointed in you." The man stepped forward with arms stiff and chest thrust forward.

"Tell me something I don't know." If Hope wanted to rile him, it wouldn't be with something he already told himself every day.

Hope gripped Ezekiel by the tunic and hauled him close

"When did you transfer your hope from the living God to your wife, a fallible human?"

"When the *living God* decided to torture me. Nobody got the message anyway, as He'd said."

Hope's breath came hot on Ezekiel's cheek. "Yahweh doesn't have to run His plans by you! You are not His counselor. You were chosen by the Most High God to be the watchman for His people."

Ezekiel's staff dropped with a clatter, and Hope's arms were the only thing holding him upright. Despair burned and clawed at Ezekiel's chest. Heaving strength into his arms, he thrust Hope away and himself off balance. He flailed and crashed to his knees.

Hard.

Pain knifed through his deadened senses.

Hope reached out his arm. "Allow me to help you."

Ezekiel's left hip locked, and he braced his hands on the packed dirt before him. Sucking in air, he fought the urge to curl onto his side and wait.

Kelila—Keli—deserved better. *For your sake. I'm trying.*

"Would you want your daughter to model your lack of conviction?"

Ezekiel glared at Hope. Were not even his thoughts private? He shoved himself upright, despite the grinding agony. Swiping at the sweat on his forehead, he cast a triumphant glance at Hope. "There, see? I don't need you."

"So it would seem." Hope's eyes filled with an indecipherable expression. "But it would have been easier if you allowed me to help you."

"I am…not…a hypocrite. If I say I am done with you, I'm not going to use you to escape a trial when I am down." The fibers from the palm dug into his hand.

Hope shrugged. "I will accept little steps."

Ezekiel braced his hands on his knees, trying to alleviate the pain shooting up his back and down his leg. Could he take that step of trust again? How many times had he instructed Kelila about the overflow of her heart? How many times had he grieved over—and despised—those who served the Lord with an unengaged effort?

His soul pricked, reminiscent of longing. "Yahweh has seen fit to harden His face against me. I am simply returning the favor." He glanced over his shoulder to see he spoke to empty space.

He didn't even have the opportunity to walk out on hope.

Lowering himself to the half wall, he breathed rapidly through his teeth. The pressure in his hip relieved slightly.

The aroma of frankincense wafted on the breeze, transporting his memory back to the temple and the joy of serving in Yahweh's presence. Days where life was simpler confronted him, a mirror to the hardened, bitter man he had become.

If his daughter modeled after him, it would break his heart, but if she hoped with confident expectation as Shiriel did, Yahweh would crush her.

Leave me be. But the thoughts would not comply. Pain and agony pushed up against the confines of Ezekiel's soul, threatening to escape—a lion intent on sinking its teeth into him and tossing him about until the jarring motion killed him. Betrayal. Could one be betrayed by the Most High God?

Approaching footsteps crunched on the dirt. Ezekiel turned and focused on Gilead's approach. Here was another affected by his lethargy.

The archer's eyes narrowed, and he scanned the area. "Are you well?" He gestured to the dirt on Ezekiel's knees.

"I…fell." Ezekiel removed his hand from the offending hip before Gilead suggested he go to the physician.

Sitting on the wall, Gilead grimaced and twisted his back with an audible pop. For once, his silent presence wasn't enough.

Ezekiel shifted. Did he wish for Gilead to engage in

conversation? *How are you doing today? Fine, thanks. I've been consulting with imaginary ideas.* He swung his gaze to his friend.

The man had also served a ruthless master, one who seemed to take pleasure in deriding him and breaking him down. Ezekiel studied Gilead's countenance. Regardless of the trials, the archer plodded on, steady as an ox.

"How did you keep going…under General Vakhtang's employ?"

Gilead's eyes widened and his chin jutted forward. "My faith in Yahweh."

"Pshh." That wasn't helpful if Yahweh was the one doing the oppressing.

"What else is there to trust in?" Gilead leaned his elbows on his knees.

That was the problem, wasn't it? Truly nothing else could be verified as trustworthy. What did one do when he who had seen the glory of God—along with His marvelous works—was smote by the very same God?

"Do you still believe Yahweh has plans for hope here in Babylon?"

Gilead blinked and eyed Ezekiel. "I do. Your message on the Sabbath, Yahweh intends to restore our nations. He has spoken it, and He will bring it to pass."

"Then why did He find it necessary to destroy it in the first place?" Ezekiel's pulse rushed in his ears.

"Do you mean, why take Shiri?" Gilead's heavy hand rested on Ezekiel's shoulder.

Ezekiel closed his eyes against the raging fire igniting within.

"You've said in the past…the scrolls indicate it was a symbol of Yahweh's great loss."

Ezekiel glared at Gilead and jerked away. "Don't you dare tell me I should be honored to be Yahweh's ambassador!"

"I'm sorry, my brother. I don't know why Yahweh has

asked this pain of you." Gilead's jaw worked. "Perhaps He desired someone to understand His suffering."

"He'll get *His* beloved back." All Ezekiel received were bothersome visitors. He propped his staff in position and shimmied upright.

The silence grew awkward. Ezekiel turned toward his house.

"Ezekiel?" Gilead rubbed his thumb across his beard. "I'm glad you're talking...we talked. I'm concerned for you."

"I'm not mad at you, Gilead. I'm sorry I'm nothing but a burden." Ezekiel shuffled toward the house.

Gilead's arms wrapped around his shoulders. "I'm here for you if you ever want to talk again."

Doubtful. Ezekiel dipped his head in acknowledgment. Anything to get Gilead to leave him alone. He limped into the house, his staff thud-clopping in stark agreement with the pain and thoughts slamming against him. He made it into the darkened interior and stopped.

He hadn't rubbed Shiriel's plant. His legs tensed. If he returned, Gilead would strike up conversation again. He didn't want to talk. Or burden his friend with worry.

Didn't want to feel.

Collapsing onto the pile of cushions, Ezekiel tried to block out everything. Memories kept flooding through his feeble walls—Shiriel caring for him with peace and a smile when he had been irritable. Her blind obedience when he told her the latest madness from Yahweh. The crushed expression on her face when he dismissed her singing and ideas for the ministry. All the times he rejected her affectionate touch.

A groan churned from deep within. He had failed her in so many ways.

"And what about You?" Ezekiel's words bounced back from the ceiling. "She trusted You."

What else is there to trust?

Ezekiel pressed hands against his ears, but Gilead's words

dove around his thoughts like a child dodging his mother in the marketplace.

Uninvited, blazing memories of Yahweh's throne room paraded across his mind. Splendor marred by heartbreak. God knew his pain.

No. God *caused* his pain.

He burrowed deep within Yahweh's judgment and vengeance, where anger reigned. Perhaps there was indeed nothing else to put trust in, but it didn't mean Ezekiel had to trust in Yahweh, either.

46

But those who hope in the Lord *will renew their strength. They will soar on wings like eagles; they will run and not grow weary, they will walk and not be faint.*
—Isaiah 40:31 (NIV)

Gilead almost broke under the torture.

Ezekiel actually initiating conversation, for the first time in who knew how long, did nothing to assure Gilead this was the right decision.

He had to tell his friend of the deception, beg his forgiveness—and watch him slip into the oblivion of his mind again.

Raking his hands through his hair, Gilead growled. Ezekiel had engaged for once. That was the goal, wasn't it?

Yahweh, restore unto Ezekiel the joy of Your salvation. Do not forget him in his suffering.

How could he pray that when he had unleashed torment on his friend?

He rubbed softened beeswax on his bow string, his nerves as taut as the string. As he concluded his task, he resolved in his heart and strode toward Tel-Abib. Storming down the road, Gilead slowed at the sound of Ezekiel shouting.

"—You say Yahweh is loving, yet in the same breath you say He is just! They can't exist together!"

Gilead peeked around the wall to see Ezekiel jabbing his staff towards Eissa.

This is madness! Should he allow his friend to turn into a monster against an elderly woman just to carry on the deception?

"You know He has to be both." Eissa's calm voice did not indicate distress, and she sat placidly in the shade of the house. "What kind of God would He be if He didn't execute judgment on sin? How would He exact vengeance for those He swore by His name to protect?"

"And what about my wife?" Ezekiel slammed his fist against the wall. "What of her love for Yahweh? Of His ways?"

"Who better to convey His message but His willing servant?"

"Then why not me?"

"What would become of an unmarried woman and a child?" Eissa's words were compassion, formed in the depths of pain.

"Are you indicating she was *spared*?"

"Love is sacrifice."

Whack! Gilead peered around the corner, heart in his throat. He exhaled. Ezekiel had only struck the wall—not Eissa—with his staff.

"Have I not sacrificed enough?"

"When was the last time you gave of yourself to your congregation?" Eissa clasped her hands on her lap.

"They are as hard-hearted as Pharaoh of old." Ezekiel grunted as he paced. "They do not deserve compassion."

"And what of your own heart? Genuine love is given when the other party can give nothing in return."

Gilead absorbed Eissa's words.

"Here you are, back around to the beginning of your argument. You meet yourself going and speak in circles, for you have no new platforms on which to stand." Frustration lined Ezekiel's words.

"My platform does not vary. Love is unchanging. Eternal." Eissa spoke with such assurance. If Gilead didn't know better, he'd believe she was Love embodied. "You may harden your heart against love as you choose, but it doesn't deny the reality. Love is everywhere. You have been given the gift of loving and being loved. It is time to share it again—"

Ezekiel brushed by Gilead's hiding spot in a rush of wind.

Gilead reached out. "Wait! I can explain…"

The priest kept ploughing ahead, never diverting his attention back.

Shoulders sagging, Gilead pounded his palm against his fist. He had successfully dug a dagger into Ezekiel's healed over scar and set infection into the new wound.

Soft weeping drew him around the corner. Eissa wiped tears from her lined face and smiled at Gilead. "I haven't given up on him yet."

"This isn't working." Gilead glanced over Eissa's head. "It's making things worse. I should have left it be."

"My boy, this wasn't a case of ripping open healed scars. The wounds may have been closed over time, but they have not healed properly." Eissa patted his arm. "The infection needed to be lanced. If not, he would have signed his own death sentence."

The balm of Eissa's words began to sooth Gilead's ragged spirit. "You are doing well as Love. You have me convinced."

Eissa's invading—yet not unwelcome—gaze gave Gilead a home. "Give it time. See how this unfurls."

"I don't know how much more he can take." He clenched his fist but couldn't dispel the helplessness.

"Ezekiel will have to go through these deep waters of pain

to realize the Sovereign Lord is with him, sheltering him, even now."

This was wisdom and truth. But this pain affected Gilead as if Ezekiel was his own son.

Lord, this hurts so badly. I wish I could say something—or that he didn't have to go through this.

And pass over the redemptive process, missing what God had planned here?

I want to shake him, Lord, he's being a fool. Sharp memories stormed through the ever-present curtain of his mistakes. Harsh words spoken because he "knew better." Oh, that the God of his fathers would help him control his tongue this time!

Bidding farewell to Eissa, Gilead sat on Ezekiel's wall. "What would you have me do?"

Ezekiel's staff ground on the dirt nearby. Gilead sprang up as his friend came around the corner, surveying the area. "Is she gone?"

Gilead blinked. "I'm…the only one here."

"Just as I think of the perfect argument to silence her." Ezekiel tapped his staff on the ground.

"Who…were you talking to?" Gilead coughed.

"Not who, 'what.'" Ezekiel twisted his staff back and forth.

Gilead wrinkled his brow, praying for words of truth. "What?"

"You saw her too, right?" Ezekiel ducked his head to peer at Gilead's face.

"Who was that?" Gilead trained his gaze on Ezekiel.

Ezekiel crossed his arms. "I know what's happening—"

Gilead hung his head. "I can explain—"

"—Love gets me all confused and then doesn't stick around for rational argument."

How should he respond to that? Gilead exhaled slowly as Ezekiel did not wait for a reply.

"Would you believe me if I said it was Love?"

Gilead coughed. He fought the urge to avert his glance. "What…You said you knew what to say to silence…Love? What would you say?"

"Vulnerability." Ezekiel growled and pounded his staff on the ground twice. "If you open yourself up to the sacrificial love, you'll soon be broken. Again. People aren't capable of loving unconditionally."

Yahweh, give me discernment. Gilead surveyed Ezekiel's expression and plucked his bow string. "You are right in saying so. All humans fail. Only Yahweh can love without conditions."

"Yet Yahweh leaves you the most vulnerable. He takes away and gives no regard to how broken you are."

"But He is with you through it." Gilead shoved himself off the wall, and his knees creaked. He grimaced and planted himself before Ezekiel. "It is only through Him that any of this makes sense. You delighted in His ways. You loved His words."

Ezekiel blinked slowly and turned toward the house.

Gilead's head dropped back, and he pressed his eyes closed. Did he push too far?

"That was before," Ezekiel's voice was wistful. "Why should I love the One who has crushed me?"

The door groaned, shutting Gilead out.

Pounding on the door roused Ezekiel from drifting on the canal's gentle waves. Slowly he swam back to shore, separated from Shiriel as always. He rubbed wet cheeks and groaned.

The pounding increased downstairs.

Ezekiel rolled over to his stomach and steadied his right leg beneath him before pushing up. *I'm coming.*

He glanced in at Kelila as he passed. Sleeping. As any person in their right mind should be.

Who could be here at this hour of the night?

Ezekiel missed the bottom stair and landed with a jolt. He sucked in air as the pounding paused.

"I'm coming! What is it?" He flung open the door, and Hope stumbled forward. *Excellent.* "What now?"

"You remember me." The man righted himself and straightened his tunic.

Ezekiel crossed his arms. "Why are you here?"

"Sometimes hope shows up at the darkest hour."

Really? Ezekiel rolled his eyes.

"You see what I did there?" Hope chortled. "Just a little play on words."

"I won't be able to get back to sleep, thanks to you."

"I'm glad to hear it. You'll have time to ponder how bereft you are without hope in your life."

"Isn't it enough that you disturb me during waking hours?" Ezekiel clamped his mouth tight on the words. "What do you want?"

"Turn your gaze to the heavens, Ezekiel. What do you see?"

A lesson on Abraham and the countless stars? Just what he needed.

"The God of Abraham made a covenant of hope with our people." The man spread his arms, embracing the expanse of the sky. "A covenant. Meaning, He will keep His end of the bargain, regardless of whether you do or not. Hope does not disappoint when you allow it to anchor you."

"Don't you get it? I don't want your anchor. If I did, I'd have to buy into the fulfillment that comes on the morrow." Ezekiel's move to shut the door was blocked by Hope's strong arm. "You forget, I know the wording. I know all the lines—"

Hope leaned forward, pushing the door and Ezekiel back. "And you still believe them. I know you do."

Ezekiel strained against the door. "That's where you are wrong. I know hope still exists. If it works for others, that's fantastic. But I choose not to be its slave anymore."

"How would you feel if I gave up on you?"

"I'd love it—" Ezekiel's foot slipped, and the door halted its motion. "Then I could get some sleep."

Hope's fingers appeared on the edge of the door. "Don't you realize you have a part in the hope of the others? You are the one called to this purpose."

Ezekiel gritted his teeth and dug in. The door crept toward the frame. "Where is the reward of hope?"

"The law of the Lord is a delight to the soul." Hope withdrew his fingers, and the door slammed shut.

Leaning against the door, Ezekiel tried to catch his breath, secretly disappointed that Hope's hand hadn't gotten caught.

"Enjoy the rest of your night. I know you will lay awake thinking of how much you miss me." Hope slammed his hand on the door, sending a shock through Ezekiel. "The truth is, you pretend you are mad at the world, but the world hasn't changed. You spout off about hope sustaining in times of trouble, and the first trial that hurts you, you retreat faster than a woman in a room of snakes."

Ezekiel pressed a fist over his mouth as ugly emotions of resentment and bitterness threatened to paralyze him. His hip locked.

Muffled breathing came through the seam where the door met the frame. "You are no better than the leaders you warn your people about. You say the righteous words, but your actions convey you are only out for your own gain, for your convenience."

Slam!

Ezekiel cowered.

"You say I disappoint you, in attempts to assuage your own guilt, because it's *you* you're disappointed in." Dissipating footsteps slapped against the worn path.

Pressing his forehead against the door, Ezekiel pounded with his fists. The thuds vibrated through his head, yet couldn't dislodge the seeds unearthed.

Ezekiel didn't punish Yahweh by digging in his heals—Yahweh took what He wanted anyway. He only succeeded in failing Shiriel and the hard-hearted flock. He slid to his knees, the rough-hewn door digging a splinter into his hand, piercing his soul. Intense longing within him begged him to cry out to Yahweh as King David did in his distress.

"No!" Ezekiel shoved iron doors against the roiling emotions. "You don't deserve my loyalty. You've not been loyal to me."

The presence of Yahweh did not rise against him and smite him. Instead, a familiar, dull blackness and aching quiet engulfed him.

47

Can your heart endure, or can your hands remain strong, in the days when I shall deal with you? I, the LORD, have spoken, and will do it.
—Ezekiel 22:14

O*n the sixteenth day of the tenth month which was in the twelfth year of King Coniah's captivity.*

Ezekiel almost ran the other way when Faith came around the corner. He rubbed eyes that were accustomed to little or no sleep, hoping he had imagined her joyful presence.

Still, she approached, and by the smile lighting up her face, intended to accost him.

"Go away."

The simple woman's face crumpled. "You are angry."

"Yes, I'm angry!" Ezekiel lengthened his stride, despite the grinding in his hip, and turned toward the river. Was there no dignity left that he could no longer outpace a small woman with short legs? "I'm angry because you keep pestering me. I want to be left alone!"

"You are afraid." Faith wheezed behind him.

"Afraid?" Ezekiel whirled around, his elbow connecting with Faith's cheekbone. His eyes widened as she flew backward in seemingly slow motion.

She crumpled to the ground, unmoving.

That was one way to be rid of faith.

Ezekiel closed his eyes. The woman—and the pain in his elbow—were real enough. He hunkered down beside her and pressed fingers against the vein in her neck.

Her eyes fluttered open and darted side to side, her gaze locking on Ezekiel's face.

"I'm sorry." He glanced around. No one was nearby. "I didn't realize you were so close."

"I never left your side." Faith touched the red mark on her cheek and winced. "You just chose not to look."

"Can you stand?"

She squinted and pushed herself to a sitting position with a groan. "I'm a little dizzy."

Ezekiel frowned and pushed back the guilt. She would recover. If there was one thing to celebrate about his body being decrepit, it was that he didn't have the strength to out and out kill her with the blow.

"Can you get to the river?" Ezekiel glanced between his staff and the tears pooling in her eyes. His hip throbbed. "I could drag you . . ."

She shook her head and began to crawl.

Ezekiel plunked his staff to the ground and muscled himself upright. By the time he made it to the canal's edge, the woman already scooped water to her mouth. If he lowered himself again, he couldn't guarantee he would rise without assistance. He leaned at an angle. "Are you all right?"

Faith scooped water to her forehead. "I am resilient."

She would say that. He shifted and tapped his staff to the ground, eyebrows raised.

"If you are waiting for me to give permission for you to

leave me, you won't get it." Faith dipped water to the back of her neck.

"I don't need your permission."

"You are angry again. I can tell." The woman plopped on her backside and squinted up at him. "You helped me. You still believe in faith."

"See here! I *am* sorry I knocked you down, but that doesn't mean I'm conforming to your blind trust once again. My eyes are open to the vulnerability you exploit."

"I give reason for tomorrow. For eternity. I make life easier." Faith tilted her chin up with certainty.

"No! You make it more difficult. If everything doesn't conform to your standards, you disqualify people." In his mind's eye, Ezekiel tottered on the brink of a gaping pit. He thrust each bellowing accusation to the woman beside him, hoping she'd get so fed up with him that she'd unleash her temper, her fists—anything—and push him into the abyss.

Why hadn't he cracked Hope in the face? He seemed to be a scrappy fighter. He'd surely retaliate and strike back.

Instead, he'd made a woman cry—caused her pain.

"You're not mad at me." Faith crossed her arms.

"I really think I am." How dare she dictate his feelings.

"No. You're mad at Yahweh."

An urge to throw his staff like a javelin—as far away as he could—rose in Ezekiel. He clamped both hands around his staff and mashed his eyelids together. If he did act in haste, he'd be stuck in Faith's presence all the longer.

Ezekiel roared so deeply, so loudly, pain cracked along the edge of the chasm in his soul. Any moment, everything within him would erupt and humble him. He swiped a shaking hand across his eyes, and his chest heaved.

He had to get away from the ledge before he shattered.

He bent over Faith and hauled the woman up by the arm. "I can help you back to your dwelling, then I need to be alone."

She turned her observant gaze to him. "You are never alone."

Didn't he know it. "Are you still dizzy?"

Touching her cheek, she shook her head and stumbled.

Is this making You laugh—me, holding onto Faith? Don't get any ideas.

What a pair they made—a cripple and an unsteady woman.

Faith directed Ezekiel to the refugee camp. As they hobbled around tents, familiar voices became clear.

"—he continues to resist all our attempts to help."

So, Hope dwelt near Faith. Convenient.

"Only a visit from your god would get through to him—" Rabgar-Nebo broke off as Ezekiel and Faith came around the corner.

Gilead and Atta turned at the expression on Rabgar-Nebo's face.

Ezekiel blinked. What business did the three of them have with Hope?

"We can explain—" Gilead tugged at his beard.

"It was only to—" Atta took a step forward then two steps back.

Out of the corner of his eye, he saw a white-haired woman rise. Love was here too? Ezekiel glanced from his friends' faces—as they talked over each other—to the faces of those who he'd thought appeared to him alone.

Hope widened his stance and jutted out his chin, Love clutched her chest, concern in her eyes, and the Chaldean officer's gaze landed everywhere but on Ezekiel.

"He helped me," Faith's proud tone broke through the chaos. "It worked. Our plan to help him worked."

Atta and Gilead exchanged guilty glances.

"What is going on?" Why did Ezekiel dread what they would say?

Hope raised his eyebrows, crossed his arms, and stared at

Gilead, who couldn't seem to glance up from his sandals.

Ezekiel's quick mind and powers of observation had diminished greatly since he no longer cared to employ them, but something was off.

He glanced to Faith, the only one who seemed willing to talk. "What plan?"

The woman wrung her hands and worry lined her face.

Don't go silent now. Ezekiel gripped her arm and gave a shake. "What do you mean 'you helped me'? Helped me with what?"

Gilead stepped forward, hands up in caution. "Release her. I will tell you everything."

Ezekiel's knuckles were white around Faith's arm. The last time he had grabbed a woman, it had turned out to be a monumental misconception on his part. He couldn't begin to contrive what assumption he had made now. He released Faith, and she ran to Hope's side and buried her face in his tunic.

"What is this all about, Gilead?" Ezekiel shook his head and stared hard at the archer.

"Did you hurt her?" Gilead approached with his palms up.

"No." The mark on the woman's face indicated otherwise. Ezekiel blew out a breath. "That was an accident. I didn't realize she was beside me, and my elbow connected with her face."

Because that didn't make him sound guilty. He tried his luck with the woman's husband—or brother. "She was dizzy. I was assisting her."

"Ezekiel helped me," Faith spoke into Hope's shoulder.

Hope put gentle hands on her face, probing at the mark. He glanced at Ezekiel. "Thank you for helping my sister."

Hope and Faith would be related.

"Now that we've settled that, would someone please tell me what business you have with each other?"

Gilead exchanged another glance with Atta. "I…found

your letters."

Ezekiel focused his attention on Gilead's demeanor. He'd never hidden scrolls or messages from anyone. He swung around, staring at the newcomers. Those letters?

Atta sniffed. "We didn't know what to do. You were so withdrawn and unengaged—"

"We—I—recruited Chislon, Eissa, and Datyah to come to you as Hope, Love, and Faith." Gilead swept his arm, indicating each one.

They weren't real after all? Betrayal knifed his ribs.

"We're so sorry." Atta stepped forward. "Keli needs…someone."

Was it better that he hadn't been hallucinating, or worse because his friends had purposefully deceived him? Or had they? Their care for him was evident.

Everything his 'spirits' had said rang true to what he knew of love, hope, and faith.

They had even convinced a pagan soldier to participate in their scheme. Ezekiel felt Rabgar-Nebo's critical gaze keeping him accountable as a messenger of the true God.

He closed his eyes and the bitter, apathetic man he'd become confronted him. How had his friends remained by his side all this time?

Gilead laid a hand on Ezekiel's shoulder. "Please forgive us."

Ezekiel scanned the faces of flesh and blood—real people. Eissa gazed into the ugliness he had allowed to saturate his soul. Warmth and compassion transferred to his insides, dispelling some of the night.

Datyah clasped her hands under her chin and leaned to her brother with a loud whisper. "I knew it'd work out."

Chislon's chin tipped up. "I hope so."

Gilead's brows furrowed deep. He twanged the bow-string across his chest. Atta sniffled.

Shame cloaked Ezekiel's soul. His friends were beside

themselves before him, thinking he would react volatilely. He exhaled a heavy breath.

His hip ached from standing too long. The discomfort of awareness weighed less than the darkness. He swallowed and tried to convey he wasn't angry. "I'd like to be alone."

Worry played around Gilead's eyes.

"To process." Ezekiel turned to Atta. "Would you mind Keli a little longer today?"

"Yes, of course. She's with Mikal's family now."

Ezekiel dipped his chin and turned south, toward the plains.

Crossing the rickety bridge over the Chebar, he felt wetness on his cheeks. So long had he walked in darkness, protecting himself from pain. Or so he'd thought. As it turned out, he'd created the perfect atmosphere for pain to fester.

The space appeared to form a thought. *Yahweh, I'm ready to talk.* "I'm still mad—so angry I can't think straight—but…I *do* miss the joy and peace you give."

Shiriel would have laughed at this whole thing and then taken to heart the symbolism—not that she would have lost faith to begin with.

A groan surfaced from Ezekiel's belly. Would Shiriel be disappointed in the way he'd behaved the last several years? His aching leg screamed for him to rest.

"I'm sorry, Shiriel—Shiri. I've let you down in so many ways. In your life and in your death." He leaned his head against his staff.

He'd also let Yahweh down.

Oh, Yahweh, I loathe what I've become. I've committed detestable abominations in my heart before You. "Create in me a new heart, a heart of flesh."

Ezekiel collapsed in the sand.

His friends' experiment had breached the defenses in his core, sending darkness and ugliness oozing as true as the tears mingling with dirt on his face.

48

"Prophesy to these bones, and say to them, 'O dry bones, hear the word of the Lord!' Thus says the Lord God to these bones; 'Surely I will cause breath to enter into you, and you shall live. I will put sinews on you and bring flesh upon you, cover you in skin and put breath into you; and you shall live. Then you shall know that I am the LORD.'"
—Ezekiel 37:4b-6

O*n the sixteenth day of the tenth month which was in the twelfth year of King Coniah's captivity.*

Ezekiel sprawled on the desert floor, spent and exhausted. He curled his fingers into the gritty sand and waited.

Yahweh had no obligation to respond immediately, yet Ezekiel's spirit twitched in anticipation. "You *are* my God. You say You will rebuild the ruined places. Does…does that mean even the mess I've made of my life?"

Clouds formed on the horizon, billowing and dark, restrained by something. Something inside Ezekiel. An issue that still lay between him and Yahweh.

If he were to right his standing before God, this hidden bitterness in his soul must be addressed. He searched for the anger he had masked with indifference. One more turn in the corridor of his mind and he beheld the roiling, black mass.

The only way to be free of this sin would be to walk through it.

Breath quickening, Ezekiel dug his palms into his eyes and allowed the darkness to surround him. The shame of having given birth to this traitorous thought was overcome with the rage that justified his position.

"You want to know my grievance against You?"

'Come, let us reason together.' Yahweh had declared to the prophet Isaiah—though He already knew man's argument.

Ezekiel plowed on. "You told Zedekiah each man is responsible for his own sin. And to Coniah, no more shall the son pay for the father's sin. Yet here I stand—my people in this pagan land—and you have set the sins of the people upon me. My vitality was taken from me as I laid on my side for Israel's sin, for Judah's transgressions. My voice was silenced that none would speak on behalf of the people. My wife was stolen from me because of the sins of the people!"

Injustice demanded a champion. Ezekiel raised his fist to the sky and bellowed to the heavens. "I told You I couldn't do this alone! I told You to allow me an assistant. You answered with Shiriel, then went back on Your word when You stole her from me!"

Ezekiel's mind bid his mouth halt, but the floodgates could not be pushed back.

"You have gone back on all the promises You spoke. You have taken out Your wrath upon me, though I served and obeyed. If this is how You treat Your servants, why would any serve You?"

If he were a dog, Ezekiel would have kicked the sand behind him to be rid of all traces of the refuse. If he were a man, he wouldn't have challenged the God of the Universe.

The sky hung ominously silent.

"There! Now I've said the blasphemous thoughts in my soul. Slay me now for my sins and be done with me!"

The whirl of Yahweh's Spirit transported him to the midst of a valley. As far as Ezekiel could see, there was no tree or vegetation.

"What would You have me see, Lord?" He stepped forward, his foot landing on an oblong white stone. The whole pile of stones beneath him shifted, clattering down. Ezekiel flailed to regain his balance and stared at his feet.

Not rocks. Bones.

He recoiled, his feet flew out from under him, and he slid down the mound of human bones. Reaching behind him, his hand closed around a large, smooth rock.

Ezekiel shuddered, trying not to think of why his fingers curled into two holes. Rocks didn't have holes. He glanced over his shoulder before he could stop himself.

He retched, but nothing came up.

All around him, bones—bleached white and dry from the sun—covered the valley as sand in the desert, and he wallowed amongst them.

Ezekiel studied his shaking hands—violated, unclean. Panic swelled through the pulse roaring in his ears. Where was his staff? He repositioned himself on hands and knees and willed his legs to support him.

His left foot slipped and he fell, coming face to face with the vacant stare of all mens' future.

"Why have You brought me here? In this valley of death?"

Son of man, you are defiled by your own ways and deeds.

A chill penetrated Ezekiel's soul. He tried to protest and prove his righteousness, but he couldn't. He'd been no greater than the leaders who had led the people astray. Who was he to stand before a Holy God?

A cool breeze traveled across Ezekiel's neck, chilling his spirit.

"Oh, God! I am a sinful man. I cannot be in your presence!" He prostrated himself on the piles of bones.

I will cleanse you from all your filthiness.

In his mind's eye, Ezekiel saw the outstretched hand of burning amber. The hand opened, sprinkling cool water over his head. Black tar oozed from Ezekiel's soul, and the hand absorbed it all.

Ezekiel wept cleansing tears.

Not for your sake but for My Holy Name.

Lifting his arms, Ezekiel welcomed the rending of his spirit, embracing the pain of his heart becoming flesh again.

I will put My spirit within you.

Yahweh enveloped his vulnerability with peace that exceeded all understanding.

Ezekiel shuddered, ashamed of the ugliness that was exposed and absorbed by healing light. His spirit was restored, and he was lifted out of the shadow of the valley of death.

A mighty, rushing wind transported Ezekiel many furlongs in each direction. The dry bones abounded with no end.

Son of man, can these bones live?

Ezekiel narrowed his eyes, desperate to understand. How could they? They'd been here for years. Yet, if they could live again, perhaps he could too. "Oh, Lord God, You know."

Anticipation circled in the silence.

Prophesy to these bones, and say to them 'Oh dry bones, hear the word of the Lord!'

Surveying his audience in earnest, Ezekiel shrugged. The people in his congregation were not much more active than this crowd.

He inhaled and words filled his mouth, "Thus says the Lord God to these bones: 'Surely, I will cause breath to enter into you, and you shall live. I will put sinews on you and bring flesh upon you and cover you with skin, and put breath into you; and you shall live.'"

Ezekiel's voice cracked, and tears flowed down his face. *Breathe on me too, God! I want to live again.*

A rattling began, faintly at first, then increasing in volume until the valley echoed with a tremendous clattering as bone connected with bone.

Indeed, sinews and flesh came upon the bones. Before Ezekiel's eyes, skin formed on the bodies, unrolling over each person like a blanket.

Ezekiel held his breath, waiting for the miraculous to happen.

The valley was stagnant. People formed before his eyes, yet lay lifeless.

Who would intercede on behalf of the people?

"Finish what You have begun, Lord. Not for our sakes, but for concern for Your holy name." His chest heaved with each breath. "You have spoken it. Do it!"

Prophesy to the breath, son of man.

The air moved across Ezekiel's neck, and he tipped his face up. "Thus says the Lord God, 'Come from the four winds, oh breath, and breathe on these slain, that they may live.'"

He raised his hands and cried out with his whole being, "'Then You shall know that I am God!'"

Life-giving breath blew over the valley, increasing in force until it howled with the force of a haboob. Reminiscent of the shofar's blast, the noise began faintly, and increased in strength, reviving Ezekiel, along with the host of people.

Ezekiel gasped with the fullness of life and spread his arms to balance against the surge of power and surveyed the exceedingly great army before him.

A deafening battle cry sounded as the soldiers pounded their breastplates in submission to the Almighty God.

Ezekiel fell to his knees and borrowed the angels' anthem, "You are worthy of all praise and glory and honor."

The vast army, once dead, joined Ezekiel's chant.

These bones are the whole house of Israel. They indeed say their bones are dry, their hope is lost and they are cut off. Prophesy to them.

Ezekiel rose and studied the warriors as they chanted.

The soldier nearest Ezekiel tucked her hair back under her helmet.

Men *and* women. All standing in awe, ready to fight before the Almighty God.

Heart pounding, he searched each face. Would Shiriel be amongst them? She was so close—he could sense her.

Ezekiel stumbled through the ranks. The vision began to fade. There were too many!

Before he could call her name, the vision dissipated like vapor.

His eyes flew open to see the darkened walls of his room.

Ezekiel groaned as fresh tears dampened the cushion beneath his cheek. *Shiriel, I miss you so much.*

"Yahweh, walk with me through this pain. I don't want to go on without Your righteous right hand sustaining me."

Hadn't Yahweh given him Shiriel when he'd cried out against the isolation of paralysis? Didn't she support him and care for him and share the messages when he could not? He thought back to the day he had been first struck down. Reflexively, his legs moved. He had called out to her in his mind, and she came to him—after Kelila managed to convince her.

Kelila was the one who answered Yahweh's prompting. Kelila. She was the one who always sensed when Yahweh spoke to him. Kelila, who helped dig a hole in the wall of the house.

He had prayed, and Yahweh had given his daughter as a support for the ministry.

Oh, God! I thought You had abandoned me all these years, yet I was the one who didn't see the fulfillment of Your promise. "Forgive me, Yahweh. You. Are. My. God."

Ezekiel rolled onto his stomach and extended his arms. Sobs racked his body. *I've tried to punish You with my silence, but only affected myself. Restore unto me the joy of Your salvation.*

Shiriel's memory—never far from his thoughts—appeared. His beautiful, caring song. Pain knifed into all his senses and tossed him about like a wave in the sea.

He could now see Yahweh's presence over the last couple of years. In his daughter, in Gilead, and even in the mad scheme his desperate friends had attempted, all reaching out, anchoring him as he was buffeted by his greatest storm.

Friends who never gave up on him when he had given up on himself.

I will put My Spirit in you and you shall live.

As sure as the promise came from the mouth of his Creator and Redeemer, He would surely bring it to pass.

Because the Almighty God could do no less.

EPILOGUE

Moreover, I will make a covenant of peace with them, and it shall be an everlasting covenant with them; I will establish them and multiply them, and I will set My sanctuary in their midst forevermore, My tabernacle also shall be with them; indeed I will be their God, and they shall be My people. The nations also will know that I, the LORD, sanctify Israel when My sanctuary is in their midst forevermore."

—Ezekiel 37:26-28

O*n the nineteenth day of the tenth month which was in the twelfth year of King Coniah's captivity.*

Ezekiel surveyed his flock on the following sabbath. The ache of compassion and a spirit crushed spread through him, threatening to drive him to his knees.

Pressing against his chest, he set his shoulders back and gripped his staff. He had to endure through the pain—the alternative of having a heart of stone was worse.

You are my God. Give me wisdom to lead Your people. Give me one more, today.

Sunlight flooded in as the door swung open and Rabgar-Nebo entered.

Ezekiel's eyebrows shot up as Gilead stepped in behind. He scrubbed the back of his hand across his eyes and glanced with pride at his master.

And the nations shall know…

The grandeur nearly pushed Ezekiel to his knees. *Thank You, Yahweh.*

Huz began strumming the kinnor, and the song of a reed flute filled the air.

Ezekiel whirled around and air left the room. He gawked at the man blowing out sound. Would music ever be pleasurable again? On the women's side, he caught sight of Kelila, watching the musicians, tears streaming down her cheeks.

He crossed the aisle before he had time to consider and rested his free hand on her shoulder. He pushed his whisper around the tightness in his throat, "Kelila—Keli—you may step out if you want."

She shook her head and flung her arms around him. "It helps me remember."

Ezekiel rubbed her back, and his eyes burned.

Kelila tipped her face up. "Do you need to step out?"

His vision blurred with tears. "I think I can make it, with your help—and Yahweh's."

"I love you, *Abba*." Kelila squeezed him tight.

He swallowed. "I love you too, daughter. We're going to make it. Right?"

Her head bobbed against him. Together they watched the flutist. Could it be he was unskilled, or did every musician automatically become relegated to inferior?

Perez spoke the opening prayer, and Ezekiel limped forward. He faced the congregation and rubbed his chest.

"My people, hear the word of the Lord." He bent to pick up the two sticks he had smoothed and written on.

He tucked his staff under his arm and displayed the sticks,

one in each hand. "This stick is for Judah and for the children of Israel, his companions."

The man in the front row covered a yawn.

I can't. They're too hard-hearted.

A nudging in his soul prompted his gaze to Gilead's master —someone who was here out of curiosity rather than duty. Ezekiel turned his face toward Rabgar-Nebo and held up the second stick. "This represents Joseph, the stick of Ephraim and for all the house of Israel, his companions."

The spirit of Yahweh moved.

Ezekiel lifted the sticks above his head and pressed them together. "As You have spoken, bring it to pass." The sticks fused together, the writing swirling and merging.

Rabgar-Nebo jerked a step backward as Ezekiel displayed the one stick.

One of the women gasped. "What does it mean?"

"Thus, says the Lord God, 'I will join the tribes of Israel with Judah. They will be one in My hand.'"

Perez took the united stick and examined it. "It is one. As if it had never been separate."

Murmurs rippled through the crowd.

Ezekiel leaned forward on his staff, pleading with the people to hear. "'David, my servant, shall be king over them and they shall have one shepherd. They will walk in my judgment and observe my statutes and do them.'"

"The Messiah!" The whisper shot across the room like a wildfire.

"'Then they will dwell in the land I have given to Jacob.'" Ezekiel scanned the crowd. He'd wasted years, not taking advantage of each opportunity.

He closed the door on guilt. Dwelling on his failures wouldn't help.

"'I will make an everlasting covenant of peace. I will establish and multiply them. My tabernacle shall be with them. I will be their God, and they shall be My people.'"

Ezekiel honed in on Rabgar-Nebo. "The nations also will know that I, the Lord sanctify Israel when My sanctuary is in their midst forevermore."

At the end of the service, Ezekiel hobbled to the back to greet his flock.

Gilead's gaze darted back and forth. He shifted his weight. "Ezekiel, I'm sorry—"

Ezekiel patted Gilead's hand and forced a tight smile. "You didn't do wrong. It was a mistake for me to enclose myself as I did. Thank you for caring for me."

Gilead embraced him. "I'm so sorry, my brother."

"All is forgiven." Truly, Ezekiel didn't feel the sting of betrayal as he should. He shifted off his left leg.

Clearing his throat, Ezekiel extended an arm to Rabgar-Nebo. "I'm glad to have you join us this morning. Did you have any questions I can answer?"

"Your God has used astounding measures to get your attention, priest. It has captured my thoughts, too."

Ezekiel hung his head. Would this Chaldean officer be here, if not for Yahweh bringing Ezekiel through this trial?

"I'm not saying I'm converting—yet." Rabgar-Nebo folded his hands in front of his loins. "I'm just curious."

Ezekiel bit back a grin. "Yahweh accepts little steps."

The words came forth as if they had originated with Ezekiel. He turned back to Gilead. "Please thank Chislon and the women for their—unusual—part in all this. Their words resonated truth I needed to hear. I've reflected on their advice, and they have been great encouragement to me."

Rabgar-Nebo and Gilead exchanged narrow glances.

Gilead coughed. "The strangest thing—"

"What is it?"

"They are no longer residing at the Jewish camp." Rabgar-Nebo tapped his leg.

Ezekiel frowned. "What do you mean?"

Gilead stepped close and lowered his voice, "We stopped

by their campsite this morning. They have vanished."

"Apart from the log we filled out when they first arrived, there is no record of them anywhere." Rabgar-Nebo scratched his cheek. "It's like they don't exist."

Ezekiel squeezed his eyes closed and rubbed his temples. Had he imagined them? He wouldn't be having this conversation with a pagan captain if he had.

"We stopped by Atta's. She hasn't seen them either."

Rabgar-Nebo brushed off his hands. "Like I said, your God used unusual methods to get your attention."

Could Chislon, Datyah, and Eissa truly have been Hope, Faith, and Love embodied?

Ezekiel shook his head. "Impossible."

Gilead shrugged.

The three men exchanged an unspoken pact.

Ezekiel pondered the possibility. Of all the things Yahweh had shown him, was it so difficult to believe?

He watched Gilead and Rabgar-Nebo depart. The Chaldean listened as Gilead spoke. If Rabgar-Nebo had any questions about the faith, Gilead would answer well.

The student could become the teacher. As it should be—Gilead could affect a greater circle of influence than Ezekiel alone could.

Thank You, Yahweh. Build up the remnant as You said You would. He turned back to the house and stopped at the door.

Israel and Judah restored.

His heart renewed.

All at the promise of a future.

Ezekiel rubbed the lavender between his fingers and breathed in Shiriel's scent.

The End

AUTHOR'S NOTE

Thank you for reading **Ezekiel's Song**.

As I was reading the book of Ezekiel, I was confounded by his story. How was a mute, paralyzed man in Babylon, meant to get the message of judgment all the way back to Jerusalem? The tableaux unfolded through 2 Kings, 2 Chronicles, and Jeremiah along the treacherous path of the leaders of Judah disobeying the Lord's commands, and judgement finally being delivered by the hand of Nebuchadnezzar. This mirrored today's society with chilling accuracy. Nations that disregard the Lord will eventually face His judgment. Hold fast to the ways of Truth and influence those around you.

Jeremiah was a contemporary of Ezekiel, but there is no record that they knew each other. Both were in the priestly service, so it stands to reason that they could have crossed paths in the temple.

Apart from the two verses in the Bible—*I take away from you the desire of your eyes"* and *So I spoke to the people in the morning and at evening my wife died. ~Ezekiel 24:16, 18*—Ezekiel's wife is not mentioned. Shiri's name and her backstory is my imagination.

Gilead is completely fictional. The scriptures say amongst the 10,000 exiles, the valiant warriors were also taken. Enter a skilled archer, faithful to the Lord who could help bear the burden of the ministry.

There is some debate on whether Ezekiel was paralyzed for the entire 430 days (around 14 months) or if he had some bouts of mobility. After all, the Lord did command him to make his bread (Ezekiel 4:9), and he was instructed to deliver the messages to Jerusalem. As I studied Ezekiel, the trips to Jerusalem appear to be in visions. I chose to keep Ezekiel bound the entire time for a couple of reasons. He is mentioned in the scriptures as having a wife (Ezekiel 24:18), and culturally, she would have been the one preparing food for the family. I also wanted to honor caregivers and those who are bedbound. Ezekiel was given a timeframe where he would regain his strength, those who have debilitating illnesses are not.

There is no record of where Tel-Abib or the River Chebar were located. I have it depicted as one of the canals bringing irrigation from the Euphrates to the outlying areas of Babylon.

I chose to have Shadrach, Meshach, and Abed-Nego as brothers. Daniel 1:3 mentions the first exile was "some of the king's descendants." This would indicate they are brothers with the same father, or perhaps cousins. The Jewish Midrash says that Shadrach, Meshach, and Abed-Nego did indeed seek counsel from Ezekiel.

This is a work of fiction, and my imaginings of how lives were affected by all the prophesies and judgements found in the book of Jeremiah and Ezekiel. Please search out the scriptures as first and final authority.

ABOUT THE AUTHOR

Author of Biblical fiction, avid reader, pastor's wife, Naomi loves reading the Bible and imagining how things were at the time. When she's not serving in various areas at church, trying to stay on top of mountains of dishes or convincing her rescue dog, Freeway, to be cute on command for Instagram reels, you'll most likely find her enjoying a good book and a cup of coffee. Naomi co-hosts #BehindTheStory with Naomi and Lisa, an author interview show on YouTube and your podcast platform of choice.

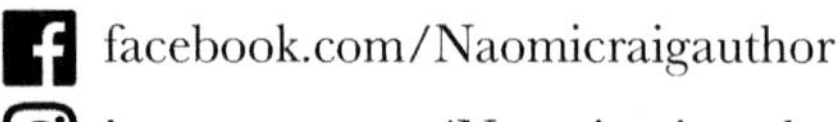
facebook.com/Naomicraigauthor
instagram.com/Naomicraigauthor

ALSO BY NAOMI CRAIG

Yahweh's Legacy

Rahab's Courage (Book One)

Ezekiel's Song (Book Two)

Keeping Christmas Collections

Keeping Christmas (Volume One)

HABAKKUK'S BURDEN

EZEKIEL'S SONG SHORT STORY BONUS

NAOMI CRAIG

1

Will not your creditors rise up suddenly?
Will they not awaken who oppress you?
And you shall be their booty.
~Habakkuk 2:7

606 Bce

"Please, Oded. Have mercy." Habakkuk fell to his knees before the door to his small hole-in-the-wall dwelling. "I need more time."

Oded's pitying smile felt like a pat on the head. "My friend, I cannot control when the creditors come to *my* door. They are demanding I settle my accounts."

Habakkuk tried to shove aside the shame that heaped upon his shoulders. *Think.*

"Abba?" The familiar dragging sound accompanied Elah to the door. His small son propped himself up with his arms, his lame legs dragging behind him on the dirt floor.

"My son needs me." Habakkuk lowered his voice. "If you send me away to debtors' prison, you would not obtain your money any faster."

Oded tipped his head and cupped his hand around his bearded chin.

"Do you know of any opportunity to earn a wage in the city?" Habakkuk sprung on Oded's hesitation. He was a decent man—surely he would have compassion.

"There is one opportunity." Oded tapped his finger alongside his face.

"Yes? What is it?"

"The caravan that travels the Incense Route. They will pay you well. I'm sure that would absolve your remaining debt. But it is very dangerous. It would be nearly three months' time." Oded shrugged. "It leaves in two days from Mamshit."

Habakkuk turned toward the door. The woman who cared for his son now stood beside Elah. Resting one hand on the door frame, Levana's eyes were lined with worry and her lips pursed as she chewed the inside of her cheek.

"Don't do it, *Abba*." Elah reached out for him. "I need you."

Habakkuk pushed himself upright and brushed off his knees. He squatted before his son and touched his cheek. "What do you think?" He sought Levana's tired eyes. "If I stay, I will be taken away to debtors' prison. Oded—"

"Oded is crooked." Levana hissed, tucking her fist in the fold of her robe.

"—has to report to those higher than him." Habakkuk stood to block Oded's view of the conversation. "It is my fault for not having enough reserved for when my son had need."

"Yes, but Oded—"

"Was kind enough to offer me credit." There was no need to delve into Oded's motivation yet again.

Levana folded her arms across her chest.

"What choice do I have? There is no work in the fields, not with the drought. Nothing that will offer a substantial wage. If I go to Arabia, I could pay off my debt."

"But you'd be away from us." Elah's small voice rose to still their debate.

Habakkuk scooped up to the boy's slight frame. He fought against the tightness in his chest. "If I stay, I would be away from you longer."

"I don't like it." Levana shook her head.

"You allow your wife to influence you?" Oded's tone edged towards impatience.

"She is not my wife." Habakkuk saw the shame flash across Levana's face before she lowered her gaze. He cleared his throat. "She is an equal. She cares for my son. This decision affects her as much as me."

Oded's raised eyebrows and tapping foot indicated he cared not for Habakkuk's justification of the situation.

Elah's small hands patted Habakkuk's face. "Don't go, *Abba.*"

Habakkuk crushed the boy to his chest and pleaded with Levana with his eyes. "I don't know what else to do."

"Then go. Pay off your debt and return to us." Levana wrapped her arms tightly around her waist and turned away.

Lowering the boy and straightening out the unresponsive legs, Habakkuk pressed a kiss to Elah's head. "I love you, my son. I'll be back as soon as I can."

Elah clung to his hand and his bottom lip protruded. "Don't go."

Habakkuk pried his fingers free and stepped aside, bumping into the bundle Levana held out.

"Some things for your journey."

Opening the sack, Habakkuk scanned the contents. His cloak. The harp that he neglected far too often. A scrap of flat bread. "I can't take this. You and Elah—"

"Take it." Levana pushed it back and lowered her voice to a wisp of wind. "Be wise in your allegiance."

The longer he lingered, the less likely he was to leave at all. Habakkuk's smile was probably more of a grimace than reassurance. "You must have faith. The Lord will provide." He squeezed Levana's hand and turned to meet Oded.

Oded clicked his tongue. "Some faith. You have abandoned the ways of Yahweh, as He has abandoned you."

Habakkuk turned his head to see Levana and Elah waving him off—as if he was marching off to complete an assignment of honor rather than a desperate mission to survive.

Yahweh, protect my household.

Perhaps Oded was right. Yahweh wouldn't look upon him when he was wallowing in the pit of his own making.

———

Oded delivered Habakkuk to the waiting caravan in Mamshit and over the following eighteen days, he rode a swift camel across the desolate desert, ever southward. The isolation of the landscape fed the loneliness flooding inside Habakkuk's chest like a wadi after the winter rain.

Thoughts of Elah—and yes, Levana—filled his jostling days atop his camel's back. With each lopsided stride, Levana's suspicions rattled around Habakkuk's thoughts. After each payment he made, Oded had seemed pained to mention the interest accumulated.

Habakkuk had never been good with figures—Levana had kept track—but the staggering amount he had handed over to Oded, surely had repaid his original debt twice over.

The uncomfortable realization wriggled through the core of his thoughts.

"Oded was right to charge me interest." Dust coated Habakkuk's mouth. He rewound the cloth around his face.

Even with interest, he'd been in Oded's debt an awfully long time.

And another thing. Why did the caravan leader wait specifically for Habakkuk unless he knew Oded was bringing him?

Oded had *purposed* him to have the treacherous journey. To what benefit? If Habakkuk paid his debt in full, Oded could no longer gouge him.

Habakkuk slammed his fist into his hand. "Oded used me as his employment!"

The camel lurched to a halt at his erratic rein movement and looked back reproachfully.

"Ha!" Habakkuk smacked the reins on the camel's neck with more force than necessary. The camel grunted and stumbled into his lanky gallop.

What justification did he have against Oded's extortion? They had never drawn up official documents before the elders. What was there to hinder Oded from oppressing Habakkuk's family for all his days?

Nothing.

Even if he now were to present his cause to the elders in the gate, why would they side with him over an upstanding member of the community like Oded?

The sandy horizon and the caravan of camels bopping before him stretched as far as he could see. His shortcomings rose as the stench of camel urine did to his nostrils.

Was there no justice for one who had made mistakes in the past?

By the time their caravan arrived in Timna's walled fortress, Habakkuk's insides had become resolute. Bitter.

He wandered through the Boswellia groves as fresh camels were loaded. The knobby trees, scarcely sufficient for shading the odd lizard with long, bent front legs, produced the sought-after Frankincense.

Habakkuk scanned the sloping hills as he thumbed the knob of dried sap on the scraggly tree and took an experimental sniff. The incense's aroma brought remembrance of the house of the Lord, and the clamor of violence outside the temple walls.

2

O LORD, how long shall I cry, and You will not hear? Even cry out to You, "Violence!" And You will not save. Why do You show me iniquity, and cause me to see trouble? For plundering and violence are before me; There is strife, and contention arises. Therefore, the law is powerless, and justice never goes forth. For the wicked surround the righteous; Therefore, perverse judgment proceeds.
~Habakkuk 1:2-4

Habakkuk assessed his new colleagues loading fresh camels while lashing the straps of his sandals tight. The days of riding on the camel's back were no more. The return trip would entail each man leading a line of loaded camels.

A gangly adolescent seemed particularly experienced as he slapped a camel on the rump, shoving it into line and tying a short rope around its tail. Habakkuk studied his every move as he confidently tied the other end of the rope to the next camel's bridle.

That is enough to keep a camel in line?

The boy turned with narrowed eyes and summoned Habakkuk with a finger. "Why do you scrutinize me so? Do you recognize me?"

Habakkuk stepped back at the hostile tone. "I've never seen you before. Are you the caravan leader?"

The boy scoffed. "Wrong."

"I'm sure I don't know." Habakkuk glanced at the men he travelled south with. Though silent, *they* were at least civil.

"Why do you study me so intently?" The boy swiftly tied the tail. "Do you have a son?"

Habakkuk whirled around and lunged for the boy. "Why do you want to know? Did Oded send you?"

The boy flailed and gripped Habakkuk's tunic with a searching stare of his own.

After a moment, the youth's shoulders sagged. "I don't know who Oded is."

"What is your issue, boy?" Habakkuk didn't like feeling as though he didn't measure up—even to a scrawny adolescent.

"Nothing. Sorry to bother you. I'm Mahath."

Releasing him with a shove, Habakkuk couldn't ignore the crestfallen expression on Mahath's face. "Who were you expecting me to be?"

The muscle on Mahath's face twitched. "No one."

Despite the comfort of not engaging and leaving Mahath's dejected response alone, Habakkuk tipped his head and followed the boy to the next camel. "What is it? Why do you appear as if you have lost a loved one?"

Mahath shot a glare over his shoulder.

"I am Habakkuk." Trust had to be earned. "I travel on this caravan to pay off the debt I amassed when my child fell and both legs were made lame. My friend—I thought he was my friend—paid for the expenses. I've been paying him back these five years."

Mahath scratched the faint hairs on his upper lip and rested his shoulder against the camel's shoulder. His gaze lingered on Habakkuk's face. "Your son is lucky to have you care."

"Mahath! Hustle, will you? We must make the first stop by nightfall."

The boy clamped his mouth shut and tied the next piece of rope.

Habakkuk jogged to catch up. "Teach me, Mahath. Be my caravan master."

A twinkle sparked in Mahath's eyes. "Tie each knot firmly. The camels will follow one another, but we don't want to give opportunity for them to escape."

Habakkuk eyed the massive crates and bundles strapped onto the camels' backs. "What do we do to prevent marauders attacking?"

"Frankincense is costly. Each night we make camp in the fortresses along the route. In exchange for their protection, we give them a portion of our cargo."

"That is extortion!" Habakkuk's roar drew the attention of the caravan leader.

"That is reality. We can't make it without their refuge and water." Mahath flapped his hand. "You will still have enough profit."

Habakkuk swallowed his retort. Each expense cut away at his chance to be rid of his debt. Another opportunity to be free smashed flat like the camel's grinding step into the sand.

Soon, Habakkuk discovered an isolation even the southbound journey couldn't compare to. All day, he trudged along, leading a line of camels. Twelve of the beasts. He craved the jostle of the camel's sway, where his deepest thought was not falling off his perch and ruminating on Oded's potential entrapment.

Now his thoughts and sins plodded with him, making their regrets his companions—robbing his presence of mind as surely as a bandit thieving from his camels' goods.

Each night he bunked with Mahath and each day he

loaded his camels and stepped behind Mahath's line. When the path curved, Habakkuk could glimpse Mahath's spritely form—full of vibrant energy. Physicalities his son would never enjoy.

On the eve of the fifty-fifth day since their departure from Timna, they made camp inside the fortress of Aqaba. Habakkuk and Mahath wandered up to the walls where the Gulf of Aqaba stretched before them to the south.

"Legend has it that is Mount Paran. The Mountain of God." Mahath pointed to a peak east of the fortress. "Where Moses met Yahweh."

Habakkuk tore his gaze away from the gulf to give it a cursory glimpse. "Hmm."

"What would you ask Yahweh—if you had the chance to go up there?"

Habakkuk swallowed his initial scoff—his companion was a sensitive one. "I'd have to consider. Only one question?"

Mahath bobbed his chin.

Mind going blank, Habakkuk shifted to the north side of the wall and surveyed the mountain. "You seem to have put a lot of thought into it. What would you ask?"

"I'd ask why my *abba* left and never wanted me." Mahath bounced on the balls of his feet and gripped the edge.

Habakkuk slanted a glance at the turmoil on Mahath's face. This explained the constant surveying of the people the youth came in contact with.

"You remind me of him. Or perhaps that is wishful thinking. How I desire an *abba* who can't wait to return to me."

Habakkuk grimaced. "I'm not home yet. There is much in my life that I have done dishonorably. I would not be away from my son if I had been smarter about my income."

Mahath scrubbed the back of his hand across his eyes and swallowed. "But you wish to be with your son."

"He is a fool to miss out on the amazing man you have become." Habakkuk's words didn't seem to go beyond his shoulders. "You are intelligent and hard working. You'd be a credit to any righteous man."

Mahath swallowed twice and sniffed. "Why don't you marry Levana? You and all your talk of righteousness."

Habakkuk's insides squirmed. He glanced toward the mountain and braced against the rampart. "It started out as a fair exchange. Levana came out of a compromised situation. She needed an escape. Shelter and protection in exchange for a caring overseer for my son."

"Ah." Mahath smirked.

"How would you know?"

"I observe people. I know things." He turned to face Habakkuk, resting his elbows on the wall.

"Well, the thing is, we've acclimated ourselves to the situation. She probably doesn't think anything of it."

Mahath snorted. "Women will think of it, trust me."

What woman didn't want to be valued as more than a live-in consort?

"Is your *ima* still alive?"

"She was trampled in the streets of Jerusalem during a riot. She thought I was involved with the wrong boys and came to find me. Looters realized she was dead and ransacked our place. I've traveled the caravan ever since." Mahath slumped away with one more look at the mountain.

Habakkuk expelled a long breath and stared at the mountain.

What would I ask You? Perhaps why Yahweh allowed such violence? "Where is the justice? Not for me—I know I have missed the mark of righteousness—but what about Mahath?"

Habakkuk turned his back to the mountain—to God—but as surely as he glimpsed the gulf, he whirled around, ready to fight.

"Why do You show me iniquity and cause me to see trouble—the plundering, the violence before me? There is strife, and contentions arise." Mahath, his *ima,* Habakkuk's own debt—all situations that had been overlooked too long.

"The law is powerless! Justice never goes forth, for the wicked surround the righteous and perverse judgment proceeds."

Habakkuk shook his fist. "How long shall I cry and You will not hear? How long will You see the violence and not save?"

3

For indeed I am raising up the Chaldeans, a bitter and hasty nation…
They are terrible and dreadful; Their judgement and their dignity proceed from themselves.
~Habakkuk 1:6a, 7

Thundering hoofbeats and cries of alarm roused Habakkuk from a deep slumber.

He threw on his outer cloak and joined the clamorous masses of people crammed in the corridor. Panic ensued as people shoved against each other in a desperate attempt to find secure shelter.

The stream of people carried Habakkuk like flood waters past the stairwell to the outer wall.

"Let me pass!" Habakkuk turned his body against the surging tide and puffed out his shoulders. People began diverting around him. He stepped sideways and stepped again until he touched the wall. He flattened himself against the wall and inched to the stairwell.

Bounding up the stairs, he emerged on the wide wall. The

approaching cavalry's pounding hooves deafened him. Terror nearly paralyzed Habakkuk and the vibrations rattled the loose pebbles on the wall. Despite the oppressive desire to cower, Habakkuk found himself at the rampart staring over the vast sea of riders.

Habakkuk's heart pounded against his chest, but he couldn't turn away from the dreadful sight. Terrible soldiers sat astride horses as swift as leopards as far as he could see.

With the ferocity of evening wolves, the chargers consumed the land with their hooves. A section of the cavalry veered off from the main contingent and immediately surrounded the city's walls. Within seconds, they had formed a siege mound and began ramming the gates.

Don't open it! Don't give in.

Bang! The gates clattered open, shaking the wall Habakkuk stood on. An arrow whizzed by his ear, and he crouched out of sight. His breathing was labored in his ears.

Screams inside the city drew him like a moth to the flame. He crawled to the other side of the wall and peered into the city. Like eagles hastening to devour their prey, the soldiers gathered prisoners as numerous as sand.

A harsh east wind whipped against Habakkuk's face and stung his eyes. He pressed his palms to his eyes to relieve the stinging. He squeezed open his eyes to find a pair of wrapped legs before him. Dread rose as he lifted his eyes up the full extent of the soldier's form to his violent sneer and cone-shaped helmet.

The soldier struck his outstretched spear on the stone and sparks flashed.

Each way Habakkuk dodged, the spear stained with blood followed.

The soldier raised the spear and lunged forward—

Habakkuk's eyes flew open to find the darkened room of the Aqaba fortress. He scrambled from his sleeping mat—there was Mahath snoring gently beside him.

Pulling his tunic away from his sweat-soaked skin and his pounding heart, Habakkuk shivered at the cool night air and felt his way to the doorway and into the corridor.

The screams from his dream—how could it have been a dream—still echoed in the corridors of his mind. He wiped his hand over his mouth and tried to still the tremors in his body. No one hindered his path to the stairwell and Habakkuk stood in the same place he and Mahath had rested the evening before.

Terror fixed his feet as if they had been mortared to the stones. His neck tensed and his breathing grew shallow. He should return to his sleeping quarters. *It was all a dream. It wasn't real.*

"It felt real." The sound of his voice startled him in the stillness of the inky night.

A gentle breeze carrying the aroma of salt water sent him into a fit of shivering. Gone was the heat of the soldier's terrible anger. All that remained were shadows lurking in his mind.

"Why does it feel so tangible, then?" Habakkuk inched his way to the edge of the wall and peered down. Nothing but two guards standing sentinel.

Mount Paran drew his attention—black against the starlit sky. Up here, Habakkuk could breathe easier. He shot a glance to the east, and the sands were still.

"Were You sending me a message, Yahweh?" Did it mean anything? Was it a test like it had been with the boy, Samuel?

"Ha. Why would Yahweh speak to me?" He turned to go back down, but something checked his spirit. He glanced back at Mount Paran, half expecting to see it glow.

Habakkuk chuckled nervously at the vast darkness. He knelt and braced his hands on the wall. "I feel like the dream meant something. That I am supposed to do something with it. Show me Your purpose, Lord."

Somehow the nightmare had something to do with his petition last night. He just knew it.

What did priests do when waiting to hear from Yahweh?

Habakkuk lowered himself to a kneeling position, then raised up to peer over the edge. Nothing. He settled down, and a pebble dug into his knee. "I have no offering. I don't even deserve to come before You. I am not a righteous man. But You said in Your holy scriptures if someone seeks You, they will find You."

Closing his eyes, he forced himself to think again of the horrors he had seen.

Look among the nations and watch—be utterly astounded.

Habakkuk's eyes flew open to search for the source of the voice. He was alone on the wall, but the Mountain of God pulsated with eye-searing light. His body tensed, awaiting without breath what would unfold next.

"Speak, Lord. For Your servant listens."

For I will work a work in your days, which you would not believe, though it were told you.

"In *my* day? This dream…this vision will take place?" Sweat formed on Habakkuk's brow as the nightmare unfolded in his mind once again.

For indeed I am raising up the Chaldeans, a Bitter and hasty nation. Which marches through the breadth of the earth, to possess dwelling places that are not theirs.

Habakkuk shuddered at the memory of the bitter face behind the spear. He had prayed for justice from his oppressors, and *this* was the answer? "You are of purer eyes than to behold evil. Why do You look on those who deal treacherously, and hold Your tongue when the wicked devours a person more righteous than he is?"

There was no answer, no impression on his spirit or audible voice.

"Those wretched heathens swept up every person in their path, like fish in a dragnet. Shall they therefore empty their net and continue to slay the nations without pity?" Habakkuk stared at the darkened mountain. "Would You let them triumph over Your chosen people and ascribe power to their false gods?"

Habakkuk waited until the muscles in his jaw begged for relief. He slammed his fist against his thigh. "Why don't You answer? It cannot end in tragedy. You have appointed the nations who don't follow You for judgement. *Your people* are meant to prosper."

He stared until his vision blurred. Squeezing his eyes shut, he blinked a couple times to restore the moisture.

Knowing full well that he resembled a petulant child, Habakkuk crossed his arms across his chest. He scowled. "I will stand my watch and set myself on the rampart and watch to see what You will say to me."

It was probably not acceptable to demand an answer from the Holy One. Habakkuk fidgeted. *Yahweh had answered his previous petition. Why not this one too?*

Without a doubt, Yahweh would correct Habakkuk's line of thinking.

He amended his demand. "I will think on what I will answer when I am corrected."

4

Behold the proud, his soul is not upright in him; but the just shall live by his faith.
~Habakkuk 2:4

Habakkuk slapped his arms as the eastern horizon began to lighten. Soon the fortress would stir and his caravan would have to load the camels and move out.

Perhaps he should have brought up his harp—the Lord might be more willing to respond if Habakkuk was playing hymns of praise.

Was it fruitless to wait? Shouldn't he take the Lord at His word and not doubt?

Uncrossing his legs, Habakkuk winced at the stiffness in his bones. He heaved a sigh. What the Lord has said, He had declared rightly.

With one more survey of the silent mountain, Habakkuk hobbled on stiff legs to the stairwell.

Write the vision and make it plain on tablets that

he may run who reads it. For the vision is yet for an appointed time; But at the end it will speak and it will not lie.

Moisture stung the back of Habakkuk's eyes. He knelt facing the mountain once again. What did it hold in store for his people? Would they be the ones gathered like sand? What would become of the cripples like his son?

"Yes, my Lord. I will write it down."

Though it tarries, wait for it. Because it will surely come. It will not tarry.

Did the Chaldeans build their army even now? Who would heed Habakkuk's report? Should he try to obtain an audience with the new king, Jehoiakim? Was there anyone at the temple who had the king's ear?

Rumor had it King Jehoiakim heeded no counsel but his own.

Behold the proud. His soul is not upright in him, but the just shall live by faith.

The words and visions poured in, searing Habakkuk's thoughts until the fortress began to stir and the day began.

All day long, the terrors of the Lord's words accompanied Habakkuk on the plodding journey northwest. Every wind that pelted him with sand assailed him with the atrocities to come.

Indeed, the path had already been set.

Visions of the current state of Jerusalem's iniquity displayed before his eyes.

The clank of the bronze bell pulled Habakkuk back to the task at hand. He had caught up to the back end of Mahath's line and had begun to walk astride of the last camel.

Habakkuk's lead animal unfurled its curved neck faster than a viper and gave a slashing bite to the camel's flank.

Mahath's camel screamed its groaning cry and flung its skinny leg straight out at the level of Habakkuk's face.

Habakkuk lunged to the left, yanking on the lead rope with all his strength.

The camel's forward momentum made Habakkuk's feet slip on the sand. He braced himself, but the camel turned his hot-tempered resentment toward him with a grumble and a swing of his powerful neck.

The force sent Habakkuk sprawling to the ground.

Let go of the rope. Habakkuk grasped for the lead wrapped around his wrist. He rolled on his back to see the camel's fat lip pulled back and its jaw unhinging. The camel only had teeth on the bottom jaw, and those were sawing from side to side.

All that Mahath had taught him evaporated like water on a hot day.

Habakkuk scrambled back. Which would be a worse fate, to be bitten, dragged, or suffocated if the beast decided to collapse on him with its bony breastplate?

Shouting penetrated Habakkuk's fixation with the camel's foul breath.

"Let go of the rope! Let go!"

Against common sense, Habakkuk tore his gaze away from the menacing face and clawed at his wrist. The rope dug tight into his skin with each jerk from the camel and the end wrapped under the rest of the coil.

The rope grew slack temporarily as Mahath wrestled the camel's head from side to side, leaning into its body with all his weight.

Habakkuk untucked the rope and flung it away from him as raw pain radiated down his arm.

"Behave yourself!" Mahath shouted, forcefully thumping on the camel's neck.

The camel screamed and its eyes rolled back.

Habakkuk pushed himself to his feet and off to the side while Mahath wrestled the camel—and the whole line—off the path toward a cluster of spiny cacti.

"Eat this and calm down!" Mahath pushed the camel's head down.

With one more rebellious grunt, the camel clamped down and ripped off a pad.

Mahath jerked his head. "Come here. He needs to associate you with this treat."

Habakkuk tentatively grabbed the lead rope and winced as the camel smacked the cactus—spines and all.

"Are you alright? I told you never to let your lead catch up with my line." Mahath paced to assess the rest of Habakkuk's caravan.

"I'm sorry." Habakkuk shook his wrist, trying to relieve the stinging. If Mahath was here, where were his camels? "Your team!"

Mahath gestured to the small line of camels. "I tied them off to the caravan in front."

He had tied them off quick enough to save Habakkuk? This youth really was amazing.

"I'm a fool." Habakkuk flinched as Mahath examined his wrist.

"I couldn't say it better." The boy tore a strip of cloth from his tunic, spat on it three times, and wound it round Habakkuk's wrist. "This whole time you are focused. Eager to get home. Except today. Why?"

Habakkuk groaned as the last line began to pass their position. "Shouldn't we—"

"Nah. You have to wait now until this fellow has had his fill—unless you wish to wrestle him away?"

"No thanks." Habakkuk passed his hand over his gritty eyes. "Yahweh appeared to me after we were on the wall. He showed me a vision and talked to me."

"Who? The caravan leader?"

"No." Habakkuk leaned close and instantly felt foolish. The camel would not spread his tale. "Yahweh. The Holy One."

Mahath's eyes enlarged like a jewel beetle's.

"He showed me…terrible things. His presence—I could see it, yet I couldn't."

The camel raised its head, still smacking on a cactus pad.

"Hup." Mahath prodded the beast with his shoulder. "What do you mean?"

Habakkuk grunted. How could mere words communicate what he had seen? "The hills bowed before Him—everlasting mountains were scattered. The rivers overflowed in His presence and pestilence and fevers went before Him."

Misgivings pranced across Mahath's face as surely as the camels plodded behind them. "It sounds terrible."

Habakkuk stopped walking, glanced back at the now placid camel, and stepped to the side. "But it was also wonderful. His glory covered the Heavens. The whole earth was full of His praises."

"What do you make of it?" Mahath's fear gave him a child-like air.

"I'm not rightly sure. The visions were opposite of each other. Wrath, yet mercy. Future events, yet a warning for those who take heed. His presence in the midst of destruction."

Mahath didn't turn his head. "Did you ask where my *abba* is?"

Habakkuk blew out a breath. "I'm sorry, my friend. I did not. All I can say about that is that Yahweh is there in the midst of devastation."

Mahath's jaw worked, and he swiped at his eyes.

Habakkuk wrinkled his nose. "I'm meant to write it all down. How will I remember it all?"

"Tell me everything. We will write it down tonight."

5

Their rejoicing was like feasting on the poor in secret.
~Habakkuk 3:14b

"When do you need to make Jerusalem by?" Mahath studied the evening sky.

"Before the full moon. How long is it to Jerusalem?" Uneasiness set Habakkuk on edge.

Mahath furrowed his eyebrows. "Nine days. We won't make it."

"How many stops in between? Can we ride through the night?" Habakkuk slammed his fist against his thigh. "I have to make the payment."

"Perhaps your debtor has miscalculated?" Mahath did not seem convinced.

Frustration curdled Habakkuk's insides. Oded had set up this scheme full well knowing it was impossible. "Why is this happening?"

Mahath leaned against the wall and crossed his arms and legs, an unreadable expression on his face.

I know You are in the midst of my devastation, but this is too much.

"What happens if we push the camels? Could we travel through the night?"

Mahath raised his eyebrows. "We'd not have the protection of the caravan, or daylight—"

Habakkuk refrained from shaking the boy. "You've made the trip. Please, Mahath. I've got to make this deadline."

"Well…What about the vision? You need to write it down."

"I have to return to Jerusalem!" Habakkuk growled and stalked away.

"The just shall live by their faith." Mahath called out. "You must honor the Lord's request first."

Habakkuk glared at his young friend and glowered while untacking the camels and wrapping their goods in the corner. Mahath was right, of course, but every fiber in his being protested.

After they sought refreshment for the camels and paid their due from their dwindling goods, they lit a lamp. The oil sputtered and flared.

Habakkuk gripped the wood border of the clay tablet.

Too late. No pay. Imprisonment. All these days away from his son, and for what? Another scheme. "I need some air."

Habakkuk stepped into the courtyard and braced his hands on his knees. "Oh God! You went forth for salvation for Your people. Can't You make a way for me too?"

There was no answer. No blazing brightness.

Weariness entered Habakkuk's bones. Who would intercede on his behalf? He returned to where Mahath waited.

"I'm sorry, Mahath. I'm not upset with you." He rubbed his eyes and picked up the tablet, contemplating the reality of debtors' prison.

The next day, Habakkuk approached the caravan master as he loaded his camels.

"Is there any way we could speed up the caravan? I must make it to Jerusalem by the full moon."

"What concern is that of mine?" The gruff man pushed Habakkuk out of the way.

"Please, my lord. My child—" Habakkuk grabbed the man's sleeve. "Can we press on at night and go on to the next stop?"

The caravan master gave a sneering laugh. "Proceed as you will. If that cargo is not delivered, you will be hunted down and executed."

Habakkuk shrugged. He was as good as dead if he didn't make the deadline. "Thank you, my lord."

"Stupid fool." The caravan master muttered as Habakkuk walked away.

"What did he say?" Mahath appeared out of nowhere.

"He released me to my own devices." Habakkuk wouldn't make it on his own—but how could he ask Mahath to sacrifice the safety of the caravan?

The youth surveyed their loads. "If we shift the weight to the back of our lines, we should be able to ride. We could more than double our pace. The ground we cover—"

"Mahath." Habakkuk swallowed the lump that formed in his throat. He wrapped his arms around the boy's thin shoulders. "Thank you. I'm proud of you. I wish you were my son."

A grin spread across Mahath's face and he practically skipped to their kneeling camels. Quick as a vapor, their diminished cargo had been shifted off their leads and replaced by Mahath and Habakkuk. The camel lurched forward raising his hind legs first, nearly dislodging Habakkuk from his awkward perch in the cargo frame.

"Hup! Hup!" Mahath prodded his lead with a stick.

Habakkuk mimicked his new caravan master, and they lurched west at an uneven jog.

Long before they approached a mountain, Habakkuk's bones and teeth jarred incessantly.

Mahath did not divert from the path, but led his line up the mountain.

Up, up they plodded, his camel straining at the line behind him. Habakkuk held on and prayed. They navigated through the harsh, hilly Negev desert with a pace that dislodged Habakkuk's idea of comfort. He almost begged Mahath to stop at the fortress as dusk deepened, but clenched his jaw as the moon grew more visible.

They made it up the secondary route to Mamshit with two days to spare. After collecting wages and renting swift donkeys, they pressed on to the northeast. With each passing minute, they passed into familiar territory. The burden to see his son pressed against his chest, and transferred into his mount's stride.

Habakkuk refused to rest until well into the night and the donkey was lathered with sweat. He climbed down and pulled the blanket off and spread it over a scrubby bush.

"We'll make it." Mahath appeared silently.

Habakkuk didn't take his gaze from the nearly full moon. He blew out a breath and tried to roll the tension from his shoulders. "I hope so." He patted the bulging pouch at his hip. There was enough there to pay off his debt once and for all.

"It will work out." Mahath stretched his arms over his head with a yawn. "Will you take the first watch?"

Habakkuk nodded as Mahath stretched out in the shadows.

By this time tomorrow, he'd be a free man—and asleep in his own house. For the first time, he allowed himself to agree with Mahath's optimism as the night stretched on.

The shadow to his right shifted and before Habakkuk could turn, he found a blade pressed against his throat.

"Didn't anyone tell you not to travel alone?" The Hebrew voice grated in Habakkuk's ear.

From the shadow, another man emerged. His eyes widened, and he fell forward.

The man behind Habakkuk loosened his hold. "What happened—"

Whiz! The air besides Habakkuk's face was displaced, and the man stopped mid-sentence, pulling Habakkuk down as he fell.

Habakkuk scrambled off the unresponsive man as Mahath emerged, tossing extra stones at his feet.

"Time to go." Mahath dropped a coin in front of each of the men.

"You are paying bandits?" Habakkuk threw the still-damp blanket on his mount's back and scrambled aboard.

"Consider it the tax for safe passage." Mahath's voice paused as he mounted his donkey.

They rode abreast of each other, their sure-footed donkeys picking their way across the landscape.

"Thank you. Once again you have rescued me. I had no idea you had such good aim."

Mahath shrugged. "I have to do something to pass the time."

6

Yet I will rejoice in the LORD, I will joy in the God of my salvation.
~Habakkuk 3:18

"Elah! Levana. I've returned!" Habakkuk flung himself from his weary beast and tied it before the house. He threw open the door and scooped up Elah's small form.

"*Abba*, you're back." Elah patted Habakkuk's scruffy cheeks.

"Who is this?" Levana's smile turned to a frown.

Habakkuk set down his boy and put his hand on Mahath's shoulder. "This is Mahath. He helped me tremendously along the way. Truly. I would not have made it back without him."

Levana bowed slightly. "My sincere thanks, young man."

Mahath flushed and knelt beside Elah's mat. "Yes, mistress."

Habakkuk drew Levana into the corner. "I have so much to tell you. But first, Yahweh has been working on my heart.

Whatever the outcome, I have been convicted to live righteously."

"What are you saying?" Levana clasped her hands at her middle.

"Be my wife. Too long I have gotten comfortable with our situation."

"It met the need for all of us."

"I want to make it right." Habakkuk moistened his dry lips. "If you'll have me."

"Yes!" Levana laughed through tears.

Emotion welled up in his chest. He glanced over his shoulder to find Mahath still engaging with Elah and pressed a kiss to her head. She wrapped her arms around his waist and buried her face in his shoulder.

"Habakkuk." Oded's voice drifted in from outside.

Pulling back, Habakkuk grinned at Levana and patted the pouch at his side. This was what freedom felt like. "Oded, come in."

"The runner told me you had returned." Oded nodded to Levana. "Praise be. I was worried that you wouldn't return before my creditors arrived."

"Thank you for suggesting this opportunity. I am pleased to give you the balance in full." Habakkuk knelt and poured out his riches before Oded.

Oded's eyes widened as he squatted down and began to count.

Feeling Levana's gaze, Habakkuk turned to see fierce pride on her face. How long had she looked on him so? How long had he felt such fondness for her?

"Oh, my." Oded's sympathy almost sounded genuine. "There's not enough."

"What?" Habakkuk restrained himself from lunging at his benefactor. "This is the amount you said when we traveled to Mamshit."

Oded scooped every last coin back into the pouch and

clicked his tongue. "I'm sorry. Truly I am. But you have to take into account your woman and child needed to eat while you were away for more than two months."

Habakkuk's stomach dropped. "You gave no indication there would be extra charges."

"What did you think, that it would be included?" Oded's friendly tone vanished as rapidly as a merchant's crop of barley in a drought. He clapped twice and two burly men with ropes entered the house. "You agreed to the terms."

"No. Please. I've upheld my end. You promised." Habakkuk shook off one man and ducked around the second. "I'm begging you."

"Is that what this is? I thought you were making a fool of yourself in front of witnesses."

"I am a fool. I never should have trusted you. You are corrupt in your calculations—" Habakkuk was slammed to the ground and his arms restrained behind him.

"I helped you stand on your own feet when your son needed help. I am your friend and hostility is the reward I get—"

"How much?" Mahath's shout broke through the melee.

Oded dismissed Mahath with a quick glance. "Never you mind, boy. This isn't your concern."

"What does he owe? Name the full amount."

Oded rolled his eyes and huffed. The price he named far exceeded the cost of food Levana and Elah would have eaten in a year's time.

Habakkuk could not lift his eyes from the packed dirt as he was hauled upright. Nothing he had done could influence the outcome. He was still a failure destined for debtors' prison.

Mahath repeated the figure and swept his arm to encompass the whole room. "You all heard. You are witnesses."

"Of course, there will be interest every day it is not paid." Oded stepped toward the door.

"But as of today, that amount will settle his debt?"

"Yes, boy." Oded grabbed Habakkuk's beard and pulled his face close. "Have you got it?"

"No. I gave you all I had." Habakkuk stared at the wall, unseeing.

"I have." Mahath counted out the coins with precision. He showed each of the guards, before slamming the coins into Oded's chest.

"But—"

"Count them." Mahath's lanky form blocked the doorway.

Coins slipped to the ground before Oded could wrap his hand around them all. He bent to pick up the dropped pieces and silently moved his mouth.

"Well? Does it match the debt?" Mahath stepped closer.

Oded's eyes darted to the left, and he opened his mouth.

"Remember, there are witnesses."

"It is enough." Oded mumbled.

Mahath did not relent. "Enough to cancel *all* this man's debt, and his family's?"

"The debt is paid in full." Oded's glare could melt sugared honey.

"We will be by the city gates with a cancellation of debt when the elders gather this evening." Levana called to Oded's departing back.

Oded didn't look back.

"Thank you for your service today." Mahath handed each guard a day's wage. "You heard this man and his family were cleared of their debt. Please join us at the gate this day as the witnesses."

The guards exchanged an incredulous glance and left shaking their heads.

Habakkuk blinked in silence as Mahath untied him. He glanced from his son's small face to Levana's hands covering her mouth.

"Mahath?" He gripped the boy's shoulders. "I will repay you."

"No need." Mahath shrugged. "You are a free man."

A free man. Habakkuk cleared his throat and blinked rapidly to keep the tears at bay. "But you need the funds to find your *abba*."

"Maybe I've found a more worthy cause. You have a real good family, Habakkuk." Mahath cleared his throat and knelt beside Elah.

Habakkuk stood dumbfounded at the overwhelming, unfounded mercy. He wiped away the wetness on his cheeks and caught Levana's gaze. She nodded toward the boys and clutched her chest.

"Mahath?" Certainty swelled through Habakkuk's chest. "I'm not your *abba*—I'd like to be. You can continue your search as you desire, but at least you will have somewhere to call home, a family who cares for you."

The youth sprang to his feet with the agility of a deer on the high places. "You mean it?"

Habakkuk sought out Levana once more and her beaming smile matched his own. "Absolutely."

Mahath rushed over and kissed Habakkuk's cheeks, then ran over to Levana, chattering like a magpie.

"What do you think, my son?" Habakkuk scooped up Elah.

Elah clapped his hands. "I've got a brother!"

"Shiri, come!"

Habakkuk smiled at the choirmaster's small family with fond thoughts of his own mismatched brood.

The little girl was about Elah's age. Her hair flowed free and the dimple in her chin gave her an air of innocence as she offered him a ladle of water.

"Thank you, child."

Shiri blushed and ran to her mother.

Habakkuk lowered himself to the ground as Master Ibraham sat before him.

"What do you have for me?"

"My lord, I know you no longer serve full time as the choir master, but…you know who I am." Which said a lot, the current master musician was gifted, but didn't care about the trials each musician had personally.

Ibraham gripped his knee with a worn hand. "What is it?"

Would the man believe his report? Habakkuk drew his harp to his lap. "I've seen a message of destruction from the Lord."

Ibraham and his wife exchanged glances. "Go on."

"I was afraid. My bones became rotten inside me." Habakkuk passed his hand over his eyes, but could not be rid of the terror. "Yahweh is establishing the Chaldean army to annihilate our land, our people."

"What did Yahweh show you through it all?" Ibraham leaned forward and his wife drew Shiri close.

"It is happening soon. In my lifetime." Habakkuk picked up his harp. "May I?"

"Of course."

Shiri clapped her hands under her chin as he began fingering the strings.

"I have to tell you, I have not always lived righteously… but all that to say, the Lord is doing a new thing in my life." Habakkuk strummed the harp, cleared his throat and began to sing.

"Though the fig tree may not bloom, nor fruit be on the vines, though the labor of the olive may fall, And the fields yield no food; Though the flock be cut off from the fold, and there be no herd in the stalls—Yet I will rejoice in the Lord."

Habakkuk swallowed but the lump in his throat would not dissipate. What would happen to his boys? To little Shiri here?

Shiri came to his knee and began humming. She joined in as he sang the chorus a second time.

"I will joy in the God of my salvation. The Lord God is my strength; He will make my feet like deer's feet and He will make me walk on my high hills."

Yahweh, may this young girl keep her faith in you. For surely, she would be tested in the great destruction.

Printed in Great Britain
by Amazon